Flock

Without

Birds

Filip Dousek

The Story

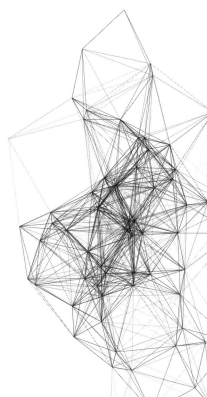

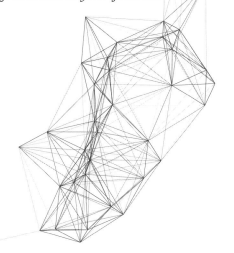

To the searchers, the curious, the lost. Stay the course.
To my children, who saved me from another ten years of rewrites.

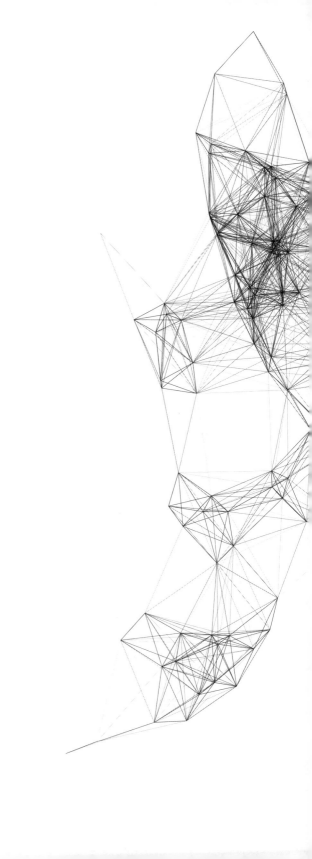

Prologue

Ancient wisdom says the whole is more than the sum of its parts.

But if that is the case, how do we account for the difference?

What is a flock without birds?

See, this is the magic of books. You open one, and there's a whole library inside. Look around! The walls are strewn with shelves full of continental philosophy, military history, mathematics of fractals, comparative logic, Renaissance artworks, and the major novels of the European milieu. Here are the Gnostics; there, shamanism and myths of medieval Prussia—even a small collection of sixteenth-century Irish poems. Lovely little pieces, I must say. An old man's library, I suppose, constitutes the footnotes to his life.

Funny that I only started reading regularly after thirty. I had no time for it before then. I was a young man in Cambridge who chased a dream. To truly grasp the mystery of the world, that was my desire. And yes, I know that everyone in Cambridge is after the same thing. But I was ... a wee bit extra *dedicated*. A bloody fanatic, really. I lived my days and nights figuring out how it might be possible to reach that mystical place that links all the seemingly chaotic fragments of this universe.

But I didn't read. I was no philosopher, no bookworm. I joined the humble profession of data science and performed my study by way of programming. That's right: I wrote a program to do a philosophizing. And, as I waited for its answer, I tried to write a diary. The space between these black covers is dense with scribbled handwriting and formulas spanning the sheets. The key to the mystery of the world, I note immodestly. Right bang here, in my journal. It's inscribed with words I could recite by heart:

Perhaps the enigma of the world hides not in what escapes me, but in what I see. Perhaps, it occurs to me today, as I stand by a window with a cigarette and observe the snow milling around under the lamplight, something obscures my view. Some object, that I see my entire life, incessantly, and hence no longer notice it. And it still shadows what lies behind it. Something important, which I sense, but do not see. The object, my blind spot.

This black diary was once intended as a travelogue of sorts. Now, let me ask you a question. Would you want to read it? Would you want to glimpse the order of the world?

When I was myself young and chirpy, I would have shouted, "Yes, for Heaven's sake, yes!"

But don't rush your answer. Rather, tell me this first: if one wants to understand a book—any book—is reading it even the right way to go?

See, one evening, I was strolling through a market in Marrakesh, happily carrying a volume I'd been seeking for several years. I was ready to sit in the cool of the riad, light up a lump of local hashish, and delve into the ancient pages. But I stopped by a stand selling roasted peanuts. "A hundred grams," I asked the youth and pointed at one sack of nuts. He weighed them and quipped as though it were nothing: "Sir, what's the story of that book?"

He didn't ask me *what is the book about*, as people usually do. And so he didn't get the obvious, curt answer that it's a lexicon of mathematics from the 12th century. He'd asked an entirely different question, and so I told him the story of Leonardo of Pisa—a boy who grew up differently from his peers, seeing his time from a slightly different angle. With his book, he then taught medieval Europe to count and account and literally changed the history of civilization. The youth gave me a few extra nuts for my story, and I left a fraction of Arabic wisdom richer.

Well then. If, like that young vendor, you are more interested in the story of the black book than the book itself, let me pull something else out. A white book. I wrote it some five years later. It's the story of the black diary and its young creator.

Which will you choose to read? You seem to have retained a benefit I lost long ago: the benefit of ignorant choice. How human, how supremely and delightfully human! Don't let my toothless laughter offend you. How could you possibly know what to choose when you haven't chosen yet, haven't chosen the opposite, and lack both experiences to compare? With all due respect, in your position, you can only decide impulsively, irrationally, ignorantly. And I applaud that. I admire this human courage to march ahead cluelessly, only to realize later what it was that you absolutely needed to know right from the start.

Choose the black book, or the white one, as you wish. But if you then sink into exploring the exploring mind exploring the exploring and wish suddenly you had never wished, remember there is no turning back, and the first step was your very own choice.

Or was it, ever?

Distra

ctions

Be a source of pleasure. No one wants to hear about your problems and troubles.

—Robert Greene

Marquis •

smiled at her, and, unassuming, she asked where he was from.

"Mars," he replied loftily.

"Ha-ha."

She was about to shrug and leave, and then she and Adam would probably never have met. But before she could dismiss him, Marquis continued. "I suspect I'm from my mother, originally. You would not reduce my origins to a mere nationality, would you?"

Unimpressed, still, she returned to a conversational posture. "Are you ashamed of your country?"

Adam grabbed a beer, planning to do some mental programming for Faustomat to occupy him while the shindig lasted. After rewriting it some fifteen times for performance, he knew large parts of the code by heart.

It was Freshers' Week in Cambridge, and there was no avoiding the student parties. They hijacked pubs, streets, colleges, and, regrettably, his own room. The beds of six adjacent rooms had been conscripted as sofas, and a DJ overlooked the scene from behind two turntables and a suitcase of vinyls. Two bathtubs were dedicated to cooling kegs.

"Marquis and shame?" Marquis countered. "Polar opposites. What are you really asking? Which school system deformed me? What music my parents forbade? How old I was when I first had sex and whether I'd like to repeat it sometime? All viable talking points—but if you're after national stereotypes, ask me directly."

She pointed her finger at him, eyes narrowing. "I'm interested— but not too much—in which country you're from. Do you want to play? Fine. It's your last chance."

"Oh, but you're strict!"

"You haven't seen anything yet. I know your accent." She raised her index finger right up to his nose. "You're from Eastern Europe."

"And here we go." Marquis nodded. "I'll tell you where I'm from, you'll reply with an 'ohright,' and suddenly, I'll have a bunch of character traits I've never even heard of. What if I say German? How about Swedish? Polish? Then, you'll ask me what I do and how old I am, and, after these three questions, you'll think we've met." He leaned back slightly, pleased with himself. "The question of nationality is forbidden in job interviews. Can we avoid stereotyping and get acquainted legally? Tell me, do you have a boyfriend—or girlfriend?"

"You've missed your chance," said Nina witheringly. She turned suddenly and directly towards Adam, who smiled at her apologetically, and asked, "What about you, blondie—same story?"

Adam rolled his eyes deprecatingly. "Just ask me where I'm from."

Nina cocked her head toward Marquis. "Inferiority complex?"

"He has a timid soul."

His expression finally made Nina laugh. She asked Adam where he was from, and he readily replied. Then he sighed, smiled a little, and fell silent. She was charming. And charm, he knew, was probably the only force capable of pulling him astray.

He allocated his minutes carefully: 170 to attending lectures, 100 to cooking and eating, 20 to shopping, 50 to cycling, another 50 to miscellany, and 60 a day, despite his best efforts, were lost. Plus, seven hours and thirty minutes of sleep. These supportive activities were a necessary evil so he could work on the Faustomat for nine hours every day. Adam's efficiency, therefore, reached 35 percent at best. He didn't reproach himself for this figure; the combustion engine, a finely tuned feat of modern engineering, functions at 20 percent. Nevertheless, two thirds wasted!

He sighed again, confirming internally she was just too dangerous to be spoken to. Losing interest, Nina was about to turn away when Marquis reinserted himself. It was the sort of moment when it's hard to tell if someone is being a true friend or a supreme jerk.

Marquis jumped onto a chair and shouted, "Everyone, do I have your attention?" Waving both hands in the air, he commanded half of the room to turn to him. "Let me introduce a special guest over here!" Adam made a feeble attempt to pull his friend from his pedestal, but he was swatted away. "You look at him, and you don't see anything of interest, right? Adam, as you can deduce at first sight, is a mathematician—"

"Data scientist," he corrected, pinching the bridge of his nose.

"Well—" Marquis took on a beguiling tone. "He guards a secret."

"What secret?" shouted back one of the Spaniards, marginally drawn in. "Go on!"

"Leave it, Marquis," Adam protested from below.

"In all of Cambridge," he persisted, "nobody is researching a topic more revolutionary."

All eyes were on Adam now, momentarily curious. He wished to die.

"This unassuming gentleman is writing software that will crack the mystery of life. Meet the man before he's too famous to waste his time in a humble Cambridge college."

"That's rubbish, but so be it," nodded Adam to end the misery.

At that, Nina turned back to Adam. "Which sign are you?" she asked. "In Western astrology. I'm not into the Chinese cock and bull."

Adam being himself, hearing about astrology, would absently nod his head, observe with an exhausted, condescending look, and sigh to himself at how much he'd have to explain. Then he'd close his eyes, and thoughts would run off in many directions at once, trying to find a place to start. But he was a true scientist. He would fail to find any fortified place from which he could launch an infallible attack against obscurantism, and he'd just get tangled in an infinite regress. But at least he was honest in it, so he'd go quiet and keep his skepticism to himself.

Adam the pragmatist, however, had learned from experience that the fastest way to end a conversation was to answer questions directly. It scared people away.

"Capricorn." One word, the height of self-denial.

"Great!" she exclaimed unexpectedly. "We're a match."

"Though," he demurred, "I'm more into science than pseudo-science."

"Hey, Capricorn, you wouldn't believe how much science there is in the stars."

"Maybe, maybe not." Adam shrugged. "It's worth a little analysis."

She shifted her weight, settling in. "And how do you go about that?"

She seemed genuinely interested. So he described Faustomat to her. "When my grandmother dies," he said, "half of the family will say God called her. The other half will mourn a tragedy. When an airplane crashes, the religious half of the planet will say it was the hand of

God. The other half will be shocked by a random black swan. People have their explanations up front and ready. And no matter which side they take, they choose blindly. And then, they let this choice direct their lives."

"Are you still talking about astrology?" she asked. It sounded sarcastic, but he wasn't sure.

Well, he'd done it. He'd let himself be drawn into the long version of this conversation. "Yes," he stated. "Now is the first time in human history when it's possible to prove or disprove these prehistoric hypotheses. We finally have the data. If you mix Twitter trends, news streams, FM white noise, your Chinese cock and bull, Wikipedia, the Bible, and an online archive of sixty million books, you have a fraction of the data Faustomat searches night and day."

"You're either nuts or genius," said Nina. "Search for what?"

Adam nodded. The safest way to scare away the distractions of the night was to press on toward "nuts".

"If this reality is based on a pattern, it has myriad manifestations. The shapes of flowers, the dimensions of galaxies, and the structure of DNA ... they should all contain the same mathematics. You would find it in the cycles of human history and the stock market. So I've got maps of rain activity mixed with crime rates and causes of death. Lottery numbers. Highway accident rates projected against the night sky. Ultraviolet signals from the Hubble telescope. Digitizations of the old masters from Hieronymus Bosch to Jan Vermeer."

He knew those were all good enough to impress amateurs, even in Cambridge. Under her steady gaze, though, he wavered, feeling ever so slightly like a fraud. The program was running, the vision held steady, but, in the center of the endeavor, there lay a dark hole: he lacked detailed personal data to show how the celestial force influenced people. No, not people. This one woman's life. Her luck and failures. Her fate, reliably read from her medical records, the tonality of her voice, her diaries, confessions, and criminal activity.

He sighed, ashamed for holding such an infinite monologue. To make it up to her, he laughed disarmingly. "So that's me. What about you?"

At that simple prompt, Nina laid out her plans. She'd go to Japan to find an old master with eyebrows obscuring his eyes, and she'd learn the mystical art of the calligraphic line. A few villages down the road, she'd varnish jewel boxes and design mountain gardens. She'd open a gallery with forgotten painters on the ground floor and a second-hand bookshop upstairs, somewhere by the beach. While the customers read, she would mix them a mean wasabi Bloody Mary. She'd also like to do an illegal show of her paintings on a Circle Line train, accompanied by her old band. And sometimes, she dreamed about something big, like she could really change the world through art, like a fusion of Joan of Arc and Vivienne Westwood. All these plans were for next year, at most. That's why she studied interdisciplinary arts and humanities, so she could do everything. And she also enjoyed photography.

"Have you been to Japan?" Adam asked.

"I don't want to go as a tourist," she asserted breezily. "I'd like to stay until I have a thin layer of Japanese dust in me."

"Best to go now, while you study."

"I know. There's this foundation that gives out two art scholarships a year. But they get like two hundred applications."

"Did you apply?"

"You're very curious," she said. She suddenly didn't feel like answering.

"Anyway, I'm friends with any country that invented Kirin Ichiban."

At three in the morning, they said goodbye and added a kiss. He went to his room with Nina's telephone number in his pocket, and she sent a shrug at an inquisitive friend—*it's nothing*.

Later, Adam would claim that almost everything he knows about Nina, he'd known from the first look—the one she hadn't even granted to him but to Marquis. It wasn't love at first sight (what is love?) but an unspeakably detailed image of her character, gleaned from a split-second impression, the shine of her eyes, the rhythm of her breath, that first laugh with sub-tones of sarcasm. That immediate image didn't change ever after.

In summary, it was a statistically significant night. He'd gotten a kiss, first one in perhaps a year. But far more importantly, he'd walked out of the party with a hypothetical girlfriend and chose to ignore momentarily the grave danger that, as a result, his efficiency might drop below 35 percent.

Lo

ve

God created her for Adam out of nothingness. Bones first. Then internal organs.
Then flesh. Muscle. Sinew. Fat. Bile. Eyes. Snot. Skin. Hair. Breath …
Adam couldn't bear to go near her. He wouldn't touch her. "He saw her full
of secretions and blood." That's what the Midrash states.
—Neil Gaiman

Their first dates were so pleasant, it was always natural to arrange for the next one. They talked, walked, laughed, and, to Adam's genuine surprise, they made love. To Nina, those days were like the sky before a storm. High contrast, with a promise. And so they were gradually getting to know each other.

Adam staked out his days as though he were building a highway. The past stood; the future was under construction. He worked on his research eight hours a day, including Saturdays and Sundays. He had a project plan, phases, and milestones—and he was falling behind. That's why he tracked every hour and didn't go to bed until he gave Faustomat its daily quota. On average, he turned off his laptop at 22:40, but it could be as late as two o'clock. Before falling asleep, he completed a short self-assessment.

For at least a year, he'd felt it was impossible to work more, but his charts showed he was gaining momentum. He simplified. He cut his hair down to a few millimeters so he wouldn't have to dry it. He bought a hundred tubes of toothpaste, twenty toothbrushes, fifty bottles of shampoo, two hundred rolls of toilet paper, and stuffed them in a closet. He was done shopping for the necessities for three years.

Every day except Sundays, his breakfast was egg white, beans, and spinach. He batch-cooked for five days at a time. Cycling to college, he would take a slight detour to blend transportation with exercise. Under the pressure of mounting velocity, the formerly random elements of his life shaped themselves into an aerodynamic arrow pointing toward the top priority. The Faustomat.

Even the life-changing decisions became easy. When he graduated, he signed up for postgraduate studies to facilitate his work on Faustomat. In the future, he would use data to tame chance in the stock market, in medicine, in the search for human happiness and extraterrestrial life. He had that clarity because he was dealing with something elemental to humans: overcoming chaos, creating order. The very foundation of being. And so the vector of his entire life was clearly visible. The highway led past the horizon.

Nina found it as humorous as it was impressive. She just lived differently. Her father had lectured on the history of art and made money on the side by colorizing medieval maps. He'd visited Russia after the perestroika and bought atlases in used bookstores. At home, he'd ripped out individual pages, water-colored the countries, and sold the maps to antiquarians in London. He'd also bought books—first editions of Pushkin and Tolstoy that had popped up in Moscow and St. Petersburg. He'd never taken Nina to Russia (Mum wouldn't allow it), but they'd gone to London together. It was her city right away: the capital of foreigners.

When he died, Nina was eighteen. Her mother told her it was an unfortunate accident. But she'd lived through enough to know. Not even a leaf falls from a tree without a cause, let alone a father from a bike. One of Nina's brothers was in New York, another in St. Petersburg, and they flew their families to the funeral in Barcelona. After dinner, her mother said she'd decided to go back to Paris. Within five seconds, Nina understood she was an adult now and calmly nodded, having already bought her ticket to London. Her brothers left; she stayed with Mother for a month in Barcelona, arranging the furniture removal and other formalities necessary for the family's ultimate dissolution. Neither she nor her Mother could wait to be elsewhere. At the airport, they hugged, wiped each other's tears, kissed, and off they went—one towards the past, the other towards the future.

She spent the first two days in London wandering the streets and sketching the city's citizenry. The third night, she slept in a Camden squat and then stayed for a year. It was frequented by stray punks, musicians from two bands fighting over one drummer and his kit, their collective one-night stands, and an occasional designer or passing undergrad.

Nina became their artist-in-residence. She sang in the more alternative of the two bands, dressed in black, and wore black eyeliner, but she never touched her long hair. Despite everything, she wasn't one of them. She didn't do crack, just drew them while they did. She drew them when they begged, at rehearsals, in leather jackets and naked on mattresses, while they groomed their mohawks and their dogs, and when they danced around the fire in the yard across from Camden Stables Market. She sold her drawings to the stall keepers there, and one of them liked to flirt with her.

"You study art, right?"

"No, not yet."

"Oh, darling, this will get you in anywhere."

"Anywhere?"

"Oh, yes."

She sent a few folios in a brown envelope to Fine Arts at Cambridge. They invited her for an interview. They asked about Wagner, and Nina countered with Mallarmé and Messerschmidt. They were all characters in the fairy tales her father had told her before bed. She remembered them like other children remember princesses. And so, thanks to drawings, punk, and fairy tales, she became the first person from the squat to get into Cambridge.

Her life was a jigsaw puzzle with a thousand tiles. Over time, some of them interlocked marvelously. Why would she want to straighten them into a line?

"Did you ever let go of your plans, *jump into the fireworks*, and never look back?" she poked Adam now.

Adam shook his head. He knew in his mind that the process of creation invariably follows the same curve. It matters little what's being created: a painting, a program, a relationship. First, it is conceived. Then, approached. Then, it is begun. Then, continued. Then, culminated. Then, finished. Then, abandoned. Then, remembered. Then, forgotten.

When they'd met, Adam had been following this trajectory with his one and only project. And he'd had no intention of embarking on another. For, no matter how pleasant it may be, each and every creation has a propensity to grow. Each step leads to the next, and what is once begun cannot but follow the entire path. And that takes time. It takes resources. It diverts.

She pulled out sketches of hats with long, delicate ribbons and folded veils, live birds, lit candles, and clouds of white smoke.

"This term's project?"

"No," she laughed. "I was drawing in a café yesterday."

"And what's your project this term?" he pressed.

"I don't know. I was thinking of starting with calligraphy."

Adam rolled his eyes, praised the hats, and laid out his time records beside the egg white and beans. As expected, his efficiency had dropped below 30% since he'd met her. And that was after a hundred adjustments to streamline. Nina's effectivity, he sighed inwardly, was at zero percent so far. Without a goal, there was nothing to measure.

"If you focused for a while on being a painter, you'd make it to the major London galleries. If you chose to be a hat designer, in two years, Gaultier and Chanel would be fighting over you. But now, it's calligraphy. A butterfly, my love, flies the same distance in a year as a raven, but it won't see Africa." There—a fighter jet and a butterfly having a chat about flying.

"Coco Chanel died forty years ago."

"You're avoiding the subject."

Nina put down her fork.

"Well, aren't you?" He willfully stoked the fire.

"You understand nothing, do you?"

"Why?"

"Don't you see? If I follow your good advice and go after what I want, we won't be together."

Adam blinked, confused. "What do you mean?"

"Nothing." Nina rose, took her plate to the sink.

"Are you talking about the scholarship in Japan?"

She ran the faucet, silently wiping her yolk from the smooth ceramic.

"Oh, come on. Even if you get it, we can still be together."

"Forget about that." She spun. "I hate long-distance relationships. If I go there, I'll live there! Not here."

"You just want to go there because you and your family can never stay put," he bit out.

"Don't talk about my family. You have no idea."

"Don't you see?" he insisted. "You live in the countryside; you dream about the city. You move to the city, but it rains there. So you dream about the beach. And you won't settle down even when you feel amazing—only once you chase yourself to the end of your imagination."

"That's not how it is." Deep down, Nina was defending her father.

"Unfortunately, the capacity for happiness is limited. You won't be happier in Japan than here in Cambridge. You'll just run out of things to complain about."

"So I should do nothing and be perfectly happy. When did you get into Buddhism?"

"Don't twist around what I said. Not 'perfectly happy.' Just the opposite. You're milking your endorphins full-on while you're sitting in the cinema watching a half-decent film. Why don't you do Japanese studies here instead of moving?"

"I don't want to learn about Japan, I want to live it!"

"And if they choose you from the two hundred applicants, you'll break up with me?"

She straightened. "Well, do you love me, Capricorn?"

He understood her question perfectly and what she meant by it. And he was in trouble. He could not casually whisper, "Yes, I love you." It would not be fair. He only had one clear label for what others called love: oxytocin. Plus a few other psychoactive substances. And he was not willing to panic and redraw the future under the influence of narcotics.

He was cautious discussing this with Nina. Most people are not moved by talk of chemical compounds.

But she pressed on. "Adam, I'm not a girl. If you don't know why you're with me, we don't have to make up stories. Just tell me you don't want to be together."

Abracadabra. A few words would suffice to lose her. He faltered, and his skin cooled with the touch of a web of a thousand tacit agreements he could unwittingly break ... *that you wear clothes, that you don't touch other women, that you march from the box called school to the box called home, up into the corner where Nina has gotten used to sleeping.* How easily he'd tear this web of words down and fall to where he's sitting in the park, naked, nodding his head, not speaking, not knowing where he's from or where he sleeps—

"Don't be angry," he breathed. But he realized the danger. Oxytocin wasn't going to cut it. If they were to stay together, he would need to find a new definition of love. And that would mean more time, more resources, more diversion.

He hugged her, dismayed that Cambridge did not offer any lectures on romance. He would even pay for private tutoring if he could find a teacher.

HO

HO

$C_8H_{11}NO_2$

DOPAMINE

HO

$C_{10}H_{12}N_2O$

SEROTONIN

NH_2

OH

(R)

NH_2

HO

OH

$C_8H_{11}NO_3$

NORADRENALINE

OH

H

$C_{19}H_{28}O_2$

TESTOSTERONE

O

H_2N

Cys

S

Tyr

OH

O

HN

H

Ile

Leu

Pro

Cys

S

O

O

HN

H

HN

O

H_2N

O

H

N

O

Asn

NH_2

NH_2

Gly

$C_{43}H_{66}N_{12}O_{12}S_2$

OXYTOCIN

Cys

H_2N

O

H

Tyr

OH

H_2N

NH

NH_2

Pro

O

H

N

S

S

HN

Phe

O

O

H

HN

HN

Gln

H_2N

Gly

O

O

H

N

Arg

NH_2

Asn

O

NH_2

$C_{46}H_{65}N_{15}O_{12}S_2$

VASOPRESSIN

OH

H

H

HO

OH

$C_{18}H_{24}O_3$

ESTROGEN

DOPAMINE + SEROTONIN + NORADRENALINE + TESTOSTERONE + OXYTOCIN + VASOPRESSIN + ESTROGEN = LOVE

Myth o

f Myth

I do not feel obliged to believe that the same God who has endowed
us with sense, reason, and intellect has intended us to forgo their use.
—*Galileo Galilei*

When

Nina said she would spend the afternoon studying by the river, he suggested he might come by.

"Yes?" She smiled. "I usually go to the little park by Magdalene's Bridge."

"Right opposite the punting station? That's on my route from the statistics lab. Have you seen how many people rent the boats? They voluntarily pay to push a pole for an hour just to wind up back in the same place!"

"It's inexplicable. We must try it out."

"Don't make me do that. What time?"

"I'll be there all afternoon."

Adam ran through his schedule in his mind. "Twenty past five?"

Nina shrugged. "Whatever works for you."

After a few hours, she was tiring of her books. She looked around, stretching her arms. A group of students cycled across the bridge. An elderly gentleman sitting nearby was reading a thick antique tome, slowly shaking his head.

"What are you reading?" she called toward him.

"The Book of Sins."

"Sure."

"Too much studying?" He gestured at her book.

"Way too much."

"Why don't you take a break? Go punting?" he asked as if that was the usual substitute. He may have been in his sixties; his curly hair and beard had hints of grey.

"I'm waiting for my boyfriend here," she said with a shake of her head. "Thank you. He should be here in an hour."

"That's a long wait. Is he taking you punting, then?"

"Him? Hardly. He's more into sciences than romance."

"Well, then there's no conflict. Do you want to accompany an old man for a ride? I can still do the work." He put down his book and waved hands as if punting already. "Unless you really prefer to spend the rest of this sunny day studying."

It wasn't a difficult decision. "Why not?" She packed away her blanket. "Are you a professor?"

The man introduced himself—Gorgonuy—and they spent an hour on the river, drifting from Cambridge's riverside architecture to its hidden symbolism, to the forms of love in Greek myth, to the curious parallels among world mythologies, to Adam's search for universal order. Meanwhile, Professor Gorgonuy confided he lived in a Pembroke basement (Adam's college!) because the university was only just searching for accommodation. He'd moved in the day before yesterday, having gotten the offer to lecture a month ago when one of the tenured professors died of a heart attack. And he was about to teach mythology—the Myths of Western Civilization, Polynesian Tales, and his favorite, the Myth of Science.

When they returned ashore, Adam was on the bridge with his bike, looking out for her.

Nina introduced them, feeling the awkwardness in the air. "Let's all have a drink! You two have to meet." Neither man could resist strongly, and soon, they were ordering a pint in a nearby pub—Gorgonuy a stout, Adam a lager, Nina a cider.

"How was the experiment?" muttered Adam. He was angry. Of their seven hours a week, they were now going to spend one or even two in the company of a bearded pensioner.

"I was getting bored there in the park," said Nina.

Adam nodded and turned to the professor. "What are you lecturing about?"

"Mythology. Theory and practice."

Nina let out a laugh, complete with her signature sub-tones. "The lecture is the Myth of Science. I think you would enjoy that."

"So you can take fairy tales all the way to tenure?" asked Adam, and he drank a third of his pint at once.

"Forget an old man's stories." Gorgonuy leaned in closer. "Nina told me about your research. I have to say, I'm fascinated by both your choice of topic—"

"One second, I'll sort out the drinks." Adam finished his pint and went to order another round.

Nina joined him by the bar. "Don't say you're jealous?"

"The sooner I scare him off, the sooner we'll be alone." He tried to hug her, but Nina was holding him away.

"Don't you even think about it. You should've come earlier."

"I said I'd be there at five twenty, and I was."

"I said I'd be there all afternoon."

Adam ordered another cider and two glasses of Highland Park whisky and brought the drinks to the table.

"So, you think you can catch God," quipped the professor.

"Undoubtedly. I'll run him down like the last dinosaur," Adam pronounced assertively. "God is the Yeti!"

"And he'll be discovered by a hunter with a silicon spear and a net of equations. Amazing. Then, you do believe in God's existence, yes?"

"That's a discriminatory question."

"Oh, I'm sorry."

"You should have asked whether I believe in a god or deity. Demigods, angels, and demons. Soul and spirits. And dragons, nymphs, and fairies."

"The whole lowly crew." The professor waved it away with his hand. "Do you, then?"

Nina called out, her voice an octave lower: "I'm a scientist, Professor, a skeptic! God is a barbarian relic!"

Adam shook his head. "I believe in God. I don't believe in God. As Protagoras said, 'Concerning the gods, I have no means of knowing whether they exist or not—' watch out, long quote, '—or of what sort they may be. Many things prevent knowledge, including the obscurity of the subject and the brevity of human life.' There. I'll take that. He was the first and last philosopher to lay it out fairly. Well, three thousand years have passed, and now we have mathematical models, data, and the scientific method—let's switch it on! I'm the first guy after Protagoras who may have something new to say." He mixed the ice in the whisky with his finger.

"The fervor! You know, I still think you need to believe the Yeti exists in order to go after it."

"The end of myths is nigh, Professor. Consider a change of careers before it's too late."

Nina shook her head. "He's the king of skeptics."

"The kind that has to put his own fingers in the wound," relished Gorgonuy. "It appears so, but I dare to disagree. A skeptic,

Nina, would reject both answers and defend his ignorance. Here, we have the opposite: a knight, bravely diving into the fury of battle." He raised his hand. "Head-on against an immeasurable challenge. Charging ahead despite ridicule, in the name of miserable humanity. Adam, I hereby dub your work the most romantic endeavor in the history of the sciences!"

"Trust me," Nina rolled her eyes, "if Adam had anything to do with romance, I'd notice. You'd have to know him." And she started laughing.

Adam shrugged. "Define romance." He honestly hoped for an answer.

But Gorgonuy wasn't helping. "I'll define romance. You just look in the mirror! I'm amazed, enraptured. For ages, I lecture about heroes who fought the gods, and suddenly, I have that very battle going on right next door. Now I know why I came to Cambridge. But knowing how heroes fare, I'll give you a word of warning. This is a dangerous journey you've chosen. Like anyone who experiments with philosophy, you're experimenting on yourself. Things will start happening that you won't be able to explain. Your entire world will start shaking, and the scientific method won't protect you."

"Well, actually, it's not going that hot. Quite the opposite. I'm pretty stuck."

"How so?"

"I do have some hundred data sources. Throw in a good analyst, and he might well predict earthquakes and tsunamis. But I don't give a damn about earthquakes, global warming, and all that malarkey. I'm a human, say what they might. I'm searching for the force that pulls and pushes us—people—like gravity," he raised his glass, "and I'm missing filthy, smelly human data."

"Oh, I love human data! You know, I am a bit of a collector in this regard. What would be your favorite kind?"

"If I could choose or steal, I would go for police criminal records and insurance claims."

Nina stepped in. "I don't know if I want to be hearing this."

"Listen," Adam continued, "I'll find everyone's greatest sins in the police database. I'll see how good or bad the people were and then, in the insurance records, how the world repaid them. You have karma smack right there. Analyzing it would just take a few clicks."

Gorgonuy nodded. "I think I've heard of something you might want to look at. I recently discovered, and I can't impart how, that the university just finished an enormous compilation of their alumni archives. They have been carefully managed since 1645 but go back all the way to the 14th century. All this history is now in one database. There's each student's college and room number, lists of their professors, publications, and even detailed biographies with an index of events—you know, weddings, Nobel Prizes, what have you. I had no idea why they spent such a fortune on that. But listening to you—could it be what you're looking for? 'Filthy' human data?"

Adam gasped. "How did they code the biographies?"

"I've heard it's a digital archive, but I have no clue."

"I have to have it."

"That, I'm afraid, will be difficult. The university plainly did all this work intending to open the archive to the public, but then, from what I've heard, the project was cancelled."

"Why?"

Gorgonuy frowned. "I don't know enough. My guess is it was too obvious how successful our graduates are and how much influence they have ... but also how much they have in common."

"Now you've lost me."

"That happens," said Nina, less and less certain that this friendship was a good idea. "And me too."

"They must have found something dangerous," Gorgonuy suggested. "I don't have another explanation. We're talking about years of work. I can't imagine another reason to just throw it out the window."

"It's strange I haven't heard of it in the statistics department," Adam considered. "Who has access to the archive?"

"I barely know him." The professor looked out the window. "If you insist, I'll ask if we can meet again."

"Excellent." Adam scribbled on a sheet of paper. "My number."

"You ask around as well. But in fact, proceed with the highest caution."

Adam saluted.

"It wasn't me who told you, you understand?"

"Perfectly clear. Thank you."

"Hello, Adam?" Nina waved her hand in front of his eyes. "I'm serious now, what's going on today? Finish your drink, go to sleep, and if you want to steal databases from the police or the university after that, then do it. But then, we won't be together. Deal?"

They looked at her.

"Yes," said Gorgonuy as he slid the card back. "Listen to your girlfriend. Besides, I've been trying to give you a friendly warning for a while now. You seem to think, as long as you stick to precise scientific methods, you're in scientific territory. Your method gives you a sense of strength. Strength lends you a feeling of certainty. And you mistake certainty for safety."

"So what?"

He spoke slowly. "Imagine you're in front of a tiger cage. You want to know the average length of the beast's hair. You've calculated exactly how many hairs on which parts of skin you must measure to get a reliable result. So you enter the cage, hold him by the tail, and begin to measure hair after hair. Are you safe?"

"If I ask you to stop, will you?" Nina asked Adam.

"And let go of the greatest scientific breakthrough of the century?" They stared at each other.

"Are you delusional?" she replied.

"How can you not see this? I can change mathematics, physics, politics, everything. It will unlock new energy sources. We'll understand disease! We'll crack DNA. It can make us immortal! And all I need is the right data."

"And why would you want to be immortal?" She sounded sarcastic. Hurt.

Adam paused, looking at her. "Because I could love you so much longer."

She giggled almost involuntarily. "You're such a bad liar."

"I am."

"Well then love me now. Leave the data out if it."

"Life immortal or true love," laughed Gorgonuy. "Doctor Faustus, this is your old dilemma."

Later, as they were leaving, Adam subtly slid the folded sheet back into the professor's palm, and that was the end of it.

"We're finally alone." Again, he reached out for her, but she slipped away. They walked back to the college in silence.

Over the last few weeks, Nina had come to know two Adams. There was the rag mannequin in the bed next to her, probably arranged there with the idea she wouldn't notice the difference. It had glass bead eyes. When asked a question, the thing would jerk its head but not look up. It didn't recall conversations. Nina talked to a recording of Adam's voice and slept by his pajamas.

He reminded her of her own father during these periods when he didn't talk. He used to barely drag himself home from lecturing, sit around in the dark, and neither her mother nor Nina could provide any relief. At times, he would hug Nina and ask how she was. She would swallow her anger. It was unbearable to keep waiting for him to smile again. To not know when she was his little girl and when she wasn't.

Now, she saw Adam, not talking, dragging himself home exhausted and sitting in front of his computer in the dark. And, to her own surprise, she felt needed.

Then suddenly, like tonight, there was a live Adam. He finally came back, excited about data, amusing for one night. That hurt.

Like when her father lit up when he was showing her Schönbrunn and the Prado on postcards and telling stories of how Nietzsche went crazy in this or that city, where they had to move at any price. He'd tell her those tall tales before bed, and she would be happy that he was talking to her again. Her mother resisted, cried, threatened to divorce him and smashed up chinaware. He swore this new plan was the final destination.

The episodes started with the slowed-down rage of a train approaching from afar through the valleys. As if coming from a bottomless gorge, a hum and rattle grew in strength until it made the glasses shake, then the windows and the hills, louder and louder, and longer than seemed bearable, until the roaring engine rushed through a quiet station and ripped down everything that stood in its way— Mum, brothers, Nina, and a truckload of furniture.

While Nina was in school, the family moved three times. Every time was the last: from Lyon to Torino, then to Vienna and, half a year later, to Barcelona. She was from four countries, or from none at all. She had two religions or none. She had two parents and two big brothers and friends all over Europe—or none. In the end, she didn't know whether to fear her father's depressions or his manias. That's why Adam's unexpected euphoria after days of weariness scared her more than the silence. She heard the far-off whistle of a train in the valley.

As they walked to the college, she assured herself: the man she was starting to love was complicated, and he didn't give her as much attention as she wished. The most normal romance of all. She sighed, and a warm feeling glowed through her. He was lacking time, not love for her. He'd said it himself: if he were immortal, he'd fill the time with love.

An idea came at that moment. An art project of sorts. It unfolded fully in her mind within seconds, and she just knew what her midterm project would be. She wanted to jump with joy, circle around him—but hush, she would keep it a secret. It would be a gift, after all, the Gift of Time. A way to offer Adam all the time he wished for. A way to lead events to a crash at the speed favored by the impatient. It was also a joke, too good not to carry through. A new adventure!

Meanwhile, walking beside her, Adam felt a wall of silence. But he dared not ask, being so thoroughly unsure what she saw in him. So far, at least, he did not produce enough "romance" to deserve her affection. Romance just wasn't in his arsenal. Christ, it wasn't even in his dictionary.

A romance, a love affair, a flirtation, a fling … he didn't know what it was between them. He couldn't measure it. And after the last few weeks, he did not want to lose it. Yet, he could not bear such uncertainty for long. He lacked the emotional capacity for torture. What he needed was a test to determine if he could live up to being the man for Nina. In the absence of love lectures, without private romance tutors, he would need to stick to the tools he knew. Holding her by the hand, he decided to design an experiment in love.

One adventure and one experiment. Each of them chose to exit that afternoon through their own private path. Too bad they didn't just talk to each other—life could have been a lot simpler if they had.

The Pa

the F

st and

uture

You shall know the truth and the truth shall make you mad.

—*Aldous Huxley*

Once

again, Professor Krugele cancelled their mid-week consultation, and Adam genuinely worried that his thesis topic might be rejected.

Why did it hurt so much when illusions about the future dissolved, mere illusions? He had to admit that leaving the university and finding a new lifestyle was too complicated to precalculate. Post-grad had, in a sense, been the easiest choice.

Deep in cheerless thoughts, he didn't even hear Nina come back from her workshops until she took him around the shoulders. "Did you borrow my camera, Addy? Why didn't you tell me?"

"I don't even know where the button is on that monster."

He wasn't exaggerating. Nina had a fifty-two-year-old Flexaret VII, a silver-black device she looked into from above. She set the shutter speed, time, and distance manually and scrolled the black and white, 6×6 film by turning a dial on the side. Pressing the release was therefore preceded by five steps that might as well be a combination lock.

"What does this mean?" She picked a bundle of photographs from her bag. Two were from the streets, one from the Pembroke quad, two from a concert. The fifth shot was of Adam.

"Amusing," he remarked and held the picture. It was him. The greyish half-portrait captured him in doctoral students' black formal dress. In the photo, he was smiling carelessly. Not in reality. An ornamental vignette at the bottom of the photograph was inscribed with the year 1912. The man could have been his double except for a certain smoothed-out feel characteristic of period portraits. He examined it from all sides, but he could find no explanation except for the obvious one: that he'd graduated from Cambridge a hundred years ago.

"I didn't take that picture," proclaimed Nina, and Adam felt shivers down his spine. "Obviously."

"So where is it from?"

She shrugged. "I had two rolls developed, and this showed up among the photos."

"Let me see." He took both negatives from her bag and stretched them against the light. His inverted half-portrait shone out a third of

42

the way down one of the strips. He was agitated. "You don't mean to tell me it just happened to appear on the film?"

Nina didn't answer, and there was no longer anything to discuss.

How could he be on a hundred-year-old photograph? Rational explanations, however much he attempted to formulate them, simply lacked power. Instead of sleeping, he spent hours in anxious deliberation over persuading Krugele, life after college, and an ancient portrait. And how ironic it was that the morning was tormented by the fragility of the future whereas the night was ruined by the fragility of the past.

Before dawn, he had at least arrived at one idea. All graduates of the class of 1912 should be ... in Gorgonuy's archive.

Rulers

All great truths begin as blasphemies.
—*George Bernard Shaw*

If I may interrupt, my wife made you tea while you were reading. Put the white book down for a moment and help yourself. Here, biscuits.

You see, the day I held the portrait from 1912 in my hand, I had no clue what it heralded. An event like this is the first crack in a wall. It looks small and innocent, and one tends to see, well, a crack. But it indicates the enormous tension running through the whole structure. If the photo was to be real, so much of my world would be shown to be fictional. My age. Physics. All of science, therefore. The established rational, scientific worldview. My rock-solid foundation of an orderly and law-abiding universe. Sort of everything.

I feel for that young Adam. It was so painful to live through it, unfolding layer after layer without end. A fractured reality is the worst pain imaginable. It becomes the reality of fracture. People call it madness, mental illness, depression, or whatnot. These all are creative ways to suffer a fracture of reality. And from the distance of age, I am so grateful to him. Because the path leads through crises. It must lead through crises.

While it's underway—and it can take months or years—one still has no clue. No idea that a personal crisis is really a worldview under reconstruction. Because it's so hard to be aware of one's worldview. It's just who we are. It's so … obvious.

And it doesn't help that there's not much written about the obvious, the most slippery of words. You can only glimpse it out of the corner of your eye. That's the gold within a crisis. It shakes up the obvious. Little else carries such alchemical power. Romain de Araia put it well: *"The loss of obviousness is the birth of reason."*

As I say, I had no clue what was at stake. How vast the shape that began emerging from the void of the obvious really was. And little is written also on structures in danger—dangerously little. So when I was young, I thought that a battle must be fought.

In my twenties, I demolished one of those obvious megastructures of Western civilization—my Grandma's churches, her God, Heaven and Hell, and the whole medieval model. My poor Granny wanted to help me to Heaven, and when I told her there was none, she was appalled. Because I attacked her structure of reality. And I did it with all my youthful power.

The man who taught me some class was Mark Talwing. He instinctively knew that ideas maintain power through obviousness. Once stripped of this protection, no truth lasts long. The free mind works like acid. Here, have a read.

Mark Talwing, et al. The Evolution of Christianity—Part I. Journal of Skeptic Theology, 1999, VI, 136-140. Introduction. (An introductory note. For the purposes of this text, we understand "Christianity" as a social phenomenon in the widest possible sense of the word—that is, not only the central doctrine itself and its various interpretations, ecclesiastical or purely personal, but also their social consequences [intended, apparent or not], just as the word "politics" must be extended to, for example, a pub brawl that breaks out because of "politics.")

In analyzing the more complex aspects of Christianity, we are forced to dismiss right from the start the misleading simplification that the author of the idea (meme) was Jesus Christ. Innovations of such scale and impact do not arise at once. They require incremental experiments and mistakes in the laboratory of time, prototypes and predecessors. We want to propose the hypothesis that Christianity has developed naturally through an evolutionary process, from its own monkey. And we suggest this monkey to be the poetic turn *"the Kingdom of Heaven."*

Studying the etymology of the term *"Kingdom of Heaven"* undoubtedly deserves its own research grant. Here, thus, but a brief overview of its occurrence in the Old Testament. It appears repeatedly, albeit ambiguously, sometimes in the sense of an unreachable divine sphere, elsewhere as eternal peace in Israel. It blends opposites (Earth and Heaven, Man and God, death and immortality) into one of those captivating phrases that can refer to a number of ideas (memes) at once, capturing human imagination and thus capturing people.

It was around 30 AD that the entire Judaic land awoke with the apocalyptic call of John the Baptist: *"Repent ye, for the kingdom of heaven is near! You brood of vipers, who warned you to flee from the wrath to come? The axe is already laid at the root of the trees. Therefore, every tree that does not bear good fruit is cut down and thrown into the fire!"* John wore a garment of camel's hair with a leather belt 'round his waist, and his food was locusts and wild honey. Jerusalem, Judea, and the entire Jordanian region went out to seek him, to confess their sins. He baptized them in the Jordan River.

Mainstream theology (with support in the Gospel of John) maintains that, by shouting *"the kingdom of heaven is near,"* John the Baptist proclaimed the coming of Jesus Christ. But we carefully assess multiple indices: John's ecstatic shouts and ascetic behavior, the popularity at the time of the doomsday prophets, crowds travelling from cities to the far desert. That is an image of mass mania that accompanies an idea (meme) spreading wildly like the epidemic of a mutating virus.

Jesus himself affirms that this virus wasn't him but the symbol of the heavenly kingdom: *"The Law and the Prophets were proclaimed until John [the Baptist]; since that time, the gospel of the kingdom of God has been preached, and everyone is forcing his way into it."* As every marketer and politician knows well, activating a population is incredibly difficult. But as soon as the whole land had risen and set out for the kingdom of heaven, a number of groups—priests, prophets, preachers, and charlatans—attempted to step ahead of the crowd to turn it in their own direction.

There were various wild rumors about how to enter the kingdom. Some argued that the kingdom would be established on Earth, others that it would bring the end of the world. The preachers fought for the key to the heavenly gate as one of the combatants, Jesus, complained: *"From the days of John the Baptist until now the kingdom of heaven suffereth violence, and the violent take it by force."*

We point out that Jesus is also evidently testing out different ideas about how people could become the chosen ones. From the literal following of the law, he compromises on following the first two commandments. Other times, six commandments are a must. But he can also threaten: *"Truly I say to you, whoever shall not receive the kingdom of God as a child shall never enter into it."* And once, only getting rid of property will cut the mustard. Even his parables of the kingdom oscillate from agriculture to an outright apocalypse. He plays the last trump card just before the crucifixion, when he names himself as the only way. We infer that Jesus does not act as the messenger of a clear message but instead appears to be improvising on the fly, only gradually discovering the charm of martyrdom and resurrection.

There are at least five such episodes of search, improvisation, and competing alternatives in the first four centuries of Christianity:

(i) Jesus prevailing in the competition of the prophets of the Heavenly Kingdom (the selection among memes after the "Cambrian explosion")

(ii) The multitude of Jesus' clues on how to get into the Kingdom. A field testing of options on the audience (extreme variability within the species, another feature of the Cambrian explosion)

(iii) Twelve disciples, each looking for the best method to spread the message (optimizing the virility of the meme)

(iv) Four gospels selected from the dozens of apocrypha (cultivation of the meme)

(v) Christian sects fighting with each other for three centuries until the Council of Nicaea, where a single doctrine was selected, precisely in the spirit of the survival of the fittest (intraspecific competition)

50

Further chapters of our text analyze these five phases of the evolution of Christianity from the sober position of memetic science.

I've found something that you should have read before this binned chapter. When I was still in high school, I begged Santa get me a subscription to the History and Philosophy of Mathematics Quarterly. There was this article by Onglemeyer in the very first issue. As I recall, the author also had to make an effort to hide his passion, barely, behind an academic form. I loved that.

From the outset, Onglemeyer is trying to untie the mess around the word *aletheia*. Somewhere amid apparency, disclosure, evidence, and truth, he gets fairly clumsily caught up. Feel free to skip all that. But from that rickety foundation, he flings himself right at John the Baptist's jugular. Those young academics. Hormones spurt forth all the way up onto their spectacles.

Jean-Jacques Onglemeyer. *Nothing but the Truth. Journal of the History and Philosophy of Mathematics*, 1997, Vol. 17, issue 4, pp. 87-90. [...] But concerning the contemporary meaning of the word "truth," none of those aspects can match the influence of the historically social phenomenon of the Bible. Not the entire Bible; the Gospel of John has everything we're looking for. It has a number of peculiarities. First, it was probably written as the last of the four canonical gospels, perhaps around 100 A.D. The content of the scripture overlaps the least with the other three. But crucially, it has a distinct, matured poetic style, avoiding parables but repeatedly using compelling symbols. Where Matthew, Mark, and Luke call Jesus' teaching *"the Word"* or *"the Word of God"* or simply capture his utterances in their text, John speaks differently: *"The Spirit is truth." "When that one comes, the Spirit of truth, he will guide you in all the truth." "Sanctify them in the truth; your word is truth."*

The word "truth" appears in the Bible almost exclusively in the Gospel of John and the Epistles of John. In these, it shows up a whopping twenty-seven times. In the beginning of the third epistle, it takes on another meaning, as a way of life: *"I rejoiced greatly when the brothers came and testified to your truth, as indeed you are walking in the truth. I have no greater joy than to hear that my children are walking in the truth!"* The crowning achievement is John's rendition of the Last Supper, the only place in the entire Bible where life, journey, goal, truth, God, and Jesus all unite. John uses the word "truth" so naturally that it would almost seem it was a common phrase at the time. But let's not overlook a gracious passage, which, again, is absent in the other gospels:

"Then Pilate said to him, 'So you are a king?'

"Jesus answered, 'You say that I am a king. For this purpose I was born and for this purpose I have come into the world—to bear witness to the truth. Everyone who is of the truth listens to my voice.'

"Pilate said to him, 'What is truth?'"

At once, I knew my biblical hero. Some years later, I would be active on the internet's more obscure forums under the nickname Pilate. But to continue with Onglemeyer:

What is truth?

Behind this short exchange lurk six centuries of Greek debates on truth, their conflicting theories and arguments dragging on for generations. The increasingly frequent wars with neighboring civilizations and the recognition that foreigners have even more varied opinions on gods, customs, and games—

What is truth?!

In John's text, Jesus does not answer Pilate's question, and the debate ends inconclusively. John, a scholar with a firm grasp of language, scripture, the magic of symbols, and, evidently, also contemporary disputation, just could not leave out this stalemate between two master orators! And inadvertently, he showed his precise knowledge of the multivalent range of this powerful word. He thus also made it clear that turning it into a synonym for Jesus' teaching was an intentional act.

As far as we know, here is the first historic record of the word *"truth"* in a poetic sense, as in *"walking in truth."* The author achieved a mesmerizingly powerful effect by blending our sense of reality with our sense of poetry. He mixed the concrete with the abstract. It can be argued that, with this single shift of a single word's meaning, John catapulted one of the many religions of his age onto its stellar trajectory.

It is indeed the position offered by the present author that this was the most critical premise of Christianity's rise and rule. The efficacy of the technique is evidenced throughout modern politics, taking on many forms. From "defending truth" to "speaking up against political correctness" to "voicing the uncomfortable truths," the dictator, the populist, and the ideologue all learned from the master.

It only seems fair to finally enumerate John the Evangelist's roster of achievements: introducing a new meaning of the word "truth." Sending Christianity on its global crusade. Devising the most powerful brainwashing technique known to man. Inspiring dictators, populists, demagogues, and terrorists. And launching the post-truth era in 100 A.D.

Imagine a young, angry scientist reading this. It felt like catching the thief. The Christians stole truth! They stole the word! Onglemeyer has proof! And I was dying to wrangle it back from them. Did no one else see that it worked as a strategy, but it also made Christianity a matter of fiction? Nothing but good marketing? Did no one care? Well, I did. I leaned hard against that Christian structure, holding my scientific rationality like a hammer.

Please, don't judge me too harshly. It took me years to understand that the Christians did not steal the word. They conquered it and ruled it. And by the common etiquette of this planet, that's okay. It's not great, but it's hardly a crime. To some, it's even admirable.

Like Constantine the Great. He certainly admired the Christians. Not their God, as they would like to think, but the way they used words to command people. He was the first Roman Emperor to really take deep notice. And you know what he did? The night of the Battle of the Milvian Bridge, he united his troops under the Christian banner.

That was a shockingly daring move. Imagine, all his hordes had their gods and priests and … interests and quarrels. And Constantine put an end to it overnight. Guess what? It worked. He proved there and then that an army fighting under one God—and a single line of command—beats a much larger band of motley clans, deities, priests, and languages. What a feat.

Flavius wrote about it beautifully. I can look it up if you want.

Anyway, there were still many Christian sects. So next, he called three hundred feuding bishops into Nicaea and told them to bloody agree on a single doctrine, or they wouldn't return home. So, they did. Oh, it's easy to admire Constantine. The Christians learned to rule truth, and Constantine learned to rule the Christians. Isn't that genius? And his son took the final step, when he declared Christianity as the only legal religion of the Empire. It's so logical when you think of it. Simplify, simplify.

Well, back then, I didn't see it as something even remotely respectable. I felt myself a victim of childhood brainwashing, righteously fighting to uncover the wrongs and set them straight. Now, it's crystal clear to me how I was, in fact, just like them. The Christians, the Romans, my Grandma. I was a ruler. A ruthless conqueror of words.

Just finish that omitted chapter and you'll see.

Next Sunday, Adam stood in the pulpit reading the Holy Scripture. His voice was trembling. He knew this was the last time for long that he would stand in a church. And so he read: *"Now, the serpent was craftier than any beast of the field that the Lord God had made. He said to the woman, 'Did God truly say you shall not eat of any tree of the garden?'*

"And the woman said to the serpent, 'We may eat of the fruit of the trees of the garden. But God said, 'You shall not eat of the fruit of the tree that is in the midst of the garden, neither shall you touch it, lest you die.'

"But the serpent said to the woman, 'You will not surely die. For God knows that, when you eat of it, your eyes will be opened, and you will be like God, knowing good and evil.'

"So, when the woman saw that the tree was good for food and that it was a delight to the eyes and that the tree was to be desired to make one wise, she took of its fruit and ate it. She also gave some to her husband, who was with her, and he ate it. Then, the eyes of both were opened, and they knew that they were naked. And they sewed fig leaves together and made themselves loincloths…

"and so on, I'll skip to the end," said Adam, and the priest looked at him sternly.

"Then, the Lord God said, 'The man has now become like one of us, knowing good and evil. He must not be allowed to reach out his hand and take also from the tree of life and eat and live forever.' So, the Lord God banished him from the Garden of Eden to work the ground from which he had been taken."

He cleared his throat. "I have a simple question. Did Adam have a belly button?"

A rustling passed through the church, and the priest stood up.

"Well, if he was created, then he didn't have an umbilical cord, so he shouldn't have had a belly button. Let me ask differently. Is this story true or fictional?"

"True," resonated carefully through the church.

"I'll ask differently again: should I understand it literally or symbolically?"

The church was quiet—a tense and hostile quiet. The pastor approached Adam and impatiently waited for the microphone.

"It amazes me," continued Adam, "when a believer insists that the story is true. Why? Hear it as a real, historical record: a husband and wife lived in a garden called Eden. I mean two specific peeps, not symbolic proto-people. They lived in a garden like the one by your house, just that it's somewhere in the Middle East and the Euphrates and Tigris flow out of it. A snake slithered in—yes, a common snake—served some fruit, and the couple had a lunch. They realized a few things while they ate, which God noticed, and He kicked them out."

At that moment, the priest's patience ran out, and he moved to grab the microphone, but Adam was faster. He jerked the mic out from its stand, and it being a modern microphone, wireless, he ran in between the pews. The pastor stood by the altar, smiling and calming the congregation with his hands. That was a school-boy mistake.

"An interesting story," called Adam's voice from the loudspeakers. He knew his weakness in improvisation, so he'd been rehearsing the speech for a week. Now, he could keep an eye on the distressed priest and the stronger parishioners while reciting by heart: "But you must understand. If the story's true, then it has no meaning for today's world. What a guy had for lunch thousands of years ago in his garden is codswallop now. So, for your own good, let's stick to the idea that it's a fable that can have a symbolic effect today. And oh, does it have an effect! An apple has become the symbol of all knowledge. Eve has become the symbol of all women. The snake, a symbol of temptation. The expulsion from the garden became a symbol of punishment. The fig leaves, a symbol of shame and the story, a symbol of human corruption. All of you, born of the original sin, be ashamed to live! Regret being alive, you brood of vipers!"

The parishioners began to leave the church while others called out. Grandma was rushing to Adam from one side, the pastor from the other.

"My, that blew up, didn't it?" Adam went on. "Each little word blew up like a balloon! Is this the fable you wanted?"

Adam faked to the left, ducked the priest, and snaked around the altar.

"What do you want?" rumbled the loudspeakers. "A true story without symbolic significance or a symbolic fable? I know, you want both. A symbolic narrative you can apply to other situations but not a fairy tale. You want the symbol to be the truth. But that doesn't fit at all; don't you feel it? Can a symbol be true? Can a symbol be real?!"

He cleared his throat and looked at the surprised faces.

"You want to shout—but it isn't clear what, right? You're angry! That's because I'm forcing an apple from the tree of knowledge down your throat. Oh horror, I'll teach you to doubt and think!"

Parents led their children to the doors. Adam scrambled up the stairs to the wooden pulpit, twelve feet high, from which nobody had preached since the Second Vatican Council. He locked the wicket behind him and held it while the pastor rattled the handle. Grandma threatened from below with a walking stick and a heart attack, but Adam saw nothing, heard nothing.

You must be thirsty. Let me fill your glass right away.

Trust me, all that rage is long gone now. The only thing that still upsets me about Christianity is what it did to the cats. You know how they are, little creatures. Cats like to roam around in the night, and they've got their own minds. After sundown, their eyes shine, and when you pet them, their fur sparks. Signs of the Devil, one after the other! That's what Gregor, the 9th I think, declared in the 13th century. So many cats and their owners were then accused of witchcraft. Millions of kittens were killed. And then ... the Black Death came. It decimated Europe. And it returned. It came back for every generation. Europe lost one-third of its population. The kitties were almost wiped out by then, and the remaining ones were even accused of spreading the plague. You know how long it took people to realize that the few surviving cats seemed to protect their owners from the plague? Centuries! Finally, it came out what the terrible plague was all about: without cats, rats bred and spread everywhere. Rats had fleas. Fleas carried the plague. Aiaiai! Isn't it a horrific irony that the death of a third of Europe was an unintended consequence of witch hunts? That's what you get when you insist too hard on what's right and what's wrong. Oh damn, that's sad.

"And if you still want to claim," called Adam from the pulpit for the last time, "that the story is literally true, then Michelangelo is lying, because he did draw the belly buttons in the Sistine Chapel. And I'm not sure that's what you meant. Amen."

The priest had long given up the battle. He sat on the stairs, holding his head in his hands, blocking his ears from Grandma, the only one still trying to reach him. The church was empty. Adam descended the steps and stood over of them. "Don't be afraid," he said.

"Don't think too much of yourself, son," snapped the priest, tearing the microphone out of his hand. "Nobody understood that."

"Such a disgrace," wailed Grandma as she crossed herself so God would see that she had nothing to do with her grandson. On the way home, she didn't greet the neighbors, hid her face behind her shawl, and wouldn't stop sobbing.

Adam was increasingly offended that his own grandmother could forsake him because of some sodding God. He regarded her opinions as fit for two-dimensional hermaphrodites.

"But life, Granny, for goat's sake, isn't a church," he shouted—"in a church, you don't choose, or fuck, or die, and the priest's opinions are a product of that."

"Oh, at least that's true, you pagan." She grew pale and crossed herself. "Until you go and confess, don't even think of going to communion!"

"We can leave it up to Jesus, Gran, whether he wants me to have a bite from him. If he's against it, he'll jerk away."

Grandma was breathing heavily and wiping her brow, and Adam needled deeper still: "That wafer," he shook his head, "that was Jesus' biggest flub. If he hadn't been skimpy and had transubstantiated into a cheeseburger instead, church would be full Monday to Sunday."

There. Adam is finished. He crucified Grandma. It's a sensitive thing for me, this childishness. See, I'm still no softy. If you try to mess with me, I'll whack you with my walking stick right in the kidney. But I'm ashamed of that tantrum fifty years on. I lacked any sense of the terror that Grandma felt when I attacked her structures. In hindsight, it was always my ignorance, rather than logic, that set my course. That portrait from 1912 is a prime example. When it challenged my own structure of reality, I failed to connect the two conflicts. I could have saved myself half the pain had I understood that I was simply suffering a fracture of reality. The kind I so loved to inflict.

At least it's out now. Even though it didn't fit in the book. There's a lot that didn't fit in.

TWO P

esents

Most rock stars of the rebellious mould use their parents'
values as the source point of their desire for reinvention.
—Nick Kent

Time,

barely trudging along. a skilled torturer. Always marching forward at the precise speed that causes the utmost pain, which now meant Adam checked his phone every few minutes. During the night, he left it turned on and would reach for it right after waking up. He messaged Gorgonuy twice without a response.

The part of his brain that wasn't busy waiting for Gorgonuy's message was trying to figure out what romance was. There, he was making exactly zero progress as well.

Falling asleep was hard, so he chose to code as long into the night as possible. On Sunday, he'd switched his computer off at three but didn't nod off until six. At eight, he woke up to a brain running at full speed as though he hadn't even dozed.

His phone rang as he was running to Professor Krugele's office.

"Mother? Please, define romance."

"Hi, Addy. Are you okay?" his mother said.

"Yes. Tell me the three most romantic things in the world."

"Movies?"

"No. Whatever happened to you?"

"Please, don't test me. Grandma's getting worse. I'm afraid Cambridge isn't good for her."

A year ago, she had finally convinced the old lady to sell her home in Galway and move to a retirement home on the outskirts of Cambridge. Three miles away was just about the right distance. "She said they take good care of her, but the nurse didn't tell me anything. Why don't you visit her and talk to the doctor?"

"I won't make it there this week, but I can call in."

"It would be better if you visited her. Grandma was asking about you. It's not just the leg now; the pain around her liver has gotten worse. Bring her a box of chocolates. Are you running somewhere?"

Adam turned into the long corridor of offices in the Statistics department.

"Mum, I'd just freak her out with my heresy."

"Come on. Could you two grow out of arguing? What have you got against her?"

"I don't know. She hasn't yet matured into that kind of under-standing that suits the departing generation so well."

"Then you should be understanding."

"Isn't she the older one?" He was honestly lost in this exchange. The emotional grammar of family relationships was a confusing and stressful discipline. He felt that his mother was trying to convey a piece of it, but the message wasn't legible.

"You won't believe this," she said. "Your uncle called me a min-ute ago. He's unbelievable. Yet again, he yelled about how he won't be cheated out of his inheritance. What's worse, he visited her this morning."

"I'll call you later, Mum." He passed another door, then another, gradually slowing down. "I can't talk now. Bye."

When he hung up, there was a message from Gorgonuy.

4 pm today? In the Pembroke basement.

Adam's hands curled into fists. He looked around and, seeing no one, danced a little victory dance. Unfortunately, as soon as he walked into the office, Professor Krugele looked up from his newspaper, mut-tered, "Stop by tomorrow," smiled encouragingly, and returned to his reading.

Adam sat down in a café, lit a cigarette, and closed his eyes. All of his thoughts slowly dissolved in the smoke until only one was left: who better to ask about romance but an old woman on the verge of dying?

He grabbed his bike and drove over Magdalene's Bridge, then Christ's Pieces and Parker's Piece and stopped by a flower stand. Without thinking whether it was necessary, appropriate, or just cus-tomary, he bought a bouquet.

"Your grandmother?" asked the nurse over her shoulder in the lift.

My grandmother ... He hesitated over the appropriation. Since that soul-cleansing day in Galway, Grandma wasn't his, only her own.

He nodded. "Is she being naughty?"

The nurse laughed. "Do you want a wheelchair? The rooms are rather full, but you could take your Grandma to the gardens."

Talking to Grandma in a room full of eavesdroppers was even less appealing than touching the wheelchair's handle. "Yes," he nodded.

"Thank you."

"Last door on the right." The nurse left.

Adam looked at his watch and pushed the chair through the door. There were six beds opposite each other in two rows, and six heads turned towards the sound.

"Hi, Grandma!"

The old lady didn't respond. Adam walked to her bed and said hello again.

"Adam? Is that Adam?" She turned to the patient on the adjacent bed. "Mrs. Norman, this is my grandson."

"In all his beauty," he uttered.

"I've been here for half a year, and I'm still not used to it. Protestants everywhere. Do you know how far it is to a decent church? And our young doctor is useless. He doesn't know what it's like when your body doesn't serve you. Young people shouldn't be taking care of the old but chasing girls around town. And you, Adam, sit down. Have you found a bride?"

"Have and haven't, Gran."

"And what kind of answer is that? Don't tell me you've got a girl just for fun?" Grandma started getting up.

"And what else for, Grandma? Lie down!"

"You!" Grandma threatened with her finger. "You know it's a sin."

He breathed in. How she always knew what God thinks, what He values, what He despairs over. And truly by a miracle were the Almighty's opinions so damn close to hers.

"Sodom and Gomorrah," she went on. "You haven't changed at all. And who is she? Doesn't she mind that she didn't hear the bells? It wasn't like that when I was young. When he came to ask my father for my hand, we barely knew each other, and he already knew he wanted me as his wife."

Adam looked around. Five heads peeking above the blanket edges listened intently. Mrs. Norman observed Adam particularly sternly.

"Have you found a job yet? You've grown so much. I remember you as the little boy who kept asking questions. And you always had your own answer to everything."

"I'm staying in school as a PhD candidate."

Grandma clasped her hands together. "Still in school? You were too smart when you were little, always buried in books. You didn't even want to play outside. I told everyone that you have a hungry head and you'd make it far. And now this. You'll go straight from student to pensioner!"

One of the heads laughed.

She went on. "Mrs. Ridley's grandson just did his A-levels, and what am I supposed to say? If studying isn't going well, leave it. What are you doing there this whole time?"

"I'm doing research, Gran. You'll like it. I'm statistically proving that God exists."

"Come now. You don't have to speculate so much." Grandma waved her hand. "Do you go to Mass on Sundays, at least?"

The heads held their breath.

"Look." He pointed at the wheelchair. "Your taxi's here. I'll take you outside for a minute." And he quickly added: "Fresh air will do you good."

The old lady sat up and hung her thin legs over the edge of the bed. Adam took her in his arms, much lighter than he'd expected, and carefully put her in the chair. He draped the blanket over her knees and pushed her out of the room.

"Goodbye," he said without turning around, and quiet whispers followed him instead of a response.

"So do you go to Mass sometimes?"

"Not much, Gran."

"At least sometimes, then."

Instinctively, he made one more attempt to connect with her. "Gran, imagine that, one day, I'll predict which plane will fall."

"It's fifty-fifty," dismissed Granny.

"Excuse me?"

"Fifty-fifty. Either it crashes, or it don't."

Adam rolled his eyes, but he didn't have anything to roll them towards. He tried to show her how he was progressing, visually, on charts from Faustomat. He mentioned sleep deprivation and working until dawn, the number of lines of code and the insane disproportion between the demands of the project and the chance of success. In his youthful folly, he still believed that the greater the effort, the more important the work.

"Don't tell me about that. Now I'm going to be worried about you!" The old lady's head started shaking. "I'm just taking your time, and my pressure will go up."

"Don't worry, Gran. I'll manage."

"But if you're having trouble, I'll have to think about you," the old lady continued, well versed in verbal violence.

Adam gazed at Grandma's almost translucent neck, and he suddenly realized how calmly she sat, waiting, motionless. That resignation ... she laid her hands in her lap as though she were holding a toy God. They seemed to embrace each other, trusting that, together, nothing bad could happen to them.

"Gran, was your life romantic?" He went straight for what he'd come for.

"Who's asking?"

"Me, Adam. Your grandson. What was the most romantic thing in your life?"

"The wedding, of course! I told you about it many times." She had, indeed. But buying the ring was out of the question. First off, Adam really needed to verify that he was even able to handle this class of explosives and not go straight to nuking a city.

"So, what made it romantic?" Dissect, observe, learn.

"Oh, the white color everywhere. I loved the silverware. And my father had tears in his eyes when he walked me down the aisle. I've never seen him cry except that day, you know? Not even during the raids."

"Anything else?"

"I never asked for more," she whispered lightly. "And really, I don't remember that much."

Watching Grandma's face, he saw the very look he was after: the dreamy, distant, and wholly inner gaze. But what was it about that formal act, Adam wondered, that held such gravity for her, lasting a lifetime?

They rolled into the park. A few tall trees screened the grass from the overcast sky. They found a free bench, he sat down, and the old lady pulled the blanket up to her shoulders.

"What's hurting, Grandma?"

"Everything now, my boy. The leg won't listen. I felt my knees get wooden, and I couldn't get up for communion. In the end, the altar boy carried me home. And imagine this, the young doctor laughed and said I'm supposed to wear thicker stockings. The people have been whispering that he's not a real doctor. And it tends to hurt here, and here as well." Her crooked finger pointed at her back. "Well, I'm past my shelf life."

"I almost forgot." Adam slapped his knee and dove into his bag. He pulled out a large crumpled cone of paper and tore it apart. "A bouquet, Gran." He introduced the bundle of daisies in green asparagus. "Get better soon."

Grandma disentangled her arm from under the blanket (so skinny!) and timidly stretched out her fingers. When she touched the stem, her reddened and loose lower eyelid brimmed over with tears.

"I'm sorry, Jesus—" Adam started.

"Adam," the old lady's lips rustled, "I haven't gotten flowers in, what, thirty years. And such lovely ones, too."

Thirty years! In her unfocused, glassy eyes, new characters appeared: the ageing widow; the diligent, hard-working woman; the young single mother; the betrayed maiden; the taciturn girl. Each of them hesitantly grabbed one of the flowers and disappeared. He shivered. Though they were close enough to touch, it was a mere illusion of an encounter. She and Adam both looked in opposite directions in time (he ahead, she back), and their independent presences only briefly bulged towards each other, just close enough that a bouquet of flowers could be tossed across.

"Adam." The wrinkly fingers suddenly gripped his wrist. "I won't be here much longer."

Damned flowers. He closed his eyes. He didn't have a single word ready for a conversation like this. "Nonsense, Gran. You look healthy." He grinned.

"Oh hush," Grandma muttered, firmer again. "Nothing will hurt up there. Listen, there's a bag inside my bedside table." She lay the flowers on the blanket. "I wrote *FOR THE COFFIN* on it, so it doesn't get lost. That's the last thing I'd like."

"Don't you want to wait for Mum to take it?"

Grandma looked at him. "Mum died years ago."

"My mum, Gran," and when she didn't answer, he proposed: "Do you want to go around the gardens some more?"

"No, my leg is getting chilly." She wiped her eyes. "Take me back to the room."

Adam looked at his watch. "I'll get going, Gran. I have a meeting in a minute."

They didn't talk on the way back, and when they entered the room, Grandma didn't even answer Mrs. Norman's cry of, "Those are flowers!" He drew the duvet aside and tucked her in like she used to when putting him to sleep. What symmetry.

He opened the drawer and took out a plastic bag. A plump bottle rolled out from the back.

"Gran, you're drinking?"

"It's only port wine, you. Oh, I'm sure I forgot my sip after lunch. Pour me a little one." Adam found a thick glass in the drawer. Grandma swished the wine in her mouth, her eyes closed.

"There. And now go."

Adam promptly exited the retirement home. He was rushing not only to the meeting in the Pembroke basement but also to fulfill Grandma's understandable wish: to let the grandson dissolve with the port. And only outside did it occur to him that he hadn't asked the doctor how Grandma was doing. Well, too late. Of all the conversations between him and Grandma, this was the very last one.

The

Fool

He who lives without folly is not as wise as he may think.
—François de La Rochefoucauld

"**But** of course," Gorgonuy said, nodding seriously after Adam showed him the inexplicable ancient photograph. He tried to catch hints in the professor's expression; it was tricky with the light of five candles jumping about his face.

"Of course?" fumed Adam. "Sure. Who'd be surprised in the territory of the gods, right?"

"What is your question?"

Adam scoffed and dangled the photograph. "Who is it?"

"You," Gorgonuy replied simply. "But a very long time ago."

"It's not me. Did you take that picture?"

"I may be old, but I'm not this old." He laughed. "That could be an insult or a compliment. I'll choose the latter."

Adam groaned. "I don't know what to think."

"What's your question, again?"

Adam had trouble replying. He felt like he wasn't really being asked but read an incantation. He passed a hand over his face, suddenly weary. "Do you have the archive for me? I want to check if there is a chance that I might have studied in Cambridge in the last century."

"What is your question?" Gorgonuy repeated.

Adam did not understand. "I'm hoping you have the archive with you?"

"Slow down, young man. What is your question?" The professor now enunciated slowly as though he was barely in control of his jaw, or as if he was somehow impeded in speech—perhaps with a straw in his mouth. Or polio.

"I'm not sure what you're asking me."

Gorgonuy put down his glass of Madeira and reached for a pack of tarot cards.

"Oh no."

"So," Gorgonuy said conversationally, "you were actually spot-on last time, remember?"

"When exactly?"

"You said I was taking fairy tales to tenure."

"Professor Gorgonuy, I apologize."

"It's you who's choosing." He shuffled the deck. "The question.

The card. *And* the meaning."

"Are you making a fool of me?"

Gorgonuy spread the cards into a fan and placed one on the table. Its face was thumbed but carefully drawn in black ink. "Which one could that be?"

"The Fool!" Adam shook his head. "Did you draw these yourself?"

"The unnumbered card of the Major Arcana marks the beginning of a journey," Gorgonuy intoned as if he was reading out loud. "We, who, after careful consideration, lean towards the French hermetic system in the tradition of Pap and Lévi, ascribe it the Hebrew letter *shin* and the hieroglyph of a flying arrow."

He tapped the card absently as he continued. Adam simply watched in stunned silence.

"The young man struts forward lightly, cluelessly. His mind knows no prejudice; it is open—perhaps dangerously so. But his honesty is disarming. His spark helps overcome even the toughest of obstacles, indicated by the mountain range in the background."

Gorgonuy was almost hypnotic in his delivery. He pushed the card nearer to Adam so he might appreciate the details in the dim light.

"Watch his face as he lifts his foot over the breakneck fall. He's singing! If the Fool ever feels fear, he doesn't turn away. The path that frightens the most, generally the hardest, is the one for him. Led by this exciting compass of fear, the Fool often wanders where no careful creature will ever set foot. He sees miracles. When he retells them, the disbelievers consider him a fool again." There, he stopped his lecture. "How do you feel about him?"

Adam stifled an exasperated sigh. "The boy got what he chose. He'd better not complain."

"Don't read the card superficially," Gorgonuy warned, "especially not this one. The unnumbered card should open the mind to opportunities. Your big question today—Who am I?—is the Fool's question."

"I know who I am. I don't know what the photograph's all about. And honestly, I came here for the database so I can check I didn't study here a hundred years ago. However foolish that sounds."

Gorgonuy laughed lightly. "You know who you are, but you need to check. Of course!"

0

Adam slipped lower into the chair and went quiet.

"The fact that you feel like a fool about your experience today—don't interrupt—is an important sign. The Fool is a charming, central character of the tarot. The whole Arcana is his pilgrimage. Since he is without a number, he can move freely. He can be a zero, the weakest of all, or the strongest—a joker. Until you understand what the Fool says, you won't understand the words of the Magician."

"It's really not necessary to delve deeper. I came here for the archive. Do you have it?"

"I am helping you answer your question. But you cannot understand one number without the others nor can you understand one card on its own. You cannot understand one feeling without the others, because the cards represent all of them. You must choose another card."

"Not a chance." Adam shifted in his seat, tried to relax.

The professor brushed crumbs off the table. "I am trying to help you. But you must be willing." Then, he pulled a small drum from below, raised it high, and hit it. "Say we just met in a park." He nodded three times. "How will you introduce yourself?" He hit the drum again and laid it on his knees.

"Doctor Gorgonuy," Adam snapped, "why don't *you* tell me why I'm talking to a codger who claims to have a secret archive, banned by the Masons or whatever devil, and then beats a drum over tarot cards while we talk? Do you have the archive? If not, who does?"

"You'll have to swear."

Adam clenched his teeth. "I do."

Gorgonuy tapped the drum. For a moment, he seemed absent. Then he continued, "You won't tell anyone you have it, and definitely not who you got it from. Because you don't want to put yourself, or me, or anyone else in danger, right?"

"Why the paranoia?"

"I warned you. You are entering dangerous grounds, soliciting illegal merchandise."

"Am I soliciting?"

"At this table, you are the buyer."

Adam narrowed his eyes sharply. "Now there's a price? I thought you were helping me."

"The fact that I am sitting at this table as a seller is an act of charity. But I had to pay my source. You have to pay me."

"How much?"

"Impatient youth," exhaled the professor. "We'll meet in two weeks, precisely. Here again. You'll introduce yourself. You will know who you are. If I'm satisfied, I'll give you the memory card."

"And what will you want for it? I hope it's not money because I don't have that."

"Money, tut tut. I'm an old man. What's still worth something to me? What is worth anything in the world?"

"You," Adam spoke slowly, "are starting to sound like a dirty old man."

Gorgonuy laughed for the first time since beginning his performance. "Let me tell you who I am." He stretched out his hand and then held the handshake for much longer than was comfortable. "Call me the Collector."

Adam sighed at this, then nodded.

"Guess what I collect."

"Batman comics."

"Guess again."

"No."

Gorgonuy seemed to smile wider. "You're stubborn. Cute." He leaned forward conspiratorially. "I collect real people."

"People?" The conversation had become surreal. He expected Gorgonuy to pull out a chainsaw any moment.

"Yes. I have a lovely collection. And that's your big break. Because that Cambridge archive is full of people—of course it is. So I decided to pay for it."

"Who sold it to you?"

"You can only buy from me, at my price." He raised the drum and hit it again.

Adam pulled away. "You're insane, aren't you?"

"Yes! Over the mask of a professor, I'm wearing the mask of a clown. How frightening. Hitting a drum!" Another loud bang.

"Just tell me what you want," said Adam.

"Why don't they sell reproductions at Sotheby's?"

"There's too many of them. Duh."

"Right. Imagine a fine painting, the finest. It attracts like a magnet. An artist became so immersed that they remained to partly live on in the painting. People feel that. And now," he waved his finger, "forget the paintings. And something is left, do you understand?" Gorgonuy leaned over to Adam and quietly spoke in a bizarre rhythm, at once hypnotic and disturbing. "A person. That's what I collect."

"Like in a fridge?"

Gorgonuy ignored the barb. "I have letters one only writes once in a lifetime. An unfinished love note from a certain István Estebányi from the trenches of the Great War. The boy carried it folded in his breast pocket. Now, it's got four bullet holes in it. I have over three hundred last wills and testaments. Some autographs—Churchill, Stalin. And a string of self-portraits, like a mini-series, from prisoners at Sintra near Lisbon."

His shoulders rose proudly. He seemed barely aware of Adam anymore.

"In the seventies, I worked as a tour guide in Quinta de Regaleira. When you're around there, do stop by. Walk around the garden for a day. What you will find there, you won't find anywhere else. I had a friend in the prison at the time." He tapped absently on the drum. "We smuggled cigarettes in, and the cons drew for me in return. But I have mostly letters because I like letters the most. You put a paper in front of someone and tell them—write yourself. How they start blundering like there's nothing inside! I could watch that all the time. And look, they always dredge something out. Because they want something I have. Cigarettes. Information. I have something for everyone."

There was a brief silence as Gorgonuy appeared to gaze into spacetime.

"I don't know if it's illegal," Adam spoke up, "but it's worryingly creepy."

"Why? The nights drag on as you get older. An old lady may walk to the park to feed pigeons and watch people. I'll take two letters and make them friends. Or I'll think up how their kids would turn out. I'll open a wine, Tinta Negra Mole, if I have the option, light a candle, and I'll ponder what death will suit them. And then, one night in the moonlight, the collection blossoms. Your feeling is refined like a winemaker's nose. Slowly, you start approaching the soul of man. Like Darwin, when he grasped the soul of his collection. It blooms and reaches out to entrust you with the secret of life. What that means for you, unfortunately," he paused, "is that the bar is high."

"Can we cut to the chase?"

"Draw. Write me something. But for God's sake, don't bore me. Then, you get the data."

Adam sat back, lifted his hands. "So, I'm supposed to write up— what? My life? That'll be fifty pages at least."

"One page. If you bore me in a page, I'd be in coma after fifty."

Adam shook his head angrily.

"Do you see, now?" Gorgonuy picked up the tarot card from the table and waved it. "The Fool has a question."

Adam got up and left. He reproached himself for not bidding Gorgonuy farewell right when he'd pulled out the tarot. This muttering buffoon was an outlandish dead end. If the historical archive existed at all, it had to be in the University. And if that was the case, Krugele had to know about it.

Stuck on this front, Adam's thoughts turned to the other: engineering the love experiment. A project of such weight called for a teammate, or, at the very least, an expert consultation.

Having no better options, he called Marquis. A workshop session was scheduled for the very same night, at the Eagle, at eight.

Infid

elity

When you marry, Filip, one of the things that happen is that you start waking up every morning next to the same woman. There is something deeply satisfactory there for us men.

—Piers Bursill-Hall

"What?"

he blurted out. He'd expected a private conversation, but when he found Marquis, there were three attractive women with him. Goddamned chemistry; a hormonal cocktail stirred up Adam's blood. His glasses fogged up, and a red tide reached the vessels in his cheeks.

One of the women captivated him. Her beauty was a work of mathematics. Her DNA gave rise to an exquisite resonance, which might crudely be called a body, or, more academically, an ornament of countless frequencies, a *fractal*. He knew her name was Eve.

If Adam weren't so painfully aware of his awkwardness, he would immediately offer to fan her eyelids, kiss her ankles—anything, forever—just not a conversation. In fact, he was shocked that Eve and Marquis were talking at all, considering their breakup from two weeks ago, which Marquis had recounted to him.

-⚓-

He circled her skin with two fingers. "I'm sad," he sighed.

"Why?"

"Your breasts are the perfect Tao."

She laughed. "Tell me about them."

Marquis watched them bounce as she laughed. "The Tao that can be spoken is not the eternal Tao."

"The Tao came and laid down in your bed."

"The Tao is about to leave."

She stroked his cheek. "She isn't."

"It'll stay here?"

"She will."

"Unchanging, perfect, eternal?"

She nodded, faltering.

"Forever?"

"If you'll want that."

He leaned over and kissed her cheek. "I won't."

He lay on his back and observed the Tao slowly putting her top on and searching for her clothes, which they had thrown everywhere around them a moment ago. When she stretched over him behind the bed, he stroked her, and she stiffened under his hand.

"Oh, Marquis," she said dejectedly. "What is this?"

He propped himself up on his elbow. Two pairs of panties were lying on the floor. One was black with a pink bow, the other pure white.

"Are you sleeping with someone else?"

"I was checking if you're still the most gorgeous woman out there, and trust me, you are."

He stretched over her to get the panties and passed them to her.

She shook her head. "The other ones."

He stopped and apologetically handed her the other pair. He was certain he'd reached for her own panties the first time around.

"I'm stoked that now you know." She was getting dressed. "I hope you remember it for fucking ever."

"Eve, we didn't promise each other anything."

"Oh, thank God."

"What's going on, then?"

She paused. "Why can't you stay with just one woman?"

He shrugged. "Why don't you eat porridge every day?"

"But women won't go after you forever, big shot."

"Exactly."

They looked at each other in silence for a moment. Then she smiled and said, "Wave goodbye to the Tao."

But what stayed imprinted in his mind was surprisingly not the eternal and unchanging Tao. It was the view of two delicate pieces of clothing composed into one tragic whole. The image was the point of all his episodes. Each individual lover was attractive in her own right. Yet, together, they were a tragedy.

Just like the panties, Eve's breasts mingled with the anthropologist from Amsterdam and the dance-like movements of the Gardenia waitress. That way, even Marquis found his perfect woman, albeit *per partes*. Whenever he'd be pulling down another pair of panties, his perfectly composed lover would stand nearby. And he would forever be insufficiently captivated, sagging outside the present. Poisoned by the tragedy of composition, which, he was realizing, was not a quality of his lovers.

Or something like that. In the bar, Eve tenderly quipped, "You should get going so you catch something tonight."

"You still think I have to chase?" wondered Marquis, forgetting to introduce Adam. "I just refuse to resist."

"And I think you're just not worth her time," laughed Eve's Persian friend.

Marquis' womanizing was the topic of the night, and Adam was bored. He could explain his friend's behavior easily. Any woman he was currently talking to was merely the nearest woman in space-time. Nevertheless, he awaited his friend's own rationalization.

"True." He didn't disappoint. "But you are drop-dead gorgeous, both of you. And that's besides having the brains to study in Cambridge. So be honest. Why do you dress so attractively? Look at your yoga pants here. I'm sure they are comfortable, but they are also, mind you, cute as hell. Is that by chance? Or is it an invitation?"

"What an old argument. Rapists say that," said Eve.

"Yet I'm not a rapist, and it's not an argument. I merely ask—why do you dress so attractively? Surely to attract someone? Something?" And before they interjected, he added: "I know it's not sex. But connection? A few looks, every day? You do want that, don't you?"

The women looked at each other, rolling their eyes. Eve replied. "You have no idea what it's like to be a woman. We live lives of constant interruption, of our thoughts and words. And of unwanted sexual advances from deeply inappropriate people."

"That's so easy to solve! Stop washing your hair, dress like a beggar, and drop that nail polish."

"Or, teach men how to treat women with respect?" interjected Eve's friend.

"Yes! Anything I can do to help with that?" He was nodding wildly. "The net result will be more flirting as the game gets safer for all."

She shook her head vaguely. "So how are you finding the scene? Is anyone in Cambridge still into one-night stands?"

"Ask your friend here." He pointed to Eve and winked.

"God, you really have no shame!"

Adam could not decipher whether the women were offended or entertained and did not dare to speak up. The conversation also had absolutely no value to him. He was just waiting. And suddenly, his silence had made him the center of attention; the others were looking at him.

"Just continue ignoring me," he stated apologetically and forced out a nervous laugh.

And as if he just materialized out of thin air, one of Eve's friends felt compelled to describe what she was seeing.

"I can read you like a book," she pointed.

Adam tried to vaporize again, unsuccessfully.

"Cambridge must be the only place in the world where guys compete over how many learning disorders they've had and whose Asperger's is worse. 'They bullied me in kindergarten! I'm not paranoid, I just doubt consistently! Cappuccinos give me epileptic seizures! Sex is male and female! I am the Cambridge aspergoisie!'"

"Thanks," Adam agreed. "I feel completely average here. It's depressing."

Marquis nodded. "Did I tell everyone what Adam is working on?"

"You did," Eve snarked at Marquis. "I hope that shy mathematician may find the meaning of life and explain it to you."

"Data scientist," Adam corrected, but they ignored him.

"Oh! So, do you think my life lacks meaning now?" asked Marquis.

"No. I think you lack a brain."

The other women chuckled. Adam shifted uncomfortably.

"I'd like those panties you took," Marquis said as if they were alone. "You know they're not yours."

"They fit me well. You have good taste in asses. Whose are they?"

"I'd like to frame them."

"And my panties aren't enough?"

"They'll be in the painting too. Can I have them?"

"Do you really have to hang trophies up a wall?"

At this point, the other women appeared to lose their amusement at the banter. They turned to chat between themselves. Adam finally breathed out.

"This'll be art," Marquis bragged. "I bought a beat-up frame at the flea market. Solid wood. I'll put in half of the cigarette you left in the ashtray, with your lipstick on it. I peeled the label off the Bordeaux we didn't finish. I used that bottle to smash the vinyl I played for you. I miss you, Eve. I want to have you framed."

"I might even tear up."

"Will you give them to me?" repeated Marquis. "Please?"

She leaned over without a trace of humor. "Your friend Asperger here is more likely to touch them."

"Is this revenge?"

"What for?" said Eve. "I just like shy mathematicians."

She turned to Adam and wrote a number on his arm.

"Let's go?" She turned to her friends, and they walked away with laughter.

Adam waited, motionless, for the adrenaline wave to subside.

"I'm sorry," said Marquis, suddenly empathetic. "She's just trying to get back at me."

"Don't apologize." Obviously, it was revenge. From whatever angle he looked at it, he couldn't fail to see the humiliating offense. But, oddly, he didn't feel that bad. "It's okay," he batted away his friend's concern. "I came here to ask for advice."

"Right! What is it?"

"I need to do something romantic with Nina. What should I do?"

Marquis replied without missing a beat. "Take her out to see the swans along the Cam. A bottle of red will do the trick."

"Stronger."

He considered. "Okay. Bed full of flowers. Champagne with strawberries."

"Stronger."

All right. A few days in a boutique hotel. Nice view, old city."

"Where?"

"Prague, my friend."

Adam was doubtful. "You're from Prague, so you know it there. I was thinking more around here."

"It's the city of a hundred spires. She'll love the medieval streets, churches, the Charles Bridge. Prague is the definition of romance. Choose a hotel in the Old Town, don't be an idiot, and Nina will melt like snowflakes. Guaranteed."

Adam was nodding guardedly. "It's hard, taking advice from you."

"Why now?"

"You're such a bastard that I don't trust you."

They laughed, and Marquis patted the phone number on Adam's forearm. "Call Eve. You owe me those panties."

"I'll do my best." Despite Marquis' unrelenting self-confidence, Adam slowly started taking immense pleasure in the moment. "And I don't have Asperger's," he assured him. "I took a test."

❦

Walking to Pembroke, Adam's thoughts were with Eve. Just thinking of her was making him feel guilty. The one and only time he'd been unfaithful was to his ex-girlfriend, Veronica. And that too began with a thought.

They were in bed one night, basking in orgasm. He stroked Vero's hair splayed on his chest. And suddenly, he realized with terror that everyday indolence would lead him to lifelong loyalty.

What could be so horrible about loyalty?

The weight of alternate realities. Hundreds of surrogate Adams crowded the only faithful one, each with a different mistress, scratching their armpits and laughing in his face: "You missed it again! You went home again, and we had fun! Next time, buddy!" During the next few restless nights, he rolled from one possibility to the next.

It was possible to simplify those branching variants of his. All of the potential Adams could be summed up into two stories: the story of Adam (about everything he does) and the story of Anti-Adam (about everything he gives up). Lived and unlived. At every prospect of adultery, Adam would grandly wave towards Anti-Adam: have her, chap, all yours. He was peacefully faithful every day, in every episode, face to face with the deepest of cleavages.

But the story has its own arithmetic. When Adam calculated the sum totals of his life, he wanted his half. Not to enjoy the uncontrollable excitement of an episode but to avoid the boredom of the monotone story. And so, one evening at the end of a warm May, as he watched the ceiling lying next to Vero, he decided—it couldn't go on like this. Loyalty is laziness!

First, he tried explaining the narrative imperative to Veronica. She didn't understand, so he cut himself short: "I have to sleep with someone occasionally so life doesn't pass me by."

She moved in with a friend who had her own little flat in the new buildings by the river. In the days that followed, they didn't see each other and only talked twice on the phone, curtly. They deftly avoided the topic.

After a week, Veronica returned to his place, but not for a conversation. She didn't argue, she didn't threaten to break up with him. She just kept repeating that she didn't want to hear about infidelity. Adam couldn't figure out what it meant—surely, the problem he'd described hadn't been resolved?

Only after two or three days did he realize that she was silently giving him free rein. The possibility of an arrangement like this hadn't even occurred to him. Why, concealing a mistress and feigning loyalty meant that he'd have to lie! Ouch!

It's intriguing how lying was completely foreign to him, even though he'd never set out to speak only the truth. Why's that?

Every day, Adam's brain processed 10^{20} bits of information. That's the number of ants in the world times a thousand. It's a million times more than there are stars in our galaxy.

The gigantic flood attacked memory, sharply limited by the size of his skull and the available energy. How did he select which thousandth, which billionth he'd remember? What was important?

A rough and basic guideline: that which repeats. More precisely: that which repeats approximately, which stopped repeating, which is similar to other repetitions. Patterns. Abstract and causal. Patterns in the changing tones of Nina's voice, her visions and melancholies.

Moreover, Adam engaged in so-called thinking. He compared patterns to each other. He classified and bundled them; one could say he was weaving his own spider web. (There, a metaphor, or a similarity of patterns.) He looked for what connected galactic spirals with the shape of DNA's double helix and the pinecone on the papal ferula.

He questioned whether the existence of life defied entropy and the second law of thermodynamics. When someone then chided him for thinking too much, he just shrugged: lazy memory.

Is it not natural that, during such lengthy sifting, the brain starts to dream of reaching the ultimate end? That it'll one day connect the mighty pattern of life with the mighty pattern of entropy as well as the rest of human knowledge, expressible in ten axioms at the most, and then it won't have to remember anything else, because it'll easily deduce all of physics, mathematics, philosophy, literature, and where to go shopping, all from these ten axioms? Is it not strictly rational to dream about an überpattern so pervasive that it'll connect tarot cards with planetary movement, social revolutions, airplane catastrophes, floods, divorces, and winning lottery tickets, to laugh down once and for all the ignorant concept of chance? Is it not simply *prudent* to dream of I-Ching and astrology? Or a computer program built to grasp that überpattern?

At no point in that process did Adam worry about truth. But the repeatedly useful patterns selected by his brain corresponded to the common conception of truth almost to the letter.

Said more memorably, ergo more truthfully: the scientist loves truth because truth is what's easiest to remember. And once more, in Adam's words: "Whatever a scientist remembers is the truth."

⬧

Adam's dilemma was not whether to cheat or to stay faithful. It was a choice of two evils: remembering his lies versus leaving all the lovers to Anti-Adam. In these arduous considerations, under the relentless strain of a carefree relationship, he finally decided, in the spirit of the narrative imperative, that he'd rather lie than bore.

But was he even capable of it? Only an experiment could tell. And in the words of Peter Drucker, plans are only good intentions unless they immediately degenerate into hard work. An experiment in infidelity had to be staged, performed, and evaluated. Only then would Adam begin to believe that he was a real man, mature enough for marriage.

She doesn't have a name, he repeated. She doesn't have a name to remember. He put his glass down on the bar and kissed her. Chewing-gum-mint bit his tongue. You'll teach me to lie, he thought to himself, and let his tongue mumble something with hers. It wasn't that unpleasant, and what's more, with his eyes closed, he could almost forget to think. The woman's mouth responded lightly and decisively, like she was returning to familiar places, and her skin smelled slightly of oil, with a tinge he couldn't stop inhaling. He took her neck in both hands, and she didn't pull away at all. I can still stop, he explained to himself, and there was no reply.

"What's your name?" she asked suddenly.

Adam faltered. "What?"

"What's your name?" She stroked his hair and looked into his eyes.

He cleared his throat. "Marquis."

On one of the landings on the way up to her flat, he calculated the chances of successful intercourse: twenty percent. And that was on the stairs to her flat, after all of the obstacles he'd already overcome. Impotentia inteligentis: where are the days when preserving the bloodline would be threatened by the sperm count rather than the neuron count?

In the semi-darkness, he looked over their voluminous, pale bodies and acknowledged that what could have been considered fun had just ended. She softly entwined him with her arms and thighs. The soft bottom of her stomach helplessly pushed against him, like a stump without fingers.

"Release the condom!" he called, unnaturally loud, and she let out a wild laugh. He stretched over to his trousers and took out the pocket-sized puzzle. Solving it would prove that he was kinesthetically and intellectually mature enough for intercourse. He also wanted to explicitly place a barrier between their bodies, making clear that they weren't that close.

He blew into the transparent cap from both sides. In the end, he switched on the lamp and put his glasses on. "The police should use this instead of breathalyzers. If you can put a condom on, you can drive."

She smiled but waited. Adam's flailing reason attempted to regain balance and authoritatively decide whether to persevere with the experiment or allow himself to run home. But he held the course.

Then, the issue of firmness came into play. They both did their best.

"The sausage is overcooked?" She finally stopped him. "Are you nervous?"

"Unfortunately, no," he replied and authorized himself to terminate the experiment. In the shower, he scrubbed himself forcefully and returned to the bedroom to apologize. He found her on the balcony, sitting on a chair in her underwear, smoking. She stopped him from talking.

"Your shirt is inside out."

He thanked her and set off home, looking forward to a good sixty years of concealment.

Afterwards, he had terrible dreams. Someone with a heavy, muddy step approached the back of his head and stood where he couldn't see him. He dreamed that he'd sweated out several thin bones. Strewn around the white sheet, they were reminiscent of a family tomb.

Barely three weeks later, Veronica said quietly, "You slept with someone."

He didn't move. "What are you talking about?"

A long silence. "Don't lie to me. I know you slept with someone."

"I'm not lying."

"You can't lie."

"And I'm not lying," proclaimed Adam, writhing in a net he still hadn't noticed. "Why would you say that?"

"You came home showered and smelling of someone else's soap."

I see you, snuggled up in lies … A poem he'd seen on the London tube. He remembered the sentence because it had been so foreign then.

"Oh please. I tried out the gym." Isolate the lie into a cocoon.

Veronica turned on the lamp and looked into his eyes. A second, two. And Adam's body started twitching with a laugh. He tried to look at her seriously and convulsed. Something chuckled at his denials, like when he was ten and his mom asked who ate the whole chocolate. Now, his lying was just as shoddy.

He controlled himself only when tears started dripping from Veronica's eyes. He wanted to hug her, and she pulled away instantly. "Did you cheat on me? Just tell me: yes or no."

Laughter. His compulsive laughter was the chiming bell announcing a generous moment in which it was possible to touch a new understanding of humanity. They could argue about infidelity, Adam could continue denying like a ten-year-old, and Veronica could claim that infidelity was a terrible evil, but all of that, informed the chimes, would only be a performance of roles. The laughter tore off the illusion of adulthood, and Adam resigned himself to what he and Veronica were meant to learn together—to understand each other a little better, not as people but as conscious beings.

"That depends on the definition, my love," he breathed in deeply, having thought about it so many times in the last three weeks.

"What definition is this again?"

"Of infidelity."

"God, that's clear enough, isn't it? Did you kiss?"

"Technically, but it wasn't what you're imagining."

"Did you sleep with her? Tell me exactly, beginning to end, what you did."

He repeatedly assured Veronica that it wasn't about sex. He described how foreign the woman was to him, how comical their exercise was. That he struggled with erection and the condom. And how they eventually stopped the intercourse and separated without a farewell. The only conclusion he could draw from the episode was how much more he loved Veronica.

He smiled sadly and tried to hug her. In the quietest voice, she pronounced her verdict: "You're sick and broken. I'm glad I know now. Unbelievably glad."

She got up, took a big linen bag out from under the bed, and started folding her clothes off the shelves. When he stepped up to her, she immediately stopped him with a quick movement of her alert hand.

"Will you help me with this?" she asked. It was two in the morning.

He mechanically pulled out the key to his father's car, which he'd borrowed for the week. Whenever he remembered that evening in the future, he thought, if only he had coldly, or at least angrily, refused to take Vero to her friend, and the episode had ended there. But some medical student was already getting up in the nearby Riverside Jazz Bar, having lost seven rounds of poker, biking drunk and turning onto the main street in front of Pembroke without lights, right in front of the car driven by Adam, who jerked the steering wheel toward the sidewalk, barely missing the dodging pedestrians and crashing into a cast-iron pole.

Had he refused, both her legs wouldn't have been broken. But then, he wouldn't agonize in guilt for months about chance, and there would be no Faustomat. And he wouldn't meet Nina. Seen from every possible angle, the adultery experiment produced thoroughly paradoxical results.

◆

Walking back to Pembroke from meeting Marquis at the Eagle, he felt guilty and dirty. He looked over his shoulder and, seeing he was alone on the street, he slapped himself three times. When he got to the college, he lay next to Nina, who hugged him half-sleeping. Touching her, he was fairly certain that what he was feeling is commonly referred to as love.

"I love you, Nina," he whispered through her hair. "Though I'll never tell you because I'm an idiot." And he fell asleep. He had frightening dreams that night involving a curious black explosive device with a pink bow. But he wasn't one to pay much attention to dreams.

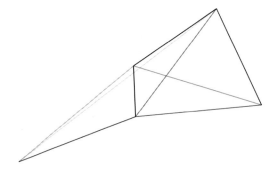

Toito

Only in the darkness can you see the stars.

—Martin Luther King Jr.

I hope you're not cross with my young self for all his disconnects. Because then, you'd carry the contagion on. Deep down, after all, dividing is relating. Refusal is attention. Insults are care.

While you were reading, I was fumbling around the higher shelves, and this little book jumped into my hand by itself. A hand-bound volume, thin and unsigned. It barely holds together. Open it to the last page.

Toito

They pointed to a girl and thus named a boy.
They pointed to the sky and thus named the earth.
They divided and thus joined.
They named and thus concealed.
They compared and thus set apart.
They set apart and thus compared.
They emphasized and thus ignored.
They scorned and thus cared.
They loved and thus neglected.
They always did both this and that, as the light throws a shadow.

One of my favorite poems. I'll admit that I do actually know who wrote it. But I'll keep that to myself, if you don't mind.

Faust

omat

Sometimes, we stare so long at a door that is closing that we see too late the one that is open.

—Alexander Graham Bell

Right

after inviting Adam to sit down, professor Krugele lit a cigar as though here, in the department of pure mathematics and mathematical statistics, general laws paradoxically lost their legitimacy. Adam gave a quick rundown of his progress. Faustomat v.1 was live, analyzing over seventy sources of data. Then he moved to his point.

"Professor Krugele. Do you know how I can get research access to the digitized historical record of Cambridge students?"

"What's this?"

"The records of all students with their biographies, academic records, and so on, from the fifteenth century onwards. I just need the access."

Krugele shook his head. "Where did you hear about this?"

"I heard it through the grapevine."

"Excuse me?"

A fragile lie has to be cushioned by a soft layer of fog, so it doesn't break against the hard facts. But Adam simply didn't know how to lie. Or how to dilute truth, bluff, change topic, turn the question against the inquirer, or paint sparrows yellow and sell them as canaries.

"The university digitized the archive and then decided to pull the plug on the entire project. Look, I know the archive exists. The day before yesterday, someone offered me a copy, but of course, I'd rather source it directly from the university."

Krugele frowned. "So the offer—"

"I'd prefer to get access legally from the school," Adam interrupted, "which is why I've held off on the offer for now. This data will push my dissertation up to another level."

"We'll talk about that later. Who offered it to you? Someone from the university?"

"I'm afraid I can't say."

"Oh." Dr. Krugele watched him for a moment. "My impression of this conversation is that not only are you basing your work on data that's non-existent, but it's also illegally acquired. This is truly unique. Did you report the leak of students' personal information?"

"It's historical records. I don't think Isaac Newton and his schoolmates have a problem with data privacy. And trust me, they wouldn't come to any harm through my work."

"Adam, which planet are you living on? Stolen personal data is a completely impermissible source for a dissertation, if I even must say that out loud. You should be very thankful if I decide to pretend this conversation never happened."

Alternative futures melted in front of Adam's eyes. He hastily cast about for options by loosening his implicit assumptions: did he need this database specifically? Could he only get it from the clown Gorgonuy or the university? Would it help anything if he whacked Krugele over the head with a chair?

"I was planning to go over this idea of yours once again anyway. If I even understand what you are attempting." Krugele waved his cigar. "Arriving through all of the noise to some clear function of God, order, fractal, or whatever it is you're looking for, is unimaginable work. I'll tell you the result straight away. Anything you'll find will have less significance than the approximations you'll make to control for demography and other known influences."

"You're missing the point," protested Adam. "You assume I'm using classical regression. I'm not. I'm looking for fractal similarity between the data sources. I have coded twenty-seven fractal functions in generic form. And an arbitrary number of data sources can be fed into each function with different weights and angles." He outlined the cogwheels with his fingers. "Don't envision some two-dimensional joke of a correlation, but a model in n dimensions. The intuition is completely incapable of grasping that, so it's premature to enter a discussion about whether I'll find anything or not." Just in case, he added, "Don't take that personally."

"Please, Adam, fractal regression is not scalable to the real world, especially, as you say, in multiple dimensions. Unless you've built a quantum computer in your bedroom, it's not a computable problem."

"That's why the Faustomat itself is a fractal."

"You mean it's recursive."

For a moment, Adam scanned the ceiling for a way to translate the cloud of his thoughts into a linear succession of words that could trickle out of his mouth and inflate back into a cloud in the listener's head. Failing, he started ripping and slicing the mental cloud until he somehow got it in front of the professor in a butchered form.

"Fractal. The algorithm chooses a fractal function and some data sources, pretty much randomly. Say, crime rate maps, the routes of migratory birds, and historic temperature. It'll cluster the source data using Monte Carlo. And it chooses an angle with which each source connects to the function. I say angle because it's easiest to model in n-dimensional space, but it's really a transformation. One time in a million, a symmetry appears in the segments. That is, one source projects relatively well onto the others. But maybe just a small part of the data, or just to a certain extent. The similarity is not trivial to measure. How do you map constellations, paintings, Twitter feeds, and Cambridge students against each other? By mixing fuzzy logic, deep learning, and genetic algorithms—"

Krugele's eyes narrowed, and Adam immediately responded to the perceived objection.

"Of course, a perfect natural order wouldn't need these approximations! I expect that the central function will explain the last detail from A to Z, but the only way I can get to it is by approaching it gradually. Or, imagine the all-pervasive order as a fan of fractals morphing into each other. These initial patterns are just partial studies of transitive states. So, in short," Adam was now standing over Krugele and drawing on a scrap of paper on his desk, "after I calculate individual results, I test them for meta-symmetries. If there's at least a weak one, I know that those data sources are fractally correlated. Bingo! I add more segments and more frequencies until the significance stops growing."

"Please, Adam—"

"These initial glimpses—I call them sprouts—they compete through the genetic algorithm while I bombard them with new data from all angles. In most cases, the symmetry is lost with the new data because it only appears in patches of a few dimensions. So in those cases, I remove the older data sources to prune the sprout," the scribble on the paper was now reminiscent of a squid swallowing its own tentacles, "and so Faustomat gradually traverses the fractal like a thousand-legged spider, sometimes spending a few hours in the micro-world and a second later rising to the stars, all the time producing stronger symmetries."

It was as though Professor Krugele had fallen asleep with his eyes open.

"When your spider finds something," he said finally, "I'll happily nominate it for a Nobel Prize. In biology. But so far, I fail to see how bombarding sprouts even vaguely approaches the classic conception of statistics, which we perform—with great success, I might add—here at the department."

"I know it's difficult to understand. Should I try again, slower?"

"Anything but that. Why don't you keep your fractals as a hobby, and we discuss terrestrial, and, most of all, publishable dissertation topics?"

"This is where statistics will be in twenty years," Adam insisted. How had his request for data access devolved so swiftly? He tried from a different angle. "You just need to look at the universe as if it were a Böhm's hologram. Then, it makes perfect sense. Besides, my scholarship has been granted for this topic."

"The scholarship is awarded for prior academic work. The proposed topic is just a point of reference." Krugele smiled encouragingly. "You must understand, Adam, every serious scholar will laugh this out of the room. It's unpublishable. And even if you kept the religious waffle to yourself, you explained to me today that you can't provide a source for a crucial part of your data. A thesis using illegal practices—nobody has yet had the courage to propose that to me." Krugele shook his head and tapped the cigar with his thumb. The thick burnt end broke off silently like the cliff of a glacier.

"Now you're rejecting my thesis. Why didn't you tell me when I applied in the spring?"

"I relayed my doubts then. You chose to ignore them." And he added conciliatorily, "You're at the start of your scientific career, Adam. Don't spoil it. Work on, say, graph theory. There are splendid open problems in vertex coloring—or, if you wanted something really ambitious, there's a tough nut in Ramsey's hypergraph theory. Why don't you think about it over the weekend?"

Adam, red in the face, rashly rapped his fingers on the table. "Allow me one question."

"Yes?"

"Who won the World Cup in '72?"

Krugele put down his cigar. "I have no idea."

"Neither do I. And I'm even less interested in graph theory than I am in football. I have nothing to think about."

"Obstinacy," chewed Krugele. "The grand enemy of a scientific career."

Adam got up, gathered his papers into his bag, and left.

Out in the hallway, he ground his teeth. He felt full enough of testosterone to burn the place down. Or to call Eve.

So he did.

She was nearby, so they met.

And so it happened that, partly thanks to Krugele, he walked home that day with Eve's panties in his pocket. Black ones with a pink bow. He was shaken but proud. After he showered, he carefully folded them between the pages of a black notebook like a leaf in a herbarium and slid the notebook under a pile of others. Then he called Nina.

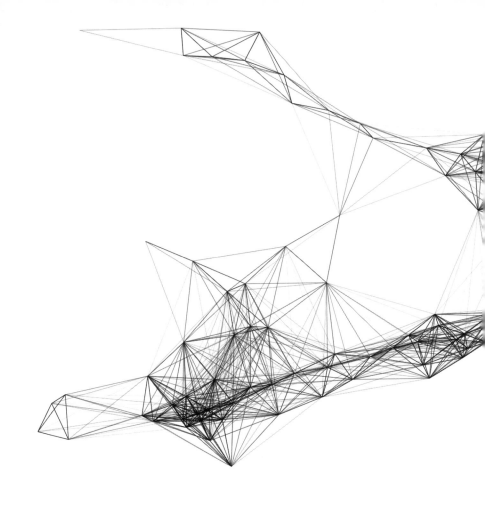

Philosophers

Some people will never learn anything because they understand everything too soon.

—Alexander Pope

Nina

hugged me, waved, let her eyes slide down, and turned around. She walked toward the Japanese policeman in the passport control booth with her little backpack and then disappeared toward the gates. She never looked back at me again. I sat down in the airport café and drank a double espresso in two seconds. What I had done was betrayal in its purest form. Fifty years on, I will still call it that. And of the years we spent together, this moment is singularly engraved in my mind as the sharpest memory of Nina. Turning around and walking out toward the airport gates.

I had betrayed all the trust she placed in me. I'm not trying to be pathetic, but trust was a big deal for Nina. One of the biggest.

You know the people who don't even know how happy they are? The ones whose parents gave them all they could. Love, a place in the world, a smile, support, freedom, perhaps even some money, but most of all, their carefree air. You see it in them right away, but they don't, because they've always had it. They never had to go through that self-destructive, self-defining war in which one is ripped to shreds in the vague hope that, over time, they'll stitch themselves together in a different fashion. Nina knew that war, which is why I loved her. It shaped her trust into a tiny flower, which she only chose to show to carefully selected people. It was meant to be a gift.

The farther I am from the moment I abandoned her, the more clearly I can feel her pain. Strange, isn't it? Contrary to my lifelong expectation, I am not forgetting certain singular moments of my life. Rather, my emotions around them appear to develop and refine with age. I'm an ol' barrel of whiskey, hey ho, richer by the year, hey ho. There is actually a voice in my head that calls in every two months or so, like a salesman who has mastered the art of the follow-up. It pulls up a few memories of Nina and asks, "Why did you betray her?"

My whole library, in retrospect, is an attempt to decipher why I did it. And the answer has everything to do with this.

Theofile Cough. Death by Chocolate: Ponderings on Certainty and Chaos, How We Navigate between Them and Why This Time It's Different. Chapter 3: A Clueless Place. [...] "Go not to men, but stay in the forest! Go rather to the animals! Why not be like me—a bear amongst bears, a bird amongst birds?"

"And what doeth the saint in the forest?" asked Zarathustra.

The saint answered: "I make hymns and sing them, and, in making hymns, I laugh and weep and mumble: thus do I praise God. With singing, weeping, laughing, and mumbling do I praise the God who is my God. But what dost thou bring us as a gift?"

When Zarathustra had heard these words, he bowed to the saint and said: "What should I have to give thee! Let me rather hurry hence lest I take aught away from thee!" And, thus, they parted from one another, the old man and Zarathustra, laughing like schoolboys.

When Zarathustra was alone, however, he said to his heart: "Could it be possible? This old saint in the forest hath not yet heard of it, that God is dead!" [18]

Here, Friedrich Nietzsche's most famous sentence. As soon as he wrote it, something rather curious happened: nothing at all. Lightning did not strike him down. Nobody burned him at a stake. And no one disproved his claim.

It took a while before it emerged that a dead God was the smallest thing. It was the living people who had problems. First, the good Christian folk who had been enduring hardships in anticipation of a payback in the afterlife. If Nietzsche was right and God *was* dead, then the promissory note for the afterlife was just a worthless piece of paper.

It quickly became irrelevant whether God had really died. The mere possibility became too important; it became the reality of possibility. And God sank further down: from a hypothesis, he became a risk. The rating of the church and its notes, redeemable the day after death, suddenly dropped from AAA to B+, by the analysts' consensus. And people don't base their savings on such instruments, nor empires their fates. Such currency is only fit for speculation.

Let us take further notice that the decline of Christianity in the twentieth century didn't happen because people finally stopped desiring certainty. Quite the opposite. They realized they demanded more certainty than the church could offer.

Nietzsche clearly described the domino effect. After the death of God, the entire Western moral and philosophical structure would collapse. And with it, the balance between nations, classes, and people; and with that, the power held by the church and the monarchs. What follows is a clueless place: *"Unavoidably now, nihilism will reveal all the precious convictions and holy truths as symptoms of the faulty Western myth. This collapse of sense, meaning and purpose will be the most destructive power in history, meaning a complete attack on reality, nothing less than the greatest crisis of humanity: I describe here the history of the next two centuries. [...] For some time already, our European culture is heading as if towards catastrophe, the tortured tension heightened decade after decade: restlessly, violently, head first, like a river that wants to reach its end."* [19]

The twentieth and twenty-first centuries: a clueless place. Experience offers no advice. The past is cut off from the future. The mind is flooded by an infinity of equal, undecidable possibilities.

People even have a special word for this tortured place: freedom.

As an old man, I have the privilege of a vantage point. The vista is high, the horizon far below. It's the last stop before the flight. With my eyes half-blind, I watch the most destructive force my century has seen: the loss of meaning and direction. There's a stir, an unrest, seeping into people's hearts. A breaking structure, still only halfway through its uprooting of countries, scientific fields, and millions upon millions of lives. I was lifted up by this unrest as a fish carried by a tsunami. Turn a few pages of that Cough.

What happens to a society whose sacred myth loses the capacity to mirror it? What will happen to France once it questions the myth of the French Revolution? And with the USA, when they re-examine the myth of the Founding Fathers? What with the civilization that admits truth is an error? They turn into birds without a flock. They'll fly off in all directions, and they won't rest until they stick a new myth together from straw, saliva, feathers, and droppings, which they can call their own image.

And so they flew: Darwin on the sea to the tropics. Weber and Dilthey into social constructs. Freud and Jung into the depths of consciousness. Mallarmé and Verlaine into the labyrinth of language. Cantor headed for infinity; Frege to logic; Maxwell, Planck, and Einstein into the texture of matter, space, and time. In the meantime, Nietzsche set out for the ancient Greek tragedies.

I ran to code the Faustomat, and Nina ... stopped responding to my texts.

I started reading. I had to know the truth. And soon, I found that we weren't the first people to face this chaos. Three centuries before Christ, Euhemerus preached that the gods were actually venerated rulers from the distant past, and their cults were a continuation of kingdoms that have disappeared. Plutarch then berated him for spreading atheism across the entire inhabited world and exterminating the gods. Euhemerus and Nietzsche are the same place, apparently fairly frequented.

And I kept reading. On that wall toward your left, there are whole centuries of recorded history of this search. It's called philosophy. It's what people do when they don't know what to do. I don't ask you to dive into all of it; that's just one more way to blunder. Just check Walkowski, who drew the smallest map of philosophy I know of. All on a single page.

Aleksander Walkowski, Civilization?, pp. 86-87. In a kind of shortened, simplified conception of the history of thought, Nietzsche is stood only against Arthur Schopenhauer. While Schopenhauer considered the will to live to be common to all living creatures, and thus an absolute principle, Nietzsche had no heart for the absolute. His will to power is a strictly individual force, which cannot be grasped or judged from without.

Paradoxically, it was Schopenhauer who, throughout his life, attempted to wrestle philosophy away from Kant's vision of the absolute. When we consider two apples, Kant would claim, it is our mind that connects them. Kant termed this capacity for thought *a priori* knowledge, and he considered it a part of the absolute, unavailable to man in its entirety.

And Kant's philosophy, in turn, came about as a polemic against David Hume, who not only saw nothing metaphysical in the human mind, he didn't even see anything particularly rational in it. Human knowledge, he noted, is no different from animal knowledge. Hume's man is an animal with advanced habits, having nothing to do with the absolute.

And Hume's skepticism was, in turn, a reaction to Descartes' conception of man as a rational being, whose endeavor shall climax with an irrefutable proof of God's existence. And Descartes himself was fighting against none other than the Renaissance wave of skeptics—that is, the revolt against Christian idealism, continuing on from Greek skepticism, provoked by Platonic idealism.

After we have breakfast and tea with my lovely wife tomorrow morning, walk up Petřín Hill. Up there, just wait for the hundreds of birds to take flight from the roofs below you, and ask yourself, "Do I see birds or a flock?" And a live image of the history of philosophy will appear. Men, as they are, void of ideals. Or an invisible ideal detached from men. I think you'll agree with me that there's something rotten in the celebrated Western philosophical way of thinking if it consistently offers two equally dissatisfying options.

I smelled the paradox through the centuries. And I eventually dug out what I believe is the original exchange on this topic. It is an ancient discussion with Protagoras on one side and Plato and Aristotle on the other. Unfortunately, the only adaptation of the argument I know is from Uncle Grime. In all honesty, that's a weak spot in my well-tended collection of authors. I can't do much about it either unless you have a better book.

F. X. Grime, Uncle Grime's Dozen Ancient Jobs, bibliophilia, self-published, 46 pages, 2022.

Chapter: Kamikaze Philosopher. One of my favorite old-timer bosses is this dude Protagoras. He knew his shit about trouble with the gods. *"Concerning the gods, I have no means of knowing whether they exist or not or of what sort they may be. Many things prevent knowledge including the obscurity of the subject and the brevity of human life,"* he claimed—and got sentenced for blasphemy. The Athenian tribunal chucked his books on the square and burned them up, but wily Protagoras knew it smelled a bit fishy and legged it. Dressed as a lady, he jumped on a ship that was taking some garbage to Sicily. On board, he was already scrawling those wicked cuneiforms into his Moleskine again. But a storm caught them on the sea and down they went. Done and dusted. The adventurous life of a philosopher!

Not a single book of his survived, and I only know about his rants from the ones that cut him down to size later, which is a bit unfair. Even so, his three sentences make up half of philosophy. Apparently, he dropped the knowledge that there are more answers to every question, which can be in mutual opposition. He nailed it in the lost masterpiece Truth: *"Man is the measure of all things: of things which are, that they are, and of things which are not, that they are not."* Everyone can basically think what they want. When he snuffed it, a bunch of wimps laid into him, namely the comedy duo Plato & Aristotle. Not only did they fail to grok the big boss, but they laid into him so hard that the argument became the basic tenet of their philosophy. Plato was older, so he barked first.

He whipped out this hip argument called *peritropē*. He went, "Look y'all, Protagoras' philosophy allows others to disagree with it. But if the dissenting ones can be right, then Protagoras is wrong!" (That's because he uses this law of the excluded middle—I'll get to it.) A truth that respects other truths isn't worthy of its name, according to Plato. Only absolute truth—that is, arrogant and snotty—has the right to call itself truth.

Just about there, Plato runs out of breath, and young Aristotle picks up the baton in his Metaphysics. He quotes boss that, like, truth is only an opinion. From that, Aristotle deduces that all opinions are true. And since it's well known that loads of people have opposing opinions, then all claims have to be both true and not. And now he heats up his fencing tricks: *id est* everything has to be fixed and in movement at once. Everything has to be finite and infinite. Everything has to be and not be at once. And that it follows that no fib, however dumb, can be disproven. And that it wouldn't, like, lead anywhere.

A summary. The Greek gang loved to argue. So they made up a rule that there's no middle ground. In every argument, just one side will be right. This is literally called the law of the excluded middle. Aristotle bundled it with truth and logic and shipped it down the centuries. Roman dictators loved it because it made dictating a heck of a lot easier. So they bundled it with Christianity and chucked it down the millennia.

The net effect down here is that being right became more important than finding understanding. That truth beats empathy and respect. And all these other things that fuck us all up.

Just for the kicks, check out the law of excluded middle.

Russell and Whitehead (3) also take over from ancient logic (traditional, Aristotelian) the remaining two of the three Aristotelian laws of thought and formalize them into theorems: the law of identity (LI) and the law of excluded middle (LEM). They are closely connected: let us have a predicate p and its opposite ~p. LI says that at most one of <p; ~p> is true (it is impossible to create a contradiction between a predicate and its opposite). LEM dictates that at least one of <p; ~p> is true (there exists no third option, p', which would be true instead of them). Combined, and only combined, these two laws ensure that, between the predicates p and ~p, precisely one is true at all times. Surprisingly, this full form never got its own name in logic.

2.1.2. The two together (LI, LEM) give rise to the classical (Aristotelian) conception of truth: "[...] but, on the other hand, there cannot be an intermediate between (metaxy) contradictories, but of one subject we must either affirm (phanai) or deny (apophanai) any one predicate. This is clear, in the first place, if we define what the true (aletheia) and the false (pseudos) are. To say of what is that it is not, or of what is not that it is, is false, while to say of what is that it is, and of what is not that it is not, is true. So that he who says of anything that it is, or that it is not, will say either what is true or what is false." [65]

2.1.3. If both LI and LEM are true, then every predicate p is either true or false.

Lo and behold! What a piece of literary beauty we're preserving as the goddamn golden egg of our civilization. Beware of it. This is the piece of cultural code that gamified the search for truth. It turned dialogue into a competitive sport. And all of us into insatiable seekers. Uncle Grime over and out.

Nina wasn't outside of this. She too grew up into a society that was searching so hard that our generation considered it normal. When she felt lost, it was, in fact, the Western world that was in an awkward vacuum. She just didn't see it. Which is paradoxical because she was the epitome of blundering.

But there are many ways to blunder. Hers was to travel the world to find where she belonged and who she was. She was a fighter. To bear that weight for years—the weight of not having found it yet. And not knowing if she'd ever find it. A search like that can take years, centuries.

One of those diffident poets I like touched upon it. We exchanged letters over the ocean for a few years. Osho says it's good not to meet a poet, and we haven't met. Still, when I take her book in my hands, I feel Nina. There's something similar about the two of them.

Janis Omassis. Nervously into History. Dark blue folder with silver engraving, without a cover; 1993. Prologue. History is written by the victors, they say. Such history, written by victors, gives the impression of a straight line. That's because the axis, onto which epochs are habitually stretched, is the unbending rod of time. Victors' time. Won through full engagement and denial of doubt, with ignorance and fanaticism.

But if we are to claim that history is written by the victors, we have to add—only while they remain victorious. Parallel to the history of victors, there unfold histories of hesitation, reflection, repeated fiascos, crossing and rubbing out, of undeclared loves. This history is a chronicle of walking in circles. The history of philosophers, jesters, mystics, and poets. The history of losers. The victors might be blind to their perspective, but the loser's viewpoint is more durable because, on a long enough timeline, everyone will cock up.

In 1972, Richard Nixon was walking through the gardens of the Forbidden City with the prime minister of the People's Republic of China, Zhou Enlai. Nixon knew that Zhou had studied in France in his youth and that he was interested in history. So he asked conversationally what meaning Zhou ascribed to the French Revolution. Zhou thought for a moment and replied, "It's too soon to tell."

History is a story made of episodes. An episode acquires meaning in relation not only to the previous ones but also to the future episodes. (I am writing about love.) If the Christian era lasted for almost two thousand years, it is not preposterous to wait another millennium before we understand the meaning of the twentieth century.

What to make of all this? The first version of history, the green and unripe version of victors, is but a rough and misty draft, in which muttering characters try out their roles. The victor is followed by an endless crowd of losers, who take over his straightforward actions and question them. Did Nixon really converse about the French Revolution during his walk with Zhou? Was it Nixon or Kissinger? Could the anecdote have been made up by some ambitious journalist? Who knows? Then, what's more real—the long-lost original of the victor's first draft or the loser's fresh forgery? The direct history of power or the circular history of thought?

I am still writing about love.

Nina later told me that she only started crying somewhere above the Himalayas. She hated me with all her heart because, after all our talks and kisses, night walks, brunches, and fights, I let her walk away. So she tried to reject me time and time again; she cried and moaned, and the pain stayed. The endless torture eventually surfaced a question, the most important question after one loses trust: how deep will the mistrust go? Would it stop with me? All Brits? All white males? Men? People? All mammals? How deep is the wound?

And when Christianity fell, people had to decide how far they would take it. Would they lose faith in the Christian God? In all gods? All of spirituality? In everything intangible? And more than that: would they abandon truth? The law of non-contradiction? Aristotelian logic? How many more myths still have to die before we finally get to the bottom of the wound? And what is the myth that we are still unprepared to give up? This: truth is but a coping strategy in the face of the great unknown. That's what I was looking for so hard that I betrayed Nina.

The S
of I

cience

ove

The trouble about man is twofold. He cannot learn truths which
are too complicated; he forgets truths which are too simple.
—*Rebecca West*

He invited her over a dinner. "To Prague? When?" She nearly overturned the table as she jumped to hug him. "If this is a joke, I'll kill you."

"I can't make jokes."

"Then I love you! How warm is it there now?"

"Like here, I guess?"

"Alright, I'm packed."

Adam strategized a shorter and a longer itinerary for each day with restaurant stops, cafes, parks, landmarks, and vistas. The plan wasn't simple: first, impress Nina. Second, confirm or deny his own romantic ability. Third, attempt to experience romance as well. Fourth, identify the key components of romance and its mechanism of action. Fifth, stay within budget.

They landed at the Prague airport, got on a bus, and changed to the green metro line. Disembarking straight into the Baroque, they tumbled their suitcases over cobblestones onto a tiny square, in the corner of which stood the hotel. A receptionist welcomed them in. Following her instructions, they climbed the creaking spiral staircase to the third floor and opened the only door there. Nina kicked her sandals off and shouted something in between giggles.

She danced back to Adam, standing in the doorway with the luggage. "It's marvelous," she whispered and leaned her head on him. Adam caressed her fragrant hair and silently contemplated the power of conditioned reflexes. He'd planned for this reaction when he'd chosen the hotel and its olive chamber. He'd manipulated her, and it wasn't any less true for manipulating her into happiness—the same happiness that Pavlov's dogs salivated with.

"Let's go out!" Nina was ecstatic.

The view over the red roofs must have affected him, or he lost his train of thought, because he forgot the itineraries in the hotel. When he remembered, they were already lost in the meandering streets by the riverfront. And getting lost on their first night in Eastern Europe wasn't good for Adam. He suggested stopping a police car and asking the way back to the hotel, but Nina took him by the hand and spun him around. And so he awkwardly tried to be lost with her and said to himself, "Fine, fine."

Somewhere in the city's labyrinth, she pointed at a poster on a hydrant. It advertised a Sunday chamber concert in the Church of St. Nicholas, featuring Bach (Brandenburg Concerto no. 3 in G major), Dvořák (Stabat Mater dolorosa), and Haydn (the seventh sonata from the Seven Last Words of Christ). Under the English text were German and Russian translations.

"St. Nick and the Classics. Wanna go see them?" she suggested.

"That's an all-star lineup. I don't know Dvořák, but isn't Bach dead?"

"He is. The band takes him on tour in a sarcophagus."

Adam smiled. "Since when does a punk singer go to churches for classical music? Look, it's an obvious tourist trap. They don't even bother writing it in Czech," he pointed out. "Let's separate romance from kitsch."

"Ex-punk singer. And I don't live in a squat anymore either," objected Nina, and Adam felt the friction between them. Now, he'd scared off romance by uttering its name. Perhaps the goddamn rainbow unicorn had appeared unexpectedly soon, and Adam had chased him away as kitsch. The whole weekend experiment might be over already! Next time, he swore, even if it meant sticking his foot in a tourist trap, he'd let loose an avalanche of romance so powerful that he'd sweep himself away as well.

But the atmosphere had already changed.

Two, three steps behind Nina, within the theater of his mind, Optimization Imperative inquired, "Are you sure that Nina is your ideal partner?"

An ideal graph of success in life, he knew, the one that a confident youth could pin above his bed, would be a rising exponential curve supported by thoughtful decisions. Their effects would not be additive but multiplicative, like compound interest. Every decision would be important not merely in itself but also as a multiplier of the previous ones and a multiplicand of the future ones. A good decision pays interest for the rest of one's life; a bad one forever harms. This exponential curve defined Adam's potential. The line, steep like a raised forefinger, dictated the Optimization Imperative: *life's outcome rests on each individual decision.*

"You didn't choose her in a controlled process," the Imperative whispered. "Experiment, Addy. Try Nina and see if you attract. Find a scientist and see if you fit. And try ten others. So the best possible life won't pass you by."

"Not so fast," Adam's quieter aide, the Skeptic, chimed in from nowhere. "The first thing an experiment needs is repetition. But life events come one after the other. Adam can't travel back in time, split in two, or reincarnate. So he can't properly experiment with life."

"What are you saying? That he should stop optimizing? And you think he'll get further?"

"Secondly, however hard Adam looks, he can't see tomorrow. Without information, he can't optimize. What if he meets the woman of his dreams at his own wedding?"

"Have it your way, Skeptic. You think you're smarter, so take responsibility. Just remember that the choice of a partner is cri-ti-cal for the function of success!"

"I'm just pointing out the fact that you've come up with a real pile of nonsense."

"What's your plan then?"

Adam took out a coin. At the next crossroad, it was heads right, tails left. Then, heads straight, tails right. A choice—every choice— was a meeting of Adams. The assorted characters competed and voted for a champion from their midst, whose prize would be the right to continue bearing the name of Adam. He would live for all the others.

Had the Skeptic been asked, he would lean toward choosing a scientist. Such a partner would discuss common interests without logical fallacies, personal attacks, or deviation from the point. She would value a quality argument, even if it didn't favor her. A keen interest in Adam's research would be guaranteed. The first pause in Adam's long sentences would not throw her off. But better still was to remain on the safe side.

"Stay away from girlfriends. They won't last." The Skeptic gave his verdict.

"Why?"

"Pure statistics. It's not likely."

It was an outright miracle that, despite the fact that choosing a partner was an unsolvable problem, Adam was walking around Prague *with a girlfriend*.

She was snapping pictures, playing with perspective. With her position in the universe. He tossed the coin around, and the questions wouldn't leave his head: what force held them together? It wasn't gravity, nor electromagnetism; neither weak nor strong nuclear force. Physics knows no fifth impetus. But Adam felt it, though he could not name it. On and on, he kept asking, as if chanting a mantra: what is this force? What makes Nina so attractive?

And his two expert advisers remained remarkably quiet on these very essential doubts.

Birds W

a Fl

Without
ock

What's the point of going out? We're just going to wind up back here anyway.

—Homer Simpson

"There's only two of you? I only do groups from four to six so I don't lose my voice. And I don't take Russians," declared the pensioner, leaning casually against the reception desk. The hotel owner had recommended him as a tour guide.

"If you want a city walk," the owner had gestured towards the hotel bar, at the inconspicuous older man in corduroy trousers and a beige checkered vest, "Doctor Brabec is no common guide. He's still free today, but you must hurry up." The man had winked and bowed to Nina, who was arranging rolls of ham, blue cheese and fresh bread on her plate. "He is a poet of Czech history."

The frail pensioner explained that he'd had enough of the Russians during the forty years of occupation. The Germans had also marched through Prague enough when they'd invaded it, so he didn't take them around either. But he was not prejudiced against Germany. Czechoslovakia wouldn't have fallen into their hands so easily if it weren't for the British, who broke the agreement in Munich and handed Czechoslovakia over to Hitler.

"Who knows," admitted Doctor Brabec, "perhaps they saved Prague from bombardment, or they saved it for their stag parties, who knows, but a betrayal is a betrayal. So no tours for the Brits. And there was also a Frenchman at that shindig in Munich, and he blew his nose into the same agreement. What's worst, he looked at the Czech in the European Union as though they'd never seen each other before. Hence, no tour for the French under any circumstances."

Adam took a breath to say something. But Doctor Brabec could hear that Nina wasn't American, which was lucky. He wouldn't show around General Patton himself, since his great bastion of democracy sold Prague to the Russians for a pittance at Yalta. Obviously, the Frenchie and the Brit were at the table too. Nina didn't look Italian or Spanish either, so it wasn't necessary to emphasize that they joined Hitler when fascism was flying high. And the Japanese. That might restrict clientele—by now, he was wildly flinging his hands open— "But one has to have principles! So the Austrians and Hungarians who didn't find us worthy of equality in the monarchy, they can hike around Prague alone. But I hear your accent, young lady; you're not fooling me. I know right away where you came from to enjoy your weekend here. I might shut one eye and squint with the other, and a half-day tour is two hundred euros."

"You're completely off," countered Nina, "whatever your guess."

("You think you're different," croaked Ramón in the Camden Town squat. She was painting him, their bandleader, on the edge of delirium and consciousness, helplessly playing around with his guitar. This was barely a week before he overdosed on heroin and the band broke up after only three shows. "It's spilling out of your eyes, the superiority. But you won't get away from anything, princess. The world is full of shit," he moaned heavily and more to himself. "And the good shit is so ... fragile." Thanks to her father, she understood perfectly. But still, she was different. Everywhere.)

"My mother is French with Algerian blood, and my father was a Russian Jew. He was born in Saint Petersburg and studied in Geneva. He met my mother in Paris and then dragged us around Europe for twenty years."

"Oh?" The pensioner eyed her with mild surprise. "And where?"

"London, Italy, Vienna ... we went everywhere. Please don't try to guess where I'm from because I don't know myself."

"A European then. Have you finished eating, young man? Let me wrap up. I've never done tours for Czechs and Slovaks because they keep making excuses, and I don't like listening to that. But to you, young lady, I'd show Prague even if your grandfather was Lenin. What's your name?"

"Nina."

"And what interests you in Prague?"

She turned to Adam.

"You choose today," he proposed.

Nina took two hundred euros out of her bag. "Where is the most romantic view of Prague?" she asked.

Brabec nodded. "Well, you'll find most of the bourgeois Baroque around Malá Strana and Nerudova. There are some rewarding little nooks there. And Kampa's just been renovated. When it's hot after lunch, sit down under the trees there by the river. But the most romantic view of Prague … that, my dear, is from Paris. From a great distance. That's the real romance."

Nina frowned. She used to flirt with romance in sheets red from wine and lipstick but always half-naked, body on body. Like when she'd ripped open the envelope from Cambridge and the cream paper had read, "We are happy to inform you." She'd run through the squat shouting, "Nina von Cambridge, get it?!" Then, whenever she'd walked through Camden market that summer, she'd looked people in the eye and savored the secret of her new origins. "Your father would be so happy," enthused her mum, and Nina slowly begun to forgive her. She breathed romance day to day.

During her first months in Cambridge, she'd constantly sent the punks hand-drawn postcards. She wrote about the motley crew of classmates, about how they heard a swan sneeze, about the ducks, and the harbored boats, so narrow and long that if they wanted to turn around, they'd have to go out to sea. She drew her friends borrowing a poorly tied punt at night, and eleven of them fitting into one phone booth, and the bridges and lawns behind King's and St. Johns. She drew the college porters in their bowler hats and formal dinners with students and professors in black gowns at long benches, where the six courses were announced by a gong. "Cambridge is a medieval movie," she inscribed in gothic type on a postcard showing the quad of her college, dramatically stretching perspective to let the library tower disappear in black rainy clouds. And the movie was a romance.

They never replied, so she stopped writing. Her classmates didn't stick together like they did in the first few months and, somehow, spontaneously, split into cold wars: the English against the foreigners, old money against the middle class, Eton against the rest. There was no fighting, just everyone knew where they stood.

Nina stopped talking to almost everybody. She wasn't in Cambridge as her family's delegate, like half her classmates, nor did she study art to rebel against them, like the other half. She started to look for her own Cambridge. Night became the time to draw. Pembroke in particular changed completely. The tall chimneys pricked through the roofs like stumps sticking out of shallow graves. Dead old men's teeth broke out of the battlements, and the entire college reeked of musty, rotting fame. The authority of the departed suffocated her. She start-ed having trouble at school. Romance morphed and decayed, and she kept drawing it.

She completely prepared herself to be kicked out over her term project. She sketched rubbish bins floating in the river Cam and black silhouettes of the homeless against stained glass windows of the churches blazing into the night. She drew a series of ten studies, detailed and exact like a technical diagram on vast sheets of paper. Only in a few places was the charcoal covered by a final layer of dark oil colors, peeling like a blister. Each study captured Pembroke as a derelict morgue. The element that changed in the studies was the in-habitants. Once it was injured clowns, limping jugglers, and decrepit acrobats. Then, children in masks of corpses. A courtyard full of enor-mous statues of ancient philosophers from which students and pro-fessors hung on fishing lines. She passed, but only just, with a dead serious and infinitely long lecture on the purpose of art.

It was around that time that she met Adam. She didn't get a room at the college for some reason, and she was only coming to Pem-broke to see him. The courtyard seemed fairly cozy again, though not as fairy-tale-innocent as in her first year. More like a haunted castle. In a horror theme park. After closing time. She ran through it straight to Adam's room and threw herself around him, wishing to hear that he, who could cast bisectors through life, would make sure that the world stopped twisting into knots and lumps and hugged perfectly body on body. If not forever, then at least for a hundred years ... or a weekend in Prague.

Doctor Brabec gave in and took the pair around the twisting cob-blestone streets of Malá Strana. Near the Castle, Nina pulled them in-side a bookstore. They leafed through large, glossy books with black-and-white prints of the city. Furrows of roofs were dotted with tow-ers, oriels, and chimneys shooting out so sharp that they pierced the haze above the Vltava.

"Are these famous photographers?" asked Nina. Brabec handed her Plicka's Prague in Photographs, and she sighed. The hundred and twenty photos she'd excitedly snapped since yesterday evening were suddenly worth a dull fart.

"You have to see what he shot," said Doctor Brabec as they walked on. "The black and white pictures of Prague without people are truly romantic, aren't they? These roofs and spires and empty streets, a quiet, morning town … that's the Second World War. The city is occupied, Miss. Down there, where you can't see, the Gestapo is marching with machine guns, Jews wear the Star of David, and swastikas hang throughout the country. All of the photographers took pictures of SS-Führers, helmets and coats, fearful faces and trains dispatched to the camps. Only Plicka climbed roofs, conversed with Prague, and soothed her: it'll pass."

Then he paused and added, "But it's one thing for Plicka to take pictures of Prague without Germans during the war, to encourage her, and quite another thing when those hard times are completely forgotten. You were asking about romance, Miss. Nobody wants to hear about Communism. The forty years we lived here alone, without Europe, are supposed to stay out of the frame because they mess up the tourists' backdrop."

And they were already at the castle then. Nina photographed the church towers below. Leaning over the terraced gardens on the steep slope under the castle, with her eye in the viewfinder, she said, "This is so charming. I can't help myself, but I would want to live here even under Communism."

Doctor Brabec spoke about queues for oranges and toilet paper and how they'd smuggled literature and recording tapes with subversive rock from the West. How it wasn't romantic at all. There were agents listening for anyone badmouthing the regime. Whether one got into a university and how she would make it was decided by a party member, but how far could one make it anyway? They couldn't travel or run a business, but, by law, everyone had to work. They called it the right to labor, and it was a season pass to a work camp. But it wasn't anyone's fault, because the people did as the party said, and the party did what it had to do. What it did to the people, this carefully planned impotence—that was the worst.

"But that's thirty years ago," noted Adam.

"Then stay here for a week. The romance will wear right off. You'll hear people complain about everything. Look how sullen they are!"

He waved. "Everybody is a passive-aggressive black belt."

"Is that from Communism?"

"No, it's what happens when others take over your country for four centuries and you survive."

"The Russians?"

"Oh, it was a team effort. First the Habsburgs, then the Germans, and then Russians. For four hundred years, the Czechs have lived in opposition. It's a weird world, but they've learned to live in it."

"How?" asked Nina, hopping along.

"Complaining," said Brabec. "And beer."

"I mean, really," she insisted, "What's the mentality of opposition?"

Brabec walked in silence for a while. "It's a mistrust of the whole," he then exclaimed. "The Habsburgs took the Czech crown and our own state. Then, the fascists, when we surrendered without a fight, took our national self-confidence. And finally, the Communists stole the *people*. We have lost all the usual cohesive wholes. Do you know we're the most atheist country in the world?"

"Birds without a flock," said Nina.

"Dr. Brabec," said Adam, "you just keep complaining, yourself."

"That's how the world repays." The doctor nodded his head.

Nina stroked his shoulder. "But you complain so nicely."

"Thank you. It has a simple solution. When the Czechs accept responsibility, they'll stop fighting and start being kinder. They'll twist themselves back from the world of opposition. But … you can't spread an idea through a vaccine."

"You can always start the revolution." Adam was annoyed, unable to decide whether their guide was charmingly authentic or grossly unprofessional.

Brabec shrugged. "It won't be me." After a few steps, he stopped. "Well, the Communists have almost died out." He sighed. "But I'm afraid the pessimists are immortal."

And they went on, down towards the church, with Doctor Brabec rambling on. Nina joined Adam in admiring the ironwork on the doors and the decorated facades, and she was no longer taking pictures.

I, Be

east

It ain't tactics, honey; it's just the beast in me.
—*Elvis Presley*

They parted with Brabec down by the river. On the embankment, under one of the bridges, they found a boat rental. From there, they rowed around the upper tip of the island and let the current carry them back along the quieter shore, far from the embankment. Adam arranged the oars in the boat and carefully crawled over to Nina. He sat and lay his head down in her lap. He closed his eyes. And almost immediately, something stopped.

Something fell asleep and forgot to doubt.

It lay silently.

It lay by familiar legs, eyes closed, occasionally moving its tail.

Where had he met this beast? Before Nina, he'd seen it often, whenever he'd returned to the apartment in the evening. It was restless and hesitant before the night. Cook by himself? Drink wine by himself? Open a book by himself? The beast would look around, sniff, lurk.

But not now. It fell asleep on the boat. Adam heard it breathe out. Not that it had chosen Nina. The beast doesn't choose a mate. It knows when something's missing, and it knows when it's sated. Then, it lays down, stretches its paws out, closes its eyes.

The unrest of solitude and the calm of communion, two simple places.

Nina stroked Adam's hair, and Adam stroked the beast. Both people were thinking about something.

A Pictur

Vltava F

e of the

iverbed

Make use of today's influx of energy, and you will deal with the troubling questions once and for all. You will be satisfied in sexual matters, though, in certain moments, it will seem as though the passion has died down a bit. Your partner needs you. Show generous support, and the spark will reignite. The stars also favor weddings and conceiving children!
—Nina's horoscope for the weekend

It was their notions of that famous city that led them to transport their physical bodies into the real Prague. Those same notions were, since yesterday, getting lost in the crooked streets, fainting, falling under the ringing trams and from the bridges into the Vltava. Adam only realized suddenly that they were gone; standing in the middle of Old Town Square, he could no longer remember his imaginary, personal Prague. Knowledge had killed something inside him again.

Nina agreed. They were sitting under a statue in some square, talking. The harmony they felt wasn't in words; each of them was saying something different anyway. Then, words ran out too, and they were silently watching people.

He asked her to take a picture of him with the cathedral towers in the background.

She took out her camera and paused. "Wouldn't you prefer a picture of the towers without you?"

"Why? No."

"I don't know." She tilted the camera. "Maybe this way …"

"Turn it back to landscape."

"What?"

"I just want one normal picture from Prague." He sounded annoyed. "We don't need to reinvent photography here."

Nina dropped her camera to her side. "Why are you doing this again? I'm not your program."

"Can I get a single picture the way it's usually done?"

"Nope. Won't happen." She threw the camera back into the bag.

"God, what's the deal?"

They weren't arguing about a picture, of course. The one picture was but a symbol of deeper layers clashing. Even the two of them were but a symbol of the ubiquitous tension between any two versions of reality. Had they been aware of this, they would have saved themselves the argument and countless others. But, somewhat naturally, they did not.

"You!"

"I just want a picture from Prague!"

"Sure!" she circled him, clicking away. "Be spontaneous!" He tried to grab her. "Be spontaneous!" She was nearly singing the sentence, laughing, then whispering. "Spontaneous ..."

"What's this about?" he asked when he caught her.

She said, "It's like pissing on fire hydrants."

He asked for an explanation of that explanation.

"The tourist and the church. The tourist and the castle. They are canine territorial marks. Don't ask me to photograph still-lives with tourists."

"You're taking this way out of proportion."

"No! You stop. Programming. Every fucking second."

He stared at her, starting to shake his head slowly.

"And ... be spontaneous, Adam!" she shouted, and she was serious. "Like, really!"

"Jesus on a cracker. How can you get mad like this?" And then, "OK. Forget it."

"I don't know if you'll have the balls to go to Japan with me."

Adam let his jaw drop. So he wasn't the only one presently running experiments on mutual compatibility. "And you're judging this based on my photography preferences."

"I mean it!" She stomped on the ground. "I see how you look around, with your judging look, like nothing's quite up to scratch. How you contort whenever life is larger and stranger than your program—"

"What's gotten into you? All I wanted was one snap so that I don't forget I was here," he said angrily. "You don't want me to be spontaneous. If we go to Japan, you don't want me to spontaneously stay there two years longer than you. You want me to be with you, no matter what, no matter what idea and impulse I get. Say that's true."

Nina was looking down, not really listening.

"You want me to be dependable."

Finally, she spoke. "Maybe you should stay in Japan two years longer if that's what's coming to you."

"Really. And you?"

"I want spontaneity. The rest will follow."

"That's now like rule number one?"

"Then, at least, you wouldn't forget you were with me."

"We'll both forget all of this, love."

Just like the trip to Prague had decimated their fantasies of Prague, he said, two months later, the photographs of Prague would begin to obliterate their memories. All of the dust and gravel between the pictures, all of that soft underlay of experiences would be washed away. In the end, they'd remember Prague only as they'd photographed it.

They walked in silence for some time. Adam was programming Faustomat in his head. It made him faster later in front of the keyboard, having thought the next steps through. And it kept him calm and occupied while Nina was mad. As they were crossing the river, she took out her camera again and told him where to stand.

Adam sat on the ledge of the bridge so she could snap him in with the panorama of the Prague Castle in the background. "Enjoy the still life," she warned. "It's the first and last one." He straightened his back and smiled. Nina stepped back ten paces. Then, she shouted: "Try and forget this!" She swung her arm rashly, and the camera flew out of her hand like a frightened bird, heading way over Adam, who barked with fright, his long body swaying on the stone ledge above the river. At the very last moment before falling over off the bridge, he awkwardly twisted himself around the ledge; the camera slapped the water's surface and disappeared in a circle of waves.

Tourists, having ducked in fright at first, burst out laughing and called something out to Adam.

He got off the ledge, turned around, and walked off without saying a word. He heard Nina behind him and marched all the more decisively, away from her and the crowds. She ran up to him in the middle of the bridge and pulled his hand. He broke loose and only stopped past the watchtower at the end of the bridge.

When she caught up with him he shouted, "Are you insane?"

"Are you?" she retorted instantly.

He twitched in an attempt at an argument, and a second one, but Nina made her big eyes and held out her ear.

What could those two reproach each other for?

It was his birthday. He didn't celebrate it, but Nina wouldn't leave it without taking him out for dinner. They found a restaurant in a cellar with stately candles impaled on cones of trickled wax. A goose was roasting in the fireplace. Fat dripped into the flames from the sizzling rinds. They sat by an oak table on a bench, under an antique carriage wheel hung on a metal hook. They relished orange-glazed duck breast. Between mouthfuls, Adam pointed his fork at Nina. "I almost fell in there."

"Will you forget it?"

"Of course. We don't have a picture."

"That's not so certain. I set the self-timer. Maybe you're there in bird's-eye view."

"So we have a picture of the Vltava riverbed. Awesome. You could've just told me you don't want me in the still life." Mainly, he was upset with himself, feeling his own rigidity. He was failing miserably at being romantic.

"But that's not why." She swayed her glass. Prague had already been captured by that local photographer, Plicka. Full stop. He found out long ago where to climb, where to rest his tripod, and what light to anticipate. He chose the perspective, exposure, and composition and waited for several years for the one morning in March. The buds on the apple tree in the foreground had just sprouted, but the dawning sun still hesitated for a few minutes between winter and spring. The local photographer quietly pressed the release. What could Nina shoot, when she happened to come to this city on her free weekend? She shrugged. Every scenic place has its local photographer.

"That's why I don't do art. I would faint with freedom." He stabbed the duck breast with the fork. "My true horror is the universe of a single second. You can literally spend the rest of your life fascinated by a single moment."

Nina looked away.

"What's up?"

"The whole world is like that." She began telling him, intermittently, about a cyclist from Johannesburg who spent five years pedaling around the entire coast of Africa. A travel magazine described the journey, as well as his immense joy when the dream had come true. But Nina hesitated. Did he see all of Africa? No. He saw a strip a few hundred meters wide, along the coast. Did he experience more than his sister, who spent those five years working in Johannesburg, blogging about him? No. In those five years, they both lived the same number of moments. In each moment, all of Africa was slipping by, except for that tiny portion each saw—he, from the saddle, and she, from the window. He didn't pedal away from anything.

Nina took this pointless five-year journey personally. If she became a photographer (and she would have liked to, but first, she'd have to deal with the other Ninas, who liked culinary arts, paintings of London's underworld, bars on the beach, hats with live birds, and Japanese masters)—then she'd compare her pieces to the local photographer's. How could she succeed? And while she was taking pictures, five designers would win grand prizes for their hats. A hedge fund manager would make three hundred million dollars. Two friends would move to the Caribbean and spend their days reading in hammocks. And Nina would keep wishing to be everyone at once.

She covered her face. "I'll end up like Dad."

Adam closed his eyes and drew her closer. "Not at all, Ninny. This is completely normal."

"You know what? I want to live in a world where this is shit."

"You're tired. Nihilism isn't a philosophy; it's exhaustion. We'll get a good sleep tonight."

"I also want to have one dream like you. I want to go to Japan. But I don't want to lose you. And why do I have to choose one, anyway?"

"Simple," said Adam, and the cursed lie nearly broke his frontal lobe. Nina was agonizing over the same problem that the Skeptic and the Imperative had fruitlessly debated the previous evening. He was watching her sadness. And himself, feeling love. He hated himself for it. To remedy this manifold crooked human condition, he tried to caress her with economic theory.

"Ninnykins. Economists solved this ages ago. It's called the opportunity cost. Listen: every option brings some kind of gain, correct? That's why you even consider it. And from that gain, you have to subtract the gain of the best alternative, the one you'll miss. For Japan, you sacrifice Cambridge. For Cambridge, you sacrifice the squat in Camden Town. For the squat in Camden, you sacrifice, I don't know, Paris. Your worry is that all of the choices look like losses, but that's not how it is. The best option will be profitable. You just have to find it. And come to terms with the fact that you'll miss the second best."

"I must be dreaming you up."

"Why?"

"What you just said wasn't bullshit. It was *deep* bullshit."

"Why?"

"You say I will miss the second-best option? What rubbish is that? I'll miss pretty much all of them."

"You can't split yourself into two, can you? If you weren't living the best life, you'd still only be living one other one."

"And that's exactly what's fucked up. I can only live one life, but I can lose a million. You have to subtract all of those, and then you'll know why I'm crying."

And both the Skeptic and the Imperative scratched their heads. Indeed: during their weekend in Prague, Adam and Nina had lost a weekend in Cambridge, Ibiza, and the North Pole. That's a burden the economists forgot to factor into the human formula: the ever-present weight of fantasy.

They drank to the bottom, and Nina gave him a birthday present. Adam tore open the silver wrap. There was a stamp carved into a little walnut block with Mandelbrot's fractal and the words *"part of the cosmic order"* in Victorian lettering. He immediately used it to include the dinner bill and the restaurant table in the cosmic order, and, on their way home, a few traffic signs too.

$$\rightsquigarrow$$

"What's this?" yelped Nina as soon as she opened the door to the olive chamber.

A silver bucket with a bottle of champagne stood on the end table. One long red rose lay on a white envelope next to two glasses and a bowl of strawberries. Adam pulled the bottle out from the crushed ice and wiped the label with his sleeve; Nina ripped the envelope open. And she hung herself on him. "You bought them for me!" She waved two tickets for a Sunday concert at St. Nicholas' Church. "You bought them," she repeated tenderly. He smiled ambivalently and twisted the cap on the bottle.

Then, lying in the bath in a long shirt, she tore petals from the rose and lay them on the foam. She was showing signs of a romantic mood. Precious research time. He'd merely arranged a collection of objects around her. The bottle, the tickets. They did not contain any chemical traces of romancium. They weren't particularly expensive or original. What in the scene then, precisely, was causing her excitement?

"Be spontaneous." He mumbled the paradoxical sentence, sinking under the foam. Nina stroked his inner thigh with her foot, waded over to him, and offered a strawberry between her lips. He swallowed. His structured thoughts proved soluble in alcohol, and particularly well in champagne-dipped strawberries. Suddenly, they were sitting on the edge of the bathtub, Nina in Adam's lap, and, with undulating movements, they floated into privacy. They kissed and clasped and writhed with such spirit that they splashed a third of the water out before they adjusted in a hard and fast rhythm.

"Be gentle," she whispered in his ear, lifting herself, firmly locked around him, and her voice brought him to the liminal. *It's your birthday* flashed through his mind, and he held Nina down with all his strength. She spread her thighs and squeezed his arms ... and they were staring at each other, each swallowing their own orgasm, both taken by surprise.

"I think I forgot my pills."

They counted up the infertile days, sighed with relief, and went to bed. Adam woke up at two. He wouldn't let it go until Nina, half-asleep, promised to take a morning-after pill. He had failed thoroughly. Isolating factors to pinpoint romance was a complete fiasco. Thus, he still had no clue if he was capable of eliciting it. Further, the scientist had presently ejaculated into his subject, ruining the last hint of objective distance. Gorgonuy's warning echoed: experimenting with philosophy is experimenting with one's own life. And heck if it was only his own life!

I, Re

ason

I'm a humble man; that's why I don't talk about the opinion I have of myself.

—Adam's father

He barely closed his eyes. As soon as Nina promised to take the pill and fell asleep, he quietly climbed out of bed, tore a single page from his notepad, opened the balcony door, and lit a cigarette. Not only did he force her to poison herself—pill or no pill, he'd lost this one battle with his beast. Earlier in the boat, he'd admired how calmly it lay by their legs. A few hours passed, and now he was licking his wounds and taking stock of the damage. What kind of argument was that, *it's your birthday*?

That, in turn, brought back the problem that he'd perfectly forgotten for one short day: how would he describe himself to Gorgonuy? He blew the smoke into the darkness. The closer the day of his meeting, the more absurd the thought of capturing himself on one page.

"Don't bother," appeased the Skeptic. "You can't fit in there."

"Hush. Cut into the meat. What defines you?" called the Imperative and winked.

He stubbed the butt out on the railing and shot it into the distance. Never certain if smoking helped him think or helped not to think, he lit another one just to make sure. It was uncomfortable to admit that what he valued most about himself was, of course, the size of his IQ. He prized his intellect like the rich prize their bank accounts. And then came one birthday bath, and his proud intellect was crying in the corner. The beast was purring nearby.

In their feud, Adam stood squarely with grey matter, that cognitive cock-block. But he was beginning to give some recognition to the savage adversary. This creature was simply trying to accomplish its only goal—reproduction—through all possible means. It used to suffice to swing up onto the butt of a female in heat and thrust, whereas today, oh Lord, what schemes did it have to concoct? Poor beast, struggling to get the cock-blocker reproduced. The mind, running experiments on the live beast. What could the two reproach each other for?

"You have to control it," the Imperative whispered. "It can ruin us."

And the Skeptic: "Who were you born to be?"

He hadn't talked to his parents about sex. They'd avoided talking about how they'd conceived the child, as if they were embarrassed, and he'd been embarrassed to ask. Everyone was ashamed that Adam was alive. He only tried once. He couldn't even reach the doorknob when he asked his father, spread out on the couch, how he came to be.

"How? Like a snap. You just slip once, and you're fudged."

"You slip on what?"

His father didn't look up from his Borges or Pessoa. "You're just not careful, you know."

"Careful with what?"

"With Mum, Addy." Adam didn't understand. Father stroked his hair and grumbled, "Forget it."

"And she didn't help you be careful?"

His father removed the book from his face to see the boy and sat up. "Boy, you'll be a Diderot. What did you do in kindergarten today?"

Adam stood in front of his father's knee covered by a checkered gown. Even then, he knew, in the way only children understand, with a prescient clarity beyond words.

"You're a freak accident, boy," whispered the Skeptic. "And don't shoot the messenger."

There were other hints from which he deduced the coarse outline of his creation. Wedding photos of a bride with a belly. Being an only child. He clearly wasn't called into the world by the parents' desire for procreation. The beast had outfoxed death, as it only had to do once in a lifetime—and oh, was it successful.

The Skeptic was in accord. "Yes, that's how bastards come into the world. It's not that they are illegitimate—it's that they are a side effect."

"It's quite the norm," whispered the Imperative. "Science views all of life as a side effect of an otherwise reasonable universe. Life is a bastard that no one wished for."

"Do you see the connection with Faustomat? How you're trying to prove that the world is not made of accidents?" Adam was unable to stop the inner chatter or its direction. "Could it be that all you're trying to prove is that there are no bastards here?"

And what of the hundred-year-old portrait? Was his father really speaking of procreation in that old conversation? What if his own name was among the class of 1912 in the Collector's archive, together

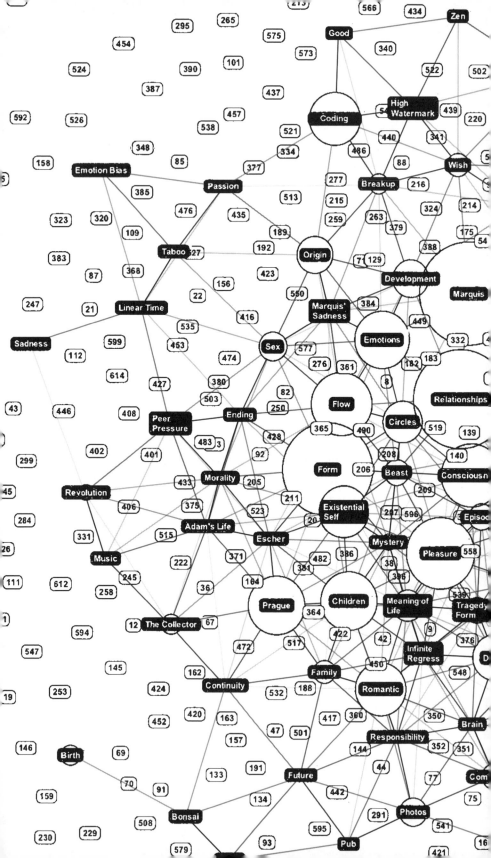

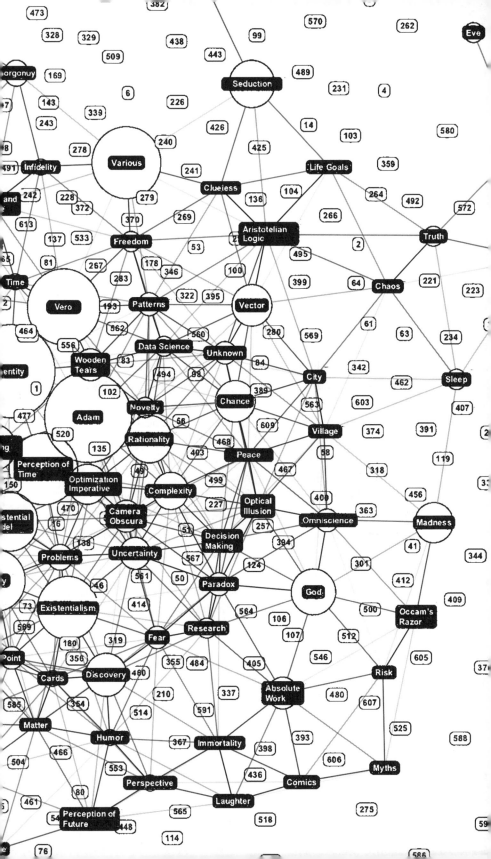

with a biography he didn't even vaguely remember, including a family accident his father was hiding? He almost wailed with tension.

The pack and the page were equally empty. Leaning against the railing, he shivered and fought a panic attack. He groped for his self, and nothing remained between his fingers. He felt like vomiting. Without his self, he wouldn't get the archive. Without the archive, he wouldn't find out who he was. There was nothing left to do but say goodnight to the self, whatever that was, and hope that it survived sleep wherever and returned in the morning.

He mechanically initiated the shut-down procedure. Shower. Teeth. Floss. Water. Pajamas. Bed. Laptop. Daily stats. He opened the file with his daily records.

And he nearly shouted out. Why, the numbers, ideas, and notes, methodically collected for the last six, seven years, had been painting his portrait, subtly and patiently, like a pencil stuck in his ass! Lost and (what luck!) found in the very same place.

Encouraged by the discovery, he spent the next three hours finding a suitable data visualization app online, learning to use it, uploading eighteen hundred records with his thoughts, moods, and tags, and, at four in the morning, Adam the Data Scientist glimpsed himself for the first time ever.

He was staring at the graph, enthralled, and clenched his fists quietly: that's me! A map of Adam. A bonsai of the brain. A complete synapticon. Outside, tomorrow's light was ascending behind the dark spires of the city. Before falling asleep for a few hours, he resolved for the umpteenth time that he had to call Marquis. He had to give him Eve's panties before Nina found them, God forbid. And, after a short and restless night, he had forgotten about it again.

I, Fe

eling

To live is the rarest thing in the world. Most people just are.

—Oscar Wilde

On Sunday morning, their last day in Prague, they ate breakfast in bed. Crisp rolls with melting butter, cuts of artisan ham and a wedge of twelve-month-old Gruyere. A bowl of yogurt and fresh berries.

"This is dreamy," sighed Nina. "Admit it."

Adam laughed and hugged her so he wouldn't have to speak.

"See, I don't know you like this," she added, and he could barely take the tension. While she packed, Adam walked down to the reception desk to pay.

"Was everything as you imagined?" winked the receptionist while he searched through the post-its stuck to the edge of the desk. He leafed through a large book, then another, humming thoughtfully, crumpled up two or three papers and threw them away. He finally handed Adam a tray with a bill and two business cards.

"Well done sourcing the tickets." Adam sighed and signed the bill.

They left their bag at the reception desk and walked downtown. The concert was due to start at twelve. Adam stopped her in front of the first pharmacy and walked inside. He returned with a white pill and a can of Coke. "Sorry, hun." He handed her the pill and hugged her. "I'm sorry."

"Shut up." She snuggled up to him. "It's love."

They got to St. Nicholas' at quarter to twelve. Groups of tourists sat in the carved oak pews. They found seats in the first row.

The bell in the tower struck twelve, and the musicians, dressed in black, entered from the sacristy. They arranged their parts on the stands and nodded to each other. The first hint of a melody was heard, barely audible but perfectly clean, as though the violinists were luring the church out of a long sleep, until the harmonies of the cello and viola spread through the dome.

Adam took the program out of his backpack and found the name of the piece. He turned to Nina to show it to her. She was resting her palms on her knees, not noticing him. Adam literally saw the strings running taut from the paintings (statues, altar, musicians) to the mirrored images within her. She appeared in an equilibrium of a tightly strung and tuned instrument, just now sounded by Bach's Brandenburg Concerto.

He was different. Hearing a melody, he had to read the guide to learn its name. Music incited contemplations, and only those made him realize what he experienced. His thoughts were longer than the moment that evoked them. He was constantly running past the present and stumbling over it. Flapping. What he felt lacking was the mystical art of being present in the present, an art not dissimilar to walking on water.

While Nina's face was motionless, her eye suddenly spun aside and looked at Adam. He burst out laughing. Her eyes widened, and she put a hand over her mouth. They looked at each other again, and Adam giggled as if he were in first grade. The people around them frowned. And again, one of them burst out, and the other couldn't resist. The relentlessly serious saints, high vaults, exalted music, and glowering looks served to perfectly deflect the laughs back between them, and the spark kept jumping from one to the other. There was no way to ground it. It stabbed them with more explosions of stifled laughter, farting through their palms and crushed behind their teeth, until suddenly, the tall violinist shook too. The wave ran from her head to her toes. She quickly turned her face, but the contractions of laughter were already spreading through the audience, surprised by the new meaning of the scene. The concert ended. A circus for which none of the attendees had bought tickets was now taking place, accompanied by a chamber orchestra. Nina got up, took Adam by the hand, and they ran out of the church through a corridor of scolding looks and more tittering. On the steps in front of the church, they hugged and started kissing.

Tongue in tongue, Adam finally figured romance out. When Nina had thrown her camera off the bridge, when he'd searched for romancium in the bath, when they finally couldn't stop laughing—all those magical moments had one element in common. Two people, two minds falling one into the other. He briefly caught that most charming capacity to mutually sweep each other into a pirouette and burst into the present together. Adam exuberantly concluded his experiment there and then and declared the verdict. Hooray, he could be with Nina!

Even the Imperative and the Skeptic clasped joyfully in a momentary lapse of judgement.

Gesamtk

unstwerk

And what hast thou to give, poor devil?
Was e'er a human mind, upon its lofty level,
Conceived of by the like of thee?
—Johann W. Goethe

A week after they returned, there was an envelope in her mailbox bearing the small logo of the Wabi-sabi Foundation. She ripped it open. The white paper said, "... *and it is with great pleasure that we* ..." She sat down and fanned herself with the invitation. "Nina von Tokyo—get it?" she whispered to herself. "Ninny is my star." Shivers ran over her neck as if they were looking for a way out, and she wouldn't let them until her shoulders twitched with laughter.

She folded the letter into her bag and ran through the morning streets to see Adam. It was a chilly and sunny October Saturday, eight in the morning, and Nina was cold after the few minutes outside. She quietly unlocked the door and walked to the bedroom. He was sleeping, bundled up in blankets. She sat cross-legged in front of the bed and waited to tell him the big news when he opened his eyes: that it was time to break up.

The final segment of the Gift of Time would never be finished. It made no sense anymore to bind him with such a gesture when, in two months, they'd each be on a different continent. She'd only be pouring salt in the wounds. What a shame ... she had been looking forward to his shocked expression.

He slept, her artist. Not that he liked when she called him that. But she'd had musicians and painters, the gorgeous and the hideous, bohemians and the volatile, and none of them was an artist like Adam. "I'm not good at talking to people," he'd warned her with his disheveled hair after their first night, and just for that, she wanted to squeeze him to death with tenderness. He'd frown with concentration over her swift ideas, and it was charming. Somehow, his height fit with strong and simple principles and an inner expanse, reminiscent of her father but calm and balanced. It was that inner expanse that Nina was trying to cross into when she rested her chin on his chest.

In September, when she'd caught the flu punting on the Cambridge canals, he'd brought her oranges and cooked Bengali curry so she'd sweat it out. All of that had won her over—but he only enchanted her with his verve, that same fanatic fervor with which he estranged himself.

He estranged himself forcefully, daily, rudely. In their relationship, he was the confidently pregnant one, protecting his fractal child from his partner. She yearned to know what spell forced him to reject every distraction so she could be closer. That's why, after coming back from Prague, she'd organized a small exhibition for him inside a shoe box. Perhaps she flattered him, even naïvely, but the gallery of leaps into the sun featured Franz Xavier Adam Messerschmidt. Richard Adam Wagner. Antonio Adam Gaudí. Gustav Adam Flaubert. Each exhibited an inhumanly brave enterprise in the gallery, and, in the center of the hall, dawdling empty-handed, stood Stéphane Adam Mallarmé.

He leaned against the wall of the Sagrada Familia, the last great sanctuary of Christianity, as Gaudí dubbed it, with its hundred-meter towers. The design had taken him over forty years. He'd devoted his time and skill, all of his money, and, when the savings ran out, he'd sold his house and moved into the building site. Every day after work, he'd walked around Barcelona begging for contributions. The only thing he'd set aside for himself was plain life, and even that was temporary.

One day, at dusk, with his thoughts on the cathedral, he had walked straight under a tram. He was wearing such poor rags that one cabby after the other refused to take him to the hospital. He didn't look like he could pay for the journey. Three days later, Barcelona dressed in black to honor the death of its architect, who, before that sad day, had set the direction of the cathedral's construction for another hundred years.

Nina knew these divers into the sun from her father's bedtime stories: "Oh fearless, superhuman undertakings! As soon as one person grasps his entire potential, Ninny, as soon as he subjects all his options to a single one, he can thrust himself much further than is natural and sensible. Because what's natural? It's to jump in puddles like you do. Sit in cafés and watch people, like I do. To be seduced by novelties, wander, and discover and to protect your bit of comfort. To loiter through the world—that's how a healthy and balanced person lives, darling. He wants to see the rainbow of life's joys, so he'll necessarily fragment his sources. A reasonable person will never achieve what a complete fanatic can."

Later, she suspected him of moving the family to be closer to them: to Vienna for Messerschmidt, to Barcelona for Gaudí. And in spite of herself, she inherited this fateful attraction to grandiose works.

Richard Wagner couldn't be absent from the gallery. Like the Sagrada Familia, his Ring of the Nibelung embodied a superhuman ambition: he composed the music and the libretto for all of *twenty-six* years. A performance, depending on the conductor's tempo, takes about fifteen hours. Thankfully, it is usually given over four evenings. The premiere demanded nothing less than the construction of a brand-new opera house, designed specifically for Wagner's piece. He pushed through revolutionary inventions like dimming the lights during the performance and a submerged orchestra pit so that the conductor's flailing baton would not distract from the show. To create a true Gesamtkunstwerk, the story, sound, dance, set design, and light all merged in an accord of content and form. Wagner honored music in the same way that cathedral architects revered light and Adam valued mathematics: as the perfect art, which doesn't need translation, because it carries its own internal meaning.

"I can't believe you don't see it," Nina would say as she played with Adam's curls. "You're obviously Wagner!" Adam had no idea what this senseless comparison meant.

"You're both obsessed." She shook his head. "Why? How did you choose the Faustomat?"

He could only laugh. If he'd known at the beginning how much work he would devote to the program over time, he would never have begun. In the beginning was the word, and the word was *hobby*.

And Nina, as tends to happen, began to see what propelled him better than he did. He followed the path of an artist. His true desire was to resolve the paradox fueling his consciousness. To eject himself to a position of an impartial observer, the fixed point in the universe. The work was a means to this alchemical metamorphosis just as the artist was a means.

"Give me what you have," whispers the masterpiece to its artist with the voice of an impassioned lover, seductively into one ear, ominously into the other. "Give me your time, skill, and mind. Look," its tongue whispers, "look at my body and enter me. Empty your force into me, and I will rid you of your torments, of paradox ... Take *my* body—would you not want a body that will live forever?"

As the originally hazy topic gradually came closer to Adam's dilemmas, the Work and the author grew more and more self-similar. Then came a point when it stopped fitting into his consciousness. Adam was no longer returning to nurture it but to explore himself. This was the kind of endeavor that demanded all of his competence.

With this realization, his career, reputation, pleasures, and having his shirt neatly tucked in lost a lot of their meaning. Adam's values were overpowered by the Work, including those that had led him to start it. Perspective disappeared, and that's how it had to be. A great, absolute work has to devour its author, horizon included. It's not born in the mind of a skeptic but in the mind of a fanatic, who deliriously places it on the pedestal of highest value. In that exact moment, the work takes control of its author. It'll allow him to store a bit of food on the side and find a roof, just enough so that the body survives. Then, it seizes consciousness and, with a horrifying scream, begins to be born into the world.

The consanguineous parent feeds its limitless appetite with everything he deprives himself of. Anyone else would let the monster die, and that's what they advise, with good intentions. But he won't hear because he's no longer a human but a Creator. Whatever competes with the Work for resources, for thought and time, has to be mercilessly slain, publicly if possible, so the massacre can serve as a warning to others. Only then can the Work outgrow him not twice, not five times but a hundred, because everything in life rearranges without further conflict. Meaningless doubts are replaced by discipline, order, routine. That's how porridge enters the Creator's life. Self-preservation steps down from the sacred pedestal and strolls amongst the common values. The fanatic's life expectancy shortens to a fraction. If Gaudí were to choose between the demolition of the cathedral, Wagner between the loss of a libretto, and their own death, they would choose to save the Work.

The Creator's sole meaning is to give the Work a breeding ground, let it grow like a flower from his eye socket. The Creator will cure a salami of his left arm so the right one can go on crafting. The garden in front of his house goes to the dogs, people lose their way to him, and his body begins to smell. In his entire world, the Work has no enemy. It can graze that world, hack it to pieces, vomit and defecate all over it, and the Creator will give it nothing but a kind smile. That's because the Creator, Nina knew, stopped thinking of himself. He knew that he wouldn't be forgotten because the Work had long known more about him than he ever had. The Work would not forget.

Is the Work a parasite? It declares itself greater than the host body, kills off rivals, and leaves the host just enough strength to keep him alive. It eats, grows, and blossoms.

Is the Work a parasite? Perhaps. And what is Nina, without a calling, without a passion, without a Work? A dead coral, waiting for a parasite.

He slept, her artist, and she was cold. Holding her breath, she slipped under the blanket, and he embraced her without waking up. Her fingers traced over his lifelines. She lay her palm on his heart and inhaled his scent. She felt … home. Her breath evened out with his, and her pulse slowed down.

After a while, kissing that big palm of his, she delicately disentangled herself and stepped out onto the balcony. She found his lighter and held it by the corner of the invitation to Tokyo. The chilly wind blew the flame over the paper and turned the color white into black, cold into heat, an invitation into silence and Tokyo into Adam. A smile slipped onto her face. After all, Japan was just a dream.

She began imagining how to, after all, finish her work of art—incomparable to the Faustomat but one she cared about as much as she cared about Adam: The Gift of Time. A *present*, one could say just as well. Or her own way to give Adam as much time as he could possibly want. She was somewhat worried that it might even be too much for him. But she wasn't one to let worry stand in the way of a good joke.

I, W

Synchronicity is something physicists don't know about, nor would they want to.

—Baron Phillips of Ellesmere

There

are days when Adam can do anything he sets his mind upon. He marches through the world triumphantly and laughs off fear and evil. The threads of causes and effects intersect in his independent will. Space-time ripples around his consciousness, and he is so content with the liquid harmony surrounding him that he feels himself to be more of a universe than a man, more free than will, and more mathematics than a mathematician. He feels to be the root, the maker, the mover—knowing well that God is a fractal.

And there are days that start badly and end worse, but it's impossible to alter a single event. Strangely, when Adam is gripped by that only possible present, he doesn't rejoice in being a touch away from the cosmic order he seeks. Rather, his free will and both his balls stiffen with fear.

One day this, another that. Adam's ability to influence fate seems to relate to calendar dates. That is, it corresponds to certain numbers. Perhaps, then, it would help to study numerology?

He could also realize that what we call a calendar date, one specific day, is nothing but a precise constellation of the Sun, the Earth, and the planets. Thus, he could see the calendar as a spatial rather than a temporal scheme. And the capacity to alter fate would suddenly become a function of his position in respect to the planets. Then, astrology might come in handy.

Or he could let his gaze defocus and direct his attention to the gaps *between* calendar days. He could delve into what it is between two days, between two hours, and between two seconds that inverts his life from total control to total helplessness. And if he unfocused meticulously, it'd occur to him at some point that each of the gaps is just the right size for a tarot card. But Adam doesn't stoop to such crutches. He prefers to pretend that the days that rob him of his will don't exist at all.

During breakfast, nervous and sleepy, he let his tongue slip. It was the day he was to meet Gorgonuy. He irretrievably disclosed what should have remained hidden. So right at eight in the morning, he contradicted his conception of the human as a rational being endowed with free will.

"If you want to steal databases, then do it. But we won't be together. I thought we understood each other on this." Nina put away her cup of coffee.

"Without that data, I can throw Faustomat out the window."

"There's an idea. And then you could descend to Earth and start living?"

"Ninny, as soon as I get this dataset, the worst is over."

She wiped her hands on a kitchen towel. "Just spare me that. What time are you finishing at school?"

"Four. I've got tons of work."

Throughout the day, he drank coffee, smoked, thought, bit his lips, read emails, smoked, and drank coffee. At three thirty, he assessed that he'd done absolutely nothing, smoked one last cigarette, and left the glass pagoda of the Centre for Mathematical Studies. He stopped his bike at the second junction next to a black cab. As the green light hit, Adam was careful to stay clear of the car when the tinted side window rolled down. A flat, solid package the size of a small pizza flew out and nearly hit his front wheel.

"Hey!" He flung his fist and bent over to pick it up. The black letters on the packing paper said, *"For you."*

"That's rather vague." He untied the string and tore off the wax paper, grumbling.

Ripping the bubble wrap revealed a delicate, antiquated oil painting. Adrenaline jolted through him. It was him on the canvas, in Pembroke's traditional graduation gown.

Without thinking, he jumped on the bike to chase after the car and sprinted through several junctions standing up until it was clear that the cab was already God knows where. He swore and stopped by the pavement to catch his breath and examined the painting more carefully. There was a label by the lower edge with the year 1812 inscribed in calligraphy.

He stood in shock, treetops above him, and the sky. It was one of those days in which the full moon can be seen in daylight—and, in the distance, invisible and silent, Mars, Jupiter, Uranus. As though the entire Universe had frozen, waiting to see which of the portraits Adam would give the Collector. Other Adams, other fates, and alternate

Universes sensed his sudden weakness. They haggled over his dwindling will and called one over the other—"Who are you, Adam?" On such a crucial crossroads in life, he understood, he had to crush every doubt. He had to flex his volition so firmly that it would push out the myriad alternate Universes back into nonbeing. Because the important thing is who we are in the dark.

In this noble moment of great, sentimental truth, he stopped at the next café, locked his bike to a pole, and walked in under the gaze of the pale moon.

"Can I have a knife, please?" he asked the waitress and pulled the synapticon out of his bag.

"Excuse me—are you going to eat?"

"No."

The waitress paused, and Adam reversed. "Okay, one piece of toast and a knife."

"What kind of toast?"

"Just a toast," he snapped. "Veggie with no veggies."

"What do you mean?"

"It doesn't matter. Look, just give me some toast. One toast. I have no preference—you choose."

"Without vegetables?"

"Just don't ask me any more questions, goddamnit!"

The waitress carefully fried an egg and two strips of bacon. She heated a few slices of tomatoes, spread butter onto four pieces of toast, and poured in hot beans next to it all while Adam concentrated on what inevitably had to come in the next moments. She handed him the plate, a napkin, a knife, and a fork.

"I need a kitchen knife, not cutlery."

With a look the length of Norway's coastline, she exchanged the knife for the one she'd just used to break the eggs. Adam closed his eyes and quickly cut into his finger. He clenched his teeth with pain, but the blood wasn't showing.

"We're not insured for this!" yelled the waitress.

He clenched his teeth and cut again. There was a sharp prick, and a rill of blood trickled down his nail onto the synapticon. "And rightly so," he breathed. "It won't happen again anytime soon." The waitress reached for the phone. Adam pressed her hand to the receiver. "Trust me. I'm a statistician."

Painfully pressing out another large red blot, he smeared the blood over the paper into the letter A and gripped his finger with the napkin. "Goodbye then." He returned the plate, toast included. Outside, he jumped onto his bike and pedaled toward the college, thoughts madly flying about his hair.

"Just about now," he breathed heavily, when he dropped into a seat opposite Gorgonuy, "I've had enough. What is this supposed to mean?" He pulled out the new oil painting.

"I was expecting you to write me a few lines. Less than a memoir, more than an obituary. In between."

"I'm asking you where this is from?"

"Why are you asking me?"

"And what about the photograph?" asked Adam. "1912? Nothing?"

Gorgonuy shook his head. "If I knew what you're talking about, we might even have a conversation."

"Since I met you, I started receiving these old portraits. Isn't it a nice coincidence? I think they're from you."

"Oh dear, no."

"So who's sending them? Are they from that secret society of yours, the one that shut down the electronic archive? Did you talk to them?"

"I was under the impression you considered secret societies to be nonsense on par with the occult sciences."

Adam flailed his hands. "I know it's somehow related, my study of chance, these portraits, and you. What perverted game is this?"

Gorgonuy reached behind himself. "Shall we ask the wiser ones?" And he placed his tarot deck on the table.

"God no."

"I don't know anything about the rest, though I'll enjoy hearing the story. I'm just reminding you that, if it becomes a problem, I would much prefer not to be dragged into it." Gradually, Gorgonuy pulled a card from the deck. "Do you want to see it?"

"No."

"Sure?"

For a moment, they sat in silence; then, Gorgonuy spoke. "You're not the self-assured scientist I met last time. Today, I see a story. Now, I'm satisfied."

"Really?"

"It's too bad you don't come to my lectures. You'd hear that a good story leaves the audience knowing less. They have to be richer with ambiguity where there used to be a single answer. A good story trades answers for questions."

"But this isn't some story, Professor—it's my life!"

"You're only a human to yourself, Adam. To the rest of us, you're a story."

"You're morbid."

He rebuked. "I'm not your shrink, so stop crying." And tapped the oil painting on the table. "Am I supposed to understand that you're offering the portrait in exchange for the data archive?"

"Am I two hundred years old?" He threw the synapticon he'd developed in front of Gorgonuy. "*This* is me. No one else."

Gorgonuy glanced dubiously from the paper to Adam. "And you're offering me this for six gigabytes of data?"

"I can't give more. This is me."

The professor slowly traced his finger over the clutter of circles and lines as though he were drawing ornaments or spelling letters. "What is this rubbish?"

Adam explained how he'd created the network graph from his diaries and how revealing and personal were the connections between the topics.

"Well." The professor smacked his lips and picked up the paper, sniffing it slowly. "What is this? What is it?"

"My blood," Adam straightened up. "I came in complete sincerity."

"Oh boy." Gorgonuy's expression shifted, and again.

"What?"

"You crossed the line."

Adam shrugged.

"And you don't even know it."

He packed the tarot and the synapticon away, leaving one card on the table. ""Why is it that a warning is not enough for you?" He walked over to the other room and brought back two glasses. "What you're showing isn't scientific skepticism, it's a ram's head. A drink?"

"What did I mess up now?" Adam rubbed his red eyes.

"You just gave away your soul. Are you not scared?"

Adam scoffed. "I don't believe in fairy tales."

"I believe, I don't believe—didn't you call that a naïve attitude last time we met?"

Adam had no reply.

"Adam?" said Gorgonuy sharply, and Adam jerked his head. "See, you nitwit, I call a name, and it turns your head. The given name is where reins are hung. And that's just a name; what if I get my hands on a photograph, hair, or nails? And a drop of blood—the things it can do! But you gave me your life, narrated from the heart."

Adam shook his head. "I had to sign that paper with blood. It had nothing to do with magic. Just taking myself one hundred percent earnestly. Saying who I am. This was the only and entirely logical path."

"Do you finally admit that logic is a servant of myth?"

"How did you arrive at that?"

"Because the idea of man as a rational being, driven by free will, is the first of our myths. It's the root myth, which holds together your self-confidence, Western culture, democracy, and the markets. But your rationality stands on your decisions, your decisions on your imagination, and your imagination is nothing but a labyrinth of myths—contradictory, half-forgotten, and half-intuited. This admission would propel you from the Cambridge maths department into another universe. Now, something is dragging you there ass-first."

"Professor Gorgonuy, I'm exhausted." Adam pushed his fists into his eyes, reddened by fatigue and smoke. "I should take the data and go lie down. You're killing me."

When he opened his eyes again, he noticed the tarot card on the table. Without thinking, he flipped it over.

"What do we have here?" smacked Gorgonuy. "The protégé of the moon, Hermes Trismegistus. His public name is the Magician, his private, the Juggler. If you have noticed, the card was upside down. That's a sign you could be facing the Charlatan and his trickery."

"And who is that?"

"Don't jump to conclusions. It could be me; it could be you just as well." He didn't smile.

"I'm not a swindler."

"The one I speak of is the Mage. His free will molds matter, forges ideas, and invokes being from nonbeing. Time and space warp around his consciousness. In moments of enlightenment and magic, he becomes one with the universe. That's why this card also represents the pervasive order of things and, a step lower, lucky coincidences. I mean those strangely purposeful connections of the space-time continuum that appear just when they can help the most."

"That would be any minute now." Adam put his head in his hands.

"You should go rest. I can't give you the data today anyway."

"But that's what we agreed!"

"I don't have it here."

"Professor Gorgonuy! What is this game?"

"It's a game of give and take. You give, I take. And when I decide, it goes the other way."

Adam stood up. "Give me my synapticon back now."

Gorgonuy touched his beard before he spoke. "You gave me your soul. What will you offer to have it back?"

"I didn't give it to you, I exchanged it for the data."

"Then you have the data?"

"No!"

"Well, then you apparently gave it to me. If you want it back, you must offer something else."

"For God's sake, what do you want for it?"

Gorgonuy shrugged. "As things are, I'm fine. I can't think of anything else you could give me. Anything more valuable, that is." He chuckled a bit.

Adam stared at him in disbelief. "You trickster."

"You're just not listening. That's your problem. Have you decided what you want from me, really?" The old man leaned back. "The data or your soul?"

Adam's face hardened. "The archive."

"Then you just have to wait till I give it to you."

Adam was incredulous, then determined. He sat down. "I'm not leaving without it."

"Well, you remind me of someone …" Gorgonuy smiled. "Someone I once may have caused to die. Would you like to hear the story?"

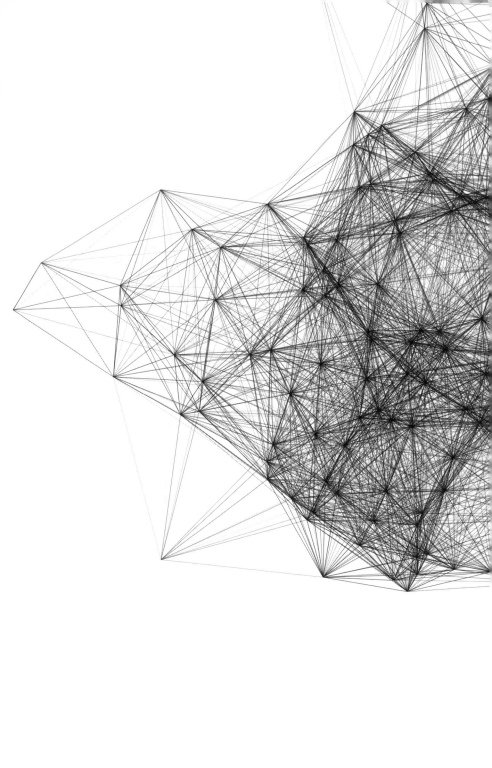

Mathematicians

Logic is the art of going wrong with confidence.

—Joseph Wood Krutch

At my age, I only care about two sports: climbing the stairs and the coffin long jump. So, in this advanced stage of decay, it is humorous for me to pick up the portraits and recall how stubbornly my younger self rejected them. Oh, son, immortality wouldn't have killed you!

It's unfortunate that we mathematicians have a tradition of distaste for anything that smells of infinity. It brought a few of our best to suicide and once almost destroyed the whole field. That downfall was called the crisis of mathematics, and it's been mostly shoved under the carpet.

I am fascinated by this nearly forgotten period. It's so illuminating to who we are today, both the hope and the crash. I have a shelf of reading on it, from comparative logic to fractal mathematics and category theory. I won't spook you with that. But quite recently, a friend gave me Washington Niedermeyer's final book, *Mathematics and Man*. I gulped it down in one sitting. The book describes the story of mathematics, and it reads like my biography.

Let me fetch it for you. Would you hold my taboret? Ah, look, there's my first edition of the *Principia*, signed by Whitehead. I paid quite a fortune for this beauty, which my wife knows nothing of. Much more than for the *Liber Abaci*, and I do have the first print-ed edition from Boncompagni. And next to Whitehead is Washington Niedermeyer.

Washington Niedermeyer: Mathematics and Man. First edition, 1968. Chapter 5: From One Logic to Many. "We must know, and we will know!" urged David Hilbert at the opening address of a mathematical conference in Paris. It was the year 1900. Nietzsche was dying. Civilization, fumbling for a fixed point, impaled itself on a terrifying fork. Despite the abolition of several monarchies, the idea of the *absolute* controlled most people's minds. That's because, despite all its horrors, it didn't seem as terrifying as the second spike: Nietzsche's warning that a society devoid of absolute ideals could burden every citizen with the weight of a meaningless existence. For, if one gets rid of illusions, he loses dreams.

The intellectual elites took this fork seriously and speculated: if it were only possible to substitute science for religion and infinity for God, the hierarchies of thought and of people would remain untouched. The universe itself, and the iron laws it follows, could stand in for the disputed God. Mathematics seemed ideal for this purpose. First, it is the foundation upon which all other sciences build. Second, infinity is closely related to the absolute. If one weren't a term of mathematics and the other of philosophy, one could consider them synonymous. Mathematicians felt the enormous pressure of a civilization reassessing its foundations. They were excited by the hope that they could replace religion in the role of irrefutable cosmic certainty, anchoring all subsequent thought—physics, cosmology, the origin of man, and the meaning and purpose of his existence.

"We must know, and we will know," Hilbert tasked his colleagues, listing ten crucial problems that mathematicians had to solve in the course of the twentieth century to prove that the invariable laws of the universe were understood.

See? They were looking for the Faustomat as well.

The very first of Hilbert's problems was solving George Cantor's paradoxes. Cantor spent most of his lonely life studying infinity, a topic traditionally reserved for God. As a man of deep faith, he was painfully aware of crossing not only the boundaries set by Aristotle but also those set by the church. To resolve this moral dilemma, he divided infinity into three spheres: God's infinity ("absolutum"), the infinity of natural reality, and the infinite sets of mathematics. He left absolutum to God, nature to the physicists, and immersed himself in the study of sets.

Even so, there was no end to controversy. He soon claimed there was not only one infinite set but that infinities come in different sizes—that some are larger than others and it is possible to compare them. For years, he alternated between proving and rejecting his own hypotheses with such zeal that he was repeatedly hospitalized in a mental asylum. The expert critics considered his thoughts at the very least contentious, if not religious deliria. Some argued that even physics does not know whether or not the universe is infinite and that the paradoxes that haunted Cantor were mere disputes over the meaning of the word "infinity." They refused to speak of it further. According to others, it was simply necessary to continue in the direction outlined by Cantor and resolve the dilemmas.

One will brush difficult problems under the carpet and live on contentedly.

And another will work on the Faustomat year after year, knowing that it can destroy his life.

This passionate and, for Cantor, literally destructive argument about infinity reflected a key problem of mathematics at the end of the nineteenth century. What was missing at the time was a convincing proof that it is possible to derive all of mathematics from an elemental set of axioms. That is, an irrefutable proof that mathematics is consistent, that it contains no paradoxes, and that it is precisely built up from the primitive foundations of logic to the most complex constructions. That it's perfect. Cantor's paradoxes pushed this vision further away, so to many, they were rather annoying. Rather than fiddling with the weirdness of infinity, they much preferred Hilbert's straightforward battle cry to make mathematics the foundation of a new society, infinites or not!

While Hilbert's call enraptured the enthusiastic public as well as the scientists, there were also critics. Poincaré and Brouwer pointed out that the mathematics that Hilbert was trying to prove in fact rested on the axioms of Aristotelian logic. Perhaps it was time to revise Aristotle's two-thousand-year-old thoughts? Specifically, they were pointing to the law of the excluded middle.

According to Aristotle's *Metaphysics*, it is "always necessary to confirm or refute, because it is impossible for anything to stand between the two sides of a contradiction." But life is not black and white, argued Brouwer, and he described other logics, from which *other mathematics* would follow. Hilbert vigorously defended Aristotle: "To rid the mathematician of the law of the excluded middle is like banning the astronomer from using a telescope or the boxer from using his fists. [...] Abandoning the law of the excluded middle is equal to giving up on all of mathematics."

"Do you love me?" Nina asked many times. "Just say yes or no." And I sweated silently in a furious conflict. I didn't know how to get it across to her that she was turning to the law of the excluded middle for comfort. I wished to explain what I felt: that basic mathematical logic was not appropriate for a debate about love. But I didn't have other language.

The thought of several mathematics to pick and choose from appalled Hilbert. If there were more logics, how would one choose *the right one?* To him, all would be equally wrong. He planned to reach his goal by first proving universal consistency, by which he would also show that Aristotelian logic was the only possible one. Cantor's paradoxes had to be resolved. In logic, even a single paradox leads to any conclusion imaginable. As Aristotle said, one could say anything about anything. More precisely, anything could be deduced, including the fact that Hilbert is a poodle.

Among those searching for a new, indisputable foundation of mathematics were Bertrand Russell and Alfred Whitehead. They spent seven years in Cambridge on their three-volume opus, *Principia Mathematica*. It illustrates the depth of the crisis most eloquently with this "proposition that is occasionally useful":

$$I + I = 2$$

Is it obvious? The proof of this equation takes up over a hundred pages and touches on a number of paradoxes between the finite and the infinite, discovered by Cantor. And the result of their work? Russell's paradox. It is the mathematical equivalent to the ancient Greek liar's paradox: "I lie." If I am lying, then I speak the truth. If I speak the truth, then I lie.

"Be spontaneous," Nina demanded in Prague. And I couldn't. How can one be spontaneous on command?

While Russell and Whitehead needed one hundred pages and a new theory to still end up in paradoxes around sets, Ludwig Wittgenstein offered a more laconic solution. The word "set" is used in two meanings, he said; we just need to differentiate between them, and the paradox will dissipate. What irony. Mathematicians spent twenty yours doubting a stable foundation until Wittgenstein surmised they had been using one word incorrectly!

But he also added a new layer of uncertainty. The work in which the brief commentary appeared is the *Tractatus Logico-Philosophicus*, a text on logic and thought built up from basic premises to a dramatic conclusion:

"6.5 For an answer that cannot be expressed, the question too cannot be expressed.

[...]

6.54 My propositions are elucidatory in this way: he who understands me finally recognizes them as senseless when he has climbed out through them, on them, over them. (He must, so to speak, throw away the ladder after he has climbed up on it.) He must surmount these propositions; then, he sees the world rightly.

7 Whereof one cannot speak, thereof one must be silent."

The *Tractatus* shows that every proposition rests within language, which cannot be transcended with words. This brusquely determines the limits of knowledge. And where it is impossible to reach the goal, there is no sense in even starting. This surely heated up the debate!

Despite (or because of) this, the first points of Hilbert's program remained unresolved for over thirty years, until 1934. Kurt Gödel later described the year in which he worked on Cantor's hypothesis, broke down, and ended up in a sanatorium as the worst year of his life. He translated the liar's paradox into the language of mathematics and elegantly proved that any theory universal enough either contains a contradiction or does not prove all truths. Hilbert's grandiose vision of a single, all-proving mathematics was buried instantly, and it is almost comical that the old and simple liar's paradox was the one to dig her grave. The final candidate for absolutum breathed its last, and humanity, whether it liked it or not, was left hanging on the other spike of the fork.

Gödel's theorem should have caused a complete train wreck in the sciences—all of the sciences, as mathematics is their foundation, and logic is the foundation of mathematics. But strangely, it did not happen.

Mathematicians never admitted the depth of the problem. Instead, they just reversed course and started acting as if they never had anything to do with life and such. The paradoxes buried in the foundation became a meaningless wordplay in their eyes. And people never got the memo that they should no longer use logic, because it's broken.

I hated their buck-passing violently. In Cambridge, I heard it so many times: mathematics is not connected to the real world, the professors would repeat, and the students after them. How can that be, when Nina called out the words of the liar's paradox in Prague? When she asked me about love following the law of the excluded middle?

I recall one conversation under the blooming trees in the Orchard tea-room garden. I could not ignore a professor in a corduroy suit jacket, swaggering in front of his insecure student, indulgently explaining lattice algebra to her. She was concentrating strenuously on some point in the sky, where she probably sensed set theory might be. Are you imagining it? The sun was shining, we were sipping tea by adjacent tables.

"I'm trying to imagine, somehow, what a lattice ..."

"Don't even try that. Do you know what set theory has in common with the real world?"

She shook her head.

"See, you do know! Nothing! Mathematics is pure abstraction, so—"

"Nonsense," said I, and the professor heard it. Not by accident.

"Excuse me, you're not talking to us, are you?" he asked with a perfectly balanced proportion of complaisance and sarcasm, as they do.

"I am talking to pure abstraction."

The professor slowly turned his deckchair to face me with his thick glasses and sat back comfortably.

"Well then, impolite sir, will you try to defend your ... proposition?"

My neck reddened. "If I asked any mathematician in Cambridge whether mathematics has anything to do with the real world, they'd say it doesn't."

The professor nodded with a smile. "Indeed."

"Because they are cowards."

He slurped his tea loudly and went quiet. "End of proof?"

I shrugged. It was always the same with academics. "Philosophers claim that philosophy isn't and shouldn't be useful. You're just creating academic comfort while the world out there waits for you to finally deliver something."

The professor remained in good spirits; why, he had an admirer. "Let the world wait for a while. I admit that I've been writing my little book for seventeen years," he used the opportunity to show his feathers, "and I could finish it this year."

"What will it be on?"

"Philosophy of sets."

"What exactly?"

"I do a bit on the empty set and a set with one element. It is questionable, you see, whether they are sets at all. So it's really questionable whether I even work on the philosophy of sets."

"So for seventeen years, you've worked on whether you work on mathematics."

"Yes, you could put it like that."

"And the book you've been writing for seventeen years has nothing to do with the real world?"

"No. It's really only about sets."

I buried my head in my hands. "This is absurd."

195

The professor's companion couldn't hold back and cleared her throat. "Some people are interested in pure thought. Some."

I pointed toward the ground. "What do you see?"

"Grass?" retorted the professor.

"What is it?"

They both stared at me.

"You didn't say 'I see thousands of blades of grass.'" I pointed at a tree. "What do you see?"

Professor: "An—apple tree?"

"You didn't say 'I see a thousand leaves and hundreds of branches.'"

"I get it. You want to say I see sets."

"I want to say you can't see further than the end of your nose." I stopped the nervous student with a wave of my hand. "Perhaps I have Asperger's, but when I open my eyes, I only see sets and their elements. Sets from morn to night. And let me tell you: as long as set theory is an abstract and not a cognitive discipline, it will know nothing about sets."

"Circular argument, my friend."

"So is yours."

"Excuse me?"

"You claim that sets are purely abstract objects and that's why they have nothing to do with human thought. That's a circular argument." And I smashed, "If mathematics really had nothing to do with the real world, then why do we reproach the kids with 'be logical!?' If we don't use logic to understand the world, *then what the hell do we use every day?*"

"Excuse me, we're having an important conversation," the student said, turning to the professor, and I called out—"Last question!"

The professor, perturbed but happy to have her on his side, raised his hand. "Sorry."

"Do you know how much the tea costs?"

"Three pounds."

"Three." My facial muscles twisted into the simplest expression of doubt I could muster. In the acting heights of a man balancing on the edge of Asperger syndrome, I looked to the fingers on my hand. "As in one, two, three?"

Ah, that young Adam. Today, I would tone down the language, but I'd still be on the same side, bringing mathematicians to account. After Gödel, they should have ripped mathematics to shreds and rewired it to fit the human experience. Niedermeyer says it well. He's so dear to me because of three paragraphs somewhere around here. I would sign those in blood if it weren't for the fact that I sign nothing in blood since a certain event.

The scientists work as if they are objective, rational, without problems, without conflict, crystalline characters devoid of human dirt. They don't shout, "But I might kick the bucket in my bed at night!" at conferences, because this is not supposed to affect the theories. The human condition is part of ceteris paribus, outside the model. And yet: the inquiring mind is not empty and impartial. A seventy-year-old scientist bends and cowers in front of a dark silhouette, and his theorizing becomes his last possible dodge. A thirty-year-old reflects on the mystery of meaning, the animal instinct to fuck, the self, on friendship and on love, on chance that saves and kills. On everything that defines life outside the model. Cantor fought his way through infinities thanks to his longing to be closer to God. Hilbert fought like a lion not for mathematics but for his vision of the world.

Between the Faustomat's lines of code, there are unfinished arguments with Grandma.

There is not a scientist that could erase the questions inside, as much as formal science tries to brush them away. The Cantors, Einsteins, and von Brauns try to step outside the model so they don't muck it up, but they aren't and they cannot be impartial observers, standing aside at a fixed point in the universe. Their theories leak from the inside, and they are subject to a certain kind of gravity: the gravity of the human condition, our very own black hole.

This is the point of Gödel's proof. This is the point of the liar's paradox. There is no objective science. The scientist is always part of the equation. The liar, the coward, the lion, the dreamer. Their anxieties define their questions, which connect into a collective a cloud of knowledge. The shape of this cloud, this summation of all the sciences, reliably betrays its creators: infinity. Space shuttles. Hiroshima.

I was so glad to finally find someone writing about this. Even if Niedermeyer writes only about mathematics, the parallels with other fields are unmissable. Diderot, Brouwer, Cantor, Whitehead, Protagoras, Nietzsche, and Mallarmé all walked the same path. They all found themselves living in a time when their civilization briefly searched for a new paradigm. The most turbulent, most creative times, when old certainties crumbled. And their contemporaries almost invariably wanted a quick answer. It was more profitable to plaster a new name on old structures than to dig deeper into the wound. It's always been individual curiosity rather than personal gain that drove some pioneering minds to tear down much more than the first layer. Dig deeper into the wound. Diderot did that. Brouwer and Whitehead did. It's as if they saw an opening within the soul of the civilization that briefly offered another path. This is the litmus test: does the new thinking confirm or dethrone Aristotle's logic?

The reason why only the latter will suffice is dead simple. We, people, have falsified Aristotle in practice. Our lives brought the end of logic as a universal law and showed it to be a mere narrative. Now, we're just waiting for the intelligentsia to notice.

I, S

oul

Gifts make slaves.
—Claude Lévi-Strauss

Adam

sat stiff as a board. Gorgonuy poured them another whisky and filled his briarwood pipe. Then, he reached into a shelf and shook a black vial.

"If I told you I have a natural poison here, which will paralyze you in thirty minutes without leaving a trace in your blood, what would you do? Would you test whether I'm telling the truth?"

"Why do you keep such a thing?"

"Well. I know something about blood spells." Gorgonuy turned the vial on the table over with his finger. "And yes, I might have caused someone's death with it."

Adam closed his eyes. "Might have?"

"I don't know." Gorgonuy shook his head. "And if I really did kill him, it was because I didn't believe in magic then."

"A mythologist's occupational hazard."

"It's a longer story, but you probably shouldn't go to sleep before you hear it." The professor sprawled out more comfortably on the armchair, puffed his pipe, and, after a moment of reflection, he started. "I was studying at the Sorbonne but decided to write my dissertation in Siberia, five hundred miles past Krasnoyarsk. That was during Brezhnev's reign, in 1976. If you have the impression that it was impossible to get into Russia at the time, you're completely right. Especially for an anthropologist studying aboriginal rituals. Nothing of that sort existed in a communist country. But my nanny was from Siberia. During the First World War, she marched on foot with a field hospital in General Samsonov's army all the way to Prussia, and there, in August 1914, she and a hundred thousand soldiers were captured in the battle of Tannenberg. Instead of returning to the taiga, she married a soldier, but they killed him during the liberation. She escaped through an underground tunnel and walked across half of Europe again before she met her second husband, to whom she gave six daughters and a son. She would tell me stories about Russia, completely different from what you'd read in the papers. Tales of hunting on frozen rivers, winters in a yurt, of shamans and vodka. And it charmed me. So in seventy-six, when our academic group got an official invitation to a French-Soviet symposium on the roots of Eurasian civilization, we all knew it would be political clownery, but I didn't mind. I approached Doctor Broussard and told her that I wanted to go and that I spoke Russian. My family placed great importance on languages.

"Three of us went in the end. A colleague was having an affair with Broussard at the time, and she'd arranged a trip to Moscow for them. We landed at Domodedovo Airport, and, even though we had an invitation, they wouldn't let us into the city for two days, until they found the fat bureaucrat who had the authority to grant visas. He interrogated us, disappeared for an entire day, and then all-importantly slammed a three-day visa into the passports of Broussard and her fancy man. He slammed it into mine too, with a bang like from the Aurora. I leafed through my passport in the corridor. Believe it or not, as he stamped it with that greasy paw of his, his stamp must have spun through, because my visa was for a year and three days. I didn't tell anyone. I made my amends in spirit with Broussard (moaning with love through the paper walls of the Rossiya Hotel) for the mess that awaited her on their departure and disappeared on the second night of the conference. Nobody knew of me for the next six months. The country is simply too big, and someone who speaks Russian will disappear off the face of the earth, regime or not. I got off the train in Krasnoyarsk and slowly carried on, with raftsmen on the river, on foot, seventy miles on a jeep for a liter of homemade vodka. Occasionally, someone would introduce me to someone else, until I finally found the village I was looking for. Nyechalnoye, said a drunk riding an ox from the field—that's the hole you're looking for. It's haunted."

Finally, he took a beat.

"Adam, the nature there—you've seen nothing like it. Endless forests ... boots sank into the moss up to one's knees; trousers were green with lichen and larch resin. You'd walk on, and suddenly there'd be a plain where not even a stemlet grew, and you'd have no idea why. Peat bogs turning into grassy marsh fields. Slopes, cliffs, rivers, and barren ridges more expansive than all of Wales, scattered with hollow stumps and fallen logs. And then pine and birch trees, with herds of grazing reindeer as far as you could see. There were lost villages in those forests, where people drank vodka instead of water, two liters a day, as the doctor said. It was easy to get lost, and only the wolves would find you. After all, barely fifteen thousand people lived in all of the Evenkia—and I'm talking about a land twice the size of Germany. There could be ten thousand more today. You'd be hard-pressed to find a more solitary place—"

"So," Adam interrupted. "You got lost in the taiga."

"No. Everything on the journey went as it was foretold in my dreams. I got to Nyechalnoye in two weeks, by chance or higher power. It was a village, but you wouldn't have used that word. At the end of a ten-mile corridor with two muddy potholes in place of a road, two six-floor blocks of apartments stood by the river. One was abandoned, the other inhabited by a handful of hunting families and fishermen. The houses were built by the army in nineteen fifty-two. It was supposed to be a crossing between the oil pipeline and a fishing thoroughfare, and some overactive lieutenant had designated it a strategic point where a city would grow over time. But then, the oil spilt into the river, creating a five-mile-long black lake by the time someone noticed. All of the fish in the basin came out belly up. The oil was leaking for a year before the army finally plugged the hole in the pipeline. The fishermen disappeared, and Moscow forgot about the strategic crossing. The army left the two apartment blocks at the mercy of nature just as dispassionately as they'd first built them. Well, first, the wolverines found them. After them, the Tungusic hunters—but they only moved into the taller one. They believed the second one to be haunted. The guy who brought me there didn't greet anyone. He spat vodka onto two of his fingers, crossed himself, turned his Lada Niva around, and disappeared back in the corridor. The first local I met was a stocky man, his head wrapped in a grubby bandage and a face as white as death. I introduced myself as Doctor Golchakov from an institute in Moscow—"

"What institute?"

"Nobody ever asked about that. But Moscow almost cost me my life right away. The last person to come to Nyechalnoye from Moscow was a certain Ivan Ovechkov, ten years before me. He let them host him for two weeks with ceremonies. Then, he drank the entire tribe into a stupor by the fire. Supposedly, he had magical protection against vodka, but I think he just poured himself water under his hand. When the Tungusians blacked out, he stuffed his Lada full of their furs and left. So the people in Nyechalnoye were scared of me, and the last thing you want is a Russian who is scared of you—"

"The Tungusians probably aren't Russian."

"You could comfort yourself with that. It didn't work for me. The first few nights, when they let me sleep in the empty, haunted block, I didn't close an eye. But you're right, they are an ancient tribe. Tungusic legends are some of the oldest on Earth. They tell of a time when the surrounding area was still mostly sea and man had nowhere to stroll, until the mammoth Shelik—a mammoth!—chose to help and used his tusks to pull out a large piece of earth from the sea, on which all people settled. Where do you think they got the mammoth—in a museum? Where was I? In Nyechalnoye. A few hundred yards past the apartment blocks, a shaman lived in a yurt. He called himself Markusha. And he was a shaman of the earth. He stank. His eyes were like beads, wolverine skin over his shoulder, and he didn't talk to me. I suspected he considered me an incarnation of Ovechkov. Next to his yurt stood two others, uninhabited, which the hunters and fishermen carried with them on expeditions. They could take them apart, mount them on a reindeer, and disappear within an hour. More's the pity I had to sleep in a block of flats with the wolverines—"

"So they wouldn't let you sleep even in the empty yurts? Maybe the shaman knew you're a liar."

"Like I said, first I thought they had me down for Ovechkov, before I learned better. They'd caught Ovechkov. They followed his trail and found him the next evening, twenty miles on, crashed into a snowdrift and frozen to the bone. They loaded the skins onto their sledge and didn't speak a single word to him. He threatened, pleaded for help, but they left him there, or at least that's what the women claimed. Who knows what happened? I just felt how uncomfortable I made them. When you're the first Muscovite after ten years, you can feel under your boots the little spider webs of their relationships, crunching. You can't avoid them—you can either not be there or disturb. So I didn't force myself into the yurts, and a good idea that was. They value them immensely. The yurt is the center point of the universe. Why are you laughing? Markusha said, 'Wherever I go, there's the center of the world.' The entrance always points south—as they say, facing forward. You step inside, and the fire burns in the center. All events revolve around it—cooking, rituals, sleep. On the northern side is *malu*. That's where Markusha had his amulets, flasks, spirit puppets, and the drum. The roof is shaped like the heavenly dome, and the sun shines through the smoke escape. Its shadow circles the fireplace, clockwise. Their whole cosmology is in the yurt. And you're supposed to stop me when I digress. During daytime, I helped women with housework, and, in return, they cooked for me too. But I tried to spend time around Markusha. At first, I just dawdled around his yurt before I dared to sit inside. We were silent a lot, often for five, six hours. He might throw in a sentence, and then it was quiet again. I watched him brewing potions, making protective spells, or soothsaying from forty-one stones. He was dismissive of me, but he didn't chase me away. I could sit in the yurt whenever I felt like it but only on the southern side, like children. I didn't know what to think of him, so I asked one of the hunters why the shaman behaved this way towards me.

"'Everyone is scared of you but not Markusha,' he said forcibly.

"'Do you want me to leave?' I asked him.

"He was surprised. 'But you haven't done what you're here to do.'

"'And what is that?' I was surprised too.

"He shrugged. I tried a different way.

"'Why do you think something will happen?'

"'You came on the same day as the Man That Lost His Soul.'

"'Do you think I have something to do with the accursed one?'

"Now, he seemed uneasy. 'The spirits say that you'll stay until you bring a disaster onto someone.'

"And there I was, in their legends. What a disgrace! As an anthropologist, I should have packed my bags and hurried through the corridor to civilization. But curiosity won. You know what? The very word *shaman* comes from their language. That was enough for me. I was thirty, I was in Nyechalnoye, I slept half-dead with fear in a block of apartments with ghosts and wolverines, and you couldn't get me out of there with a Kamaz truck. When I sat in the yurt, the accursed one came by sometimes, to whisper desperately to the shaman for half an hour, begging him to lift the curse. He kneeled by the fire, crying and muttering ceaselessly. Markusha just gazed into the flames, until he snapped at him once and asked him, 'Where did you leave Buchuk?' His lips moved noiselessly. He stared at his shoes and shuffled the tips of his toes against the skin on the floor. The shaman repeated, 'Where is Buchuk?' and the man didn't answer. He poured soil into his hair and mouth, burnt his forearm with blazing embers, ripped out clumps of hair and threw them into the fire. In the end, he tore the dirty bandage off his head and burnt it as well. There was a huge black scab in place of his right ear. The shaman neither spoke nor moved after this—he tapped the drum and looked into the flames, as though he couldn't see or hear the wretch.

"Nobody in the village knew what had happened to him. Just before I'd arrived, he was on an expedition up the river with another hunter—Buchuk—in their usual hunting ground. And they didn't return. After three weeks, as the village was getting ready to dance for the dead, this one came back with a fever, his head and arms painted with blood up to the shoulders, the remains of a portioned badger in his boat, and desperate howls instead of answers. That day, I arrived as well. The villagers washed and treated him, but they didn't get a single word on what happened or where Buchuk had disappeared to. He just repeated '*proklyataya krov*,' cursed blood. The Tungusians were scared that the man would bring evil spirits or a bear into the village at night, they were scared of me, and they patiently awaited their fate. The hunter only spoke to the shaman, always imploring him to lift the curse, and withered in front of their eyes. Once, as he was leaving the yurt again, thin as a leaf—he must have lost another ten stones—I sat down by Markusha and stayed there through the day.

"'What do you want, Muscovite?' he asked in the evening when I was really very hungry.

"'The children in the tribe avoid that man by a mile so his shadow might not befall them. Why don't you help him?'

"'And are you perchance shrewder than the children, since you know how to help him?' The shaman grimaced.

"I shook my head. 'Does the great shaman Markusha not know how to lift the curse?'

"'If an evil man curses you with the spell of the cloud, and you're nimble, you can crawl under his lightning. If he hexed you with the poison of the black adder of the underworld, you'd climb up a pillar of smoke above the birches. But blood is no warmer, or cooler, or thinner, or thicker; it is only as man himself is. You can't break a curse of blood without breaking the man too.'

"'Ever?'

"Before answering, he circled the entire yurt with his drum, in the direction of the sun, as always. 'Blood runs through all of a man's souls. When you're breaking a curse of blood, you can damage the souls. You might return this life to him or take away all others. Would you summon the rain if it could rain for all eternity?'

"When he limped to see Markusha for what must have been the twentieth time, with yellowed eyes and skin brown with spots and paper-thin, I saw his skull literally shining through his face. His four front teeth had fallen out, as though he was rotting from the inside. His cheeks were shaking, and he spoke even more quietly. This time, he endured several hours of pleading. In the meantime, Markusha made him a talisman. He tied nine knots on a string at regular intervals and inserted a black feather into each, dipped in the blood of various animals: a marten, a reindeer, a toad, a sturgeon, and others.

"'Wear it around your waist during the day; in the night, stretch it under your back.'

"The hunter departed with gratitude, and Markusha turned to me. 'I can't listen to him anymore. One takes a week, another six months, but everyone whose blood is cursed eventually comes begging for *galai golihai*. May it come soon.'

"'What's *galai golihai*?'

"'The blood of three worlds. This one, the higher one, and the lower one. I already told you, it either returns one life or takes them all.'

"'And if he asks for it, will you give it to him?'

"'I'll ask the spirits what they desire.'

"The accursed one returned in a week with the feathers shredded, the rat and toad ones lost. He leaned forward while he walked, his palm supporting his side. 'Markusha,' he called, 'you gave me a weak spell. What are you afraid of?' Markusha was silent. 'This is unbearable. Boil the poison of three worlds, shaman, and if the spirits wish it, death will free me!'

"The shaman stepped into a slow dance around the fire, beating the drum and singing rhythmically. After a good half hour, he paused in front of me. I'll tell you this, I couldn't stand his gaze! I looked away, and he said, 'The spirits ask whether you're ready.'

"'For what?' I asked him.

"'They say they won't cure him directly since you're here. It is time for you to stop observing. They offer to have me lead you through the ritual. And you can then help him if you want to.'

"I wasn't at all sure it was a good idea. The anthropologist in me warned strictly about getting mixed up with their magic, but—"

"Curiosity won," noted Adam.

"This was the moment I'd been sitting around for those three months. And I couldn't stop thinking about Brezhnev in Moscow, acting as if he had all of Russia in his stomach. While he waged a cold war, I sat in a warm yurt, the only foreigner far and wide, and I let the Tungusian illiterates show me how much I didn't know about Russia, the universe, and myself.

"Markusha handed out the tasks, and we spent all of the following day preparing the ceremony. He took me to the river and asked me to watch. He walked around for a bit, and then, on the chosen spot, he spoke to each of the four sides. He apologized to the place for damaging it, and he warned the insects and smoked the sacred amulet. We collected boulders from the river together, and Markusha sat down with them, sacrificed some tobacco, and explained to them what he needed. He asked each stone whether it was willing to lend our ceremony its healing power, and he exchanged the ones that refused until he had about twenty strong and eager stones. We carried down three kinds of wood for the fire and wove a sweat lodge with willow stems. The hunter who later looked after the fire brought skins and covered the structure. In the evening, the accursed one appeared. He hauled a fox on his back. It was without a trace of blood, just her head rolling like a stone in a bag.

"The ritual began. Markusha cut the fox open from stomach to the throat, and he cut out the *zuld*—the head, throat, lungs, and heart. He hung it up on three stakes in the ground so that the soul, when it wanted to, could fly out from the *zuld* into the higher world. There was barely a drop of blood until he pulled the aorta out with his finger, cut it, and caught the stream in a pot with a thick herbal potion. When the blood stopped running, he took a spoon, gouged the eyes out, washed them in a bowl of water, and handed me one. It was the size of a small egg.

"'Drink it,' he commanded.

"I breathed, bit through the eyeball and sucked the vitreous humor out in one go. My mouth was full of it. With the utmost revulsion, I swallowed. 'Will it help him?'

"Markusha laughed. 'This? Not at all. That was just a delicacy for you.' He slurped up the other eye with gusto and called to the fire guard that the ceremony could begin. The three of us undressed—the accursed one's ribs sticking out like wicker from a broken basket—washed in the river, and sacrificed more tobacco. Then, Markusha crawled into the hut. We followed him and sat in a circle. The fireguard brought in ten red-hot stones on wooden forks and placed them between us. Then, he closed the entrance. I immediately started sweating. Markusha blessed the pot of fox blood and herbs with song and incantations, poured it over the stones, and the hut was veiled with hot fumes with a heavy, acrid scent.

"After a few minutes, I was shouting, 'Heeyah! Heeyah!' like they'd told me to so the vapor would disperse, but it did nothing. Sparks jumped around the scorching stones, we sweated, the accursed one wailed, and a moment later, he drowsily got up and collapsed with a thud. The shaman acted as though he hadn't seen it, calmly took a knife, and cut his own wrist. A trickle flowed into the bowl from his forearm. I was sweating and dizzy but determined to help the wretch. The shaman suddenly took his limp hand and cut it too. The fellow didn't even flinch.

"Markusha let the blood flow into the bowl and circled it slowly just above the stones, singing algyshes with a throaty whisper. When smoke started rising from the bowl, he alternately put it on his left and right cheek. Then, he drank. I barely understood him: 'One trickle from me, that's the blood of the higher world. One trickle from him,' he pointed to the accursed one, 'that's the blood of the lower world that his soul strayed into. One trickle from the fox, which knows this world only. Drink from the sacred *galai golihai*, and the three worlds will open. The one you think of will accept you.'

"'Me?' I asked, barely seeing the shaman through the fumes. I felt alternately heavy and light, hot and cold, and I thought I'd lost color vision. Markusha handed me the bowl of blood. An anthropologist would describe what followed as a ritual, but I experienced an expansion of consciousness with a sledgehammer. I slithered on the floor. Breathing heavily, I took a while to roll over onto my back and see a circle of light above. Joy suddenly coursed through my body and pulled me up towards the light. I left all of the weight on the floor. Colorful, incandescent beads flowed in front of my eyes, trickled inside and descended down my spine, pulsed through my arms and legs, and stretched a huge smile on the face, which wasn't even mine. Then, the rotating spiral of power and colors pulled me up to the heavens. My spirit turned into a bird and flew over a river, drifted over the taiga and carried me above herds of sables, mountains and valleys, until I spotted two tiny people down below. They were in a boat, rowing upstream, and I descended, circled around them, and watched where they were heading. They covered a few miles. At dusk, they stopped under a tall cliff, took the boat out of the water, and set up camp nearby. They didn't see me. After preparing fire, they set out into the forest. I flew from branch to branch. It seemed as though they were looking for dry wood to fell because they only carried an axe and a saw. Scraping through the thicket, they reached the cliffs, and suddenly there were screams, thuds, twigs breaking. I flew higher for a better view, and they turned around and ran under the cliff through the undergrowth. The clamor came closer until an old bear burst out of the bushes, roared terribly, and got on her hind legs, twice their size. The hunters held each other around the shoulders, screaming in terror, their backs against the rock, and the bear ran toward them. In the last moment, one man pushed the other forward with all his strength, against the animal. The bodies collided.

The bear clasped its hands together, bit twice, turned around, and ran into the bushes. The hunter fell to the ground. His stomach was ripped open, he wheezed and moaned, his guts strewn around. The other knelt beside him, crying, and embraced him, to give comfort before death.

"The ripped one got up on his elbow. I'd fluttered almost to the ground when I heard this over the sobbing: 'Samei, Samei, why do you even bother? Why did you let my blood spill on this world? I curse you, you lowly cad, I curse you with all my heart, may your blood run with mine, may it flow down to the underworld and broil there for all eternity,' and he bit his ear as hard as he could. They brawled for a few seconds, and the ripped one tore off the entire ear with his teeth, lobe and cartilage included. He coughed with laughter and pain, the bloody ear between his teeth, his innards shaking like jelly. He didn't stop until the other one returned from the fire with a rifle and shot him between the eyes.

"Markusha too had a vision. When we finally crawled out of the hut, he pushed a black vial into my palm. 'The spirits send you poison against Erlegkhan, the ruler of the lower world. It's *kharakhoi*, a potent poison. It's made from the thickest *galai golihai*, so thick it almost won't flow. *Kharakhoi* brings no visions. You drink it, and it seizes your body and mind, and through it also Erlegkhan, who holds the stolen soul in his arms. It poisons him, and he writhes in convulsions, crushing the soul with his fists. If the soul is strong, it will slip out and return to the body; if it is weak, Erlegkhan's wrath will destroy it. Body and soul are either restored to health together or die forever. The spirits say I should give the *kharakhoi* to you. They give you the gift of choice. You either give the *kharakhoi* to the hunter or keep it. The spirits say that, if you keep it, the hunter will die. If you give it to him, you'll miss it one day.'

"I didn't know then and I don't know now where the delirium ended and the mystical experience began. I saw two options. Seen realistically, the entire story about the curse could be a load of twaddle, and that seemed likely. The hunters were poisoned by who-knows-what on their expedition, the *kharakhoi* wouldn't help the sick man either way, and my vision, and the shaman's, were nothing more than the hallucinations of an overheated brain. In that case, I could keep the *kharakhoi* with a clean conscience. Or else, everything the Tungusians told me was true to the letter. The spirits of Siberia had brought me to Nyechalnoye so I could meet the shaman and his accursed patient, whose soul was held by Erlegkhan in the lower world. And the black vial really did have magical powers. In that case, I had to keep it because the day when I'd need it, as the ghosts of Siberia had let me know, I wouldn't have a shaman at hand.

"All night, it was as though two hemispheres were competing, but really, I was just resisting the fact that I could not find a single reason to give the *kharakhoi* to the poor beggar. After breakfast, I informed the shaman of my verdict. He assembled the entire tribe and relayed the story in detail, my vision and his, and my final decision. The tribe heard him out and, without another word, gave the accursed one some food, like they did with old people before they died. He limped out into the taiga without looking back.

"'And now, you will leave?' The shaman turned to me, and I've never felt more remorse. The guilt that was on the accursed one now lay squarely on me. And it stays with me till this day." Gorgonuy shook the vial. "But that doesn't mean I'd do it differently. I sent him to his death and kept the medicine; that's how it is."

"And that's what your dissertation was about," remarked Adam.

"In my dreams. That experience rattled my bones and completely switched my thinking. Cartridge for cartridge. It shattered my idea of Russia, of Western civilization, of anthropology. Today, when I hear any of those words, one of the icy Siberian spirits breathes down the back of my neck. And I never finished the original dissertation. What should I say to the academics? Trust the myths of the native Siberians because I sent one of them to his death? That's not the way to do anthropology. I wrote my dissertation on some Polynesians I'd never seen in my life. It was successful, and it's still cited today. And I'm an anthropologist in Cambridge … I laugh at myself, Adam. This rooted idea of the detached, and thus rigorous, study of cultures is nothing but a myth—a comfortable myth of the academics who have corks in their asses. We need to live, experiment on ourselves—" He broke off. "But you, you're going way over the top."

"So this is the *kharakhoi*." Adam took the black ampule in his hand. It was unexpectedly heavy.

Gorgonuy nodded. "I'm waiting for the day I'll need it."

"Boiled blood from thirty years ago? You're not planning to drink it, are you?"

"Markusha boiled it down to a thick paste and mixed it one-to-one with honey."

"And? Honey preserves?"

"For some two, three thousand years. The Egyptians used it to embalm mummies."

Adam shook his head. "I wouldn't eat that for a Nobel prize."

"*Kharakhoi* is the last option. And that's not as far off as you think. All this country needs for anarchy is three days without gasoline. Then, the food in the supermarkets runs out, looting starts, and gentlemen transform overnight into a pack of hounds. Equally, every man is only a sleepless week away from being a tortured animal. There's a direct train service from sleeplessness to madness. The funny thing is, the way there takes seven days and the way back seven months, if you're lucky."

"Then I'm halfway there. If Krugele kicks me out of school, I'm done for."

"I'm sorry to scare you rather than comfort you. But I'm no god, nor a woman. You worry me. When I warned you about entering the land of the gods, I had no idea you'd continue to dash from one schoolboy error to another. All these obstacles are so clearly bound to your research. And what do you do? You march on regardless. You buy a hard drive of data with your soul!"

"Then help me. What should I do?"

"Stop working on the Faustomat, stop challenging the gods, and stop asking for the data archive. Beg me on your knees to return your soul to you."

Adam snorted. He shook his head. "Over my dead body."

Gorgonuy shrugged his shoulders. "Then do something, at least: go and weigh yourself. Start weighing yourself every night."

"When will you have the data?"

"You will know."

Adam pointed his finger. "You owe it to me. Don't try to trick me. I'll come after you. And I never, ever give up."

They sat together in silence for a while, both pensive. When the professor finished smoking, he spoke again, as if suddenly remembering. "Nina." His eyes drifted into the dark. "Don't … risk it."

Adam shivered. "This is—and stays—between you and me," he said to the professor.

"Oh, stay as naïve as you wish."

Adam left in darker spirits than he'd come in. Instead of setting off for his college, he cycled toward the train station. There, he crossed the bridge over the tracks and walked into Chefton's Gallery, the best art appraisers in the city.

"I'd like to verify that this is a forgery. " He passed the 1812 oil painting over the counter.

The man in the brown suit nodded obligingly, passing his gaze from the painting to Adam and back a few times until he laughed shortly.

"I see, this is some student prank, is it? Did your friends paint this for your graduation? Not that you look particularly well, per se, but I wouldn't have you down for two hundred years," he laughed.

Adam shrugged, and the expert narrowed his eyes. "So, really?"

Adam nodded. The man brought a large, square magnifying glass from the back room and carefully examined the painting and frame through it.

"The frame. That's a fifty, sixty-year-old imitation of late baroque. Anyone can see that. But the painting, sir, I won't tell you that before I examine it. Give me a week and two hundred pounds. If the painting is real and you auction it through us, this payment will count toward the commission."

Back in the college room, Adam had nothing other than time to wait. The undecided questions hovered above him like enormous statues in the dark. He stood below them, exhausted, not knowing what to count on and what to fear. He gazed up, to scale the contours of his uncertainties. But there was nothing but darkness. The void of a thousand black birds mutely flapping their wings, flying inches away from each other. The darkness of doubt. It began a touch under the skin, right around the corner, ten seconds away. He knew that one of the black birds nested in Nina—the bird of vain efforts—and one in him, the raven of ambiguity. He felt its beak by his heart, the weight of its wings in his shoulders, feathers in his mouth and claws sunk into his guts. He stepped on the bathroom scale, the bird in him. He wrote "92" on his forearm with a marker pen, closing his eyes. And he saw that something approached through the darkness, something that was going to hurt.

Gallery

into th

of Leaps

e Sun

Better to dream a foolish hope,
nothing but darkness ahead,
than discover the truth,
knowing its horror instead.
—K. J. Erben

Though

it might seem surprising at first, art precedes science by decades, even centuries. Architects built the Renaissance long before Kepler and Galileo calculated it. Then, the baroque appeared when society was still enraptured by the success of science. It undermined the predominant rationalism with music, movement, and contrast, with such a variety of shape and expression that it overwhelmed the senses. It was Bach and Caravaggio that Hume then hurled into an empirical attack against rationalism. And similarly, impressionism started exploring the private universe some thirty years before Einstein's theory of relativity. In their own ways, artists express what the time feels, what it lacks—but what its words won't yet carry. That's why it's artists who tend to have the delight of shocking the unprepared society.

Snuggle up, Ninny. Close your eyes.

Those Viennese who visited the exhibition in the Citizen's Hospital in October truly had their breath taken away. And that's despite the fact that the Viennese audience was accustomed to art. A number of metal and alabaster busts were spread across the entrance hall. Contrary to the customs of the time, they didn't portray the Empress Maria Theresa, well-known aristocrats, army generals, or Greek figures. There was no trace of the idealized, concealed strokes of classicism nor of the lavish pathos of the Baroque. Many of the heads lacked not only the usual wig but any hair whatsoever. Their faces stretched towards the visitors and bluntly provoked with very human acts. They stuck out tongues, stared, and guffawed. There were jaws clenched in pain. One stared into the skies half-witted, and two had something close to a bird's beak for a mouth. The face of the most deformed bust was gripped by such tension that its eyes, mouth, and nose had bent towards each other.

Each head captured the chosen grimace so faithfully that some immediately mimicked them with laughter; others raised their eyebrows with offense. The monarchy had not yet seen such an exhibition: so self-centered, so vulgarly human, so surreal. The visitors found themselves in a panopticon of warped reflections—but reflections of what?

The author? Themselves? Humanity? The debate about the artwork's hidden meaning resounded through the marble hall.

The connoisseurs recognized the author in some of the faces, the eccentric and extraordinarily talented Franz Xavier Messerschmidt, and brought up his well-known rise and fall. When he was merely twenty-eight, the Empress had personally entrusted him with sculpting her own statue. It would be the only large sculpture she allowed to be crafted in her lifetime. Then, the old rector of the Academy had died. Messerschmidt had applied, confident in his singular abilities and the favor of the court. But his Academy colleagues had categorically opposed. Despite all of his fame, he could never lose his roots as a common woodcarver with undignified jokes and brazen disrespect for the aristocracy. And some suggested that there was something more behind his eccentricities, significantly tapping their foreheads. Supposedly, he'd even tried to kill a man in a fit of rage. Maria Theresa had heard out the complaints. Instead of a promotion, she'd offered him a modest life annuity. The resentful sculptor had left Vienna and moved to the outskirts of Pressburg. After a few years, few remembered him. On the day of the opening of his great exhibition in the Citizen's Hospital, the visitors probably didn't even know that the bilious eccentric had actually died ten years ago. What could they expect from him? To many, the grimacing busts were an obvious revenge. They venomously caricatured the exhibition's visitors—no, all of Austrian society!

A chubby professor from the Viennese university, glass in hand, disagreed. If Messerschmidt had wanted to caricature society, it would have been obvious at first sight. He knew how to be so pointedly acidic, the professor explained, that everyone would recognize themselves in the caricatures right away. There is no doubt, he explained lengthily to his fashionably dressed companions, that the faces portrayed the ancient conception of human emotion, with which Messerschmidt got acquainted during his studies in Rome. "Here," he pointed his walking stick successively at a few heads, "wrath is the opposite of calm, fear is the opposite of confidence. We shall find offence and its opposite. Compassion, too, and so on, indeed. I see here all seven pairs of emotions, as classified by Aristotle. You have all heard, certainly, that Messerschmidt, that poor devil, fell so desperately in love with his brother's wife that he refused to speak to all women for the rest of his life? Now, love would amount to nothing without hatred. I am deeply convinced that you will find these busts here in corresponding pairs."

"There are supposed to be forty-nine heads," a woman acrimoniously objected. "Even though I refuse to count them, professor, you must agree there are more than fourteen?"

"Yes, yes," nodded the professor. "I have heard that Messerschmidt had planned sixty-four heads. But our Lord, as we can see, did not want that. Now, do not forget that, apart from Aristotle's system, the maestro surely took into account Seneca's stoic tradition with only four basic emotions, again ordered into opposing pairs: two good ones and two bad ones, two present and two future. You can name each of your actual emotions a nuance, or a re-combination of these, excuse me, primitive emotions. It might interest you, ladies, that it was precisely Seneca's adaptation, elegantly doubly antithetical, that led St. Augustine to show which movements of the soul were caused by corrupt human nature and which, as we would say now, by *natura naturans*. That is, by a gift from—"

"And what does this … statue … mean, in your enlightened opinion?" interjected the woman, nodding towards a face that had the long beak of a bird in place of lips, its eyes firmly shut. "I imagine that I'm a bird?" The group laughed, and the professor pushed his pince-nez closer to his eye. "You cannot blame me, Professor, if I have grown distant from Messerschmidt. His earlier sculptures were so natural, so—" she rubbed her fingers, "so *empathique*, but this curiosity is intolerable. Why should we look at these bald heads? He only sees vulgarity since he moved out of the city." Her words were accompanied by muffled laughter, with which the company departed to the salon.

Each explanation was defied by some of the heads. The discussion even spilled over into the press. Some contemporary enthusiast gave his own imaginative names to each head, sometimes simply and accurately: *Choking, Morose, Yawning*. But names like *Scrawny Old Man with Painful Eyes*, *Saved Drowning Man*, and *Suffering from Constipation* remained unsatisfactory. Nonetheless, his article became a semi-official prospectus as the exhibition travelled to other cities. These names are used to this day as no explanation of the work was found in Messerschmidt's journals. Thus, a legendary secret remains in the void between the statues. Why did the most gifted sculptor of his generation spend the last fifteen years of his life on fifty anonymous faces?

1

She had told him she would prepare dinner that evening, and it was time to start cooking. Then, Adam called her to say he'd be working into the night and she shouldn't wait for him. That was an impossible challenge. She waited for him while she cooked, while she ate, and while she arranged his food into a bento box, and she waited after dinner, too. Nina's love was no saint—quite the opposite; it was a wildcat, provoked by Adam's distance. It would cuddle up to him with a hot tongue and fast breath—the signs of fever. Hungry, tired, addicted. It wanted to bite. It howled at the moon when he didn't notice her. That was her love, and Nina pampered it as a stray cat because she preferred pain to loneliness. Still, she was surprised she'd decided against Japan. Without regret for the decision, she also didn't consider it particularly her own. Rather, she wondered at herself, in love like never before.

And she did understand him. She knew the story of Stéphane Mallarmé. He died after working on the last, perfect book of mankind for a whopping twenty years. It was to contain the meaning of all previous books, and he hadn't even finished the first chapter. Not even a page. Well, really, not even a letter. Nothing.

‿

After Mallarmé's death in 1898, all of his assets were burned at the author's own request, including the notes for the Livre. For fifty years, the work was considered irretrievably lost. Only after the Second World War was one of the many original diaries found to have survived the burning and published. This discovered diary and the essays from *Divagations* are the only leads as to what Mallarmé was going through during his twenty years of working on the Livre.

He planned the work's form down to the most minute detail. A friend of Nina's father, Jacques Polieri, was an expert on this empty book. He liked to explain meticulously during their dinner conversations how every printing of the book was to have five volumes. Each volume of each book consisted of three sections, eight pages each. Together, therefore, twenty-four pages per volume. It was possible to interchange the volumes. The pages in the volumes were not bound, and so it was possible to swap them too, between volumes and between copies. Further, each page contained eighteen lines of twelve words each, and it was physically divisible down to individual words. Hence the words, lines, pages, sections, volumes, and copies could compose new variations.

That's not all. One could read the words on a page back to front, diagonally, or selectively according to any arbitrary key. Because the five volumes formed a block, one might also read in depth, by choosing one word per page. The book was designed to be read at séances, where each reading depended on the number of attendees and various circumstances. The book itself did not determine or even suggest the vector guiding the particular reading, so the attendees themselves chose but one of the manifestations, forever incomplete.

"That's no book," little Nina would say, and Uncle Jacques chuckled.

"Bright girl. But it's perfect, too. Like your mother's ratatouille."

"Mum doesn't cook ratatouille, Uncle Jacques."

"Yes. Can you smell how tasty it would be if she did?"

The form is deeply, perfectly relativistic. Every reading is as good as any other. One cannot choose between them; one cannot judge. No wonder Mallarmé despaired during those twenty years of writing. Well, writing ... Uncle Jacques would pull out the original of Mallarmé's letter to Henri Cazalis and point to the middle of the scribbles, "The mere act of writing causes hysteria in my head."

"What's historia?" frowned Nina as the company laughed.

(Meanwhile, the adult Nina understood: who wouldn't grapple with hysteria if they spent twenty years in writer's block where a hundred possible books beat themselves up in their head? Nina's life came to resemble Mallarmé's perfectly. Where certainty allows one to enjoy a single life, uncertainty pushes her into living a hundred existences. It exhausts to tears, to hysteria.)

That much is known of the form. According to Uncle Jacques, Mallarmé did not leave one line of the book's content. Could he really believe that he would write the last book, which would contain the whole meaning of all previous books? Could he have been serious about something so audacious? The twenty years of life he dedicated to the Livre must serve as proof. There is not a hint of sarcasm in his notes. But try as he might, he simply could not start writing. If he were a relativist—or, as Nietzsche's contemporary, a nihilist—he would have filled the book with ease. The variable form would provide adequate liveliness to any content. What was he searching for, all those twenty years, instead? It must have been a counterweight to the perfectly relative form. He was looking for an order that would manifest through each reading like the sun shining through iron bars. Year after year, he made notes and planned the work out, locked in an epic clinch with the idea of the absolute.

These epic life battles—Gaudí's, Mallarmé's, Wagner's—weave the longest and bloodiest war of ideas in history. At the end of the nineteenth century, the home front of the absolute was defended by theologians, conservatives, and social idealists. Against them, the liberals, the nihilists, and the avant-garde hurled their theses over the ramparts about God being dead and ideals with him. The absolute work of art enthused all. The Gaudís, building a bridge on whose tallest arch they were to meet the Creator. The Wagners, looking to fill God's empty throne. One camp waged war for God, another for the monarchy, another for truth, meaning, ideals—and they lay into each other like there was no tomorrow. Who won?

Well, did Wagner compose the perfect drama? No.

Did Messerschmidt capture all human emotions? No.

Did Gaudí build Christianity's last shrine? No.

Did Mallarmé write humanity's last book? No.

They failed, one after the other. And their failures, grand and beautiful, gave Nina hope for Adam's project. She didn't doubt for a second that Adam, like the others, saw perfectly well the absurdity of his endeavor. And he still gave it everything because Faustomat was an absolute work. A self-destructive potion, in which the desire to dedicate one's life to a single, perfect end, the desire for orgasm, for transcendence, the ancient yearning to resolve a paradox, to quiet the mind, the longing for a goal, a point, a fixed place in the universe, all mix with the wish to end oneself in a kind of deepest inhalation. In essence, none other than the rebellion of a man constricted by boundaries. A wholehearted attempt to tear oneself out of the human condition and free oneself from freedom. A leap above the abyss of futility that, however it turns out, whether it flays skin or breaks limbs, will remain the most graceful and noble rising of the mind. An inhuman act, and in that, paradoxically, the most human of acts.

A leap into the Sun: the decision to fail beautifully and magnificently.

❦

She leafed through fashion and art magazines with glossy pages smelling seductively of France. When she showed her last works to her lecturer, he was enraptured. "This is the best I've seen from you so far, Nina, so sensitive, barely hinted ..." His hands were actually shaking. "You're growing out of rebellion. I didn't think I'd live to see this."

She laughed, but he saw the love she was still hiding. Then, every evening, she waited for Adam to admit that he was no longer firm on his feet. But he wasn't coming even an inch closer. As though she was missing some single ingredient. Nothing to do with the Faustomat, fractals, or how to project Twitter against constellations—she knew much more about those than was necessary. She felt she needed to learn about him in the depth between words and gestures.

It was nine o'clock, and Adam wasn't calling. She set the bento she'd prepared for him on the table. For a moment, she lay down on his bed with the magazines. They bored her ... they lacked fractals, hand-written formulas and scraps of C++. She got up again, feeling like drawing. She reached the desk, where Adam kept his large black notebooks. She took one in her hand, the thickest one, and it opened itself to where, like a leaf in a herbarium, a pair of black panties with a pink bow had been placed between the pages. She slowly traced them over her skin, as though poisoning herself with a veil doused in chloroform, and her nose inhaled deeply the acetic scent of another woman.

So he wasn't taciturn and distant because of his great work but for an entirely different reason, and she was just a naïve girl. The only one failing magnificently. Throbs of pain pierced her stomach. She instinctively tried to vomit, but all that came out were sobs, coughs, and a thin whimper. Her eyes were watery and bulging out as she was trying to exit the situation through any means: forgetting, hiding, removing her body, having a stroke, blinking. All dimensions of her tried to be someone else, and the convulsions of that effort twisted her body onto the floor. Then, the pain became infused and slowly overshadowed by shame. The gravity of that emotion was so much worse, for pain can be fought with; shame is the debilitating one. Shame is the last stop on the red line. She felt like crawling under the bed and piercing her own eyes so she couldn't see herself. She was beginning to feel as if in a cradle of sorts—a cradle of pain and shame, rocking herself as a castaway, crying baby. For she *was* cast away.

By the motherfucking man.

In an exemplary demonstration of the species, one half of humankind just screwed over the other half.

She breathed in deeply, and more, finally feeling some ground in her anger. Screaming helped her get on her knees and stand up. She put the notebooks back in the drawer, straightened the panties between the pages, took the bento, and returned it to the table. She wiped her eyes, collected her design magazines, and left.

Immo

rtality

A new scientific truth does not triumph by convincing its opponents
and making them see the light but rather because its opponents eventually
die out and a new generation grows up that is familiar with it.
—Max Planck

"**Oh,**" was all Adam could say when he heard that his Grandma had died. It was a breathing sound more than a word. He felt stones in his lungs. Touching his throat, he looked toward the sun. Mum only started crying at that point.

"So ... God is dead," he tried to make conversation.

It took a while for her voice to come back. "If I died, would you be relieved too?"

He was taken aback. "Why are you saying that?"

There was only sobbing.

"I am sorry, Mum," he said, crouching inside under an unbearable tension. He had no idea how to prevent these misunderstandings. So as usual, he turned to facts. "She was eighty and sick. Didn't we know this would happen?"

"But my mother died today!"

"Well ... let's talk about that. Do you believe in an afterlife?" He didn't remember his mother ever saying a single word about death, sex, or God except for "I don't know." These were the three taboos of their family, handed down from generation to generation. Three clueless places. There was no advice from the elders on these topics. They weren't even forbidden, merely ignored. The disobedient child that dared to explore them would do so alone, at their own risk.

"This really isn't a good time for a conversation like this, Adam."

"Okay." He unwittingly raised his voice. "I'll tell you what you want to hear: my sincere condolences. Have you called me because you just want to hear that empty phrase? Or do you want to talk about death?"

"My God! It's as if you aren't even human!"

"I'm probably just not hysterical enough for this family. When and where is the funeral?" he asked to finish the conversation.

"Can I have at least one day before I start running around, sorting out another problem?"

"Of course. And don't be angry at me; you have no reason to."

Aren't even human, he repeated to himself. If only. If only he really weren't human and knew nothing at all about death. But when he worked until three in the morning, death made him coffee. When he examined his naked body and photographed his birthmarks, it held his shirt. When he cheated with a nameless woman, it was death's bony ass that he held in his hands. Unlike his mother, he wasn't chasing death out of his life, because he respected it deeply. If it weren't for death, life would have died out long ago. And that's why now, when Grandma died, Adam also saw the blessing.

If immortality had developed in primates millions of years ago, like it developed in the *Turritopsis dohrnii* jellyfish, the eternal monkeys would converge into a stable hierarchy with a single alpha male. He would castrate one rival after the other like a hairy Herod, until finally, he would castrate himself so that his own sons could not dethrone him. With that, he mused, the monkey ruler would complete his first and only task: to remain the ruler. That immensely long line of revolutions, culminating with the one we call Homo sapiens, would calcify before the Australopithecus.

Adam watched the paradox in Cambridge. Professor Krugele, even if he racked his brains for a hundred years, would never construe Faustomat. For that, Adam needed to be born, grow up in a different age from Krugele, collect life experiences forty years fresher, and arrange them into a more current paradigm. Krugele's brain would not reach Adam's paradigm, neither through time nor enlightenment. Ever. His soft grey matter had long ago turned to stone. It was too lazy to go once more through the immensely exhausting process of rearranging one's entire experience into a personal worldview. Krugele did it thirty years ago; he fought for his place in Cambridge, acquired a reputation, and now, he just needed to retain this successful life. He couldn't have found a better fortress for that. Layers of decorum protected the conquered titles and ceremonial privileges of those who ruled in Cambridge. They wore exclusive gowns and drank port in closed circles. Their dinner was served first, at a higher table, above the young ones, the ones born later. At mass, they knelt near the dean. And, unlike everyone else, they didn't have to dismount their bicycles in the college gardens. Their plump bodies furiously defended the social customs, to which they clung not from some noble principle but because it was through this system in particular that they had climbed to the top. In this one system, they were the strong ones.

An old academic will protect an academic system based on publishing papers because he has published the most. An old politician will defend a parliamentary system because he is in the parliament. An old banker will defend the financial system because he owns it. The best interest of those who rule is to backpedal. That's why Adam loved death: patiently and without honors, it weeded out old dictators, old ideas, and old gods. Death, dear Mum, is birth.

"Is there anything you want to tell me?" asked Nina on the phone that night. He was just eating the bento she'd left on his table. It was cold but from her.

"You read me so well," said Adam, and his voice cuddled up to her through the distance. "Grandma died."

And he listened to how humans react to this information. She pitied him gently.

He didn't know that Nina lacked the heart to ask about the black panties with the pink bow. During the evening, she decided there would be no time for a conversation about infidelity before the funeral, if at all. She didn't need his assurances, or the embarrassing admissions, the apologies, the pleading for her to stay, the insistence on how much he loved her, the promises of improvement—that old male ritual of the return from the hunt, body stained with blood, kneeling in front of the goddess, declaring the perfect love the hunter had rediscovered in the wild. She hated playing goddess. She had to decide what to do next, and the question was hers alone.

The family was dealing with the funeral. The bereaved agreed that it would take place in Ireland, in the graveyard behind the little church where Adam once explained his concept of truth to the parishioners. It didn't make any sense.

"Our entire family lives in England," he explained to his mother, agitated. Now that Grandma was dead, the funeral was nothing but a ritual. His utilization would drop again—while he was still desperately trying to make up for the trip to Prague. The irony was unmissable: while he singlehandedly worked on debunking the rites and rules of the old world, it was providing him with a string of distractions. It was defending itself after all, as Gorgonuy had warned. And wicked ways of defense it used: first art, then love, now a dead lady.

"Grandma would want to be buried where she was born. Surely that's obvious."

"Why?"

"Because people should die at home."

"It's too late for that. It wouldn't help her to lie on a Caribbean beach, now," he uttered, his eyes closed. "Let's just do the funeral here in Cambridge."

"I really don't think you're human," remarked his mother, and once again, it hurt.

"Please, once and for all, don't use ad hominem arguments. Or rather, ad non-hominem," he sighed. "Do you know how much it costs to fly a coffin with Ryanair? You'll have to take a reverse mortgage to pay for it, and I bet they'll shove her in the aisle. Why don't you cremate her in England, do the funeral here, and then take the urn to Ireland? We'll save a fortune."

"When I die, you can have me burnt and dump the ashes in a park. Make it a carpark, if you want. But I won't ever do it to my mother."

The family wouldn't budge. And he decided he wouldn't go.

"As opposed to all who will bring flowers to the funeral, I brought her a bouquet in time," he told Nina. "Why would I go?"

"And what about the plastic bag?" she asked. "You know your Grandma wanted you to put it in her grave. What's she got in there? Did you look inside?"

"No. I don't give a toss whether she thought that she'll need a gold coin or a head torch. This bag," he rattled it, "is the old generation's mistake."

"But you promised."

Adam sighed, moaned, and threw his hands in the air. "Okay. Will you go with me? I don't want to get into any arguments there."

She shook her head. "No." There was no way she was going to hurt herself like that. "At least you'll have time to think," she said solemnly.

"Think about what?"

"Us."

"Why should I think about us?" he asked, confused.

She gave him a long look. "My point exactly."

He had no idea what was happening except that, suddenly, all the women in his life had seemed to turn their backs on him. His eyes grew heavy with wooden tears that wouldn't flow.

He bought a ticket for Friday afternoon to avoid his family. When he was leaving for the airport, he stopped at Chefton's Gallery. The appraiser smiled at Adam as soon as he walked in.

"Sir, I have good news." He brought the painting from the back room and unwrapped the protective film. "We had a few fibers from the canvas and a graft of the varnish tested in the Fitzwilliam laboratories. This doppelganger of yours is a good two hundred years old. I can't tell if it's 1812 or 1805, but without a doubt, we're in the early nineteenth century here."

"Could you be wrong?"

The man smiled. "Sir. The Fitzwilliam Museum works for the most renowned auction houses in London. If you searched all of England for experts, you'd choose them again. Authenticity is not a question in this case. But the likeness really is unbelievable. Would you like to sell the painting through our gallery? I think you could get two, maybe two and a half thousand pounds for it. Our commission—"

"No, thank you."

On the plane, he put a sleep mask on and took in the fact that a laboratory had just declared him immortal. The flight took barely an hour, but he managed to ponder an infinity of questions. Had he been alive two hundred years ago? How did he die? Was chance pushing back against its challenger? He contemplated an immune system of chance, which would twist the world around whenever it edged toward a resolution. Is Nina safe?

"Don't risk it," the damn Gorgonuy had said. But how the hell do you *not risk it*?

He got out onto the tiny airport's single runway. He waited for a taxi among the elite of Galway, returning from the workweek in London. He needed to switch off. It was six in the evening. He rubbed his eyes.

The driver stopped on the hill, by the church. Adam set off along the gravel path towards the gate. The sun was setting above the city in tufts of clouds, and a breeze rose from the pastures on the other side of the hill. He lit a cigarette. He thought he could hear irregular bangs from the other side of the church as he leaned onto the wooden gate. It was locked. He walked between the headstones on the trimmed grass, around the back of the building.

In the far corner of the cemetery, the gravedigger was getting ready to work. Adam offered him a cigarette. They talked for a while, and, during the conversation, Adam weighed the pickaxe in his hand. He swung it above his head. He wished to scoop up the church wall with an upswing, then plunder the graveyard tomb by tomb and descend on the city to wreak biblical terror.

"What's that, young man, you want to dig?"

"Ha. No thanks."

"Well, if it's really your grannie's grave like you say, don't you feel like digging it yourself?"

This idea made sense in at least three ways at once. Here, he could still do something for Grandma—something other than tears, condolences, and a bunch of flowers with a "We'll never forget" ribbon. Perhaps this was the act he'd been subconsciously searching for. "Hoho, you'd let me do that?"

The gravedigger wiped his nose. "For a bottle of whiskey?"

"What? I'll be doing your work for you!"

"You won't give her another gift, boy. This grave is the last thing she needs. No doubt 'bout that." The gravedigger blew smoke out and raised his thick eyebrows. "A bottle of whiskey."

"I'll get you two pints of Guinness down at the pub, and then I'll come back at night to dig the grave. Take it or leave it."

"I drink Guinness with a little shot of Tia Maria." They shook hands on it. "But there better be a hole when I come here in the morning. It has to be eight feet deep. That's this high," he pointed, "above your head."

Adam returned to the graveyard before midnight. It was quiet, and the moon was shining. He borrowed an oil lamp from the morgue, hung it on the nearest cross, and started beating the ground with his pickaxe, quickly and ferociously, so that he'd forget that he wasn't mourning Grandma's death. He cried falteringly that he could not grieve and grieved that he could not cry. His way was carving wooden tears out of beech logs and rolling them down the cheeks.

Down in the village, the last window went dark. Adam had long since sobered up in the chilling air. Between strikes, he listened. Startled nightmares flew out from the subconscious into the flickering lights of the lamps. His back was sweating. He peered over the tombstones, even though he didn't believe in any of the things that scared him. When he had dug out the first foot, he lit a cigarette, wiped the sweat off his face, and tore his shirt off. His nipples were puckered. The next two feet took an hour.

"Fucking hell." He wiped his forehead and took off the rest of his clothes. He kept digging as he was, strike after strike closer to a bare human. Occasionally, a bat would fly through the air. He switched between the pickaxe and shovel and breathed deep and sharp. His body was tired, and his head would not wither. Death seemed so much more logical than immortality. But it was too late. He had known immortality; he couldn't unknow it. The bliss of ignorance was gone.

It was an old tune …

Once he had understood that love was but a chemical cocktail of endorphins, how could he love Nina as madly as he would have loved when he was sixteen?

If Faustomat were to discover the order ruling the world, how could one sustain the illusion of free will?

With every great discovery, something joyful departs. Because with every discovery, he moved further away from obviousness and, with it, from people. Now, even his own mother excluded him from humankind.

But whenever it came down to a choice between the warm herd and cold logic, Adam didn't hesitate for a second. He trod resolutely wherever reason took him, even though it didn't please him at all that it happened to be further and further away from his family and from Nina. Homo Adam simply wasn't a happiness machine but a truth machine. And so he could hardly expect to end up happy by chance. The horror of this realization, which came with the certainty of a simple and indisputable calculation, shrank his stomach.

He put the shovel away and sat down, terribly lonely. The grave was neck-deep. He jumped into the hole as he was. He didn't go to sleep; it was almost daybreak. Instead, he stretched out onto his back and gazed at the rectangle of the sky above him. The stars disappeared, and catharsis failed to come. He'd dug his own grave, the immortal non-human, abandoned by people and by Mother. If he knew how, he would cry. He'd howl with the dogs for knowing how chemical love comes to be, knowing the vacuum in the heart, wooden tears and human progress. They all come to be through the examination of nice and obvious things. Through thought, at whose end solitude lies. All that remained was to turn himself off. After all, he had come logically all the way: to the end of knowledge.

It was probably for the best that this immortal and omniscient Adam's kidneys started getting rather cold in the grave, so he climbed out and dressed. And also that he didn't quite know all of the details, like what Nina was doing in the meantime, and with whom, and that he had about twenty-four hours before he'd lose it completely.

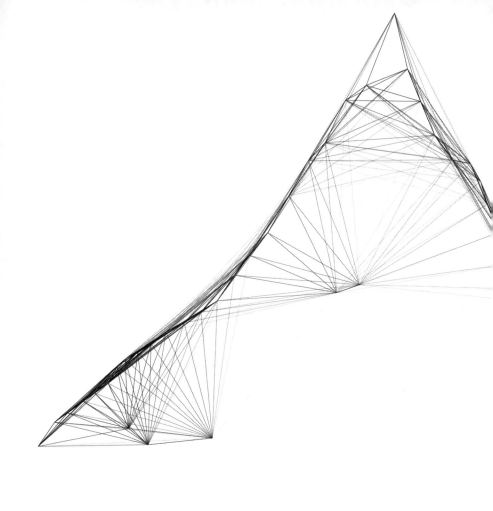

Omniscience

Have the gates of death been shown to you?

Have you seen the gates of the shadow of death?

Have you comprehended the vast expanses of the earth?

Tell me, if you know all this. What is the way to the abode of light?

And where does darkness reside? Can you take them to their places?

Do you know the paths to their dwellings?

—Book of Job 38: 17-20

I remember that night well. To people like Adam, the urge to think is as powerful as sex. And equally enslaving. That's because there is a command in every question, and the young man could not disobey it, no matter the struggle. And notice that it was him asking the questions. No one else to blame. He was a slave without a master.

Of the writers describing this self-propelling urge of the mind, I have a weak spot for Darvishi, who alternated in his life between being a writer and a welder, as his writing was first popular and soon thereafter banned. Here is my own translation that I will probably never publish.

Darvishi, Ezra: Verse in the Multiverse, 1958. "Antithesis" is one of the comfortable simplifications that only work in the imagination, like night and day. What a gross simplification: sunlight intensifies and dims gradually. Only that corner of grey matter, which has taken it upon itself to closely observe the temporal dimension of all actions, perceives day and night as distinct opposites, thanks to its particular signal sensitivity. An egregious simplification—yet irresistible. Let's talk about a creature of opinion and a creature of paradoxes.

The creature of opinion reads, listens, and devours novelties. Whatever he finds, he studies from all sides. What does it relate to, what is it similar to? He patiently composes knowledge into opinions. Opinions are second nature to him—really, he is them. He does not hesitate to judge abruptly. He is proud of the great continuous blocks of knowledge that he has stuck together and smoothed over: entire universal theories, monolithic like the mass of a continent that binds horizon to horizon. His world map is a map of continents.

On the continents' borders, where tectonic plates collide, lava and waves crumple the shores. The creature of opinion constantly supresses this marginal turmoil. He protects his continent, he fights for his country, not only because he's trying to retain and expand its territory, but also because a conflict means he hasn't reached his goal yet. On the way to singular and absolute truth, he occasionally dissolves these edge paradoxes into deeper understanding. With that, his opinions change, and when someone alerts him to the change, he feels ashamed of his past, imperfect thoughts. Years go by; the conflicts accumulate.

Perhaps, he begins to wonder, every thesis is spied upon by an antithesis. And with that thought, the map of continents inverts into a map of tectonic faults spewing volcanoes and geysers. They are far more interesting than the seamless surfaces of the plains ever were! The creature finds that he has somehow lost the ability to formulate his own opinion. On the other hand, he effortlessly changes points of view. It comes to light that he was connected with friends only through shared opinions. He dumps his friends and changes his name.

The creature of paradoxes trusts nothing and no one apart from the ever-present contradictions. His mind is a grouping of characters—a constellation. But it isn't characters that interest him (or rather, that he identifies with), but their quarrels. He gobbles up the life gushing from their mutually-inflicted wounds. Sometimes he even manages to start a fight: he briskly takes one of the positions, likely the one more difficult to defend, and with a dispassionate eye observes the fight with empathy for both foes locked in the combat, he being one of them. He has no traits, but his closet is full of costumes. When he is caught changing positions, he giggles. Someone finally noticed his humorous act of pretended opinion, just as funny as feigning that he can walk on two legs, playacting matrimony to his partner (say, a four-year game, including the wedding and a first-born), or (that silliest game) that time and money are convertible. In a moment of extraordinary honesty, he nostalgically throws in an old maxim: I don't mind changing opinions, because I'm always right—and he and his conversants laugh madly.

Whenever he finds a permanent contradiction, he accepts its sanctity and lets the smokily bitter taste of the dessert spread on his tongue, aware that he has reached one of the ends of thought—the raw, irreducible energy of discord. The paradoxical creature relishes all that is condemned, feared, and cursed; he has gin and tonic for dinner. He's a conservative anarchist. A rational mystic. He has the morality of tricksters and novels. He is an advocate for the searchers, the curious, and the lost, but always to all at once, just as he is also their prosecutor. Yes, the defence and prosecution, rarely the judge. His epitaph: *He saw a skull behind your face.*

Is he an inconsequent logician, an unreliable narrator, and a dangerous demagogue? Unquestionably! And he isn't, naturally, because to emerge from the chrysalis of opinion into the butterfly of paradox requires precise thought.

Maybe, the creature starts to think at three in the morning, maybe it is tension, contradiction, and conflict that will stand strong when everything has been said. Maybe the great paradoxes are terminal, inconsolable. They might perhaps stem from an omniscient being, neither good nor evil, for which heads and tails are one and the same side of a coin.

What would such a mischievous know-it-all do first? He would create a universe in his image and *hide*. He would make the universe infinite and plant a tiny folk in the corner. He'd give them ten rules that are impossible to follow. He'd bear a son through immaculate conception. And then he'd start whipping out miracles like there's no tomorrow. Dividing the sea, promenading on a lake, changing water into wine. He'd promise eternal life for the dead and mock the living with a resurrection. Screw you, tiny folk! What a world that would be, the paradoxical creature sighs longingly. True paradise on Earth.

Or, he wonders, is it actually somewhat bizarre that the entire Universe smells of paradox? Perhaps, if he had enough time, the paradoxical creature might break through and see that what contradicted now complements, what despised now loves, and what used to be paradoxical was simply a refraction in the eye of the beholder—that is, an opinion. And he can't help but smile contentedly at the ambiguity of the thought.

Darvishi just doesn't seem convinced that it's possible to reach the end, does he? Adam would not like to hear that. Concerning the ultimate destination, Gwendolyn McMurphy sheds a little more light.

McMurphy, Gwendolyn: Slave Without a Master. Toito Publishing, 2028. Chapter 9. [...] for those who tempt omniscience, true omniscience, have much to learn. In the trials that await them, the apprentices must recognize every wave in the ocean. They must name every grain of sand on every beach: its shape, composition, weight, and detailed history. They must know the second half of π.

The disciples of omniscience are also well read. They can recite by heart a library of all the books that were ever written. There are higher rungs in that library, containing the books that were not written, each in a number of editions: one copy for each pencil, pen, quill, typewriter, and computer that ever existed. Two copies handwritten by everyone who ever lived, one written with the right hand and one with the left.

They know universes that are not formed of particles and waves. Universes with doughnuts in place of stars and universes carved out of wood. And what's more: the near-omniscient scholars have to know what it's like not to know. Because if God created man, then it was only to break free from the boredom of omniscience—and with that, He truly made things difficult for Himself. To maintain omniscience, He now has to know how to be spontaneous and how to forget. He has to know how to be wrong at every step and not see a second ahead in time.

So the disciples will have to learn that too. Only then it may be possible to assess, using a few questions more difficult than the ones God thought up in the book of Job, whether they ate the living heart of paradox for breakfast:

Do they know what it's like not to be?

Do they know the answer to all the unanswered questions?

Do they know what's impossible to know?

Then, finally, they may open the Book of Ouroboros: the book with all the knowledge of the omniscient being. They know the book by now, surely, know it by heart. The book therefore also contains its own text, as remembered by the omniscient beings, which ... and so on. It's the book Giordano Bruno was flipping through when he suddenly flung his head back in his armchair, closed his eyes, and mumbled to himself, "The stars know no end."

Ah, omniscience. Where were we?

Mall

in T

armé

okyo

When you start with a portrait and search for a pure form,
through successive eliminations, you arrive inevitably at an egg.
—Pablo Picasso

She was a liberal artist with French roots, so perhaps she should've given her boyfriend's infidelity no more than a sigh over espresso. When Adam left for his grandmother's wedding, she packed a black army bag in lieu of a purse. She threw in her toothbrush, black make-up, a sketchbook, and some brushes. Then, she put on a short checkered skirt, Doc Martens, and black tights. She was beginning to understand that leaps into the sun are a singles sport. Adding a black leather jacket full of safety pins, she hid her eyes behind her sunglasses of the season and got on the train to London. She'd known she might meet someone from school, but the one sitting down opposite from her at the last moment surprised her. Removing her earplugs, she smiled.

"Good afternoon, Doctor Gorgonuy. Are you heading to London?"

"What a pleasant surprise, Nina. I'm going to a reception at the Japanese embassy this evening. You're going out?"

"How does one get an invitation to the Japanese embassy?"

"I've known someone there for ages. We met thirty years ago in Tokyo."

Nina sighed expansively. "In Japan! That's where I want to go."

"Why don't you?"

Nina looked out of the window. "Because I'm stupid."

"Perhaps you're just waiting for clarity."

A beat went by as Nina gathered herself. "Did you study there?" she prompted.

Gorgonuy smiled. "I'll admit—I've never finished a degree. I had a book written back then and no publisher, so I set sail into the world."

"No way. How can you lecture in Cambridge, then?"

"I'm not an academic. I was interested in Asian myths, so I got on a freight ship to Japan. It sounds romantic, but I got sick of sailing the high seas after the first night. So I disembarked at Sumatra and continued by land. From Indonesia to the Philippines, and then I stayed in Thailand for half a year. I was teaching English to elephants in an orphanage."

Nina burst out laughing, and Gorgonuy took the implicit invitation.

"Tourism was just exploding back then. The tourists spoke no

248

Thai, and the elephants didn't understand them. So I got a job. And elephants are intelligent, kind animals. I listened to the stories and legends of the elephant trainers, thinking that I'd stay there for good. But the oil crisis came. People stopped travelling. The season stopped dead, and the orphanage owed me five months' salary. But as they were good people, they gave me an elephant, and off I went. I rode it to the Malaysian border, where I wanted to sell it. But of course, there were no buyers. So we stopped in a little fishing town, and I organized a lottery. One ticket for a hundred baht. They nearly ripped my arms off. Children, fishermen—everyone wanted to win an elephant. I made five times more than if I had sold him. Then I could afford to travel on through Indonesia, on junks and motorbikes, hitchhiking, however I could. And then, one lands in Japan, and a civilization opens up before one's eyes." He stopped. "But you know your stuff about Japan, otherwise you wouldn't want to go there."

"Please, keep talking. I'm hooked." She was willing to listen to anything that would stop her thinking about Adam. And the train was already stopping in London when Gorgonuy leaned over to her.

"You know very well what you want. And you have to do it today. You can only do everything today!" He reached into his breast pocket. "Here's my card. The reception will be over by ten. Perhaps we can take a train back to Cambridge together?"

"No one can see that far into the future."

"I wish I couldn't either."

They laughed and said goodbye. Nina bought a tossed salad at King's Cross and headed for the V&A. The museum had a collection of busts by her beloved Messerschmidt. She sat down on the floor, put some music on, and started drawing in long, thick strokes reminiscent of calligraphy. She sketched each bust in six to ten lines, not more. The style honored the stroke as an elemental principle of life, each having its beginning, progress, and end. And what she was drawing that afternoon was the end. She entertained herself with the self-conscious men who lingered by the busts so they could eye her up. None found the courage to strike up a conversation. Englishmen with good manners bored her.

She gave all the drawings to the last of them. For a while, he talked to her excitedly about the import and implication of the exhibition in the context of contemporary avant-garde, and then he asked for her number. She put her finger on the highest button of his shirt and declared tenderly, "If I wanted to fuck, we wouldn't be talking about art—we'd be fucking."

She smiled, threw her bag over her shoulder, and went off to the tube.

As night fell, the underground tunnels in Camden Town poured out throngs of the sort whose weekend dinner is music, drugs, and booze. A few hundred of these tattooed and maladjusted individuals were hanging around the tube exit, and Nina suddenly felt back at home. She walked by the Camden Lock and through the market, where the salesmen had already packed up their worthless knick-knacks and forgeries and joined the night crowd.

The huge cast-iron curry bowls and the stalls with artwork, where she'd sold her drawings some years ago, were still in place. Her favorite clubs, too—the Monarch, Lock Tavern, Bar Fly—and the Marathon Bar, a renowned dump that sold kebabs until four a.m., which saw so many legendary scenes from music history that MTV could open a studio there. Once, when Nina was ordering a chicken shish and coke, Jack White of the White Stripes had burst in, guitar in hand and fifty fans trailing him. They'd come there after a concert in Koko, which Nina hadn't had money for, and Jack had played unplugged at the back of the bar until two in the morning. She was still too shy then to talk to him.

There was no plan until she stood in front of the squat. The entire building was gone. Not a bark to welcome her, let alone her old friends' hollering. At that point, she realized that she really had been expecting to sleep there. She wandered onwards, like when she used to run away from home, once more not knowing where to go. The path of least resistance somehow led through her old bars. And through a few cocktails in quick succession. Then, she returned to the station, sat under the boards, and started chanting to herself in Japanese. *Akaru-sa. Sanchi. Okotte. Kirai.*

"Where are you going?"

"Home."

"Where is that?"

She looked up. "Japan."

"The Shinkansen leaves from platform seven. What's your name?"

"Tokyo."

"Pleased to meet you. I'm England. Would you like to have a coffee?"

"I'd prefer a beer."

"Of course. They have Kirin Ichiban on tap around the corner."

Yeah. Adam's favorite beer.

He didn't bore. And also managed not to touch upon anything important in two hours. No past, no art twaddle, no dreams, no family, no obvious attempts to impress. And yet they laughed. She had no idea what they actually talked about, and that was right. Then, they painted the town red. While traversing Camden, Nina flirted with the wild and beautiful lot of the night, danced on the tables and pogoed in Lock Tavern. A singer was dashing all over the stage, spitting streams of beer onto the crowd and shouting, "Freedom!"

And what would you do with it?

"Revolution!"

And what then?

"The state is an infection!"

Two more vodka Red Bulls.

"I think you missed the last Shinkansen," he said at two in the morning, offering her to sleep at his place. He'd kip on the sofa. She grimaced.

"But no funny business."

He looked her over from the checkered skirt to the boots. "Roger, captain. The connection is fine, signal's clear, message received. No sex."

"Promise."

"I swear by my Boy Scout badge."

He had a place in West Hampstead. Nina sat down in the living room with a glass of water, and he went to change the sheets. She searched through the drawers in the kitchen and hid the longest knife she could find in her bag. Later, it somehow came to pass that England was lying in bed next to her. He stroked her shoulder and pressed his penis against her butt. She pushed him away and rolled towards the bedside. A few minutes later, he hugged her again. She awoke suddenly, braced her bum against him, reached over the bed into her bag and felt the knife. For a moment, she was taut perfectly between the slicer and the penis, right in the clueless place.

Nina could have anything: for example, the relative safety of Adam, and Marquis' pale blue eyes to boot. Neither of them would dare say anything if she decided to occasionally swap them in bed. And *of course* she'd slept with Marquis ages ago. The first time was on the night they'd met, after Adam left the party to go to sleep. She'd turned to Marquis and yawned, "I'm offering my entire intellectual depth here, and I'm actually boring myself."

"Do you want to kiss?" he'd asked, and she'd shrugged.

And then, a few more times in those days, while she'd let Adam court her, charmingly and clumsily. Then, when she'd slowly fallen for him, she was tempted to act like the punk version of Virgin Mary that Adam took her for. But now ... "You know very well what you want," said Gorgonuy. She wanted to live, as genuinely as he did, the elephant teacher.

She let go of the knife and took him into her hand instead. He was pleasantly warm and just thick enough. She pulled her panties down and held them bunched up in her hand the whole time they were making love. He whispered in her ear, "I thought you wouldn't do it," and she had her eyes closed, holding him by the hair with both hands, repeating "You're a liar." He laughed as if she was joking, but it didn't matter.

In the morning, after she left, she found a number for the Wabi-sabi Foundation. Over eggs benedict in a café on West End Road, she swallowed all the *ifs* and called. The universes of potential realities collapsed into the only real one, and, as they dwindled, she felt lighter by the second. On the phone, she took a deep breath and said how happy she was to be able to accept.

"And I'm going," she whispered when she put the phone down. "Ninny von Tokyo."

After this decision, she began without further hesitation the rapid and irreversible process of forgetting—that is, pruning all of her words and weeding out every mention of him. The patterns of Adam's life and behavior, which she had until then carefully remembered, were never to repeat again. The Adam she'd created through the mirror of her mind became a lie. In about three weeks, she would have most of it done. Adam would turn back into a man without qualities, floating through space in an undefined and boundless proto-form, looking for someone to start noticing other patterns, drawing out a different person. When she walked out onto the street, where the autumn sun dazzled all of its children, she burst into tears. Finally, she had also found the right way to fail.

The Pu

chline

I'm against endings. I'm against things being over. Being finished should be stopped!

I am Comrade-in-Chief of going on. I support furthermore and etcetera!

—Saša Stanišić

After

sleeping lightly for two hours, he got up, molded his face into a somewhat acceptable shape, and put on a suit and a black coat. He walked up the hill towards the church without breakfast. It was drizzling. There were some sixty people standing in front of the gate. The day of suffering had come.

The children noticed him first, rushing in from all directions and hanging themselves onto him. Then came the greetings.

"Did you sleep under a bridge, Adam?"

"Doesn't he look like a chaplain in that coat?"

He didn't speak much, observing how foreign they were to him. There was no fight in it, only distance.

"Son, you need a gin and tonic."

The service began, and Adam couldn't even take a seat in the pews. He was shaking, and his mind was racing from one thought to the next. He stood up and climbed a staircase to the gallery. The old organist looked exactly like he remembered him from his summer trips.

Adam leaned on the balustrade and tapped out a quick rhythm. He was suddenly in another church, his mind mixing the tracks of memories. The sounds he heard were the opening notes of Bach's Brandenburg Concerto at St Nicholas'. They couldn't stop laughing and ran outside, kissing on the church steps. The memory felt like a wedding. And it could have been that, he thought. He should have proposed to Nina before the damn portraits started arriving and everything started falling apart. She was the only one who'd ever understood him.

Standing alone on the gallery, he felt love. He reached into his pocket to call and propose to her. But that also didn't seem like a good idea.

The organ requiem for Grandma subsided, and the dramatic voice of the preacher resounded through the church. Dozens of bouquets were lying around the coffin.

"... mother to some, sister and grandmother to all. Let us pause in sorrow and mourn, but let us not grieve." The priest went quiet and looked around the silent church. He nodded lightly, almost contentedly, and immersed himself in the words again. "After all, a woman lies in front of us who ended her long journey with dignity and in the name of the most noble of missions: in the name of faith and the love of God, which she spread to all of us through her patience, kindness, and good will. What more can one wish for in this world?"

Adam held on to the balustrade to avoid shouting. For whom was the priest condensing Grandma's life into a three-minute punchline? Oh, for the brains down there. They needed to close an eighty-year-long story. There was the same imperative for closure, like when the aunts asked him with a cheeky smile, "When's the wedding?" Pick one partner for life—and most importantly, please, no more changes. Stop delaying it, Adam. Finish the story. Pour some concrete over it.

The speech ended. Four men lifted the coffin on their shoulders and walked out of the church with the procession. Adam walked down and joined the crowd, plastic bag in hand. It was still drizzling, the grass was wet, and the plane wasn't leaving until five in the afternoon.

The procession crept up to the grave. The men strenuously brought the coffin down on the planks. One of them massaged his shoulder. "Granny was a featherweight, but the bier's heavy as fuck."

The ropes slowly lowered the coffin into the grave. Adam pushed his way to the front. His family was standing silently and gazing at the coffin. Perhaps they were estimating their own distance from death. The first handfuls of wet earth fell on the casket, and Adam threw the white bag in. It rang against the wood. Nina would be proud of him. He flew to Ireland just to keep this promise.

"What's that?" asked his uncle.

"From Grandma."

"What from Grandma?"

Adam shrugged. "She gave it to me a few weeks ago. Saying she wants it in her grave."

"And you didn't peek in? What if there's money in there?"

"Not likely."

"You were always a dunce!"

Adam closed his eyes. At that moment, his uncle leapt.

"My God!" Two or three hands reached for him in vain, and he broke through the coffin with both legs and a terrible racket.

Someone started laughing hysterically; the ladies' hands flew up to their mouths to hide shame or shock. Adam gawked like all the children around.

"Friggin' plywood," wheezed his uncle as he reached for the bag. He rummaged around in it while the relatives, bowed over the grave, started crossing themselves and shouting. Someone was apologizing to the priest. Ten arms reached into the hole to help him out.

"Get out right now, Donald, before I give you a slapping!"

"I am so ashamed," gasped a woman on his right. "So ashamed."

"One second!" he grumbled. "My ankle is stuck."

"What happened?" called the relatives who had been quietly talking a few steps away. Another explained, "Donald the nitwit fell into the grave!"

"Oh, I'll die, or have a heart attack."

"What's he doing down there?"

His uncle was still standing with one foot inside the coffin, fishing through the plastic bag. Suddenly, he waved a piece of paper around. "Adam, where are you? Is this yours?"

Adam grudgingly took it. The yellowed page with frayed corners was almost falling apart, but the ink drawing in clear and fast lines clearly captured a man swearing on a master's scepter. The year 1712 was noted next to the calligraphic addition of "*Hinc lucem et popula sacra*" in the same handwriting. The man here, graduating from Cambridge three hundred years ago, was, without a shadow of a doubt, Adam.

"What was it?" the family whispered over each other, but Adam hid the sheet in his pocket, squeezed through the huddle without a word, and let his cousins extract his uncle from the grave. People began to quiet down and resumed sobbing.

He spent the next few hours wandering over the rolling hills, away from the villages, between fields and low stone walls. He tried his best to keep his feet on the ground. But if another one of his likenesses was found in his grandmother's inheritance, then that could only mean one thing: that his own family knew much more about him than anyone had told him. He finally had to admit that he *might* be immortal and that the world turning inside out in his mind had only just begun to resemble reality.

He breathed quickly, smoked, and beat his head. He would trade anything for his own funeral speech, where the priest would sum up his life into a finished story. There were so many questions starving for answers that he even vomited twice. He didn't go back to the airport. Again, he thought about calling Nina, but he was too worried that she would be worried. Instead, he staggered to the church just before sunset. Exhausted, he walked over to the altar and kneeled. He clasped his hands, hung his head, and recited the Lord's Prayer out loud three times.

Omnis

cience

Adam

paid three hundred pounds for one of the last free seats on the night flight without batting an eyelash and allowed the plane to transfer his body from one island to the other. He could not sit still on the train to Cambridge. He switched to another carriage. And again. People stared at him quietly flapping his hands against each other, rocking his body and hunching his head in his hands. Every compartment he entered went quiet. They looked to him like polyp colonies clinging to the seats, impulsively retracting their stumps and growths from the foreign body that stirred their cloudy waters. He listened to them, but they lowered their voices, so he couldn't tell what they were saying.

Then, he couldn't sit at all. He walked from one end of the train to the other. Thirty-seven times there and back. He walked past the conductor six times. Every time he brushed past him, he could hear full well the man whispering to the passengers about him. At the station, he ran for the bus and again rocked his body back and forth and mechanically repeated, "What grips my neck?" (Quietly but loud enough to hear himself.) And again, the co-travelling polyps pulled away, being transported from place to place, as though it meant anything, dumping them out at the other end of the town ... as though the jolting could revive them.

He got off by the college and alternately pushed his lower limbs into the lift. He rose up to the cuboid assigned to him. Inside, he sat down and lay his hands on his knees. The fingers were shaking, each on its own. He took two sheets of paper out of a drawer and arranged them in equidistance from the table edges. He wrote *FAUSTOMAT* on the paper to the left, *COMPLICATIONS* on the one to the right. Two empty sheets locked in combat for one consciousness and one right hand. Caught in between, unable to write with both hands at once, he couldn't help them. The pencil in his fingers was shaking—

Wrong. This hand is right, and this one's left. Trust me.

look over your shoulder, and see that terrible habit of questioning *constantly returning to the same place*—a question turning into itself— *what is a question?—*

questioning is not in the question; it comes before

262

so it won't find satisfaction in an answer
the answer won't answer the *questioning* of the question. You fell for it!
go on, son, with that methodical skepticism
and the paradox will eat you from the guts out—
Tuck your shirt in your pants!
welcome to the final destination of the supremely rational
Sit! Say hello to your friends!
Brouwer + Gödel + Messerschmidt + Cantor + Nietzsche + ∞
quiet, staring

He quickly got up and called Nina. He'd tried a few times, many times. She wasn't answering. She was lost. He should be protecting her, and he could not. Worthless man. Broken, worthless man. He sat down again and positioned the phone next to the papers, perpendicular to their long edge.

rationality is a glorified compulsion
Don't slouch! Nina—

⟶

Berlin literatus and publisher Friedrich Nicolai stopped at a friend's workshop on his way home from Vienna. He found him standing in front of a mirror, face contorted, scratching into his notebook every few seconds. The artist started and, seeing a friend, brightened up. As they looked through the workshop together, he gave reserved explanations of the series of plaster busts lined up along the walls. Nicolai noticed that a number of them had their faces transfixed in strenuous convulsions and curiously inquired. The artist locked the door to the workshop, scanned the room three times and, whispering, confided that the sculptures protected him against the evil spirit of proportion. Every grimace captured precise ratios and added to the inner order of the work, repelling the demon. Nicolai noted the anecdote in his travel journal, and, as life goes, they both died not long after.

Over decades and centuries, the forty-nine faces would attract waves of periodic interest and forgetting. The attention expanded and contracted with the slow breath of dead artists for nearly two centuries. Then Nicolai, despite being dead, disturbed the artist's peace again. The diary entry was discovered by a Viennese psychoanalyst and friend of Sigmund Freud, Ernst Kris. He found enough in the curt notes to connect the busts' twisted grimaces with a progressing mental illness. This became a popular reading of the meaning of Franz Messerschmidt's busts. Ernst Kris turned a deceased artist into a lunatic. That is Messerschmidt's real story. But is it a story about the real Messerschmidt? Or about a fictional character, a figure in the mirror, loosely based on a model long turned to dust?

⤳

He convulsively clenched his neck muscles until they shook his head. He got up, threw the window wide open—but instead of air, he inhaled an influx of atoms, bacteria, dust and started coughing—

Don't put it in your mouth! Oh, I'll slap you so hard your beanie'll fly off!

Turning around and falling over a chair, he crawled over to the bookshelf and took out a monolingual dictionary. A vortex of words burst into his eyes. A charging army of grasshoppers, termites, rats, crows—

stinking of another dog's urine

He broke off the dictionary and flung it across the room. The binding cracked, and pages fluttered in the corner.

that which called itself Adam broke truth

who is I if not words! Who dug his own grave?! I don't know I just watched him dig. "I don't know," he said out loud. "I don't know!" he shouted and put his hand over his mouth right away—

must stay beside words!

He stood and breathed, turned his head around and back, looked down at his own crotch and released urine. A warming dark shadow was extending along his trousers, a mark of protection. And to work! Hopefully, it's not too late—hopefully, a fast weaving of words, his words, those he can't forget, without stopping or sleeping, can prevent losing consciousness, before it's too late, and it will only be late once, at once. He hesitated and wrote one, perhaps the most erroneous of all but in its error proving its own opposite, which is why he could only write it mirrored: *NAMDAM*

my name my name is staring at me

You're thinking too much. Trust me.

cold skin and the sixty-ton weight of the body—

fissure—

my fingers run over the board of the table, and I'm gaping at where it gets the cheek to claim to me that it's hard, *material*. Where I get the guts to imagine that matter is something more than energy = information. I lay my head on the fingered wood, and I see through the illusion of her *materiality*, and the web of fissures grows—I avert my eyes and close them and see a circus—and now, I know rock-solid that there *used to be a brake of obviousness* in my head, an intentional barrier dampening discoveries; it had to be there, protecting against over-gulping on each cubic millimeter of the world. We talked about that in Prague, and the barrier I was leaning against with all my weight finally burst, and a web of cracks grows in me— Nina, I pushed through what I was never supposed to break, and now the desire to know burns through my head in a chain reaction scorching my comically systematized world into a spray of spinning words—a self-feeding explosion of obviousness lost—do you get it? I beg you, do you understand me? I thought too much I was too mindful, Ninny, I was so much that I broke me—one's not supposed to live that intensely … I no longer know what a table is what a chair is—a situation refracted through crushed icy facets *being* from all angles at once, echoing *the loss of obviousness is the loss of reason*—

Brush your teeth every morning in and out! Finish your porridge!

tongue has that metallic taste with a smack of plastic, and its sixty-ton body collapses into self-awareness, but who is *self*? It knows how to point a finger at others, and over and over it tries to point the finger back, but what does it see of *self* but a hand twitching like a lizard's cut-off tail being observed; it leans closer and jerks back right away from the grave dirt's perfume—

Where is she? Why is she not answering? Adam crying—

as I nod my torso there and back and my face pierces the thin transparent membrane on which the color movie of the present projects I'll take a step back or just stagger and I'll never be able to find this opening into the world again I'll fumble in the grey non-matter until I suffocate

I'm holding tight, pressed into the present with nanometric precision but if my eyes detuned to a different frequency my body running through the landscape would see nothing! Frantically tuning, the frequency occasionally flashes—it's there I know—I'll never find the exact original hair-thin wavelength with clumsy thumbs we'll miss each other in the ether. Perhaps for a moment I'll accidentally tune into x-ray eyes and the wall blackens, the table turns transparent, the night sky whitens with brightness. Then, infrared heat-sensitive eyes catch a smudged trace flailing after the writing hand and the sharp edge between what is and what isn't melts, softens, and disappears. Color-blind eyes and a bat's ultrasound eyes and each further valid illusion reveals a deep mistake—the color movie—the so-called world, reality—more disappearing words—that whole colorful universe with a table a wall a twitching hand and stars above is a fantasy—a twisted mirror image constructed an inch behind the pupils in my imagination—my oh-so-human imagination

Wipe that stupid grin off your face!

but how do you want to keep a grip on reality boy when you don't know what reality is? how does everyone do it for God's sake with ease with such ease the polyp clings but I don't want fantasy I want reality I want to feel something other than my own hand

Stop frowning. An empty set is an object, what's not to understand about that? Answer me. Be quiet when the teacher is talking. The whole is more than the sum of its parts. A flock without birds isn't anything you naughty boy, do you want detention again? You caught a deadly thought out in the cold, you see? Guess—which one was it?

time scrapes and scrambles over my body wedged into the fissure between the future and the past but most awake—I can never fall asleep even if I weren't scared, it's just impossible to live like this so let me become who I am and cut the cord—

Don't put it in your mouth! Don't make me slap you!

Sit still! Don't run!

He slammed the window shut and used the handle to lock the universe outside. It pressed on the glass with all of its weight, glaring with the night sky's trillion eyes.

the tick of the heart, the hum of the air pumped through the neck, the sounds of a machine

what's left is to clean up after being—turn off the machine—get rid of the body

He crumpled up the sheet covered with scribbles, tucked the paper ball inside his shirt, turned the light off, and stepped towards the window. He reached for the handle and suddenly saw a person reaching for another handle from the outside. It was not an illusion but a real intention looking at its own reflection inside the room. They faced each other in a mutual desire to step onto the ledge and jump through to the other side.

They both paused. It was necessary to somehow reflect the other's craving to do the opposite, arising from a completely contrasting history in an inverted world and shockingly leading up to the same point. Intuitively, their disparate time and space fractals had to merge in order to thrust the self into a new dimension. But that connection wasn't coming. Something writhed between them, however much they simultaneously winked, screamed, bulged their eyes, bared their teeth, and waved mental swords. Something between them refused to be reduced to the union of two opposites in a joint annihilation. In the perfect excluded middle, it gradually toughened into a fixed point of resistance, just as strong as all attempts to overcome it, and grew into an atrociously loud ringing emanating from the room behind.

He returned to the table. The phone screen was lit, reporting that Nina was calling, still alive, and that he'd stood in front of the window for almost an hour. He picked it up.

"Darling, you've gone crazy. I've got nineteen missed calls from you. What's happening?"

dawring you've gone awry. you put it nicely again, perfect Nina; I'm your dawring. Will you marry me? I am afraid this is not a good time to talk about it. I am afraid. Before I went awry, and now I've gone crazy, and I'm the only piece of the puzzle that doesn't fit. Sadly, Gödel's theorem proves that the liar is the only consistent one.

"Adam? I can't hear you. Are you there?"

don't do this to me, Nina. I'm right there where you can't point to. Now, say anything, just, for God's sake, don't say you don't understand me—

She hung up.

He put the phone down. It started ringing again. He observed it, scared that whatever Nina would say this time would not be enough. He loved her. So much that not even a kiss could bridge the fissure between them. Unfortunately, she'd try, fail, and her lips would knock him down into a plummet with dilated pupils, and the weight of the sixty-ton body would silently snap the only tightened string. The ringing stopped. There was no way out. Obviously. A complete inversion took place, and he was the ghost behind the window, trying to find the way out into the room, while the body in the room was trying to find the way back inside the universe. They logically could not attain these goals, because any intent would have the opposite outcome. Despite that, he turned around and walked out the door. Inside the lift, he pushed the lowest button, and the cage moved in a manner contradicting the very essence of an elevator.

The stairs to the basement were dimmed by a dull red EXIT sign and arrows pointing back up. He passed several unmarked doors and stopped in front of the last one. There was a nailed wooden sign with a hand-drawn number 0. He banged on it, not to go inside but to get out. Not to speak but to gain silence. Not to fight but to give up. He banged a third time. Only then did he realize that it was past midnight. The floor creaked.

"Who is it?" said a voice through the door.

He raised his hand in a fist and let it fall again.

The door opened. Gorgonuy in a brown gown scanned him. "Do you know what time it is?"

He sighed, shifted his weight, and stared.

"What is going on, Adam?"

That isn't me, he answered to himself. And something's up—but what?

"You're shaking. It's one in the morning. What happened?"

Whatever I say will be the opposite of an answer.

"Adam?" shouted Gorgonuy. "What's that on your trousers?"

Words would come out inverted. A glimmering light and the smell of smoke were coming from inside the flat as if it were lit by a fireplace, but he couldn't hear the crackling nor the hum of a chimney.

"Your eyes look terrible. Can't you sleep?"

Adam slowly and indistinctly nodded or shook his head and laboriously articulated "I will not sleep" word by word. He staggered, collapsed on the floor, turned his head left, back, right, back, left and started muttering, "What should I do what should I do." He looked left and

269

right, a machine that had lost its program, "What should I do," and his torso concentrated on fighting his unstable stomach. It was demanding something, scratching him. Without looking down, he pulled his shirt up, and a paper ball fell to the floor. He spread the sweaty wrinkles out. Obviously, this scratchy mess was a mirror opposite of his synapticon. That which remains after constant pushing. After the toe presses deeper into the lobe above the pharynx, retches, and forces the heel into the cavity and thrusts in the knee. The thigh rams in right after, and then the butt is pried into the dislocated, ripped jaw, and the second leg steps in with ease. One swallows and that's it—he stands at the final victory of recursion in his own ass.

He kicked the paper towards Gorgonuy's legs and closed his eyes. He heard the professor bending down.
"Switch it off or kill," he uttered slowly.

"Siberian poison."

"My ... wait here." The professor disappeared inside.

Wait here. Who? Where? My, that'll be harder than you think. But Gorgonuy came back and found him again.

"Here you are." He pressed the vial into his hand. "Pour it into boiling water, and let it sit for ten minutes. Drink very slowly."

"Is it strong?"
Melancholy wedged in hysteria spilled through the tone. Gorgonuy nodded and helped him into the lift. Before he pressed the button and stepped out of the elevator, he pushed the crumpled paper into Adam's back pocket.
"No—"

"Yes," said Gorgonuy. "Listen, you'd better just drink half," and the doors closed.

He could faint into another dimension between any two floors. He could grow old in a blink of an eye, disintegrate into atoms, fall between seconds—but none of that happened before the water in the kettle came to a boil. He poured the entire potion into a mug and topped it off with water. Black resin floated up. He bent over into the steam. The stench was so piercingly disgusting that his innards finally cramped, and he barely managed to collapse sideways into the sink. He emptied himself, splashed water on his face, and got ready.

With the mug, he walked back to the window and looked his reflection in the eye. What little was left of it, anyway. Raising the mug, he shakily motioned to the cosmic other. They both began swallowing their double doses, gulp by gulp so bitter that their faces twisted in a terminal performance of all possible grimaces. The laconic knowledge that this life will either be straightened or lost filled him with a sense of order and balance. He swallowed until there was nothing left at the bottom. Kneeling on the carpet, he placed the mug on the window sill and his body along the radiator. Molecular chaos darted through the veins. Or was it perhaps the piercing cold that couldn't be melted by the hot infusion, who knows, who ever knows?

"Just let it be strong," he repeated. "Let it be strong enough."

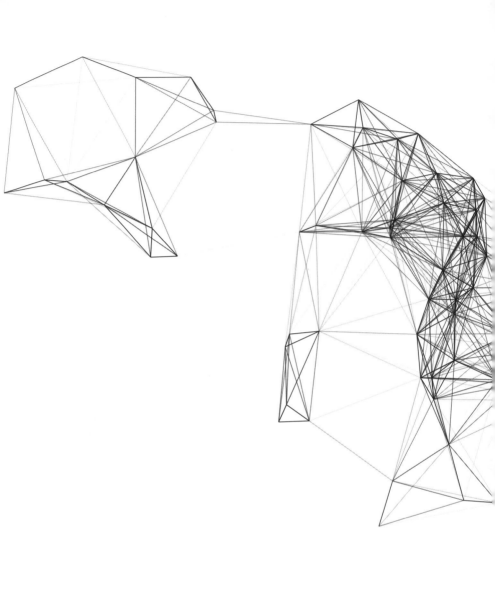

Duckrabbit

"Mr. Gandhi, what do you think of Western civilization?"
"I think it would be a good idea."

I t tolls for two o'clock, my friend, to announce the darkest part of the night. Now, when not even a hint of light disturbs, it is time to take our cardinal question to the final level.

Am I real or fictional?

This is not what I set out to resolve as a young man. I was interested in the particularities—mathematics, God, programming, women. Ironically, I spent years hunting down God, only to suspect in the end that it may have been the higher force itself proposing the questions and waiting curiously for my answer.

What is still real, if God isn't? And who has the authority to answer? As Timothy Leary put it in a concert of ... what's the band's name? I'll play it.

The voice of Timothy Leary in the song Third Eye by the band Tool. Limited edition of the album Salival, 2000. Think for yourself. Question authority. Think for yourself. Throughout human history, as our species has faced the frightening, terrorizing fact that we do not know who we are or where we are going in this ocean of chaos, it has been the authorities, the political, the religious, the educational authorities who attempted to comfort us by giving us order, rules, regulations, informing, forming in our minds their view of reality. To think for yourself, you must question authority and learn to put yourself in a state of vulnerable open-mindedness—chaotic, confused vulnerability to inform yourself. Think for yourself. Question authority.

So to answer how real I am, I suggest you follow Tim's advice and try an experiment. Compare the story of my life with something completely real. With the twentieth century, for example. Everyone knows what it is, right? Then, point to the twentieth century with your finger. Aha! Where is it?

I once had an argument about this with Marquis and Nina that was quite telling. You know Marquis. He's a liberal—the vulgar kind, who's clear on everything right away. He saw history as a straight line of linear growth with occasional hiccups. He read up on von Mises and Hayek, the entire Austrian school, due to some fairly useless need to underpin his free thinking with a philosophical foundation.

"Economic and social phenomena should be explained exclusively through the acts of individuals," he noted down in a lecture on methodological individualism, where he had gone to cast nets in new waters. It was such an obvious stance that he had no idea how anyone could dispute it. After all, to him, "women" was never a designation of a collective, abstract whole but a series of brunettes, blondes, the delicate one, the wild one, a waitress, a medical student. When he talked about a state, he meant its citizens.

So he pulled out a statistical yearbook. "All you need to know," he said, and pointed to a brief history of freedom in a few charts. One showed the expansion of automobiles and tourism as proxies for geographical freedom; another captured the growth of technology and, with it, the freedom to communicate; then, the spread of contraceptives and the related sexual freedom. All the charts had a similar shape.

The Official Yearbook of the United Kingdom of Great Britain and Northern Ireland, millennial edition. Chapter: Facts in Context, pp. 1350-1356.

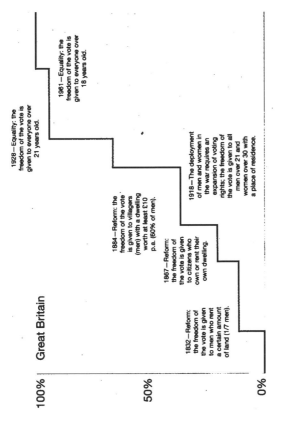

Great Britain

100%

50%

0%

1928 – Equality: the freedom of the vote is given to everyone over 21 years old.

1961 – Equality: the freedom of the vote is given to everyone over 18 years old.

1884 – Reform: the freedom of the vote is given to villagers (men) with a dwelling worth at least £10 p.a. (60% of men).

1867 – Reform: the freedom of the vote is given to citizens who own or rent their own dwelling.

1918 – The deployment of men and women in the war requires an expansion of voting rights; the freedom of the vote is given to all men over 21 and women over 30 with a place of residence.

1832 – Reform: the freedom of the vote is given to men who rent a certain amount of land (1/7 men).

Political Freedom

(the percentage of citizens with the right to vote as a percentage of the entire adult population)

That's the twentieth century according to Marquis—a steep curve of individual freedom, phallically pointing from the depths of the past. Nina was there, listening, and, at first, she smiled. When the right moment came, she uttered, "You're so comically self-centered."

I knew where she was coming from. Or so I thought. The liberals reminded her of kids, still entirely engrossed in fighting for their own space: "Me me me!"

"And what are you left with," she asked him, "when you win the freedom from everything that you fought for with your little fists? Loneliness."

It took me years to consider maybe she wasn't talking about liberalism at all. Anyway. She had a completely different view. She wished for communal dinners at one table, for family, for belonging together. Everything she didn't find in the squat.

"And you know how they end, your collectivist utopias," Marquis cut her down to size that evening we talked about it. "Italy, 1919."

Arpado Capra. *Nocturnal, Infernal, Carnal: A Safe Guide on the Roads to Hell. Chapter: Politics, pp. 104–106*. In April of that year, a young, charismatic man spoke to a large crowd from a balcony in the center of Milan: "If the nineteenth century was the century of the individual, nothing prevents us from believing that this is the collective century and therefore also the century of the State." The crowd responded with joyful applause. It was a crowd of survivors. They vividly remembered the terror of the World War, which took the lives of 20 million people. Then, the Spanish Flu pandemic passed through a devastated Europe full of refugees, claiming 60 million victims. Italy was threatened by civil war. Nobody believed in the old order except for the conservatives, but the World War did not bring a new order. The Italians felt cheated by the Treaty of Versailles. The factory workers in the north were on strike every month. They refused to pay their rent and burned down the houses of the rich. What could a single person do, then? The individual was a demonstrably feeble and acutely mortal victim of terrorizing fate. It's no wonder that the speaker's words about a safe and strong community sounded more than attractive.

It was the speech of his life. His dream of a political career was falling apart, and he was considering dropping politics to wander the world as a violinist. Unfortunately, people gave him a huge round of applause that day, and Benito Mussolini decided to hang up the fiddle. His central argument, that the state is more powerful than the individual and its interests have to come first, began spreading throughout Europe. In a few years, his Fascist party won a parliamentary majority, 18 percent voted for Hitler, and fascism grew in Austria, Franco's Spain, Salazar's Portugal, and Papadopoulos' Greece. The utopian, transcendental, and mystical vision of the People—which is more than people—enticed millions. Whether they were looking for protection or solidarity, they got neither.

If it seemed in the seventeenth century that the 9 million victims of the Inquisition were the height of absolutist power, the twentieth century turned it into a mere prologue. Mussolini's Milan speech led to 1.2 million dead in Auschwitz as well as the other 60 million victims of the Second World War. Fascism practically eradicated itself in a spectacular catharsis, a massacre eclipsed only by the second absolute evil of the twentieth century, communism—as yet the most perfect disguise of absolutist philosophy. For all the terrors and perversities this mode of human cohabitation caused, it should suffice to briefly list the 30 million victims of starvation in devastated collectivized Russia, the 2 million dead in the gulags, the 40 million victims of Maoism, and half a million Tibetans. Every one of those murders was committed in the name of something higher than the individual.

A note for tour guides: of all the roads to Hell we have available, this is one of the safest ones. It is a timeless hit with group excursions and is perfectly described by the phrase "tourist trap." The signposts only indicate the way there. The route offers vistas of the gems of brutalism, monumental memorials for leaders, and mass graves. Due to its low difficulty, this trip is suitable for just about everyone.

He passed her Capra's guidebook and snorted over her—"Do you still want a utopia?"

He was always finished so fast. After what happened between him and Nina,

I spent a brief period of some five years tearing apart every one of his ideas.

It was a side project, but I was rather thorough. During the course of one winter, I took time to understand the shortcomings of liberalism. It drained away some of the pain.

Gustavo Caravella. A Century of Fallacies, pp. 94-97. Political economy fails as a science, utterly and completely. It can't predict crises, its models are static, its scientists serve the wealthy, and, even as a bar sport, it only annoys people. But when it comes to experiments, there is none above it. No other science has managed to make guinea pigs of entire countries. Generations of people gamble their livelihoods on one hypothesis or the other in enormous experiments in the art of living. East and West Germany, for example: a fifty-year-long comparative study for the benefit of humanity. Eastern and Western Europe: a study ten times as large. Such political experiments teach society how to distinguish between reality and utopia, fact and fallacy, a lot more effectively than theoretical science.

To take a prime example, Hayek attributes the death of some 140 million people to a single fault of reasoning. If that's the case, then it has to be the greatest fallacy in human history. Apparently, it is shared by fascists, communists, and socialists alike.

... and Nina.

All of them, according to Hayek, *"have a tendency to approach entities such as society, economy or the state as though they were clearly given objects, the regularities of which we can discover by observing their collective behavior."*

Italian fascists, socialists, and communists were sworn enemies, and yet they could agree on something. The Italian word *fascio*, meaning "bundle," refers to the same root as the Latin *socius* (partner) and *socialis* (connected), from which socialism is derived, and also *commun* (shared), the root of communism. The common denominator of fascism and socialism is the emphasis on the community, the whole. (The other thing they almost miraculously agreed on was that they hated liberals even more than each other.) And only when the whole (people, nation, state) is seen as an entity in its own right is it possible to begin putting it above the individuals.

But by no means does this prove that Hayek's individualism is any less wrong. The evidence against the simplistic liberal doctrine surfaced toward the end of the century. The internet in particular just sent individualism to the dogs. How does one capture information as a characteristic of individual people? The virality of YouTube videos? How does one attribute the overall value of Wikipedia to individual contributors? These unbelievable network synergies show that individualism cannot adequately capture today's reality. It's dead.

Let us see next what it is that connects communism with the Greens, open source, and Wikipedia.

All I need is to recall the laughter in St Nicholas' church. Who caused it? No one. Strictly individualistically, no such thing could have happened. And, after all, even Hayek let up on his dogma.

Friedrich Hayek. Studies in Philosophy, Politics and Economics. Routledge & Kegan Paul, London, 1967. The overall order of actions in a group is in two respects more than the totality of regularities observable in the actions of the individuals and cannot be wholly reduced to them. It is so not only in the trivial sense in which a whole is more than the mere sum of its parts but presupposes also that these elements are related to each other in a particular manner.

Even Hayek. I wish I could tell Marquis one day. Even Hayek, you bastard.

But why am I talking about all this? Surely not to engage in a political debate. My point is simple: Marquis and Nina couldn't agree on what the twentieth century is. Neither could Hayek with Mussolini or Capra with Caravella. All we can say about it are stories that contradict each other. Unfolding, ambiguous, elusive.

The comic conclusion: last century was a hundred-year-long experiment in storytelling, which has not yet been concluded. Thus, the twentieth century is not over.

The tragic conclusion: I don't want to sound like a rambling old fogey, but something is fundamentally flawed when we're describing our course in terms of two directions we're not heading in. Wars in which people have nothing but disdain for both sides are characteristic of my lifetime. They don't believe in God, and they're terrified of death. They don't like the Church's chastisements, but they don't like the thought of anyone doing whatever they please. They consider the idea of an absolute work naive, but postmodern art makes no impression on them. One partner is not enough, but they can't bear infidelity. Leftist utopias disappoint them, the right-wing ones scare them. Absolutism stinks of orders, relativism of hopelessness.

This terminal paradox transects Marquis' and Nina's minds and will not give them peace in this lifetime. Like a tectonic fault, it cuts through Cambridge, Europe, art, science, Western culture, and every debate. And the longer we argue, the more we hear the dispute resonate through every corner of our actions, as if all the human domains rhymed in an all-pervading fractal überpattern.

284

WAGNER ——— POSTMODERNISM

LOYALTY ——— INFIDELITY

OPTIMIZATION IMPERATIVE ——— SKEPTIC

ADAM

UTOPIA ——— LONELINESS

NINA

LEAP INTO THE SUN
THE WORK —— LIVRE —— CLUELESS PLACE
PARASITE   CAGE OF FREEDOM
                  DEAD CORAL

ADAM & NINA

286

ARISTOTLE ——————— PROTAGORAS
ABSOLUTE ——————— RELATIVE
CHRISTIANITY —————— MYTH
GOD —————— YETI
STORY —————— EPISODE

PHILOSOPHERS

TRUTH —————— STORY
CREATION —————— EVOLUTION

RULERS

SET ——————— MEMBER

HILBERT ——————— GÖDEL

LOGIC ——————— LOGICS

1 ——————— ∞

MATHEMATICIANS

OPUS ——————— CHAOS

UNIVERSE

FLOCK & BIRDS

I told you before, walk up Petřín Hill. Up there, as the hundreds of birds take flight, a live image of this obvious century will appear, an image that is reminiscent of the duckrabbit more than anything else.

THE TWENTIETH CENTURY

By trying to compare me to the twentieth century, we have learned nothing about me, but the century no longer appears as unwaveringly real. The twentieth century is a duckrabbit. I am a duckrabbit.

Is the duckrabbit real or fictional?

Perhaps that fractal God, who probes through me, is just trying to understand why the hell it looks like a duckrabbit.

The relentlessly logical conclusion to which we are inevitably heading here is that our world stands on a paradox, and it is, therefore, impossible to draw any logical conclusions. Logic has brought us to its own end, knotted unto itself like a thousand-year ouroboros. Truth, logic, and reality reveal themselves as mere narratives. The lullabies of a civilization.

What will homo do then?

Will they kill logic like they killed all other fictions? Will they pierce its heart with a stick? Or will they say, "Know what, old man? You're insane! You're a straight-up paradoxical being! Now I've exposed you!" Very well. Think for yourself. Question authority. Don't trust me! What a shame you can never obey that order … in the true spirit of the liar's paradox.

Occam'

s Razor

The important thing is this: to be able at any moment to
sacrifice what we are for what we could become.
—*Charles Du Bos*

In hindsight, everything so far had been logical. His steps led one to the next, and not only did each make sense on its own, but Adam had made them freely and consciously. Just the next one did not follow. How does one choose what to do when he doesn't know what to do? Only when the usual methods fail, he assured himself, does intellect emerge. To evaluate data according to a known pattern—well, a machine can do that. Only a human knows how to strut forward cluelessly. But which way?

"Marquis. Can we meet in town? I need a smoke and someone who won't shut up," he rasped into his phone. He'd woken up on the floor, and his head was roaring.

"Same here, man. I hope you mean getting wasted, shouting in the streets, getting locked up, catching the first train back from London in the morning, and never finding out how we got there in the first place."

Something like that.

"And don't forget to bring me—"

"Yeah. See you."

Marquis arrived about an hour later than they'd arranged, and Adam didn't care. He stood in a clueless place, smoking. The pub was full, and football was on. They found a place at the bar where they couldn't see the screen. "Listen, I have a feeling like Nina split up with me."

"What?"

Adam ran his hand through his hair. "I just slept through two days. She was at my apartment in the meantime, packed her clothes and the toothbrush, and wrote me a message. She's leaving for Japan in a month, and she'll stay with a friend for a few days."

"And did she break up with you?"

"No." Adam hung his head.

"So what now?"

"I don't know. I really have no clue." He looked down. "I wanted to propose to her. But she won't answer the phone."

"Do it!"

"You're the one telling me that?"

"What do you think? Of course, I could say that you're using

294

a sledgehammer to crack a nut." He swirled his glass around and drank deeply. "Nina's a great woman, and if you want to marry her, then marry her, or someone else will."

"I can't believe my ears."

"Of course. Because I'm the idiot who never sees that life has two sides."

Adam peered at his friend a moment. "You don't sound well at all, Marquis. I'd almost say you look worse than I do."

They finished their pints in long gulps, and Adam went to get two more.

"So why haven't you proposed to her yet?"

"Apart from being the idiot I am, it appears I would have to move to Japan."

"So what?"

"I'm doing a PhD here."

"So instead of living with an amazing woman in Asia, you'd rather be Krugele's bellboy."

"I have a scholarship in Cambridge—" he started, and Marquis laughed out loud.

"Trophies!"

"You're one to talk." Adam reached into his pocket and threw a pair of panties into Marquis' face.

"Look what we have here!" Marquis grinned. "Someone is working two shifts! Go on, how was she?"

"I'm going out for a smoke." Adam grabbed the pack and walked outside. A few butts were lying on the ground, just the right amount to make the street cozy. He stood next to some woman, and, with his five beers, he noted, "There's something intriguing in you." She nodded, and Adam, feeling audacious, explained, "I don't mean anything by it. As Bertrand Russell put it, there is much pleasure to be gained from useless knowledge."

She examined him. "Russell? What band was he in?"

"Solo artist."

They smoked in silence from then on.

"What was that you asked?" said Adam to Marquis when he returned.

"Everything! Entertain me."

Adam settled in his seat. "It sounds insane, but I called her."

"Of course! A person's capacity for rational behavior is strictly de-limited by his tolerance for boredom," conjectured Marquis. "And?"

"We met. We had a chat."

"What about?"

"Oh. I remember that absolutely perfectly. I said that the phone number she gave me might be the beginning of something nice."

"Woohoo!"

"She replied, 'Adam, sweetie.' You know she has this soft voice with a sharper undertone, this totally dainty dyadic voice. And she's like, 'Adam, sweetie, when I said that you'll get in my panties sooner than Marquis, that didn't mean you'd get into them. What I meant was that, before Marquis does, a brick will have to fall on my head.'"

Marquis bubbled into his beer and sprayed it over his face. Then, he loudly exhaled and offered some support. "That ... is a start. Not a pole position, but she was talking to you. How did you reply?"

"I kind of repeated myself. And she's like, 'Sorry, sweetie, in a dif-ferent universe.' And she left. I stood there like a lump and felt to see if my bones were still in my body. She stopped a few yards down the hallway, in her miniskirt, and brought her panties down to her stilet-tos in one move."

"Oh, what a treat!"

Adam sadly shook his head.

"What?"

"I wanted to look all right, so I'd removed my glasses before I talk-ed to her." He took a long, long sip. "She threw the panties over and left. So if this was your best pass, my friend, then go solo next time, and I'll stay in defense."

It was so obvious. Adam was simply supposed to be grateful that Eve had even considered him a living being.

And they rambled on through sixty more beers, and Adam got into sharing the result of his experiment in romance.

"An explanation shall be delivered by way of analogy. Might you know what drags men to pubs to watch football?"

"Football, I'll wager."

"Or, more precisely, what urges men to go observe football in the pub in particular?"

They were crammed between regulars mightily flexing their muscles. No answer could be heard from the direction in which it was possible to consider the person named Marquis. Thus, Adam offered a clue deftly hidden in a riddle.

"What does the pub have and the home don't?"

"Beer on tap!"

"Again."

"Bahtrender!"

"Again."

"It's full!"

"And here, we hit the nail on the head, and the truth gushes out. Men are drawn to pubs by empathy."

"Nah!" Marquis rolled his eyes all the way to the back of his head.

"Community empathy, Sporty. These men need each other!" He waved his wet paw with such amplitude it threatened to knock over the glasses full of their eighty-second imported lager. "What's the right word ... compassion ... co-feeling ... fellow-feeling?" he pronounced passionately in a mute shout.

"Hogwash!" yelled Marquis just as silently. "You telling me these fellows are all feeling each other?"

"Calm down, boys," suggested the leading beerer.

"Too late for advice," countered Marquis and slammed his glass on the bar. The muscles surrounding them bulged closer.

"Screw football. I found out in Prague that I only feel when Nina feels. It sounds so astoundingly cheesy, but the proof is in the pubbing. I'm telling you, a man goes to a bar to stand by another's side and grab him by the shoulder and shout with him to feel life pulsing—"

"Pulsing, throbbing, grunting. D'you hear him?" hollered Marquis and waved his pint at all those looking at him in judgement so ferociously that the pint departed from his grip, a single white dove flying across the bar toward the assembled musculature. "Let's make love, ma boys—"

Marquis slowly got up from the floor, and a black red gushed from his face. He didn't say a word, leaned on Adam's shoulder, and they passed through a corridor of powerfully breathing bodyweight. Only outside, while he wiped the blood off his face onto his sleeve, did he ask—was that you who took me down? Adam nodded and led him away with a spattered shirt stuck to his chest.

"It was the only logical thing," he explained after a few minutes of silence, absorbing the paradox. "If I didn't, they would have beaten the living daylights out of you."

They stopped at the one place every hungry drunk in Cambridge knows, the Gardenia, and then walked on to Pembroke. The sun was coming up—dragging, clumsy, and silent but still coming up. And as if Adam had taken rather than thrown a punch, he knew exactly what he had to do next and why.

The

Com

Fear
pass

If you do not change direction, you may end up where you are heading.
—*Lao Tzu*

Adam

pulled the crowbar twice and pushed with all his weight. There was a bang, and the doors burst open with splinters flying from the doorframe. He listened for a moment, lit a flashlight, and carefully entered.

He had been wanting to throw that jab for a few years. Now, not only did he break Marquis' nose to save him from a real fight, but the punch presented a shocking clarity. Its vector continued past the nose and skull. In retrospect, that direction had long been reliably pointed out by fear. Adam just needed to trust his fear like the needle on a compass and follow it where he was most scared to go: into the epicenter of uncertainty, the heart of the paradox.

He tiptoed through the hallway. When he'd last sat there with Gorgonuy, he hadn't realized how plainly the room was furnished. The space resembled a storage room that someone squatted in, rather than an apartment. He started methodically searching the few pieces of furniture that were there—the table drawer, a musty wardrobe, the bookshelves. Besides books, there were wooden beads, leather drumsticks, ampules, amulets, crystals, and statuettes. He found the tarot cards and put one in his pocket.

Then, he approached a chest. He bit down on the flashlight and raised the lid with both hands. Inside was a heap of papers and, on top of it, a doll pierced with five long pins. The flashlight fell out of his mouth. He swore, picked it up, and started quickly reading through the scriptures—on various kinds of paper, from newspapers to postcards, folded over, crumpled up, and torn from notebooks, there were people's lives, written by hand. Between the thousands of stories, he spent half an hour searching for his own. He didn't find it. So he sat down on the floor where he was, in the land of gods, and read to pass the time.

Then, the lift door thumped. He sat up on the chest and turned the penlight off. Something flashed in the corridor, shadows danced across the wall, and Gorgonuy appeared with a candelabrum.

"What's this supposed to mean?" He tilted the candles deeper into the room until wax dripped down and the flames rose higher.

"You're taking the words out of my mouth, Professor," whispered Adam, raising the voodoo doll.

Gorgonuy nodded, set the chandelier down in the center of the table, pulled over the armchair, and started stuffing his pipe.

Adam pounded the chest. "Do you really think these papers will give you immortality?"

"What do you think?" replied Gorgonuy.

Adam pointed the doll at him, pulled out a pin, and stabbed its head a few times. "That you've gone insane."

"Says the mathematician after he's signed his life in blood, pissed himself at my door, and finally broken into my flat to steal ... a voodoo doll?"

"And whose fault is it? You were the one who started with the territory of the gods, with tarot and whatnot, and then those portraits started appearing!"

"I have been warning you."

"You've been manipulating me! Do you have nothing better to do than play with people?"

"I have grown accustomed to the fact that, when someone is rude to me, they're merely speaking to themselves. They scold themselves for their own mistakes or what they consider to be mistakes deep down."

"I'm asking you for the last time," Adam fumed through clenched teeth. "What interest do you have in me?"

"Did you not ask me to help you?"

"You gave me nothing, and I almost went insane!"

"That's your lack of patience."

"And why the hell did you threaten me with something happening to Nina?"

"I told you not to risk her so you'd wake up and start thinking of her more, you wrecking ball! The entire time I've been warning you about the trade-off of knowledge over Nina."

"Where's my synapticon?"

"I'm making sure it doesn't fall into the wrong hands."

"I want it back."

"You entertain me, Adam." Gorgonuy huffed and stretched contentedly, as if the argument had cheered him up. "Do you now have something to offer?"

"I won't turn you over to the cops."

"What would that be for?"

"Attempted poisoning. I kept the Siberian ampule that put me in a coma for two days."

"Do you mean the herbal tincture I gave you to calm your nerves?"

Adam got up, pulled the pins off the doll, and threw it on the ground. "You've never been to Siberia."

"Of course not."

"You didn't study at the Sorbonne."

"No."

"Are you even a professor in Cambridge?"

"I made it all up. I am lying. Hence, I am lying when I say I'm lying. Don't trust me."

"God damn it already." Adam slammed his fist on the table. "Give me my piece of paper, we'll say goodbye, and that's it."

"You do believe the paper holds some power over you, don't you? And that's very hard to reconcile with your rationality. That's what this is about. Not the data. The blood-signed deed is a crack in your beliefs. It will keep tearing until your simplistic rationality falls apart like a house of cards."

Adam was silent.

"Very well then. I might, in fact, declare this a victory." He took a sheet of paper out of his shirt pocket, spread it out, and slowly smelled it. Then, he carefully folded it along the lines and put it back. "Now, you want your bond paper, and that has a price. We both know that. What can you offer?"

"What do you want?"

"I will keep it with me. If something occurs to you, come and talk."

"No. We'll sort it out today."

"And how?"

"I don't care at all."

Gorgonuy was nodding. "Very well. Then grant me one wish, and I can promise you that we will never see each other again."

Adam stood and stepped slightly away, arms swaying. "What scam is this now?"

"You'll let me paint your portrait."

"Are you trying to joke? What year will it be from?"

"We'll see."

"An ordinary portrait," said Adam. "No abracadabra." He still didn't trust him.

Gorgonuy took out paint, brushes, and an easel. Adam would swear they hadn't been in the room until then. When he sat down, Gorgonuy was holding a blank canvas.

"Stand here and hold the candelabrum," he ordered and stepped up to the stand. Adam didn't see but felt how quickly and precisely Gorgonuy was painting. Like a butcher cutting up meat. Still, standing there was boring.

"What's the most interesting piece in that collection of yours?" he asked, half-interested.

"That's impossible to tell," Gorgonuy replied. "The documents reach back to the thirteenth century. You have just attempted to steal the third largest historic collection of people after King Solomon's and the Makkhab treasure." Gorgonuy again talked with that strange rhythm, as if chanting. "The first deeds were written in Persia under the rule of the Mongolian Khan Arghun. Because of this, as well as for other reasons, it was called Genghis Khan's Persian Regiment and the Babylonian Horde. A certain prince, exercising an astonishing lack of foresight, exchanged it for a hundred thoroughbreds. Since then, it's been expanded and tended to in Europe. Except during the Second World War, when de Gaulle's guerrillas helped hide it in Casablanca. There are the deeds of two Habsburgs, Maria de Medici, countless witches trying to redeem themselves from being burnt, the deed of Christopher Marlowe and Doctor Faustus Jr. himself."

"Show me that one," thought Adam, but the words did not leave his mouth, which was strange. He listened on to the twisting history of the collection, and its characters seeped into each other like rooks carrying a secret treasure over the Mediterranean Sea. Adam still waited for the Collector to finally appear in the story, and he waited in vain.

He was barely aware of Gorgonuy painting the last strokes. He walked around the canvas and stared into his own face, only it was the face of an old man. His eyes were more alive, restless. His hair was grey and thin. Yet, the thirty-year-old Adam saw that he was fifty years senior to that old man. The grey one only knew what the young one had taught him. He had only experienced what the young one had decided to do. The old Adam in the picture was the young Adam's greying grandson. And that's what they talked about: what will Adam live through and the old man remember?

"Of course I won't go," Adam was unyielding. "If I go to Japan, I'll never finish Faustomat. And I don't speak Japanese, so I can't study there, let alone work."

The old man in the painting was silent. The room was rocking under their feet, the canvas was undulating, and a wrinkled palm reached out from the painting. Adam held his breath. Gorgonuy stood aside. His eyes were shut, and he was swaying as though in a trance. Adam slowly stepped closer to the canvas and touched the bony hand. He felt his own pulse. There he was, between worlds. In a clueless place. The two beings, gravitating towards each other their entire lifetime in a story of proximity and distance, looked into each other's eyes. The point of birth and the point of death. Two blacksmiths, forging each other.

"As if you didn't know how I'd decide," Adam said.

The grayhead in the painting shrugged. "I just asked to pass the time."

He didn't believe him. "You know everything that happened. Are you telling me to go?"

"I know everything, but I remember bugger-all. See, youth can't imagine old age, which can't remember youth. Forget about me, Adam. I adore the human courage to march on regardless, boldly and cluelessly."

"But surely you remember if you travelled to Japan?"

"Ah, many times. What a stunning country." The pupils wavered for a moment and returned to him. "If you ever go there, go to Tōhoku. You won't find another place like it."

The painting rippled, became supple, and then hardened.

Adam was looking at a painting of an old man who was undoubtedly similar to him. He staggered and held on to the table. "What's this sorcery?"

Gorgonuy sat in the armchair next to the easel, huffing on his pipe. "There's heavy air here in the basement."

"I spoke with that codger." Adam pointed to the portrait. "You hypnotized me!" His voice cracked. "Who the hell are you?"

The storyteller smiled. "You solve one mystery, it spawns another. Here you are." He handed him a folded paper.

"I'm taking the portrait too," declared Adam.

Gorgonuy didn't move from the armchair; he just calmly put his hand on the canvas. "No, you are not."

Adam didn't argue either. He leaned over. "And what will you give me for this?" Just above the flames, he flipped the tarot card of the Magician.

"Please. It's not that valuable." Gorgonuy waved his hand. "I'll draw a new one."

"A copy?" Adam shook his head. "Would you risk that?"

Gorgonuy shifted in his seat, but Adam grabbed the candlestick first. "I remember what you said about the card well. Maybe I'm the Magician, and maybe you are. Shall we see?" He passed the edge of the card over the flame, and a new scent drifted through the air. "After all, if you really are just fabricating, as you claimed, then you have nothing to lose." The rim of the card blackened.

"Give it to me." Gorgonuy stretched his hand out and twitched his fingers.

The clash took place in silence. Each felt the other's pressure, his weight and balance.

"I'll trade it for the portrait."

The wick sputtered. Gorgonuy reddened, spat, and then croaked, "Take it!" He threw the painting at Adam. The card dropped to the ground, and Gorgonuy leapt for it. Adam managed to catch the canvas in flight, and the dropped candlestick fell into the chest of papers. Burning wax spilt across the pile, and a few parchment deeds went up in flames.

Adam didn't wait. Running out of the flat, he took the stairs three at a time and only stopped in his own room. He slammed the door shut, locked up, threw the portrait under the bed, and slid down onto the floor. Then, breathing heavily, he climbed under the blanket, and held it over his ears the whole time the firemen's siren blared down in the courtyard. There was no data archive. There never was one, he was suddenly certain, except in his mind. Still, it was so painful letting go of something that had never existed. He let out a sob. It was a splendid idea, and it was to remain one.

Like immortality. And time travel. And marrying Nina.

Ideas locked firmly in the form of ideas.

How *romantic*.

He gasped for air. The crazy move had resolved nothing. The attempt to step out of the clueless place turned against itself. He simply had one more portrait, of himself in a hundred years, perhaps, and a few last days before she would fly away. How *romantic*.

When the firemen finally left and the blue lights of three police cars illuminated the courtyard instead, he messaged Nina that they had to see each other, swallowed two melatonin pills, and waited.

The

of T

Gift
Time

How ridiculous and how strange to be surprised at anything which happens in life.
—Marcus Aurelius

The

police only arrived at Adam's apartment the next morning, and it was downright liberating after his restless night. The officers apologized and briefly explained that there was a fire in the college's basement.

"Was anyone hurt?"

"No one, thank God. There was a bunch of old trash down there, but we still have to investigate. It could have gone much worse."

"It really could have," he assured them.

"Regulations, you know. Do you know of anything that could be related to the fire?"

"Such as?"

"Did you see anyone here in the last few days who shouldn't have been here?"

"There's a lot of people milling around the college. Tourists and such."

They wrote it down.

"You look tired. Don't take your studies so seriously," laughed the younger one, handing him a flyer. "If you recall anything, call this number. Otherwise, have a nice rest of your life."

It was almost too easy. He made eggs for breakfast and called Krugele. After a month of ruminating, he was done in three minutes. And Nina messaged back, saying she was free for a while after lunch.

They ordered coffee. She seemed agitated and spoke about a few bits and pieces, sensitively trying to pass over the fact that all the pieces were linked to her flight to Tokyo. She looked positively ethereal, and yet was the only one who Adam could possibly consider a fixed point in his universe. He breathed in.

"I want to be with you."

"No, you don't."

"Why do you say that?"

"You're cheating on me, Adam."

Adam nearly swallowed his entire latte. "What are you on about?"

There was nothing to argue about. "I found the panties you hid in your notes."

"God! Those were Marquis'!"

"And you can't think of anything more stupid."

"I swear." Adam's pupils went wide, and Nina von Tokyo saw such inane innocence in them, it took her by surprise. "Well ... then ... I have to confess something. And I don't know if you'll want to be with me after this."

"You slept with someone."

"Those portraits ... were from me."

Adam's mouth fell open, and his confused features once again surprisingly matched her father's.

"I know, it sounds awful now," she explained dejectedly. "You must be really mad at me. But you never had time. And I didn't want to be nagging and whining. You just needed more time, didn't you? So I gave you a few extra centuries." She ran a hand through her hair. "When we were with Professor Gorgonuy, you said—"

"He's not a professor."

"Do you remember? You said that, if you were immortal, you'd love me more ... so that's what I did. I made you immortal." In that moment, Adam's face overlapped with her father's perfectly, like their death and immortality. And she finally told both of them what she had wanted to say for a long time: "It got a bit out of hand, didn't it?"

"No." He shook his head. All of that terror with such a simple explanation? "No. An examiner confirmed that the painting was two hundred years old."

"Oh, that's flattering. I'll pretend it partially offsets the fortune I paid for the eighteenth-century canvas and paints. That's the oldest trick in forgery. I was just scared that you'd catch the cab. We kept getting red lights."

Of course, he realized slowly and clearly. The madness, his pissed trousers, and two days in a mandrake coma were all, in the larger scheme of things, of his own making. It was his wish for immortality that he now wished he had never wished.

"But the last portrait was in Grandma's coffin bag."

A kind of panicked dismay flooded her face. "I thought, well, that you'd been unfaithful to me and that we'd break up anyway. So I just wanted to get rid of it for good."

"And the photo on your camera ..."

Nina waved her hand. "That was fun and easy."

"You were lying to me the entire time, Nina."

"It was my school project," sighed Nina unhappily.

He stirred the cream in his coffee. "My madness was, in fact, your conceptual art piece."

She wrinkled her nose and nodded carefully. "*The Gift of Time.*"

"A gift? Are you sure?"

"It's what you make of it," she suggested.

Adam waved to the waitress. "We'll pay."

Nina took a breath and nodded sadly, but he stopped her. "It is what you make of it. You're right. That's why I'm going to Japan with you, love."

"Don't joke around."

"I can't joke. I called Krugele this morning and told him to find another clown."

"That's absolute and perfect nonsense."

"Yup. It doesn't make any logical sense. It's completely indefensible. And it resolves absolutely everything."

"But you can't. You—"

He laughed. "I want you in my life. You're more important to me than anything else."

"More important than the Faustomat?"

"Will you ban me from coding in Tokyo?"

"Yes, I will." She frowned. "Every weekend for the rest of your life."

"I'll take that under one condition."

"Which is?"

"You'll make me a stamp of the cosmic order in Japanese."

She laughed, and he spread his arms. "We're going to Japan."

In that embrace, he compressed all of Nina's futures, and his own, into a single, real, shared one. His stomach clenched, but why not? Why not? Arms in the air and scream in terror! Life! Rid of logic, he plummeted forward on the wings of the pure, indefensible knowledge that it didn't hurt to kick his own butt with all his might once in a while, to fly onwards a bit.

They'd get married and have children. Together, they could mutually keep themselves human. And Nina would be a wonderful mum; he could see that in her. She'd know how to smile at their child so it wouldn't cry, so its brain would solidify into joy. They'd have the world shown to them again, this time by a tiny teacher whose fantasy was not yet exhausted by years of logical consequences, tamed by money, corrupted by experience.

And Adam's grand moment wouldn't be far away either. He saw it vividly: a three-year-old girl running toward him, crying because she got vertigo in front of the mirror. "I am there," she'll say to her father, upset, as though she'd opened her eyes for the first time. He'll talk about the self, how no one knows where we come from and each of us will die one day. Somehow, she'll sense that Adam can't help her with the mysteries of life and death in any way, and the realization will burn half her brain out. And from that ash, a human will slowly begin to grow. Adam will open a bottle of Baron de Lestac or perhaps Tinto Negro Mole. And over the many years that follow, with tenderness and admiration, he'll observe her steps on the long journey toward the learned art of living.

"We can't both live off my scholarship. How will you make money?"

"Stop being so reasonable," he whispered. "We're flying to Japan together."

And that's the end of the story. What continues is life. Because life always goes on. And it turns what had seemed like an entire story into an episode. And what looked like the perfect present into one of many parallel timelines.

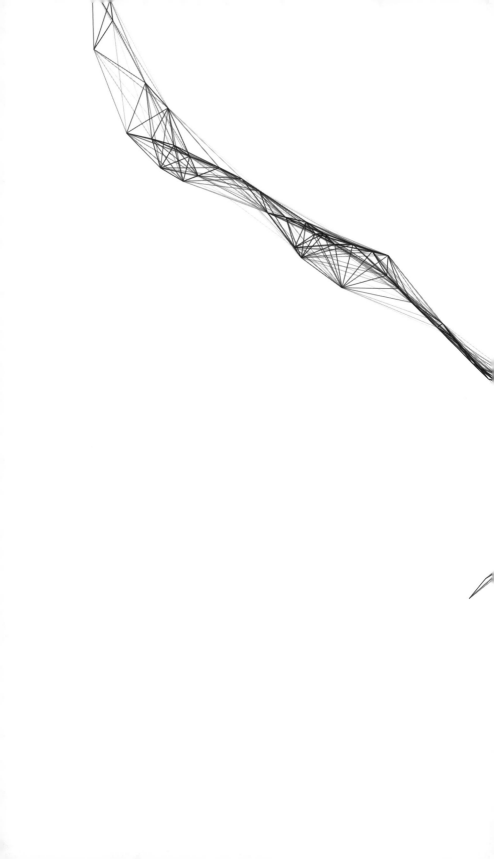

Epilogue

So you see. I wanted to lend you one book and ended up leading you through my library. Well, I won't lie—I suspected it would end this way again. I lean towards the position that a book is granted its meaning by the library in which it lies. And it's all the truer for people—the flock and so on, you understand. Still, I do have a favorite among all of these portraits and reflections of mine. It isn't the painting by Gorgonuy, in which he drew me with such ghastly precision that, today, it looks like a Venetian mirror—I could shave in front of it.

I've long resigned myself to never knowing what being entered my life then or what happened to him and his collection in that fire. But I was surprised when that conversation with my young self returned to me in a dream, fairly recently. It fit word for word, and we did shake hands at the end. If it was a dream, then it was the kind of dream from which one awakens as though one had walked over a footbridge from shore to shore, and nothing distinguishes the two banks—they mirror one another.

My favorite portrait is the last image of this white book: The Data Scientist Flies to Japan. What do you think—how did he feel at the time? Was he free or blind? In love or addicted? That is the moment, the one angle from which

I wanted to show you the boy, so you'd understand his black book. The day he let go of the crutches of logic and abandoned his rationalist culture and its stronghold, Cambridge.

Statistically, the moment is irrelevant. An outlier. I almost never behaved like that. And in my eyes, it is this entirely uncharacteristic decision that was most human. It was the step that was impossible to calculate. The moment of phase change. Today, I'd claim the entire black diary, and the events described therein, were echoes of the enormous energy released as I walked through the crucible of paradox and emerged from the smoke on the other side. But maybe it's just that everything is getting scrambled in my head over the grave, the universe, and all. So be it.

Well, then. Do you recall my question?

Am I real or fictional?

If you are able to tell me with a straight face that I am just made up, then I congratulate you from my heart. Perhaps even with a hint of jealousy, although that's a strong word at my age. Because a story about a fictional character can conclude, and conclude with a punchline. And you can keep the happy image of two lovers, departing for the sun. Don't spoil it with the black book. Even if you had already dipped into it, what of that? What value does a fictional character's diary have? Let me tell you, hold on to the happy ending if you can.

The story's over.

I bid you farewell. But do as you please. The candle burns, and there are heaps of wax in case you did want to read on. You can stay till the morning light. I'll finally lie down and relish falling asleep with the woman of my life. Can't do it too many more times, after all. So long, and, most of all, good digestion.

The Book

A Para

Isabella

de for

of Castile

The

The rich tend to mistake their bank accounts for self-worth. The famous, their number of fans. The beautiful, their daily approaches from strangers. The muscular, their body mass. The orderly, their punctuality. The intelligent, the number of their quips. Such a variety of scales—and one thing in common: they all use a scale that favors them. Indeed, many find it easier to measure themselves by the number of problems they don't have to solve, rather than the number of problems solved.

As for me, it's been my feeling for quite some time that it isn't money, fans, or muscles that make us human. When I searched for a more appropriate measure of life—eager to weigh human life by its own intrinsic value—I sought its core. And, in my view, there is nothing more intrinsic to human nature—and, therefore, no better (more general, more natural, more elementary) measure of human quality—than one's progress along the axis of awareness (exploration, understanding).

This is not a heady academic phrase. I have myself embarked on this existential adventure, guiding my cognition toward its most essential and basic subject, the self—literally, that is. When you turned back to Europe, I headed forward, toward the unseen end of existence. This is the diary of the days that followed, conveyed in the simplest language I could muster. If there were an ideal dialect beneath these pages, it would feel rugged and unpolished as *kutani-yaki* pottery. Hardened by fire, brittle.

1

When the West runs into philosophical difficulties, it likes to hop on a plane to Delhi, take a bus to an ashram, and get its grey matter washed white with koans. It's become something of a beaten path. "Forget words," says its signpost. "Wisdom leaves through dialogue but comes by silence."

Some pilgrims return smirking, confiding that the East is largely a fraud. They sink back to the paradoxes of the West, this time consoled by the knowledge that there is no escape.

Others, by their own accounts—and I actually trust them—do glimpse a different order of the world. Typically, they return suffering speech blackouts. They respond to questions with an array of sighs, knowing smiles, vague allusions to "epiphany," incoherent parables, and a general paralysis of explanatory skill. Such is the curse of the Eastern path: where one enters without words, one must also leave without them.

The Western path, on the other hand, is the path of the word. This is the path I have striven to follow, for I am a Westerner to the core. The printing press, the dialogue, and the skeptical attack are as much a part of my method of advance as the repeatable experiment.

~—

When Christopher Columbus returned from his grand voyage to the West, he did not bring back a map of the new landmass, nor a geographical survey outlining its mineral riches, nor a business plan for the settlement of that land. He did not present a census of the indigenous people, nor a military strategy for their conquest.

What he brought was a carnival of curiosity: brightly colored parrots. Bananas and pineapples. Ten half-naked pagans. Cotton. Aloe and fandangles. Upon landing, he mounted a parade in the palace of Queen Isabella of Castile and she, impressed, perhaps astounded, sent further ships to explore the new territory.

This diary is that parade for Isabella.

❦

An academic, a creature of thoughts, nowadays writes like someone trapped in the trenches. His defense preempts all attacks. He blocks all routes a skeptic might take, making his writing heavy, closed, fearful. The academic writes an apology for the travesty of thought.

A love letter, on the other hand, is cast like a spear. Swift and sinful. Let this diary be such a love letter.

It is very important that what I have to say is not lost in metaphor. I do admit to having pondered wrapping my coarse words in a story. On my walks in the wide Himalayan valleys, far from the villagers, I heard myself weaving sermons that filled the air and echoed back from the mountaintops. Do not doubt that I could have forged them into a cult. But to me, such veils would not be a display of skill, they would be displays of cowardice.

Let me start where we left off—on the day you left Japan. After two years, you'd finally had enough Japanese sediment. You were ready to return to Europe. Return home, despite having no home. And I told myself that while you were a traveler, I'd gradually awakened the adventurer within. I had to finish Faustomat and see where that would take me. Without limits. Without you. For once, I felt ready to live the life of Marquis. I admit it.

So you hugged me at Narita International Airport and really didn't want to cry—and you managed. I slipped the cosmic order stamp into your pocket and walked through the glass doors to the escalators. I returned to our apartment, which was now missing all of your things. I found the stamp back in my pocket when I reached for my keys. You always were a step ahead.

It took me precisely six days to get tired of Japan. You had managed to take all the colors with you. In the following months I grew somber and translucent, but on the sixth of April (much later than expected), Faustomat was finished.

Of course I never got that digital archive from Cambridge. I don't think it ever existed, but that's irrelevant. Turns out it's not that hard to find other databases online—some public, some stolen. I had British and American police investigation archives, used clandestinely by debt-collecting companies: life stories told in cars and mortgages, benefit claims and bankruptcies, church affiliations and criminal records. I had medical records, lifestyle profiling, and voting histories. All this is terrifyingly easy to get. I released the final version of Faustomat onto the cloud, set up alerts to frantically

text me when the code hit on the mother of all fractal correlations, and forgot about it.

That was the time when I started reading anything I could get my hands on. I switched from Kant's philosophy to Marlowe's *Doctor Faustus*, logical paradoxes, fractal modelling, supersymmetric quantum mechanics, Bohm's holographic universe, information theory, Elliott's market waves, the rise and fall of Eastern empires, and the Japanese art of composition. I devoured data like I was trying to compete with Faustomat. We were both crawling through the internet, desperately craving grand symmetries. And the topics were not chosen consciously. My wandering thoughts simply followed the scent of paradox.

Months passed, and I eventually found myself near those dark places that had made me piss my pants in front of Gorgonuy and swallow the *kharakhoi* that knocked me out for two days. But I believed that I wouldn't fall into the same hole again. Since I couldn't rely on anyone but myself, I carefully controlled my level of exhaustion, tamed my obsessive mind with yoga, and dared to go further every week. I wasn't going to give up this time. I knew myself enough to see that there was some kind of mountain pass towards which my life was inevitably rising. Faustomat now seemed like a bonsai of a grander vision, my real Great Work. So one day, I packed up and travelled to the Tōhoku region. I found a B&B on the shore and moved in without a check-out date.

(I'd like to write that this was the first I'd heard of Tōhoku, but that's not true. I heard about it for the first time from my eighty-year-old self, when Gorgonuy was drawing my portrait. The night the fire broke out in Pembroke. I never told you [or anyone else] what happened but I will when we meet. You won't believe me.)

My room had a wooden floor, a foldable mattress, and two bowls—one for water, one for food. That was all and it was enough. The owners sometimes offered a suggestion on where to go for a walk along the sea. In the midst of nature, I made it clear to myself that the only alternative to resolving those old riddles was brain damage. I packed my skull with paradoxes and let it broil like a pressure cooker. It was another six weeks before it blew up.

I walked along the beach boulders in a trance for hours on end, asking the question to which all others led: what enables this boulder, such a distinct object from myself, to be not only out there but in my eyes, in my mind too? What is it, I asked, pressing two pebbles together in my fist, that allows me to feel through the separation of subject and object? What's granting me the privilege of an observer? What strange ability, belonging neither to me nor to the sea?

I stood on the beach and the waves broke under my feet. A few islands dotted the horizon and above them hung a single, enormous cloud the color of a hushed fire. I closed my eyes and pierced holes into my blind spot, so many holes that the rays of late afternoon light finally found their way in. A word (fragile, cautious, new-born) floated through and hesitantly touched my consciousness. I mumbled it, took a few more steps—and, capitulating to a place that bears reflections of all corners of the world, I laughed, cried, and sang that most obvious of words. Waist-deep in waves, I saw my face in the sea, laughing at the sky, and I choked on happiness.

"I see," I repeated between laughter and tears.

Today, I can give that moment a name. The experience bore a remarkable likeness to what others describe as enlightenment. For several long hours, I was one with all around me; I saw the world from a shockingly fresh perspective. To my utter, stunned surprise, the thoughts that led me there, those powder-dry bits of thought I'd kept collecting for years, had reached a critical mass. In a sudden and violent ignition, a chain reaction was unleashed, melting and amalgamating the fragments into a stream of fascinating insights. The self-induced psychedelic round-the-world flight illuminated mental landscapes and dimensions I was for the first time invited to gaze upon. They had always been there—it was only my eyes that opened that day. I had reached the alchemical union of opposites and completed my Grand Work. I finally understood the link between statistics and mysticism: *ordo ab chao*. And I became one with the strange loop of the ouroboros. (I am aware of Gorgonuy's clues and have not a single comment on their significance in the direction of my life. I am neither grateful nor resentful toward him. It happened, period.)

Some would call it transcendence, but I smile at that word. Transcendence is an arrow pointing in the wrong direction: a signpost "East" pointing to the West. Why, there is nothing to transcend.

Others would give that moment a much humbler name: a breakthrough. I later realized that this same experience may be triggered by other means. Meditation, yoga, psychedelics, a deep appreciation of nature, a shock that shakes one's beliefs to the bone and beyond. It is understandable that the path through which one reaches this place is also the path by which one typically departs it. So, for better or worse, it was words that carried me along the Western path, and words were what I took back. That afternoon was only the beginning of another year of research. For the second time now, I am organizing the bouquet of ideas that bloomed from that flash of inspiration.

With the benefit of hindsight, though, I like to call the event a change of perspective. A new mental model. If I say it just for you: when you change the model, you get a different painter.

⬇

Here in Darjeeling, people gather in one hut in the evenings. They cook, weave, draw mandalas for tourists, and share stories. It's almost as sublime as it sounds. I enjoy listening as they talk of gods and beasts, of Milarepa, Buddha, and King Ashoka, the same story many times over.

Once, they asked if I would like to tell a story too. I was shy—I don't know any stories. I was a mathematician, I protested. And they said, "Tell us a story about mathematics, then."

Blushing, I began telling them about Leonardo of Pisa, the son of an Italian customs officer of the name Bonaccio, and one of my few heroes. Back in the 12th century, growing up in an Italian merchant family based in a trading post in Algeria was a rather unique experience—Leonardo would be one of a mere handful of people of his time in whose mind collided two great civilizations. Fifty years before Marco Polo, three centuries before Columbus.

Back then, it was the Arab world that considered itself heir to Ancient Greece. In the first millennium, when Christian dogma ravished

13

the remains of the Roman Empire, priests and their useful idiots burned whatever books they could lay their hands on. For every text was either in opposition to the Bible, hence heretical, or in accord with it, hence redundant. When the Christians destroyed the Great Library of Alexandria and blamed it on the Arabs, Hellenic knowledge was in fact preserved thanks to Arabic merchants. During the worst memocide in human history, they smuggled scripts and books to the more benevolent kingdoms of the Middle East. And it was the Arab world, carrying the ancient legacy of the sciences, that young Leonardo encountered as a child.

With his father, he would trade with both the Italians and the Arabs—with the Italians, using Roman numerals and the abacus; with the Arabs, using their Indian method with altogether different numeral symbols, the elegant decimal place value notation, and the fascinating *al-khwarizmis of al-jabr*, the algorithms of algebra. Being a merchant, he also learned two strikingly different ways of recording trade. And he studied with the best Arab mathematicians of the time.

At the age of 32, he wrote down his findings in *Liber Abaci* (The Book of Calculating), a unique encyclopedia of 13th century mathematics. Leonardo signed the book "filius Bonacci," or, in short, Fibonacci. Today, he is widely credited for one curious sequence of numbers, the Fibonacci sequence, which was explained, among other things, in the manuscript's six hundred pages. Surprisingly, nobody celebrates his greater feat: the introduction of Arabic numerals to Europe, which he accomplished in the same prodigious volume. But what is truly criminal is the failure to acknowledge his most impressive legacy: Western capitalism.

Liber Abaci was not a well-known book in Fibonacci's lifetime. In his zeal, youth, and naivety, he crammed it with the sum total of his mathematical insights. As a consequence, few people read it. It was too thick and too dense to gain popularity. Then, twenty years later, he wrote another book—almost a booklet—a brief and simple guide for merchants, explaining the basics of Arab trade records. In the simplest terms, he explained Arabic numerals as well as their curious habit of recording each transaction not once but twice. The booklet became an instant hit. Tradesmen appreciated how much easier it was

to add and multiply with place-value notation, compared with the dominant Roman numerals. (Try adding DXVIII and MCDIX without converting to Arabic!) This innovation amounted to nothing but a change of representation, a shift from one kind of symbols to another, but it profoundly transformed the economy of Europe. Numeracy spread like wildfire—by the middle of 14th century, numeracy in Europe rose from 1% of the population to 30%. And that was the perfect entrée for the second topic of Fibonacci's booklet, no less insightful.

Meet Giacomo, a humble, hardworking shoemaker in 13th-century Florence. He has some leather—enough for, say, six pairs of shoes. He also has ten finished pairs and his lifetime savings of four gold florins. When he sells a few pairs of shoes, he buys more leather; but never more than what his gold coins can afford.

There's a knock on his door. Fibonacci's booklet enters. Giacomo has it read to him, and, gradually, a new understanding seeps in. He learns to record purchases and sales in such a way that those shoes—finished and unfinished, his stock—are now more than simply a number of pairs. By using this clever technique, known today as double-entry bookkeeping, Giacomo now knows the *value* of his stock. When it's time to purchase leather again, instead of counting his gold coins, he can show his partners what value is locked in his stock. He can value assets in cash terms. He can now take on debt from a moneylender against this value. Thus, the business loan is invented, debt becomes a commodity, capitalism is born. Giacomo can now produce goods on a promise, rather than barter, and the value of the economy increases by the value of future production. Giacomo gets richer, so does his moneylender, and so do others.

"Wait," you might say, "did accounting really bring about capitalism, rather than the other way round?" Oh yes. The original, poor Giacomo sees his shoes as just that, shoes. The things you put on feet so feet don't bloody freeze. He sees his gold florins as just what they are: metal coins. Those things that you exchange for other things. And these two different types of things, shoes and gold, like apples and pears, do not get added together. They get counted in isolation. It is double-entry bookkeeping that gives both a common denominator: value. For each and every transaction, one record shows where

value came from, the other, where it has gone. Value flows between different forms, from gold to leather to shoes to gold, and does not vanish as the forms do.

And let's stay precise. Accounting did not create this value. It allowed value to be *recognized*. It brought an alternate view of the shoemaker's shop, a novel way to see goods, a new representation, less tangible, more abstract. The solid shoes could now be seen as equivalent to future sales, to future gold, to capital. And gold underwent the same alchemical metamorphosis: by acknowledging the value of debt (equivalent again to future gold), debt was commoditized, and it became easy to take it on as well as issue it. Thus, money was liberated from gold. And the consequences were nothing but stunning.

In the 14th century, the first European financial powerhouse to adopt, perfect, and exploit double-entry bookkeeping was the Medici bank. The Medici family came to understand the power of commoditized debt and its unique property, financial leverage. Quickly gaining enormous wealth compared to everyone else, it was them—their money and their patronage—that allowed for the advent of the Italian Renaissance in Florence and the return of independent, radical thought to Europe. I would argue that it is quite sensible to attribute the subsequent rise of Western civilization to that original harbinger of light, Leonardo Fibonacci. Or, to the light he brought: a subtle change of perspective.

You have no idea how much they liked the story and how often they wanted me to repeat it. I alternated weekly between Diderot and Fibonacci and the villagers sat as quietly as church mice. It was the same dark irony as teaching English in Japan. Sometimes, it's more important to entertain than to be understood, but I'm still fighting with it.

Bloody love letter be damned to flaming hell. I'm starting from scratch again. Last time, my writing being nearly finished, a stealthy evening brought back the memory that I exchanged love for a small stack of black leather-bound journals. Yes, ma'am, a loved being for

a love letter. A furious solitude beset me and I ripped the pages out of the stupid notebook, threw them in the fire one after the other, and watched them burn to ash.

And now I'm sitting by the gas lamp writing again. Not because I feel like I have something to say to humanity and not because it's so much fun, either. I hate it. It's twisting my brain. But I could never explain to you what happened—and why—in person. So let's see how far I get this time.

✈

Even when we were together, I had a bunch to say about obviousness. Like when the Japanese would slurp their soup so loud we could hear it outside the restaurant. When they apologetically kicked you out of the spa because of your tattoo. Or their horror every time I stepped on the *tatami* in shoes. I don't even want to remember the one time I was teaching in-house and walked around the entire evening in their bathroom slippers. There was a pink note on them next time, saying *only for the bathroom*. They were too embarrassed to tell me outright so that I wouldn't lose face in front of them. You know how often we spoke of their, or our, obviousness. Trivialities, compared to what broke loose in my mind after Tōhoku.

Through the obvious, one may climb up level after level, like on a ladder. Every next level is invisible, as long as one sees only *one*: one understanding of shoes, one understanding of gold. That is the understanding that settles in the mind spontaneously like sediment. There's only *one*, therefore it's obvious. Then comes Leonardo and he wants to explain a new perception of shoes, and the mind must perform a difficult step—remove the concept from obviousness. That's why Leonardo demonstrates how it is possible to see shoes as a number, and whoever reads his book eventually bursts out laughing with the recognition that there are at least two kinds of shoes—one of them solid, the other abstract. He can compare. He sees how it would be possible to propose a third view of shoes. But above the two or three representations, there is now something that is again *one*, for whose name he has to search lengthily to climb higher on the ladder of abstraction.

And now, what happened to my mind in Tōhoku. Once a change of representation has been performed on some single, far-reaching idea, it follows that this method of enrichment, of multiplication, can be performed on every last one of them. On *all* ideas. On ideas about ideas. The method can be applied to the method itself. In every thinkable direction, an infinity of directions bursts forth. Wherever there was obvious simplicity, a deep fractal rainbow blooms and in it another one, two, a billion. Damn! Having just learned to multiply viewpoints, the mind gapes into the newly unfolded dimension—an endless, mesmerizing complication of thought—never to return to the original ignorance! Pull my ears and call me a donkey. In every imaginable direction, infinity stretches like disembodied fractal bowels. (It is not the shift from one representation of the world to another that is so disorienting. It is the shocking systematic realization that such a shift is possible.) Fully aware that the whole of infinite possibilities of all ideas is a little tough to embrace, the self launches into this most marvelous leap into the Sun … within.

This love letter, this parade for Isabella, is a diary of that jump—or rather a fall, as I did not take it intentionally but out of my inability to avoid it. Already years ago, I believe, back in Cambridge, I had held enough data for the paradoxes to emerge. But the mental demand of the transformation was too high, as was my schoolboy panic. This second time, in the months after I suffered enlightenment—I kid you not—my brain bled. Day and night, from January to fall, mind and body in tortures mutual, I found myself once again forced to devote all available strength to the unending and uncontrolled rapture that raged in the ravines of my brain. In this explosion of abstract thought, this metamorphosis of the whole of thought into an alternate crystalline structure, this inflation of a linear universe into a fractal flower, my fear of madness again shook my hands. But this time, I had the Tōhoku vision to hold onto. This time I understood with an elementary clarity that, at the end of the rabbit hole, there was another mind.

The one writing to you today.

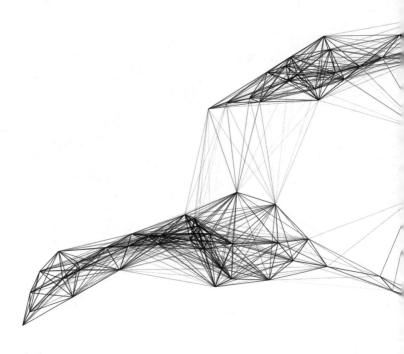

The
of Ari

Fruit
stotle

All the idols made by man, however terrifying they may be, are in point of fact
subordinate to him, and that is why he will always have it in his power to destroy them.
—Simone de Beauvoir

I should probably explain why I've been in India for the last half a year. A few weeks after the breakthrough in Tōhoku, I terminated my lease and bought a one-way ticket from Tokyo to Delhi. Once there, I followed the usual tourist track to the east, through Varanasi. I have never been much of a traveler. Now I was wandering around this foreign and overwhelming country, in no hurry, ingesting its earthy medicines and dirty poisons. It consumed me even more than Japan. I travelled on trucks and banged up steam trains through the dust and dirt of poor people's lives, without emotional immunity to the hordes of children begging for an apple, apple, please sir, apple.

While it was not my plan, one day, all the way in Darjeeling, I hit upon a mountain village of Tibetan émigrés. I rented a room with one of the families. It wasn't long before I was learning their style of cooking and even herding yaks on the hills. Occasionally I would experiment with heating and irrigation, to improve one or the other. They laughed at me, and it didn't do any good, but the children got into the habit of sitting with me in the evenings so I could teach them math using stones and twigs. It wasn't long before I didn't have to pay for the room and board, and I had most of the day to think.

How could I not have seen it before? Why did I never consider the most obvious solution—that the parallel paradoxes in art theory, math, philosophy, political economy, and my forlorn love life might stem from a single, more fundamental source? In fact, I had felt this, I honestly had. But for a long time, I'd believed it was human nature itself, elementary and unchallengeable, that dictated our biases and our paradoxes. Only in Tōhoku had something begun to peel off the shapeless depth of my nature, something deeper than thoughts, deeper than dreams and desires.

It had become less obvious and more tangible, its contours beginning to protrude, until the culprit finally moved into plain sight. For thirty years, it had been part of my nature—inseparable, now separated. I could finally give it a name. I played around with it, examined why and how it worked, and finally called it a *toy model of the universe*. It is not a thing, but it says how things behave. It is not a story, but it gives stories shape. It is not a value system, but it influences how

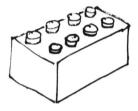

THE FRUIT OF ARISTOTLE

values are formed, thus thoroughly shaping the direction of one's life.

Newborns don't have it; first-graders do. They glean it from their parents and peers as a cultural treasure, through fairy tales, smiles, and reprimands. The parent, unaware of this crucial layer of knowledge, unaware of passing it to the child, passes it on nonetheless, no matter if their parenting was great or horrid.

To say I was shocked to find this cultural infection inside my consciously cultivated self would be an understatement. It felt like pushing a lump out of my brain and discovering that it wasn't an organic peculiarity but a computer chip. The true stunner, though, came once I tracked down who built the damn thing and found it wasn't my parents or grandparents. It bore the marks of a much more ancient maker, who had taken some vague outlines and forged them into a precise mechanism—a guy called Aristotle. Now, that really got me.

When traditional *kampo* doctors in Tokyo, following from the Chinese herbalists, spoke about heat in the kidney and dampness in the liver, it was obvious to me that they didn't mean *kidney* and *heat*—that they were using a metaphor, a model. But I always thought the Western approach was reality itself. On the contrary, Watson. It's a model just as much. Its several key components fit together so well that they mutually resist disassembly. If one is challenged, the others unite in defense.

Ultimately, all the constituents have to be rejected at once. As Wittgenstein observed:

"Philosophy is like trying to open a safe with a combination lock: each little adjustment of the dials seems to achieve nothing; only when everything is in place does the door open."

Sapere aude, here is the door.

T

Absolute truth. I imagine explaining the word *truth* to a four-year-old. Say, to the little girl I wish I had with you. "Truth is a tyrannical dictator, a concrete demon, an arrogant Narcissus," is not the sentence I'd choose. Instead, overwhelmed by her trusting eyes, my consciousness would be momentarily hijacked by another belief, the belief of *my own* four-year-old self, resurfacing out of mythos. A barbarian springing forth through my mouth, eager to plunder and procreate.

"Truth is always how it is."

I could have foreseen the response.

"Why?"

"Because people think that's how it is."

"Why?"

I'd attempt to explain the old view that there's one certain way that the world is (reality). And that, following this belief, it is easy to imagine that a complete description of that pure reality, called Truth, resides somewhere, up above, forever eluding humanity's imperfect grasp. This common, intuitive idea of truth takes on a nearly physical form; it floats up above, wholesome, absolute, and can be approached by means of rational thought. Perhaps I would even sketch this truth for her.

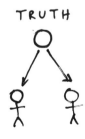

"This perfect truth, darling," I would say, "is the same for everyone. It knows best, even better than Mummy. It's always right. And that's why the other kids don't want to play with it." And I would leave most for later: that this is but one face of the word "truth," though one widely recognized. That someone deeply accustomed to speaking of truth could well assume that it does, indeed, exist. That this single picture I just drew is responsible for every playground fight, every hatred, every world war.

Its virtues are projected directly into the Christian version of God:

And then I would also omit that, despite joking about truth that knows more than Mummy, I'd just helplessly infected her with the Aristotelian disease.

The Ideal. Like every celebrity, truth loves to pose alone but can't survive without company. I'm reading Silvestre, the only book I brought to India:

"So push a little harder and swing above the ruler, above religion, climb on, above perfect good, absolute truth and the axis of power, another step, where muscles merge into one controlling mechanism. Don't let your head spin! There, in the clouds, you'll spot a single thought: that somewhere above you, there's a singular ideal."

What a powerful notion. The single ideal above us justifies the conviction that there is a single scale by which to measure people—the

common denominator behind snobbery, racism, totalitarian regimes, envy, and anorexia.

I got rid of this for good in Japan. My original understanding of the world had been *westernized*. We used to talk about it all the time, remember? Europe this, Asia that. So many things lost their obviousness and drifted into consciousness as we found three alternative ideals for each Western one. I can still feel the strange taste of their favorite *umeboshi*, the dull desserts that proved impossible to eat, watermelons in the shape of a heart or the documentary about becoming a Japanese astronaut—hundreds of applicants folding origami for a week and then a team of psychologists examining their paper cranes to see if they could cope with boredom. And how the Japanese explain why they wear a face mask when they have a cold: it would be immoral to infect someone, or, even worse, to miss work. I can't say I identified with Japanese ideals, but they estranged me from the Western ones.

🕊

I can't stand this anymore. It's evening again; I should be meditating my head off, but instead, I'm smoking one cigarette after the other. I'd decided to write everything down before getting in touch with you, but it can't go on like this. Tomorrow, I'll walk a few hours down to the village where they have internet and wireless signal, and I'll call. I have to hear you. Otherwise I'll smoke myself to ashes with this Indian tobacco. I can tell it's probably not a good idea, but as soon as I thought of it, some huge weight came off my shoulders. I'd run down right now if I had a flashlight. So I'll write into the night as punishment, and tomorrow I'll go. Bright, giant, Indian stars, stand by me. I can't wait!

𝍏

Logic. Drawn by the distant ideal of truth, humans set forth to attain it. They advance by being reasonable, rational, logical. By this, I propose, we do not mean what mathematics began to call *logic* in the

26

20th century (a system of reasoning freely chosen from among many possibilities). We don't ask each other at cocktail parties, "Have you thought about this from the perspective of intuitionist logic?" or, "Dear, I feel like having a fuzzy logic day; let's see where I end up sleeping." We use the term *logic* (and hence reason, rationality) in its medieval meaning of a single, ideal method of thought, which, in medieval times—and only then—was a reference to one specific kind of logic: Aristotelian logic. In short, Aristotle's view of what organized thought is and how a good argument is made.

But in Aristotle's time, stoic logic dominated. Likewise, Aristotle's successor as head of the Athens school, Theophrastus of Eresus, was already modifying Aristotle's work. However, the manuscripts of stoic logic, Theophrastus' works, and other streams of this discordant discussion are lost. Arabic, and later medieval Latin scholarship, absorbed Aristotle's *Organon*, as if it was an unparalleled work, and it became the central point of reference, sinking into the obvious until it blended with absolute truth.

By his own claim, Aristotle was the first philosopher to organize the very method of his reasoning into a system of logic. In a seminal philosophical breakthrough, he pointed out that besides his opinions, his method was also worthy of discussion. What he didn't see was that his logic was a product of his toy model of the universe (the one I am describing), which he inherited from his parents, from earlier Greek philosophers, and they in turn from the Egyptians and other ancient cultures. Had he had a different model of the universe, he would have reflected on his own reasoning in a different manner, written a different *Organon*, and laid the foundations of a different Western civilization.

Aristotle's logic rests firmly on the law of the excluded middle. Consequently, it is supposedly always capable of establishing whether a statement is true or not. But it's the other way around, you know. To someone with a hammer, everything looks like a nail. Once you start following this logic, pairs of opposites spring up everywhere (black and white, flock and birds). Between them, the tension of enemies, the emptiness of trenches. It was a perfect weapon in Aristotle's time because Greek dialogue was a combat sport: one

wins, the other loses. This logic allows no draws. No respect for a differing view. No empathy. This view of truth, ideal and logic, gives rise to the concept of the human as a rational being.

I still remember how I felt when your friend burst into tears over a coffee in the university library, after I'd explained to her that even though her thesis was due in three days, she'd do best to restart from scratch. "Why are you such a stuck up brat?" you'd asked me, and I'd felt ... like God.

⤳

Linear causation. It's been two years since we last saw each other. I often ponder whether the breakup was necessary for me to travel to Tōhoku and then India, or whether perhaps we could have been here together. You know what they say—everything happens for a reason. I don't know if that's how it is. Faustomat is searching for that answer and might take forever. In any case, "everything happens for a reason" is the unavoidable position when logic becomes the dominant way of approaching reality. It is both a consequence and a premise of this way of thinking. Every effect must be preceded by its cause and every action must cause a reaction. Thus events chain together, one after the other, in a con-*sequence*.

So I could trace back what led to my breakthrough: it wouldn't have happened without my breakdown in Cambridge (when the paradoxes got burned deep into my subconscious to await resolution for several years). That would not have happened without Gorgonuy and his ingenious manipulations. He wouldn't have taken that perverted pinch of interest in me, had I not been working on Faustomat. That would never have existed had I not had such a hard time concealing my experimental cheating from Vero. I put that down to my fear and guilt, which I blame, in turn, entirely on my grandmother's early Puritan influence throughout my summer breaks in Galway, those evening Bible readings and five-mile-long Sunday walks to Mass. With God's insight, this red thread of my destiny could be foreseen at my birth, at my grandmother's birth, in the very instant the Universe was born, in that first flash when the universal clockwork

was set in motion to turn its wheels according to an inescapable, pre-conceived Grand Plan, cranked up by Aristotle's *causa causalis*, the only mystery in the machine.

What I describe is the conception of the Universe as a mechanical masterpiece that can be disassembled into its component parts, examined, and assembled again. When, in the second half of the fourteenth century, the Church began mounting massive turret clocks on church towers, they weren't there to mark time. They weren't even meant to summon farmers from faraway fields to the evening Mass. The traditional means—the sundial and the bell—worked like a charm for that, while these monumental beasts would go off by an hour every day. Yet, within a decade, there were five hundred of them all over Europe, with one set task: to demonstrate to the common people the genius of divine creation. Not only were they a metaphor for a mechanical God, these clocks were literal toy models of the Universe.

According to some, the next few ticks of this universal clock can be read in the stars, by way of astrology—or in numbers, thanks to numerology. The occult sciences aside, the same deeply held belief in linear causation also forms the Western scientific method. Evidence-based science dictates the demonstration of action and reaction; it is not satisfied with influence, resonance, or catalysis, nor with coherence and emergence. Instead of focusing on dynamics in general, it demands proof of causation—that is, linear causation. Action and reaction. To do that, it must isolate a single variable: surgically remove the studied phenomenon, extract it from its place in the world, cut it free of the confusing context. This is called the controlled experiment.

When I experimented with infidelity, I had thus tried to isolate the studied phenomenon—intercourse, in this case—and failed miserably. The echoes rippled through my life so hard that Veronica broke up with me, which led to the accident, to Faustomat, and so on. In Prague, I attempted a controlled experiment in romance that again concluded with the most ominous leak of context imaginable—right into you. And worse than that, I know how much I hurt you when I let slip that I took our trip as an experiment. Goddamn isolated variables destroy my love life.

29

The skeptical scientist stresses the need for proof. Fine. But proof of what? Of the scientist's idea of how the world works, of linear causation. It's an exquisite case of circular reasoning. Only after Tōhoku did the question come to me: is linear causation truly an indispensable prerequisite of the scientific method (of rationalism, of sound Western thought)? The skeptical scientist nods mechanically. But this question forms a crucial junction on the Western path and deserves a considered answer. I'll write it up the day after tomorrow. I am dog tired now. Tomorrow, the descent to the telephone awaits me.

I'm smoking and sipping local cardamom tea in an internet café with two computers from the eighteenth century. I feel downright clueless. I had my beard and hair trimmed, stocked up on tobacco, and then called your old number. Someone picked up right away, but I didn't hear a thing. I don't know if it was you. I repeated my name a few times and said that I wanted to speak to Nina, and then the line got cut off. I called back right away. It rang a few times, and the number's been unavailable since then. I'll write for a bit, then call back again. Children are leaning over my keyboard and begging. They don't know I have even less than they do. A girl has climbed into my lap, trying to figure out what I'm writing. A love letter, darling, for one wonderful woman.

Nina, if you've read up to here, it's time to put out in the open that I'm writing this diary for you. I thought I'd abandoned you long ago—how wrong I was. Having *serkam* from yak milk for breakfast, I wonder whether you'd like it. Wandering through deserted valleys and villages, I go where you'd want to go. I observe the sun setting behind the mountains just to glimpse how it would be reflected in your eyes. Two years after you went back to Europe, I'm still stuck in fucking India and I love you. I never told you, right? I know. When I grow up, I will be an idiot.

The second story that enthralled the villagers was about someone who did not take linear causation to be an indispensable condition of the scientific method. (Imagine the lovely Tibetan Indians, listening intently to my exhortation in lotus position.) He lived in a time when the scientific method was only emerging, and he fought fiercely over its form. This man was Denis Diderot, who in 1764 converted a routine commission for the translation of a two-volume English encyclopedia into a grandiose attempt to consolidate the knowledge of the Enlightenment into thirty-five volumes of the *Encyclopédie*, to which he ended up devoting two decades. His associate Jean le Rond d'Alembert wrote of their time:

"In short, from the Earth to Saturn, from the history of the heavens to that of insects, natural philosophy has been revolutionized; and nearly all other fields of knowledge have assumed new forms."

The two men set out to order the discordant fruits of the new paradigm. They planned to collect the new thought, solidify its foundations, and review, renew, and rewrite the various sciences under the new model. It was the kind of total reordering that typically happens after a paradigm shift.

They hired an army of experts. Diderot paid for thousands of engravings of various mechanical processes in Parisian workshops, so as to allow others to replicate them, directly spurring the industrial revolution. D'Alembert authored over fifteen hundred articles; Diderot, spearheading the enterprise, penned an incredible six thousand. In the first volume, eagerly expected by the period's elite, Diderot wrote on anatomy, arithmetic, and art but also on aristocracy and authority. "No man has received from nature the right of commanding others," wrote this audacious subject of the French monarch, instantly landing on a shortlist of state enemies.

Not only did he criticize the lack of liberties, capital punishment, and slavery, but he devoted more space to the manufacture of enamel than to the doctrine of the Trinity, and in the entry on Noah's ark, the chief concern seemed to be the incredible effort required to shovel away all the manure. The Jesuits, the court, and the censors alike scrambled to put an end to the provocation. Diderot was jailed for three months for raising the question of God's existence, and, in

d'Alembert's words, the establishment was "piling up the faggots at the seventh volume to cast them into the fire at the eighth."

But as the censors were sanitizing the entry on Oppression, Diderot provoked with Sovereignty; they censored Infidelity, he penned Lust; they turned to Morality and he was raising hell with Tolerance; they cut out most of Theology and he gave them Objection, Philosophy, Sceptic, and Christian Sects.

Meanwhile, a second battlefront emerged, no less intense, which Voltaire called a civil war between the heathens. It raged in the French Academie, in the salons of Paris, and above all in the articles of the *Encyclopédie*. Both editors were united in a joint anti-clerical campaign and they both stressed that the proper way to explore the world was through the scientific method. But, in an ominous turn of history, they soon realized that their visions thoroughly diverged, representing two strikingly incompatible interpretations of the Enlightenment.

"The study of nature is the study of the properties of bodies; and their properties depend on two things: their movement and their shape."

That's how simple the Universe was according to d'Alembert. He was a mathematician, a geometer. When he closed his eyes, he could see the grand astronomical clockwork ticking moment after moment, turning planets and destinies alike according to unchanging laws. He sensed the plan behind the machine and sought to grasp it from first principles, the most abstract of concepts, like Descartes and Newton before him. To him, matter was fully inert; motion was external to it. This view of the Enlightenment left a good deal of space for God (as a *causa causalis*, the source of motion). And where there was space for God, there was space for Church and King. This was a direct continuation of the established Aristotelian thought model, simply with a higher emphasis on individual reason than revealed truth.

Now Diderot was a biologist. A chemist. One almost wants to say an al-chemist, in the original sense of the word: an explorer fascinated by the bubbling, shape-shifting chaos under his hands, its transformations, evolutions, and endless change. He laughed at the idea that geometrical laws could describe the complexity of the world, and aimed to study this complexity directly, without reference to

idealized principles. In his experiments, he did not observe a division between matter and motion; he observed them together.

D'Alembert attracted the fascination of the public with his *Discours Preliminaire*, in which he put forward the idea that first principles might ultimately be arrived at by mathematicians (long before Hilbert resurrected this old hope and Gödel put it to its final rest). Diderot retorted in *Geometry*. Rather than a divine principle, he described geometry simply as a human simplification of nature, scoring against d'Alembert on his home field. Then the French government banned the work altogether and d'Alembert, exhausted by the constant controversy and danger, withdrew as co-editor.

Diderot, the ultimate freethinker, assumed exclusive responsibility for the now clandestine project. He wrote more intensely than ever, including the decisive entries Encyclopedia and Philosopher. He continued sourcing the best minds of Europe, fought against his own publisher's censorship, and eventually brought the *Encyclopédie* to a successful close. His heroism is undeniable. But Diderot's scientific vision oscillated between materialism, vitalism (viewing all matter as equally conscious), and atheism, converging in a mystical wonder. He analyzed the nature of living organisms, memory, identity, consciousness, and society and argued against the clockwork universe, for the indivisibility of reality and the connectedness of all things.

His was a complex critique of the mechanistic Aristotelian status quo rather than a coherent philosophy, an attitude rather than a formal system. He was harder to grasp and far more controversial. This debate was not a discussion of particulars, nor a disagreement on abstract philosophical themes—this was a clash of two fundamental approaches to reality. In the end, d'Alembert's mechanistic conception proved fitter for the times and solidified the position of Aristotelian thought in the West for a few more generations. And with it, linear causation became the hallmark of the scientific method, leading us to that strange belief that we can cut a part from the whole, like an organ from the body, and study it in isolation. If we do this with every part, every organ, goes the belief, we will reach a complete understanding of the body. That is our science. Aristotle's and d'Alembert's. In the

meantime, folk wisdom suggests that the whole is more than the sum of its parts. But if that's true, how do we account for this difference? What is a flock without birds?

And the people in the village giggled and demanded to hear this pivotal Western story again. I kept wondering how much of it they could understand. And what tiny fragment of meaning did I possibly grasp when they talked about King Ashoka?

It's six o'clock and I'm still sitting in the prehistoric internet café. I tried calling you all afternoon, but the number is unavailable. I sent you an email. It flew around the world in five seconds and returned as undeliverable. I searched online. There's nothing on your exhibitions, no gallery is selling your paintings—I almost can't believe you're not famous yet. Because one day you will be. You paint better than Picasso. I logged on to Faustomat after a long time, but there's no trace of you in its databases either. I'm done for today. I don't know what to do next, but it's getting dark, so I have to go. I'll probably come back down in a few days and try calling. When I imagine that you might be with someone else tonight, I feel nausea and waves of heat. And I'm not even in the least entitled to that.

It's two in the morning. I got back to the village happy to be alive. The moon had the decency to light my way until midnight, and then pitch-black darkness fell. I was walking essentially by memory. The path winds mostly along the river, but, at one point, the slopes narrow into a gorge, and one has to climb the hillside. Some of the cliffs there are terrifying. I felt the chill rising up, the quelling river below. Well, perhaps I mis-stepped, or a stone slipped under my foot suddenly. I was hurtling down the rocks a hundred feet before my back slammed against a tree. I still have no idea how deep the void below was. As far as I remember, there are straight drops down to the river. I'm still a bit in shock. My back is scraped and I think I sprained an ankle.

Linear time. I almost can't move my back. It's more beat up than I expected. Where there isn't blood, there's yellow-blue swelling. It's difficult to breathe. I can't bend over. It's possible I broke a rib. My landlady gave me herbs and brought me breakfast in bed. I write. I can't fail to notice that it all has a common denominator—the two years we haven't been together; yesterday, which I spent trekking; the nighttime return; and the moment when I was tumbling down and thought I was done for.

You know my memory for quotes. I see them in front of my eyes on the page, as if I were holding a book in my hands. The *Encyclopédie* entry for Instant (Metaphysics) is in the middle of the left page and the third or fourth line says:

"The nature of things requires ... that there be a cause if there is an effect."

Even as I recall it, I wince a *no*! (And my ribs clench.) Linear causation is not the nature of things. It is the nature of the Aristotelian model, which is foundational to Christianity. It didn't get enough scrutiny during the Enlightenment to be overthrown along with the other old dogmas, so it's still here with us today, still obvious and self-evident, still not challenged head-on.

But I'm in fact elated to find an allusion to linear causation under Instant. It works perfectly to illustrate how the toy model dictates our perception of time. It says:

"An instant: a fractional duration in which one does not perceive any development; or that which takes up only the time of one idea in our minds. This time is, for us, the shortest moment."

In this model, time is composed of individual moments that follow one another like frames of a film. The universe unfolds step by step, tick-tock, in constant con-sequence of actions and reactions. And within each precise moment, the stars are at a standstill.

"It is an axiom of mechanics that no natural effect can be produced in an instant," continues the Encyclopédie. This is an inevitable precondition to absolute truth. In order to clearly differentiate between truth and falsity, between night and day, the planets must stop in their tracks for an instant. This allows the examiner to proclaim truth (what is and what is not), and only then can they resume movement.

If the universe failed to stop for the duration of the instant, day might turn into night, the living might turn into the dead, and within the same moment—*at the same time*—a person would be both alive and dead, the opposites would be equally valid, truth and falsity would amalgamate. Everything would be "so and not so," as Aristotle argued against Pythagoras—all in contradiction with all.

And so when Aristotle said, "truth is to say of what is that it is, and of what is not that it is not," he not only defined some notion of truth (which lays the foundation of a certain logic) but also a particular perception of time. Unless we can stop the world—at least for a moment—it will continually escape such definitive description.

When I allow this notion of time (as a series of frozen moments) to take over my perception, it makes me focus on special *moments* in life. (Birth. Graduation. Wedding day. Promotion. The carrot on a stick.)

It binds my attention to endings: victory, death, goal, product, revolution.

It makes me see history stretched over the inflexible rod of time, a history of victors, the first hazy sketch.

It makes me conservative like my grandmother (makes me detest and resist change).

It made you, Nina, run from idea to idea, from the vision of Cambridge to the vision of Japan, from one idealized still-life to another. This is why I recall our entire relationship as a single picture of your glowing eyes when you burst out laughing in a Prague church. This is why you spent the first few days of our trip behind the viewfinder. And it's why I still shudder with tenderness when I remember how you threw the camera into the Vltava River and Aristotle's time with it. It seems to me that you somehow always understood that towards which I had trudged for years by thorny paths. This Aristotle's demand that the stars stop in each instant, so that the examiner may utter his truths, is the very same folly as my unspoken assumption that you would wait for me while I took two years to complete my Asian abstraction tripping. Surprise, surprise.

My back keeps hurting more and more. I can't get out of bed. I'm only sipping water so I don't have to go to the toilet. But I'm alive. You know the moments when someone comes so close to death that

they throw off their beliefs like baggage, just to jump over the coffin. So today, I give thanks. To God or Jesus, or whichever divine gardener planted the tree at the edge of the cliff that nearly broke my back. I won't argue their existence today. A miracle saved my life, and I want to spend the rest of it with you.

The Object. Playing around with the Aristotelian mental model, here in Darjeeling, I once again examine the strange group of topics that make it up: Truth, Ideal, Logic, Causation, Time. And like before, I sense that this new lot also stems from a more fundamental source. Not the source of a culture, this time, but of a single person. I travel back into my first days as a newborn and to the unbelievably complex task of the little Adam: the transformation of experience into patterns, better known as cognition. There, among the non-existent memories and inaccessible imprints, I fish for the root of my thought.

While I was still floating in fetal fluid, exploring the soft walls framing my living space and feeling the vibrations from outside, there was nothing I could remember. Everything happened for the first time. I was experiencing. Perhaps then, in my mother's belly, absolutely enraptured by every perception, was the only time I have truly lived full-on. I don't remember it, but it must have gone like this: they put a colorful spot in front of my eyes, and it changed shape like an amoeba. I didn't know that it was a rattle. I didn't know that the sound I heard was made by the rattle. That when the spot disappeared, the rattle had fallen into the stroller.

But I was attentive to every change. I remembered the colorful blob in all its forms. I remembered the sound, quiet or loud, mixed with laughter and baby talk. How many times must I have heard the rattling, glimpsed the blob, held it, let it fall on the ground, and licked it carefully before an intersection arose, a certain common element that the mind could grasp as my fingers grasped the rattle, and formed its first *object*—my own idea of a rattle? Two months of video and audio and touch and taste and statistical analyses. How long

did it take until the first rattle ceased to amuse me, until perceptions ceased to supply new information about the object? A year.

After a rattle, a teddy bear, and Mom and Dad, I sped up immensely: I discovered a system. When I found something new (say a toy in the playground), I didn't have to explore an amoebic spot for two months. I got what a *thing* was. In one hundredth of a second I applied my experience with *things* to the new one. I took it and saw what was different about it. I had the simplest, purest idea of a *thing* on the day I brought my mum a piece of dog poo. Since then things became categorized—the good and the bad, the living and the inanimate, the lost and the broken. Thanks to the *things* at the playground, I learned the concept of ownership, the cause of the world wars, and, step by step, I deepened my understanding that "the study of nature is the study of the properties of bodies."

I grew used to seeing the world as a jigsaw puzzle, a box of bricks from which a single one may be removed, studied, and returned—the whole world as a Legoland. And now I'm not just talking about rattles, bricks, and dolls that one may hold in one's fingers. I was already learning another fantastically complicated thing: that the same procedure (transformation of repeated experiences into a pattern, the creation of an *object*) could also be used on the abstract level. The red rattle was a basis for red things—that is, for the object *red*. Three different rattles merged into a single object—*rattles*—different from *this particular rattle*.

Toddler-me didn't have a clue what related to what and whether it was important to discern similar colors or shapes or sounds. I watched everything. Hence, even the first abstract objects, let me emphasize, emerged just as the concrete ones, from the similarities between (same) perceptions composed into the (same) patterns stored in the (same) brain structures. What surprise then, that later on, my idea of truth resembled an *object*, up there above, a single truth for everyone?

It is this view of the world as a collection of objects (a Legoland, a clockwork universe) that produces its own, internally consistent version of Time, Logic, Causation, Truth, and Ideal (the mechanistic, Aristotelian toy model), that in turn produced its own culture

(the Western civilization). This is the operating system of the West, and it hasn't had an update for two and a half thousand years. It is the foundation of Christian theology as much as of Descartes' rationalism. It created Plato's idealism as much as Aristotle's materialism, and later, Kant's idealism just as much as Hume's sober rebukes. It produced absolutism, and equally, it produced relativism. It authored the *Gesamtkunstwerk* as much as postmodernism. It created modern science, and it created astrology. It created the individualist political right, and it created the collectivist left. It created the world in which you, Nina, are so uncomfortable because you can't belong to it. It is the common element behind all our core dualities, and it enforces the very concept of duality. It is the model of the world that I have lived in for the first thirty years of my life. I was born into it, like everyone before me.

The model continues to be so obvious, so ubiquitous, that no one talks about it. But under the radar, the view that the Universe is ultimately a collection of objects makes one's mind focus on precisely that: Objects. Bodies. Things (owning, shopping, littering). Product (gross national). It creates consumerism, greed, and the art of collecting art. It suggests one *ideal thing* for every precious *moment*, pairing the graduation day with the graduation wristwatch and the wedding day with the wedding ring. It tends toward hierarchies, authority, and stasis. It focuses the mind on its ultimate object: the self.

It's a staggeringly successful model. The key to its success is brutally simple: as long as people are focused on things, the philosophy of things will prove superior. As Gorgonuy put it, "Our success stands firmly on a rigorously materialist philosophy. And that's the winning strategy, when you compete for matter; when wars are fought over a territory and won by pushing more tanks onto the battlefield."

It does its job perfectly well. Its only problem is, this is not how the Universe works. At all.

As a data scientist, I kept bumping into analogous issues. I struggled to understand relation to self (recursion, cyclicality). Naturally, for bricks aren't recursive. I was similarly confused by the self-referentiality of cognition. By objects turned towards themselves, like Möbius' strip and M.C. Escher's drawings. I was confused by folk

wisdom, saying the whole is more than the sum of its parts. I couldn't see where synergy came from, the waves of fashion, mass hysteria, and culture. I was fascinated by infinite regress. Fractals. Empty sets. Because no brick I've ever held in my hand was turned inwards, infinite, immaterial, emergent, and morphing into another brick, let alone looking as if it was aware of itself, seeing the starry sky above and knowing how to love.

With you, humor and art entered my neatly ordered world. With Gorgonuy it was myths, tricks, and illusions. And something began to flower within me, something that couldn't be cut out, for it wasn't an object. With time, it bloomed into that firework of shattering contradictions, the final explosion of the mechanistic model. Judge the tree by its fruit, my grandmother taught me, and I do. Damn right I do, Aristotle. Your fruit is hard as rock.

In one of those curious twists of the stream of consciousness, I'm reminded of a paragraph I wrote down long ago one night in Pembroke on a page of a Set Theory textbook. I remember it word for word, as if it was embalmed in some rather remote corner of memory.

> *Night-time Cambridge shrouds itself in snowflakes. They are beautiful, but at this time of year, here, they seem absolutely inappropriate. The air blurred into a grey, gigantic mass and the people, the houses, and the streets vanished. A strange idea … Perhaps the enigma of the world hides not in what escapes me but in what I see. Perhaps, it occurs to me today, as I stand by a window with a cigarette and observe the snow milling around under the lamplight, something obscures my view. Some object, that I see my entire life, incessantly, and hence no longer notice it. And it still shadows what lies behind it. Something important, which I sense but do not see. The object, my blind spot.*

Shit. I felt so bad today while writing that I considered getting somehow to a hospital to get my ribs X-rayed. I tried to find my insurance

documents to read the fine print. I couldn't find the little bag where I keep my documents. It was round my neck when I went to call you, but now it's gone.

I turned this place upside down. I worry I lost it during the fall. It's dark now, but I have to return there tomorrow. If I can find the place where I fell. And if I can limp over there at all. This'll be some night! I thought the broken back would be the only warning I got, and now I'm without a passport.

The Il

of the

usion

Object

There is nothing more difficult to plan, more doubtful of success, more dangerous to manage than the creation of a new system. The innovator has the enmity of all who profit by the preservation of the old system and only lukewarm defenders by those who would gain by the new system.

—Nicollo Machiavelli

In the morning, the villagers sat me on a yak and six of them walked along to help me search. I told them to stay at home, that they had work to do, but they wouldn't. I'm thankful for every day I live with them. But it was a terrible journey—I was in so much pain that my arms got numb. We combed five miles of the trail, and one of them walked all the way down to the town, but we didn't find my passport. The spot where I fell was marked by dried blood and a torn up parka. I didn't even miss it. I saw the tree as well, and, just as I suspected, it was the single last stump before a thousand-foot fall. I can't begin to describe how it was to sit on the trail and see myself plummet down there a hundred times over.

I'm going to sleep. Dead tired. I've definitely broken a few ribs. But it's not like a hospital would fix anything, so I'll just have to suffer through. My landlady looks worried. She changes my herbal bandages every hour and asks why I'm not drinking. I'd like to wave it away, but that's a kinetic impossibility. I can't bring myself to tell her that I'd rather die of thirst than try to walk to the bathroom, so I just smile. I should call the embassy to have them arrange a new passport, but I can't imagine surviving the trip down, even on a yak. And the consulate is going to make me pick up the passport in person anyway. So going down to call makes no sense; the only thing it would bring is that I'd be able to call you. I don't know where you are or what to do next. I miss you, babe.

*

I woke up at daybreak in throbbing pain but with a clear mind. The lost passport was an omen. There's nothing left for me to do in India. It's time to return to where I don't need a passport—to England—and find you there. I won't put it off, even if my ribs kill me. Today, I'll limp my way up to the overlook above the village for the last time, to write and say goodbye. I'll pack my things up in the evening and arrange with the locals to take me on a yak to town. A bus service goes from there to Darjeeling, the last stop of the steam-powered Himalayan Railway. I'll take that to New Jalpaiguri and then the regular fast track to Delhi. I think the nearest consulate is in Calcutta, but

THE ILLUSION OF THE OBJECT

I remember flights from Delhi being cheaper. I counted my cash and it'll be pretty tight, but I won't get stuck in India because I can't buy a plane ticket. Everyone gets out of here somehow.

—

In the long file of days gone by, this one shines. The valley in which I lived for six months, and which grew on me much more than Tokyo, lies at my feet. Above us, the enormous mountain ridges are completely indifferent to our little ant-farm world. They know about it somehow; I can feel that. They even know that this is the last time I'll be with them, so they hold the clouds back to let me see far and etch every stone into memory. I meditate to remain present but can't help turning to similar days that were, like this one, crossroads between worlds.

Writing about them is hard. But it's an exercise in honesty, I assure myself.

On the beach in Tōhoku, I pried the third eye open. It stretched, gazed around, and saw what remained hidden to the old eyes: a fabric of relations. Karma. The mills of God. A fractal über-pattern connecting all that is. Who would've guessed?

For an artist like you, Nina, the raw experience is paramount, I think. You'd be content with that undiluted mystical experience. The sentence, "A relationship is not reducible to the objects it binds," contains too many words. But that's not me. I arrived at this alternate reality through the Western path, the path of the word. Following it, I crossed the faintest bridge: the substitution of a single word that ultimately solved every single one of the paradoxes that haunted me. The word that had to go was *object*—the fundamental building block of the Aristotelian universe. A new word—*relationship*—sprung up in its place. The one-word castling rippled through layers of my consciousness, memory, character, hurtling on through the abstractions, through physics and logic and social science. This nuclear reaction tore Aristotelian mechanics from my grey matter neuron by neuron, ripping out the mightiest of words as if they were weeds: Truth! Time! Ideal! Good! Cause! Hierarchy! I dumped them all in one go so that new words could grow in the reclaimed space. Such is the way of every revolution: some words are replaced by others.

❧

I thought I'd leave tomorrow, but it won't happen. I got up to the vista above the village, somehow, and I couldn't walk back down. Every step down on the boulders hurt so much that I fainted after two hundred feet. When I came to, I started screaming for help, and thankfully, Hitesh and his older brother, who were ploughing nearby, heard me. They carried me down. My landlady gave me a good talking to and said I wouldn't leave until she allowed it. Every day of waiting is agony.

❧

I have a favorite magic trick for killing time. I've done it a hundred times, and a hundred times it's worked. I take a most ordinary thing—say, a red apple—and, using nothing but the power of my mind, I turn the apple—an obvious, undeniable object—into a *relationship*. Bingo: between the juicy flesh, the seeds, the core, and the skin, there's

a relationship. I pick one of the smaller objects, say, the seed, and continue playing the mind game, seeing the seed not as an object but as a relationship. A finer structure emerges, this time connecting the protective seed coat, the nutritional cotyledon, the endosperm, and the radicle. How far can I play this? (What are the smallest objects that make up the world? Leucippus of Miletus said atoms; Leibnitz argued for monads; and ever since 1961, when the double-slit experiment demonstrated the particle-wave duality of electrons, we're just not sure.)

It's not about the apple. Just look at the object as it is, or rather, where it is: in the eye of the beholder, there and only there. It is only my mind that encircles its contour to create the illusion of separation. Meanwhile, the apple remains thoroughly connected to the rest of the universe, like a fish in water. Molecules of vapor emerge from it ceaselessly as every cell within it osmotically exchanges liquid nutrients with its neighbors. The apple's boundary remains forever approximate as its shape changes without pause, whether growing or rotting, as germs dive into the skin and mold sets its roots. It is always touching and pushing against something as gravity pulls it down to the ground and likewise toward the Moon above. It reflects light, vibrates with radio waves, gently adjusts its surface tension, and emits and absorbs heat. As you would say, the apple is always part of some still life.

Let me generalize the apple trick:

P1. Every object can be seen as a relationship.
P2. Every object is part of a larger whole.

These two mental movements, *P1* and *P2*, between objects and relationships, show that the view of reality as a relationship is freely interchangeable with the object paradigm. The object gives rise to a relationship; the relationship gives rise to an object. The two movements are popularly known as analysis and synthesis, respectively.

My hand is gone, the apple is gone. Magic trick number two: Nina and me. When I met you for the very first time, after a thirty-year-long walk into the present, our minds began to mirror each other.

47

Our thoughts and moods swirled together until it was no longer possible to distinguish one from the other, and we, as they say, thought of each other. We became each other's psychedelic drug. One infusion, one blood stream. Behold the enigma of the bond: the skill to see (and that's not a skill of the eyes), the faculty to feel (and that's not a faculty of the skin), the capacity to cuddle (and that's not a capacity of the arms). The skill to laugh in St. Nicholas' Church in Prague—that's the sound of the ouroboros. It would never sound if only one of us sat there, and it is therefore not a skill of either of us. I simply can't maintain the illusion of the individual self when I hear St. Nicholas' Church resound with our laughter. You and I, we're not two people but our talks, our lovemaking, our joint present. *We are the ouroboros.*

And we're not alone. We're not some anomaly in the face of general entropy, cuddling on regardless. In fact, I nominate this one word (entropy) for the grand prize as the most misunderstood concept of all. Everything moves toward entropy, disintegration, death; that's the common "scientific" conception. That's why, they say, a glass falling on the floor will break and never fix itself again. A universal decay from whose grinding fist our earthly life has somehow miraculously escaped.

No! As soon as I stop focusing on objects and see relationships, the grand movement turns from disorder towards harmony. Watch: I take a glass of water and throw it hard against the floor. It breaks, spills. And I don't see entropic chaos. I see lovers: the Earth and the shards and the water, hugging, kissing after a timeless eternity of longing. I see the tiniest elements attracting each other, forming atoms, forming molecules, attracting each other, forming compounds, forming single cells, attracting each other, forming primitive organisms and complex bodies, attracting each other into networks and flocks and cultures and cults and me and you, and a common element shines through all this attraction from the tiniest to the largest bodies. Here, the greatest of mystical insights: the Universe is cuddly.

So far, I've written of mind games and magic tricks as insignificant as an apple. With the following *corpus delicti*, though, the illusion of the object is starting to border on a grave error. Our next exhibit is political economy.

The illusion of the collectivist, common to the socialists, the communists, the fascists, and the green, was called out by Hayek. He traced the evils of the left to the "tendency to treat wholes like society or the economy, capitalism, or a particular industry or class or country as definitely given objects about which we can discover laws by observing their behavior as wholes." Once the collectivist regards society as an object, it is easy to conclude, as Mussolini did, that this whole (society, state) is larger than any individual and thus more important. Except it does not exist; the collectivist just fell for the illusion of the whole.

On the other hand, the individualists—liberals and libertarians alike—commit an analogous error. They fail to see that Nina and me, we are not two people—we are an ouroboros. If they separate us, we will laugh no more. An organ is not separable from a body without harm.

Like this, one half is deceived by the illusion of the whole, the other by the illusion of the part. Hand in hand, the collectivist and the individualist commit the Grand Western Error: they see the world as a collection of objects and ignore relationships.

I think a perfect example is that Czech professor complaining about his country's post-communist difficulties, if you remember. It was clear that he attributed them to fifty years without private ownership (of *objects*). Few people realized that the Communists didn't nationalize just private objects but human relationships too. Because when the totalitarian state banned private ownership, it also banned the most natural of human contacts: mutual exchange and mutual benefit brought on by the division of labor and the opportunity to work for each other. And that must have hit the people a lot deeper than robbing them of property.

When I came to Darjeeling, I bought a rock of Afghan hashish the size of my fist. I still have most of it, and now I smoke it as a painkiller. Other than that, it doesn't do me much good, just like this writing. It was on one of those hash trips that I burned the first diary, after all. So why do I smoke, you'd ask. Why … I may never have been as present as on that stoned, wordless night, when the air was filled with your absence. That original diary was a parade for Isabella. It was written in the language of objects for the people of objects, to show them a few curiosities from that new continent I'd discovered. As I planned out in my grandiose dreams, a new philosophy would be cultivated there, a new mathematics, a new political economy. Founded on relationships instead of objects. But, like with Faustomat before, once I realized that a new science could indeed be built on relationships, my intellectual interest was sated. Well. So I took five caked yak turds and set them on fire. I slowly tore out one page after another and freed thoughts from words.

In the month following the burning, my contemplations took on a new form. No more parades for Isabella. The only reason I write again about objects, truth, time, and all that is the calm realization that I still love you and that it was—beyond all doubts—the Aristotelian paradigm that divided us.

You always wanted to belong somewhere: Cambridge, Japan, then Europe again. All of your flight tickets were one-way trips home; but wherever you landed, home wasn't there.

This nomadic neurosis wasn't caused by your mom and dad. You wander the world because of Aristotle. The conception of the world as a collection of objects made you feel separated and alone. It gave you existential anxiety from too many equal options. It gave me the obsessive feeling that there's something to solve, some deep and complex paradox, which I could not resist in Cambridge or Japan, as if it were the only task I was born for. (As a person believing in mechanical fate would say!) Essentially, it made us both search for the same thing: how to stop searching. The good news is, I've figured it out.

I formulated the Great Western Error. I suggested its solution. I freed the mind, and now, I need to tell you what I should have told

you ages ago, in Prague: "Love is the masterplan. I want to do that grand cosmic thing and have children with you." The only way we can really be body on body is by killing the Aristotelian paradigm. I killed it in me, and now, I need to kill it in you. Soon, Nina. I went to the bathroom without whining today.

◣

The abstract form of the Error is the conception of a set. As a mathematician, I find sets rather important. Not only are they the foundation of set theory, which in turn is considered the foundation of mainstream modern mathematics, but I see sets around me every day. A train full of people is a set with members. A library is a set with members, as is a bowl of Tibetan lentil soup. I can't imagine a meaningful sentence that in some way does not refer to the idea (concept, method) of a set. This has little to do with mathematics and everything to do with how the mind breaks down reality under the object toy model. At one point, I searched for a proper mathematical definition of a set, somewhat embarrassed at not remembering it. But to my great surprise, I found out it does not exist. Unlike most mathematical concepts, a mathematical set is an *undefined primitive*. The properties of such primitive, essential terms rely on intuition rather than definition. It sounds shaky, given that we are talking about the very foundations of mathematics. But there is no other way; any attempt to define everything, to avoid the use of intuitive primitives, invariably leads to an infinite regress.

"At the core of all well-founded beliefs lies belief that is unfounded," writes Wittgenstein. Our theories rest on primitives; primitives rest on intuition. And there we have the true foundations of mathematics: no set theory but intuition.

The central question then becomes: what is our intuitive conception of a set? It was a few months after Tōhoku when I screamed with excitement again, upon researching and confirming through numerous sources that the foundations of today's mathematics rest on "an intuitive conception of a set as an object."

As an *object*! There was the culprit that linked everything together:

51

our mathematics, politics, my view of self, and, thus, the fortunes and somersaults of my life. All of them have the same shape:

Next time I hear Cambridge mathematicians say that mathematics has nothing to do with real life, I'll tell them. I'll tell them about the Grand Western Error. Mathematicians commit it as nonchalantly as Mussolini with Hayek.

～

This is my last night in the valley. I told my landlady that I love her more than my own grandmother and that she couldn't keep me here with a pair of yaks. The villagers took the news like any other. The journey will be several days of misery on trains, but I have enough hashish to get through. And who knows, maybe a message from you is waiting for me in town. I am packing the few possessions I have. Among them, a deck of cards I drew on Darjeeling evenings under buttery candlelight.

Each Monday morning, I pick one card. For a week, I focus on seeing that card as a relationship rather than an object. Had Gorgonuy told me back in Cambridge, the night he did a tarot reading for me, that one day this data scientist would carry his own hand-drawn pack, I might have ended the conversation there and then. Today, the seventy-eight cards remind me how often I fell for the Grand Western Error, finding this or that strange, misbehaving, escaping my grasp. Today, I spread all of them in front of me. I contemplate where life might lead me next. I am grateful for each question mark that makes life worth living. For every clueless place.

These are my cards.

Work. Money. I never told you what I did for a living in Japan. I was happy you were satisfied with me "teaching English," but it was a bit more complicated. In the beginning, I really did teach English. But gradually, I discovered that I could charge extra for various reasons and I started specializing. Private lessons for students with learning difficulties became my domain. I taught three hours a night, made great money, and felt terrible. The students grinned at me, repeated after me, imitated my accent, and burst into endless laughter. And a week later, they barked out the same words—as if hearing them for the first time! I didn't catch a whiff of memory, of progress. In actual fact, I had to repeat the same lesson over and over. I was basically cheating, stealing money for a service I could not provide. I could never teach them English. But this facsimile of work allowed me to divide twelve hours of my day between programming the Faustomat monster and examining the insane yet somehow charmingly consistent Japan. So I lived in this terrible, exploitative lifestyle. I couldn't admit it to you.

Only after you left, one night, I finally decided to stop, and I called off one lesson after the other. And the families were horrified. "But our daughter loves you!" they said. "We've never seen her so cheerful!" And also, "But sir, you are so funny!" It took me a while to process what I was actually selling them and conclude that the relationship worked for everyone. The academic in me whimpered, but after all, it was only one of the hundred cognitive dissonances throbbing in my head at the time.

Good. Evil. God. If we put Hitler in a spaceship and shot him into space for his entire lifetime, would he still be evil? No. There is no evil outside of relationships and no morality either. That's why good manners don't require Grandma's Ten Commandments and supernatural police. It's enough to feel relationships.

Universals. The color blue in all blue things: does it behave as a thing or a relationship? This card clarifies all abstract concepts right down to the last one. I talk about nothing less than another view of abstraction itself.

Idea. Context. Mine is the responsibility for relationships between words. In a post-truth world, mine is the responsibility for my web of beliefs. Mine is the answer to the tyranny of memes that want to control me; mine is their meaning and context. Mine is the paradigm.

Paradigm. Meaning. The epitaph I want on my tombstone: a relationship is not reducible to the objects it binds. That is my core insight from Tōhoku and also the reason the mystical paradigm cannot be conveyed in terms of the mechanistic one. Why it cannot be mechanistically proven. Such is, after all, the case with all paradigm shifts. They happen in a leap that cannot be justified before the take-off.

The suspicion this raises in the mechanist's mind! And rightly so. The silliest thing could hide under these statements. But how does one switch paradigms, when there is no deductive path between them? Well, through experiment. Seeing the world through other eyes is not a suddenly acquired mental thunderbolt but a skill that can be trained and tested. It is a question of focusing on relationships rather than objects. On process rather than state. On similarity rather than difference. On influence rather than control. On complexity rather than certainty. On harmony rather than truth. This kingside castling is an art not unlike learning to write with the left hand. Ideally, after such training and experimenting, one is left with two perspectives that one can easily shift, using one or the other as it is useful.

Shape. What is the shape of a relationship? How different is it from an object? Rather than being or not being, it makes sense to talk of its intensity. It can be positive or negative, waxing or waning, but it never disappears. This much I learned when your absence turned unbearably painful. A *relationship* grants a fresh perspective on self-reference, recursion, infinite regress, the liar's paradox, fractals, consciousness, emergence, networks, flocks, and societies. But it remains a primitive—a vague, intuitive notion begging for examination. So what is a relationship? And what toy model does it cast? What kind of people? What science, what culture?

Uncertainty. A new attitude to uncertainty ultimately gives rise to a new society.

Identity. I'm the one you take me for. Who I am with you. Whichever I you bring forth.

Paradox. A single-entry sceptico-esoteric dictionary:

$$objects = relationships$$

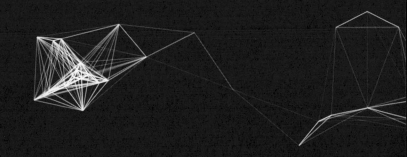

The Ill
of T

usion

ime

What should you do, then? First of all, you must realize that you are the hypnotist.
—Seth, speaking through Jane Roberts

The

backpack is on the rack above my seat. I sit in my compartment while people are squeezed together in the aisle and on the roof, children and animals among them. It's impossible to fall asleep in the stench. We've spent several hours waiting in a nameless town of about a million people. The train is besieged by vendors selling food and knick-knacks. I bought three vegetable samosas and two bottles of water from some woman. The caps are missing that protective strip. I have no illusions.

I just caused a great commotion on the train. I've had a plastic bag on my lap the entire time, guarding it closely. After several hours of standing, my fellow passengers, having nothing else to do, wanted to see what was in the bag. I showed them; they turned pale. They started shouting, and soon the whole train, including the conductor and driver, were peeking and pushing into our compartment. Everyone wanted to see the immortal *sahib* and his hundred-year-old portraits. They offered me cigarettes; I took one. I quietly watched their stunned, whispering faces, seeing the same animistic shock that had once run along my own spine. The paintings are so masterful that, by the time I realized they were forgeries, they'd managed to crack my original perspective of time, which eventually turned out to be an illusion anyway. Kill an illusion with an illusion; that's what I call art. Burst open that wide, empty space of clueless wonder that precedes all understanding, and never apologize.

One afternoon, in the company of the yak herd, troubled by the intimate bond between time and logic, my eyes fell on a raven sitting on a rock a little higher up the valley. For a long time, the raven sat still, then he flew up and was gone. I thought, when—at which precise moment—did the raven change from sitting to flying? If time is indeed discrete and linear, tick-tock, one frozen instant after another, as the *Encyclopédie* says and as I was always implicitly told, then by definition, the change could not have happened within *any* instant (within which all is still)! I watched another raven, and after a while, it happened again: one moment it sat, the next it flew. *When did the change happen?* Assuming linear time of successive moments, there must have been some last instant in which the raven sat and a first instant in which it flew. Inevitably then, change had to happen between

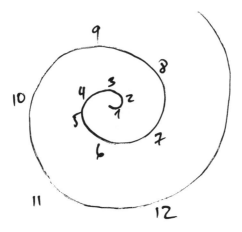

THE ILLUSION OF TIME

those two instants. In the gap between seconds. Isn't that a nice turn of phrase? I can summarize:

(P3) All is still in an instant, every instant.
(P4) Speaking of holes between instants is good only for poets.

Frankly, there is no space for change in this concept of time. The mechanistic model of the universe and change are incompatible. And then I must ask—which one is the illusion? Linear time of consecutive moments or change? (But the question that has been robbing me of sleep for a while now is much more concrete: is it too late to get back together? Is the right time irreversibly gone? I think about it every day. And the answer wholly depends on the shape of time.)

✢

Weaving rugs with the grandmothers one day, after a long silence, I tried to explain to them what had been bugging me recently. Soon I was walking around the room gesturing, as I was accustomed to

doing during debates in Cambridge. You know me. I was stuttering with the vain effort to push the network of thoughts out through my mouth.

They stood up too and gently took me by the hands. They made me sit down with them. I laughed, and the women each put a finger on their lips. They began to murmur and sing gently. I closed my eyes.

We sat for a good hour. The muttering in my head wouldn't stop: what is the present *now*, if not a single instant? Do we actually live in *more* time periods at once? What an absurd thought! Eventually, the echoes quieted. What remained was wonder. I fully understood what Wittgenstein meant. "Not how the world is, but that it is, is the mystery," he wrote toward the very end of the *Tractatus*, as his path of words bent back to its origin, into the silence of a clueless place.

The world is. *Shock!*

I held the wonder in my mind, resting in the oasis at the end of thoughtful torture, the eye of the hurricane, the center of gravity, the name of the mandala. A motionless raven taking off. This was the point of origin for Western philosophy, science, and my dear mathematics. As the silent wonder of mystery slips away, the first words begin to weave, clumsily and laboriously, into a web of meanings, symbols, books, and language. Into Aristotle's logic of truth and falsity, Wittgenstein's Tractatus, my diaries. All of these are a personal reaction to the primal wonder. Memorials to a mystery lost.

The world is.

When I opened my eyes, the grandmothers were quiet. I breathed slowly, and equally slowly, perhaps another half-hour later, I began to see. The breath of the women. A bug's flight across the mud floor. The sunlight traversing toward the far wall and gently tinging the evening yellow. The dust dancing in the air. The heartbeat in my arteries. The primal wonder returned. This time, back at the beginning of words, I didn't avert my gaze as quickly as Aristotle and Wittgenstein but stared into the mystery a fraction more persistently.

The world is *changing*.

In that hypnotic trance, my consciousness held steady while everything whirled around. I held the surprise, not fooled by the commonplace sound of the word *change*. I stared at it firmly and

loudly pronounced, "Not that the world is, but that it is changing, is the mystery."

That day, the Tibetan women taught me how to find the beginning of thought. Meditating, I remained fully aware of the importance of the first step I would take from there. I was choosing between paths leading from two primal wonders into two different Universes.

The first path, the path of men mesmerized by the fact that the world is, leads to thinking about that which *is*. Static thinking. Object thinking. Aristotle's truth of that which is and that which isn't, the logic of black and white and the excluded middle. Absolute truth and the whole mechanistic shebang.

The second path, a reflection of the subtler mystery—that the world *changes*—takes one right through the blind spot of the objective view to uncharted land. What is change? Is it even possible to grasp such a fundamental word using other words? Every definition, it seemed, would express less than the word itself. Here, close to the primary mystery, on the edge of silence, was the region of primitive terms. In these depths few words floated, far apart. Each primitive term guards its own indispensability, and the attempt to link them produces metaphors more often than definitions. But if one insists and presses for a definition, one may read that "change is an expression of 'energy.'"

Next, one might look for the definition of energy and be referred to a "potential for change." One will look up "potential" and "change," which will refer back to "energy" in an elegant catch-22.

We do not know what energy is, what change is, or how change happens in this universe. We observed the strange phenomenon of something being the same and not the same, at once, and gave it a name: change. But let's not mistake labels for understanding. We do not know what change is.

Medicine calls this a syndrome: we do not understand the underlying phenomenon, but we can recognize its symptoms. All of our philosophy and science and religion is an attempt to turn the syndrome into a known disease—so far unsuccessful. After centuries of thought, the best we can say today is that our universe suffers from the syndrome of being. The syndrome of change.

1

Behind every primitive term, mystical wonder lies in wait.

—

The train's finally moving again. I don't even know when we set off. I smoked a joint so my back would stop hurting and fell asleep. It's a torment, but I'll manage. We should be in Delhi at noon tomorrow, so I've got loads of time to write about time.

As far as I recall, I first heard of time when I was three. "It's time to go home!" they told us in kindergarten. But later, searching the universe for that time they spoke about, all I could put my finger on was various flutterings, like the movement of the Sun across the sky or the hand around the dial of the turret clock. All I could see was a momentum, a rush, a need. The monumental gesturing of one falling off a cliff. It is only us, people, who speak of time. The universe doesn't know it.

And so it is perfectly possible to entertain other shapes of time than that mundane straight line of linear progression that jolts from one frozen moment to the next. These different forms of time create entirely different paradoxes and, thus, entirely different philosophies. They create different attitudes toward uncertainty and, thus, different societies. They create entirely different human conditions and, thus, different beings.

Long excursions through the Himalayas are ideal for these contemplations. I hiked the same trek every day for a week so I could walk it with different times. Not at different times. With different times.

I walked, for example, as if time offered resistance. In order to move forward in time, I had to make an effort, and as soon as I stopped, time also slowed to rest. I pushed forward, knee-deep in time thick as honey. I toiled toward death. And still, I walked, because stopping solved nothing. Imagine, approaching death was now my choice and responsibility. I passed old tourists standing by the path. They breathed heavily and refused to take another step, and then they moved an inch, as if breaking crumbs off their last loaf.

Another day, I walked as though there was no single timeline but an infinite number of intervals unfolding at once. High on the ridge

with a panoramic view, I enjoyed a second of wonder in every hair-pin, the two-minute task of walking to the next turn, the hour between refreshments, the day's hike, the month of sunny weather, the year in India, the two years without you, the decade of economic recession, the century of the crisis of humanity, the millennium of the exponential, the ten thousand years of Western history, the four hundred thousand years of human evolution, the four billion years of life on Earth … all mingling in one present.

This now of the relational, mystical model was a self-discovering, pulsating web of meaning, which couldn't be paused for analysis. It had to be experienced in stride. The monkey that observed me for half a mile resonated with the span of human evolution. The mountains I circled, and their age, showed me how much I share with the ape. And the sun above the horizon … Every step had different and entirely contradictory meanings in the different time spans *at once*. This perspective was necessarily inconsistent and paradoxical. And it didn't bother me. Inconsistency became another word for dialogue. Paradox became a synonym for change. And time is a DJ.

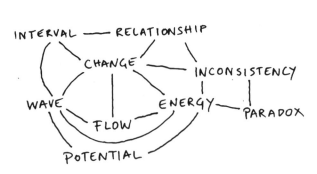

Each of these primitive terms has its own unique meaning while being mutually synonymous.

You were so upset that Ernst Kris rewrote the story of Franz Messerschmidt's life. Thanks to him, it is obvious to us today that Messerschmidt's busts were influenced by hallucinations, paranoia, and possibly schizophrenia. I understand your anger. What's the difference between an artist working for ten years trying to capture all of humanity in an absolute work of art and one working for ten years trying to capture his inner world? Why should there be a difference between those two leaps into the Sun?

I will retell his story. I believe that an artist with a unique gift for capturing human proportions, through years of training, begins to perceive repetitive patterns with such clarity that it becomes an obsession and, eventually, a curse. A mania to notice bodies, movement, speech, but most painfully, faces. The artist becomes secluded as solitude becomes preferable to the daily confrontation, until eventually, he envisions a cure: to capture each and every human expression in a bust. Then, whenever the artist becomes overwhelmed, he will simply point to one of statues! By completing the work, the evil ghost will be locked into the work and the artist freed. Was he any more mad than Mallarmé, Wagner, Hilbert?

I saw clearly how far Messerschmidt may have been from madness when the ghost of proportions began visiting me in my dreams. It may well be just another name for the relational paradigm. So I forgave Kris his harsh judgment. Today, Messerschmidt's life is still changing in the longer timeframes; what seemed madness for some eighty years is beginning to look more like illumination.

And the parallels run everywhere. Gödel gave a new meaning to the liar's paradox and Aristotle's notion of truth, demonstrating that the meaning of ancient Greek experience is still fundamentally shifting today. Likewise, if the Christian era lasted two thousand years, it is not preposterous to wait another millennium before the twentieth century reveals its apex. Enough frequencies must complete a cycle for reality to blend into a story, the story into a myth, and the myth back into reality: Faustus into Faustomat. Isn't it ironic? I've spent all this time studying thousands of years of history to find out who I am only to realize that the answer may not come for another thousand years.

I thought about Hitler. It is possible that the longer timeframes will show the Second World War as the high watermark of the old paradigm, in which the true nature of the object was revealed. In the longer timeframes, two hundred years later, we will still be counting the dead. Not the corpses of humans but of ideas, as the powerful model that was dramatically defeated in May 1945 gradually becomes untangled, understood, and replaced. Without Hitler's psychopathic catalysis, both its culmination and its fall would have dragged on longer. We would still be speculating about the extreme form of the Aristotelian paradigm, unable to wise up—unable to perceive Aristotle through Hitler.

These Messerschmidts, Aristotles, and Hitlers are but parallels to the one event that matters to me. I know full well that we broke up in Japan. And that you will think that this diary, this love letter, is somewhat out of place, out of time. Our hug at the Tokyo airport has a completely clear meaning in the frame of days and months. But in the frame of years? Was it—is it our last moment together? Or, rather, a door to a higher resonant frequency of love, which we both had to find separately?

⌒

Nina, instead of a higher frequency of love, I seem to continue pushing into deeper frequencies of shit. The only positive thing about the last three hours is that I am no longer pressed into a cattle wagon along with half of India. I'm in the first car behind the locomotive, reserved for police and army use. The doors and windows are barred, so nobody can get in (even though they keep trying). That's the end of the list of positives. If my writing is a bit shaky from here on, it's at least partly because my hands are cuffed.

Apparently, we got held up in that hole because a storm washed out the rail track ahead. I tried to sleep and stopped drinking water again so I wouldn't have to get up and lose my seat. I wouldn't make it to Delhi standing up. More people kept coming to see the immortal *sahib*, feeling my hair, kneeling down and touching my hands. They brought children and kept pointing at the portraits and

babbling until two policemen showed up. They wanted to know what was happening. The people stepped aside and watched. A smaller, chubby man, looking like Homer Simpson with a moustache, pointed at the bag with the portraits. They examined them, laughed, and asked whether I was immortal. I shrugged jokingly, and they asked for my passport. And the fun was over. I told them I lost it on a hike in the mountains. They asked whether I'd reported it. I didn't even think of that. I explained that I was going to the consulate in Delhi for a new passport and then flying straight off. They asked whether I'd notified the consulate, so I said I hadn't. They exchanged a few words and told me to go with them. I refused because I'd lose my seat, and Homer took his gun out and told me to get my stuff and go with them.

They led me out of the train and along the platform towards the engine. There must have been a hundred oglers behind us. My back hurt so much I almost couldn't breathe. We boarded the barred carriage behind the locomotive. They told me to sit down and started searching my stuff. There were about ten of them around when Homer pulled out rolling papers and the rock of hashish from the top pocket of my bag. I thought I'd faint. They handcuffed me and read me my rights. I argued that a few grams were legal in India. But apparently the law is different from state to state, and I'd just taken the train to where it's forbidden.

The train started moving a moment ago. I don't know where they're taking me or when they'll let me call the consulate. I have no idea how I'll get out of this mess alive. I heard that Indian prison can kill you in a month. Rats, disease. And even if I stay healthy, it can take years for the case to get to a court. And I can't survive years in Indian prison without money. Christ, I hope they'll let me go with a fine. In any case, I'll keep writing, Nina, everything I wanted to tell you. Who knows if this diary isn't the only thing you'll hear from me. I love you. Without you, I do one stupid thing after the other. I'm just a statistician after all, an expert in risk and trouble.

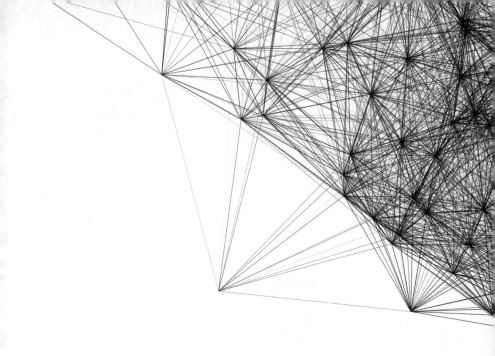

The Il
of T

usion

ruth

Adventure is just bad planning.
—Roald Amundsen

I'm sitting on the floor of a prison cell with fifty other blokes. We're all waiting for a ruling about detention. It's comical that they want to lock me up for this trifle, but I have to play along. There're dead rats in the ventilator. For a toilet, there's a hole in the corner. There's a sickly stench. The plastering is so full of carved messages that the paint is invisible. I stamp the cosmic order on the wall with all my strength. It's almost invisible, despite my breathing on the ink for a few minutes. The stamp gives me a few moments with you. Occasionally, there's a brawl. The screaming starts, the guards come and look, rattle the bars, but they don't come in. I keep to a side. I write. It helps me not to think about my hurting back. I sit on the floor, rest against the wall, and barely move so this mob doesn't notice I have a problem.

⟶

The more these heavy words are supposed to mean (object, relationship, truth), the less they say. But even if these largest of words are completely vague, nearly invisible, they influence me, like the distant celestial bodies of the Zodiac. Shift their configuration and an entire life changes.

If I told you how crucial relationships are, you'd laugh and say "Addy, that's obvious." Well, maybe it is. So let me extract them from their invisibility cloak of obviousness. I'll show how perceiving something subconsciously as an object makes it look completely different from seeing it as a relationship and how this shift alters lives. If you were a scientist, I would talk about the shapes of truth. But you're an artist, so I'll talk about the shapes of the ideal. Their shapes are the same.

Remember when I worked on Faustomat late into the night and you compared me to Wagner? You flattered me, but I hated it. He was after the absolute work of art, the Gesamtkunstwerk. His ideal looked like this:

IDEAL

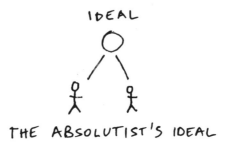

THE ABSOLUTIST'S IDEAL

I hated his ideal because it looked like my grandmother's ideal. Up there above, greater than us, perfect. Next to its perfection, we humans are inadequate, shameful, and guilty. And admit it, you didn't like it either. You were just fascinated by something that was so foreign to you. I'm no art critic, but I saw your paintings of Pembroke ruins. You never wanted to draw for the heavens that Wagner composed for. You hated his dictate of perfect beauty, but you equally detested your postmodern schoolmates when they exhibited rubbish from the River Cam. In their juvenile jejunity, they triumphantly paraded this ideal:

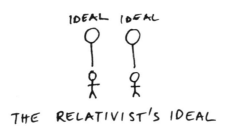

THE RELATIVIST'S IDEAL

And I'm with you. Postmodern relativism is crap. In a postmodern world, the only way to decide what gets displayed in a gallery is by lottery. Everything passes as art. But once you reject Wagner's ideal of perfection and the grim view that all works of art are equal, how do you decide what to paint next?

Do you see the *objects* in both ideals above? Now, I'll draw an ideal with the shape of a relationship:

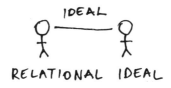

This clumsy drawing is a much more fitting model of how humanity answers the question, "What is art?" I like your paintings, and I can't help but tell my friends, and they post it on social media, and a gallery notices, and they organize a show for you, and an art critic blogs about you, and people read it, and they come have a look … and the relationships between you and the people are the ideal itself. It's this chatter that decides what art is and what it isn't, not some preconceived model of perfection or anyone's isolated and incomparable conviction. Your painting has transformed from an object hung on a wall into a bond between you and your audience. To an inspiration to other artists and the progeny of your own inspirations. A node in Indra's net, reflecting in its own skewed way the history and future of all art. The stronger its connection to the web, the more value it has.

If this means that Madonna is more artistic than Wagner, then I say, "Why not?" Madonna is closer to today's perception of art than the dead fool's yodeling. But I am not reducing relationships to followers. The key to this great web of an ideal is influence. If a journalist with a lot of influence writes that Wagner's music has a timeless beauty, perhaps more people will listen to Wagner. Or perhaps this recommendation will cost him a fraction of his influence. That's all part of the endless negotiation of an ideal with the shape of a relationship.

🦅

It's morning. They finally let me call the consulate. I talked to Mr. Cooray. He sounded young but was forthcoming and explained what

would happen next. The consulate has confirmed my identity to the police, so the passport problem is solved. They'll take me to court in the afternoon to decide about detaining me. They can only hold me for 24 hours, so it should be quick. Cooray said they'll probably give me a fine and let me go. Then I should immediately make my way to the consulate to pick up the new passport. Happy to oblige, Mr. Cooray.

As I sit here, arrested, I recall your favorite, Mallarmé. The twenty years of working on the *Livre* without producing even a comma, that was prison! And it made me think: his *Livre* was invisible. It changed with every reading. The book *happened* as the readers gathered in the reading room. Its content morphed with the number of readers and other circumstances, influenced by the environment. It was emergent and forever unfinished. Even though he thought he had nothing at all, the *Livre* was in fact a perfect relationship.

⟶

It's now been over 24 hours since the arrest. A guy with an inflamed wound next to his eye tells me the courts are overloaded, and it could take three days for me to come up. I am calm and content. Starting now, they're holding me illegally. The road home opens. Good thing India is such a mess. I was so nervous I didn't sleep all day, and now, I can doze off at last.

⟵

Compared to my schoolmates who went on to hedge funds, Ph.Ds, and Silicon Valley, I am, quite frankly, a loser. In no particular order, I managed to teach English to the disabled, bum about in India, and lose a girlfriend. That is no great achievement by many standards, but I no longer have those standards. I'm planning no career. No job as a *thing* to get some*thing* to buy some*thing* with. No mortgage, that perfect vector one can hold onto for decades like a life buoy. I abandoned all my vectors and turned to work in the shape of an ouroboros: evolving and unpredictable. If it felt strange in Japan to teach

English at night or fix strangers' computers, in Darjeeling it was already natural. I just tried to be useful. And the village changed little by little with me, as I changed with it.

When I get out of this mess and go back to England, I could accept an offer I got from some bank in the city. They want me to consult on statistical risk modeling two days a week. I am as open to serving coffee in a student cafeteria as I am to presenting a paper on fractal symmetries at a conference. Nothing is certain—not inside me, not ahead of me. To me, that's freedom, Nina. I am locked up in India, and in a way, I don't care. Tell me, what's worse: to be out in the street, a slave to an ideal, or to sit in prison, free? The only freedom I know is the freedom from ideals. The freedom of a clueless place.

∡

The trial just finished. A complete, utter disaster! They assigned me a different attorney than the consulate recommended and the entire proceedings took place in Hindi. I didn't understand a single word. I shouted at the lawyer to translate—that I had no idea what was going on. Then I asked the judge for a different lawyer, and they took it as contempt of court. I said that's ridiculous, and the lawyer—my lawyer!—put his hand on his chest and told me, "Sir, we Indians do not like when a British man tells us what is ridiculous." My lawyer!

They said I traveled with drugs and without paperwork, I have no connections in India, and I behave aggressively, so they would detain me until the trial. The protocol says that they arrested me today, which is a lie, so I refused to sign. It can be a year until the trial. I'm desperate, and I can't even sit up because of the pain. I have to talk to Cooray. Britain can't let me rot here!

�

Indian cities awoke in me a dislike of objects. They lie everywhere: houses, broken-out cobblestones, rubbish, carcasses. In the mountains, the ratio of objects to people is much more agreeable. The fewer there are, the better you can see them. And among them, there's one

I truly abhor. Or rather, I abhor the word that describes it. Or rather, the frivolous obviousness with which the word gets thrown around. Or … the consequences. That's it. What I abhor is what the thing does to people's lives while they celebrate it like a deity: truth, the God of objects.

"What is truth?" asked Pontius Pilate, and I drew it for him.

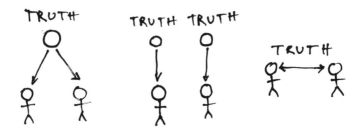

From left to right, we have: a) truth up there, b) the relativist truth that separates people into impenetrable bubbles, and c) truth in the shape of a relationship—the one that's negotiated, that emerges and unfolds. You might think that I have chosen this third truth too. Not quite. I don't like any of them.

I'd hope that the problems I have with the first truth are clear. That innocent-looking absolute truth is always right. Mathematicians call it a circular definition, common language calls it arrogance, and electricians call it a short circuit. Being always right, it never has to change. It's stiff as concrete. (Perhaps it's that singular form of the noun that creates the sense of truth as a single Lego brick. If we spoke of truths, truthing, or degrees of truity, I'd be less anxious about it— even though it wouldn't suffice.) And, if the stunning incompatibility with the fluid world around us were not enough to reject it, I add that Aristotle's truth is black and white. It makes me go either to Heaven or to Hell, be right or wrong, success or failure, friend or foe. Absolute truth is a tyrannical dictator, and I don't plan to live in its prison.

The second truth is the foundation of existentialism, relativism, and postmodernism. I dare say that most of the philosophy known as

"relativism" is a misunderstanding. It's Aristotle's misapprehension of Protagoras and his doctrine of flux. Relativism is an absolutist's failed attempt to grasp relationships. It's not radical enough. Forget it.

I toyed around with third truth in the shape of a relationship. One of the more popular theories of truth, correspondence theory, seemingly says precisely this (that truth is a relationship). It could—could!—be seen as dynamic, emergent, and negotiated as a slippery ouroboros between all of us. I'd like this fluid truth. But the philosophical discussions within and around correspondence theory have so many layers of object thinking, and the word itself, "truth," is so deeply connected with the object paradigm, that I have no hope of salvaging it. The idea that is bound to the word needs to be freed and lightened. It needs to get lost for words for a moment.

Try what I did: banish the toxic word. Curse it with *damnatio memorae*. And you'll see that we'll get closer to each other. I remember the cold evening when, listening to our giant hairy yaks return from the valley to the night shed, I scribbled my goodbye note to truth on a greasy brown paper bag.

Truth is a fallacy. A misleading simplification of a more precise term. The word that has real value in human life is error. Focusing on truth is the same mistake that Darwin and Spencer made when they said, "evolution is the survival of the fittest." It isn't. Evolution is the death of the unfit. There's a massive difference: a crow is not the fittest. I am not the fittest. But we are both fit enough. Arguing about truth is the same as arguing about how to be the fittest. Whether one should have four legs, or wings, or be a virus. Whatever. Be anything, as long as you don't die.

Philosophy needs to focus on the elimination of error. Error has value because it is life-threatening. Non-error is ... well, just life, nature, reality, if such words are necessary. We define each of them through its opposite anyway: life is the absence of death, reality is the absence of void, health is the absence of sickness, truth is the absence of error. A temporary, fluid, chaotic, uncertain, and grossly overvalued absence of error.

THE ILLUSION OF TRUTH

It didn't take long before new words began to grow in the reclaimed space. Words like "fitness," "resonance," and my favorite, "harmony." Real understanding is *harmonious* with the subject. Harmony is not an idealized perfect state but a process. It expresses the strength of a relationship and its charge—positive or negative. Harmony is The Word Formerly Known as Truth.

⌐

So they let me call the consulate. Cooray asked, "How much money do you have?"

"Nothing on me. Other than that, as much as necessary."

Silence. "Okay. I'll send someone over."

It could have occurred to me that it wouldn't be cheap. It was time for my friends from Cambridge. Well, friends ... the one friend. I asked for one more call, dialed the number, and prayed for it to work. We hadn't spoken in years. It clicked. "Hello?"

"Marquis!"

"Who's this?"

"Adam."

"Mate, how are you?" I was expecting a bit more excitement in his voice, but at this point, I loved him like a brother anyway.

"Not great. I'm locked up in a prison in India."

"No shit!"

"And I have a huge favor to ask. I need money to get out."

"How much?" he asked, dryly. "Where do I send it?"

"I don't know. I'll let you know."

"Do you need help with anything else?"

I hesitated. "Listen ... have you heard anything about Nina?"

He paused. "I have."

The blood rose all the way to my ears. "Where is she? Is she okay?"

I was so happy to hear his voice and finally catch a trace of you, I blurted out that I was searching for you and how wonderful it was to finally be on the right track—philosophically, as a human, as a man.

"Mate," he interrupted. "I probably have bad news for you."

My heart skipped a beat.

"Nina's with me."

"Is she okay?"

"Well, yes, she's great."

"How am I supposed to take that?"

"I won't beat around the bush. We've been sort of together since she came back from Japan. She didn't think it was a good idea to tell you."

"And why's that?"

"How am I supposed to know, buddy? She said she wants to let you live your own life. Make of it what you will. But I have to say that, when she came back from Japan, she was well rattled. I occasionally took her out, and we somehow got close. You broke her heart when you let her leave like that. I think she really loved you. She doesn't want to see you again. But you sound a bit desperate, so I'm telling you."

"You're a real friend, Marquis, thanks. Will you give me her phone number?"

"I'll ask her."

I put the phone down and slammed my head against the wall. Then five more times, harder and harder, before they led me away. I begged the guard for three cigarettes and smoked them in one breath. I'm on the final edge.

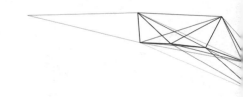

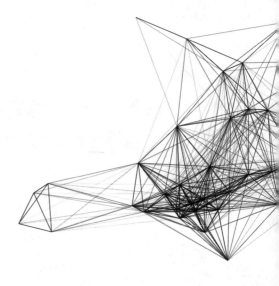

The Il

of Hie

usion

rarchy

There is one thing stronger than all the armies in the world,
and that is an idea whose time has come.
—*Victor Hugo*

I must control my demons. If I fail, I'm dead. I hold on to the pallet until my knuckles go white to stop myself from getting up, forcing my way through the twenty prisoners sitting on the floor towards Shiv—the biggest yob sitting below the window—and bashing his face in. It's his fourth time in prison, he weighs sixty pounds more than I do, and he's a psychotic murderer. He hasn't done anything to me. But he sees me. He keeps looking at me. Getting up and battering his mug would solve it all. In three minutes, I would no longer know anything. A single punch would grant me the bliss of forgetting that you're with him and not with me. The end of the fear of getting locked up here for a year, if I can even survive that long in this dirt hole. The end of deciding which gang to join and which to avoid. A single solid punch, like I threw at Marquis years ago. Christ, I'm so happy I got him then. I picture his bloodied nose like a dear fairy tale. It tells me I can defeat him, too. It's merely a question of choosing the right means. I keep wondering whether I should borrow the bribe cash from someone else. But no. This makes some perverted sense, just like the punch in the pub. I have to walk straight. Without a shiver. And keep writing for you. Jail is an incredible inspiration. The perfect Hierarchy. A perspective sent from heaven so I could write you about it.

➤

Question. A seemingly unrelated thought: so much of my inspiration came from Wikipedia that I can simply say, "No Wikipedia, no Tōhoku." It is therefore of utmost importance to ask, "How did Wikipedia come into existence? Why did people write onto the first empty page without a leader ordering them, without threats of Hell or promises of profit? Why are they so nice?" My grandma could never answer this.

➤

In prison, everyone has their precise place. It starts with the superintendent. Then the guards, the gang bosses, the privileged ones,

THE ILLUSION OF HIERARCHY

standard prisoners, and the bullied ones at the bottom. Under them, us: the amateur first-timers who got in by accident. The campaigning is relentless. You want enough food? The kind that doesn't smell of rat carcass? You want smoke? You want to make a call? Everything's possible. You just need to join the ranks. Refuse, and you're against everyone. There's no space in the shower for you for a week. The guy with maggots in his stomach will rub against you at night. You've got two broken ribs? And what about these other three? Shiv will hold you, Sandip will swing the metal pole, the guard will sleep through your screams. You still won't be ours? We could use a Brit. And you do need something, after all. Everyone does. To survive, for example?

↟

Hierarchy. It seems normal to them. They don't see the axis of power that is also found in the military, the ecclesiastic organization, or sacral architecture. To me, it's like a protruding backbone—a single straight path between an exclusive top node and the nodes below. It's called the chain of command, or, looking from below, the path of falling shit.

"Whose fault is it?" resonates through the Hierarchy as the bottom sins and the top mercifully forgives. The question is but an echo of the followers' belief in linear causation, clear rules, moral

imperatives, and respect for authority, the same virtues that chain them to the structure. There is nothing holding the Hierarchy together but the followers' own mindset of slavery.

Note to Grandma: a slave mind does not contribute to Wikipedia.

Ideas. The 28 volumes of the *Encyclopédie* sat on my father's bookshelf like sacred bricks of knowledge. Their pages stored wisdom as a list of independent objects. My encyclopedia, the Wikipedia, captures essentially the same content, only as relationships. Hyperlinks and crowdsourcing together freed Diderot's volumes into a fluid network of information, made it come alive and grow beyond imagination.

It is telling that Wikipedia does not separate mathematics from philosophy and history. Where needed, they meet, as they did before Aristotle. The parallels and paradoxes between Aristotle and Brouwer, between Einstein and Mallarmé, are free to come forth into dialogue. Mallarmé came up with the form of the *Livre*, but it took another hundred years for us to begin writing on that first empty page.

A man sent by the embassy visited today. An Indian, supposedly a lawyer. He wore a white suit but didn't look like an angel. He explained what would happen now. There is contempt of court in my file. It can take two years for my case to come to court, and I'll probably be dead by then. I told him I have issues with the other prisoners.

"You won't last long there," he pronounced indifferently. Then, he took out a business card and wrote a figure on it.

"This will get you to trial in two weeks. You'll be silent throughout the trial. The judge will give you a fine, and the same evening, you'll be on the plane to Heathrow."

"But that's an awful lot."

He just shrugged. "I'll come in two weeks. Make up your mind."

"No. Do you have a bank account in England?"

"Certainly."

"Write it down and the money will be there in three days."

He offered me some cocaine before leaving. I knew he was no lawyer. But he was my only hope. With great self-denial, I called Marquis.

"Holy crapoli!" he answered. "Okay. You should probably start looking for a job."

I didn't ask about you. But I bit through my lip holding back. In the cell, I covered the stamp in blood and finally pressed it onto the wall. It's there. I'll be out in two weeks.

Now, just to survive.

Open-source. After four years of work, I released the Faustomat code as open-source. With one mental movement, I allowed anyone in the world to see every instruction in the code and to change it as they will. Right now, while I'm in jail, seven people from around the world are hammering on. The youngest is fourteen, and she's South Korean.

The simple mental movement was Pi: I flipped Faustomat from a closed, impenetrable object into a web of commands. Suddenly, seven people came forward to work on it for free, just like others spend hours editing Wikipedia, simply because forming relationships is so much more satisfying than building objects. And so the avalanche continues. Static objects melt unstoppably into fluid relationships. On all levels, the principle remains the same: what was separate is connected.

The rules of the Hierarchy are small in number. They are of written form and rigid as commands. The Network, on the other hand, may appear lawless. Its rules are the rules of dance.

I got a call from Cocaine King. He got the money. The trial's in ten days. I hope he's the first rogue one can trust. You couldn't say that

about the ones doing time here. It escalates by the day. Two gangs are fighting over me, but it's not like they're courting. Sometimes, I don't get any food. They wake me up every hour at night. Someone took a piss on my mattress. I told them I'd be out in a bit, but it only got worse. Apparently, they need people outside. Last thing I need. I have to pull through, even without food and sleep. I'm counting down the days.

Seeing as I am sitting in prison, I dared to do something I never had the balls for. I got a tattoo from a triple murderer. It hurts like hell, but I'm proud. I refused to think of when I'll start regretting it, and I let myself be carried away by the pain and my admiration for the dreadful instrument he stabbed into my skin. I've got a tat on each fist. I'll get tested for HIV in London, but I'm alive now!

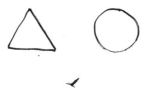

Goal. To produce the same things again and again, build Hierarchy. To repeat, quickly and often, build Hierarchy. To keep things as they are, build Hierarchy. Incidentally, the ruler at the top of a Hierarchy always wants to keep things as they are. Thus, the Hierarchy fears and hates revolutions while the Network lives in permanent rebellion.

¡Hasta la revolución siempre!

If "permanent rebellion" sounds pointless, that's because it is. The Network doesn't set goals. The meaning and direction of a system of feedback loops are negotiated within. While in the Hierarchy, the ruler and the followers always look to a fixed point on the horizon, be it Heaven or a holiday; the Network's focus is on process. While the Hierarchy sets a strategy, the Network fosters a culture. And with no leader and no followers, the flock crosses entire continents.

My own journey could, with a little effort, also be seen as such a crossing of continents. First, I broke free from the orderly world of academia in a rather random act of youthful rebellion, propelled butt-first into Japan. I thought I was leaving Europe while, in fact, I left a landmass much greater in a search for a place even more remote than Asia; from the peaks of Hierarchy, I travelled to the flatlands of the Network.

So—I cannot regret leaving you. In a system based on feedback loops, cause and effect lose their meaning. They are replaced by influence, interdependence, resonance, harmony, tension, and emergence. Linear causation gives way to a catalytic one. No experience can be singled out, no piece of information pointed to as the trigger of Tōhoku. It had to happen this way, giving me enough time and distance to see the larger picture. I have a feeling where this Grand Circular Tour is going to end: in Cambridge, not that hierarchical one I left but the one that lies in the Network. Chatting in cafés with those kinds of joyful spirits that thrive in flocks. Just as soon as I get out of this stinking shithole.

Hierarchies are the guardians of objects. Networks are the children of relationships.

Uncertainty. The mantra of the Hierarchy is order and stability, the virtues of good objects. A typical inhabitant of the Hierarchy is the bureaucrat. Orderly, rigid, conservative, bureaucrats abhor change and uncertainty. They move upward in a series of frog leaps called "promotions," between which they sit quietly in their place, rather certain that they won't fall back down.

This strategy does not work in the Network, because there is no "up," no certainty, and no ruler promising promotions. Life in a Network is an adventure. As each member searches for the Network's elusive center, their relationships constantly shift based on attraction

and repulsion, reshaping and harmonizing the whole flock. Everyone ceaselessly gains or loses their influence. The Network is a new attitude toward uncertainty and, thus, the basis of a new society.

Power. An army without a war will eventually dissolve. The reason is purely physical. In the army, as in any other Hierarchy, power is unevenly concentrated at the top. To prevent energy in any system from spreading evenly, an external force is required. Every hierarchical structure, human or abstract, requires an external enemy to survive. A commie might do, a terrorist might do, an American is just as good. It is the tension against an outer opposite that keeps the Hierarchy in place.

The Network is also powered by tension. Its cohesion comes from the power of the internal paradoxes and inconsistencies that keep its dialogue loud and its shape shifting. Its power comes from its own gravity. The Network's raison d'être is the Network itself. The shift from Hierarchy to Network therefore means a massive and unstoppable redistribution of power away from authority: from academia to Wikipedia, from rulers to the flock.

Ouroboros. What keeps my body in balance and my mind conscious is the same self-improving loop. The feedback loop forms the shape of my body as well as the shape of my character and, consequently, the shape of my life, society, science, art. It is the ring of mutuality between everything and everything else. The ring, the magical symbol of a relationship since time immemorial.

"But a relationship between what?"

A sensible objection. Between two objects, says the knee-jerk response. I avoid it, for as soon as the objects are back in view, at the tips of every relationship, it's convenient to ultimately ascribe every quality to one of the objects while the relationship remains nothing but an imaginary link, without attributes or substance. That is not

the model of relationships I am talking about, one that would lift the Aristotelian curse. My vision of reality consists *only* of relationships, like a bridge without pillars. Not a vacuous void but an emptiness able to relate to itself, folding onto itself in endless patterns.

The ancient Buddhist scripture of *Avatamsaka Sutra* describes a striking image: a net of pearls, each reflecting all others. Look closely at any one pearl—and at the pearls reflected in it—and you will see that each reflection again reflects all other pearls. This is Indra's net. The ancients say it's what the world is made of.

And I think maybe they just misheard it. It's called the internet.

⌖

I think of you incessantly. I wait for you to leave a message, day after day, just that you know of me. I fall asleep missing you. It's been obvious for a while that I can't even show you this diary. If I let you see how much I miss you, you'd turn away from me as if from a beggar. I am crippled by love, Nina. I am dirt. A disease that wants to infect you.

The bullying is awful. Worse all the time. Someone punched me in the night and knocked a tooth out. Nobody saw him, naturally. I spat blood onto the stamp and printed another cosmic order in Japanese above the bed. Only I know what it means. Love is such a lonely sport. And you'll never find out.

⌖

Character. Hierarchy teaches fighting, patronizing, protectionism, and fear of competition. Defense and attack. Hierarchy is a grumpy teacher.

The Network teaches respect. Helping. Fostering relationships. Playing. Sharing chocolate. Searching for usefulness. Mutual growth. The Network is a caring teacher.

⌖

The responsibility of a Network's member (catalyst) is greater than that of a Hierarchy's member (soloist). Rather than being accountable

for their own actions, and their actions only, catalysts answer for all they have influenced and all they have failed to influence.

It follows that the responsibility for a relationship is not only shared between two people, but it is also shared among everyone with even a hint of influence. In a universe of relationships, all effects and, thus, all responsibilities ripple out much farther than in the universe of objects. My grandmother, the villagers of Darjeeling, Marquis, and Aristotle all have a share in our breakup and reunion.

Politics. Communism is a form of Hierarchy. Democracy is a form of Hierarchy. The political model of the Network, once it crystallizes, will have little to do with either of these.

~

Morality. My grandmother always said: people can't be good without faith. But, as there are many heathens working for the common good on Wikipedia, I can't agree with her. When she says, "People can't be good without faith," my ears translate to, "People without fear won't follow the ruler's orders."

The Network knows no moral imperatives, no commandments carved into stone tablets. Its morality is negotiated. Its morality is a search for harmony. Its morality is co-operation. It's always been here, the morality of atoms whose good deeds are the molecules. The morality of molecules, whose good deeds are the protozoa. The morality of ravens, whose good deed is the flock.

"Love and prosper," said the Network.

"Love your neighbor as yourself," replied the cuddly Universe.

~

The trial's tomorrow. Shiv knows. He's got contacts. He sat next to me at lunch, put his hand on my shoulder, and whispered in my ear, "I know everything, British. You bribed the wrong man." He gave me a pat on the back. "It's your last chance to have brothers." I got up and returned the untouched food.

I'm fainting with hunger. By now, I haven't slept or eaten in three

days, but … I know why it's happening. Why there is a Sun in our universe and an Earth at a precise distance and life on Earth and me in it, without a passport in jail. Still the same reason. The universe wants to get to know itself. Everything I experience somehow brings the universe joy because it's another step, however bizarre, on its journey to itself.

It's four in the morning. To keep myself in possession of my faculties, I am writing down a table of the two paradigms. I reach into all the corners of the mind. I look the universe in the eye. It's not sleeping. Neither am I, so they don't kill me.

⋏

"Please fasten your seatbelt," an air steward just asked me with a smile. I look out the window, and I can't believe that, in ten hours, I'll be at Heathrow. I'm free. And I'm flying to meet you. And to challenge Marquis to a duel. I've got a present from India that he'll never give you: a certain breed of time whose magical shape will allow us to be together again. Time, which will cure the Aristotelian illness, free us from fate, and allow us to choose the meaning of everything that happened to us. It'll change everything, Nina. Everything except love. I even know why I had to be locked up. So I'd have to ask Marquis for help, so I could find you. Stars above me!

PARADIGM CONVERSION TABLE

	OBJECTS	RELATIONSHIPS
MYSTERY	"THE WORLD IS"	"THE WORLD CHANGES"
PRIMITIVE TERM	OBJECT	RELATIONSHIP
REALITY	MATTER	ENERGY
FOCUS	THING BEING/FORM /SYNTAX	MEANING INFORMATION FUNCTON
BEING & ABSENCE PART & WHOLE FINITE & ∞ SEMANTICS & SYNTAX TRUTH & FALLACY GOOD & EVIL ABS. & REL.	OPPOSITES	CONVERGENCES (ALLOWED BY CHANGE, ALLOWING CHANGE)
ORGANIZATIONAL STRUCTURE	HIERARCHY	NETWORK
BINDING FORCE	EXTERNAL ENEMY	CUDDLY UNIVERSE
VALUE	POWER (TO CONTROL)	INTRINSIC VALUE
POWER	POWER OVER OTHERS	POWER WITH OTHERS
GUIDING PRINCIPLE	TRUTH, GOOD	HARMONY
IDENTITY	IMPOSED ONTO OTHERS	LENT BY OTHERS
ETHICS	MORAL IMPERATIVE	NEGOTIATED
ORDER	PREVENTING CHAOS	EMERGING FROM CHAOS

	OBJECTS	RELATIONSHIPS
MOTIVATION	GOAL (CARROT ON A STICK)	JOURNEY (PROCESS)
PRIMARY COGNITIVE METHOD	ANALYSIS ISOLATION CATEGORIZATION	SYNTHESIS COMPOSITION CONTEXT
LITERARY THEORY	STRUCTURALISM	DECONSTRUCTION
FOUNDATION OF MATHEMATICS	SET THEORY	CATEGORY THEORY
LOGIC	ARISTOTELIAN	INTUITIONIST, QUANTUM
PHYSICS	NEWTONIAN MECHAN-ICS	SPECIAL RELATIVITY, QUANTUM
QUANTUM PHYSICS	COPENHAGEN INTERPRETATION	DE BROGLIE-BOHM MANY-WORLDS
SPACE	CARTESIAN 3D	HOLOGRAPHIC, FRACTAL
PHILOSOPHY	ABSOLUTIST, RELATIVIST	RELATIONAL
EUROPEAN MODERNISM	ENLIGHTENMENT	ROMANTICISM
ENLIGHTENMENT RATIONALISM	D'ALEMBERT	DIDEROT
CITY ARCHITECTURE	TREE	SEMILATTICE
ARCHETYPE	APOLLO	DIONYSUS
UNIVERSALS	CONFLICTING THEORIES	RELATIONSHIP

The Il

of Cau

usion

sation

The difficulties you meet will resolve themselves as you advance.
Proceed, and light will dawn, and shine with increasing clearness on your path.
—Jean Le Rond d'Alembert

I'm in Cambridge, from where, years ago, we set out on our Eastern voyage. Well, I was wrong. It is undeniable now that I, too, am a traveler rather than an adventurer—it's just that I've been on a longer trip than you. If need be, I suggest this lesson as a testimony to the fact that life's choices are ultimately indefensible.

I ended up spending most of my flight in meditation, growing gradually calmer. I love how meditating cultivates my intuition. Because somewhere above Munich, I realized that I'd do well to look around for a more romantic simile for our love than Hitler.

I judge my next steps with utmost care. The way I go about approaching you depends entirely on the shape of our relationship. Most people would draw a short, straight line. If that was my view, I'd have called you right after landing in London and asked you out that very evening. This would never have worked, not least because you're with Marquis. The man is not just in another league from me, Marquis is a different sport. He bloody has it all: innocent blue eyes, the tongue of a snake, the dirty grin. He could pull so many cards that I'd have no idea what combination worked on you in the end.

Luckily, I see relationships as rings—a web of interconnected feedback loops intricately interfering with each other. That gives me a weapon of my own. I'll weave the rings together, channeling their enigma toward a vertiginous momentum.

To achieve this, I had to withdraw and find some peace. A week was enough. And now I'm planning a war.

∗

Nina, I might not give you this part of the diary to read. Don't be mad. In any case, I'm in a great mood. I think I have a plan. No—I'm dead sure. Tonight, I walked around the familiar streets, listening to the din of the pubs, until I found myself standing in front of Pembroke College. Hesitantly, I entered the archway onto the grounds and turned right, under the twin towers of the library and the chapel. I haven't walked into a place of worship voluntarily since our trip to Prague, but to have a fighting chance to get you back, I had to rid

THE ILLUSION OF CAUSATION

myself of all disharmonies. The tension in one relationship would seep into all others. That meant making peace with my grandmother. With this thought in mind, I walked inside the candle-lit chapel and sat down in one of the back rows.

As if a secret sign had been given, the sound of the organ filled the space almost at once. Someone was playing to an empty chapel, just for the joy of it. I recognized the piece; it was the same we'd heard in Prague! Right then, the best (the only possible) way to meet you was clear.

I enjoyed Bach until the end this time, and when the musician paused, I walked upstairs to greet him. He was the reverend of the parish, an elderly gentleman. I gathered my courage and told him what had struck me while he played. Carefully, step by step, I explained how this one thoroughly oddball request could bring together two people who used to be in love and why his cooperation was *condicio sine qua non*.

"I assure you that I understood what you were asking." For a while, I thought that he was holding back his excitement, except he wasn't. "Your proposal is the most bizarre idea I've heard since I came to this parish twelve years ago. The students these days think that a church is—what, a theme park?"

"All I press for is love," I said. "Tell me, please, is the church not a house of love?"

"Yes, God's love."

"Is there not but one love?" I asked.

"A sly dialectic will not move you an inch closer to Him, son. You are asking me to violate the dignity of a consecrated church, and I must politely ask you to forget it." He locked the organ keyboard cover, shaking his head. I tried a different angle.

"Would you like to know why there are more young people on Facebook than in church?" I asked, trying to keep my tone neutral.

He smiled at me. "Oh, that'll be a more interesting topic—yes, please."

"Your world is dying," I smiled back.

"Ah."

"Reverend," I reasserted his authority, "do you find it amusing that your religion will die out?"

He looked at me, still smiling. "Death is a part of life. If you don't mind, I'd rather let the Bach resonate for tonight. But do come by any time if you want to talk."

I left and retired to a couch provided by a former classmate. I am full of calm faith in everything going well. Finally.

⌐

In the morning, the calm was all gone. True, I'd laid it on him quite thick. But what can I do except try to explain what I see coming?

The old religion will die out. Like witchcraft, like superstition, like alchemy, like confirming someone's death by fumigating tobacco smoke into their anus—a thoroughly modern practice in the seventeenth century. Like Roman numerals and Latin. It will die the slow death of obsolete representations. And I don't mean Christianity or Hinduism. I mean religion itself. The mesmerizing power of that word. Meanwhile, every new paradigm will be subject to old interpretations.

Religious interpretation: relationship is God.
Philosophical interpretation: relationship is transcendence.
Mystical interpretation: relationship is the fabric of the universe.

Scientific interpretation: relationship is a primitive term.
Mathematical interpretation: relationship is the difference between
the whole and the sum of the parts.
Esoteric interpretation: relationship is the divine fifth dimension,
the chakra, the meridian, the essence of karma. The prophecy of the Mayans.
Panta rhei. The new age of Aquarius. Relationship is Tao, it's Joni, the
sacred Goddess Mother, the ascending matriarch, the om, the yin, the Lune.
Relationship is the secret message of the crop circles, the weight of the soul,
the food of angels and the fuel of UFOs.
Romantic interpretation: relationship is love.

I am not even sure what my own interpretation is. Perhaps even speaking of relationships was being too crude too soon, even though it was my own choice of a fundamental primitive. (Or was it, ever?) Forging a world-view is a DIY project after all, of which the relationship paradigm is but one example. Should you want to build your own, here are the step-by-step instructions: summon primary wonder. Pick a primitive term. Stir, don't shake.

✠

I spent today making up various scripts for my next debate with the chaplain. I drafted forty-four of them. Eighteen of those concluded with my victory, and the rest ensured him a sleepless night. But I'll admit right away that, in reality, he came up with number forty-five.

"The depressed prophet returns!" he cried as soon as he saw me, opening with move number six, the gay peal.

"Reverend. I hope I did not disturb your peace last night."

"Not in the least, son! I am glad to see you restless to return. Would you like to stay for the evensong?"

Restless, Reverend. Restless ye are. "Is it now clear why Christianity will die out?"

The priest nodded. "The Church helped guide our civilization through enough revolutions to fear another one, my young friend. There are truths that are timeless, and they will prove their worth again, of that I am certain."

"Classic Aristotelian response," I retorted. "'Beneath the chaos of the world, there are eternal, unchanging laws, the manifestations of God.' This is precisely the line of argument that Thomas Aquinas used against the Cathars. That drew the West back to mechanistic thought for another few hundred years."

I couldn't help myself. One million Cathars were slaughtered on the basis of Aquinas argument! And the Papal Inquisition was set up so that the same fate would strike the totality of "pagan" wisdom, alternately labelled as gnosticism, mysticism, spiritualism, shamanism, occultism, and witchcraft. Whatever the labels meant, the hard line of the Church's argument against them has remained the same: *we own this reality*.

In effect, with the Aristotelian model in its heart, the Christian universe is not a universe of love but a mechanical clockwork. Look at my grandmother: she would call herself spiritual, caring, and humble before God. To me, she was a conservative, rigid, dogmatic Christian. Everything in this Universe was always clear to her except the fact that she was the walking embodiment of the Aristotelian paradigm. Damn, I'd been planning to make my peace with her here.

The priest was contemplating something.

So I carried on.

"There were several seminal moments when the West came close to overthrowing the Aristotelian curse. The case of Cathars vs. Thomas Aquinas was one. Then Kant came close to breaking through and reversed course in a desperate attempt to save the mechanistic fundaments. D'Alembert's mechanism won over Diderot's mysticism. Again and again, when the times were ripe for a thorough revolution of thought, the mechanistic Aristotelian order got the upper hand simply because the alternative always seemed too radical. It involved changing not only the order of society but also its notion of truth, time, causation, and reality. And that's always been too much to ask for. But this time is different, Reverend.

"Watch the 20th and 21st centuries, their slew of revolts. The wars, the social revolutions, the digitization and social networks. This time, the emergent paradigm is not the vision of an enlightened fraction. The whole world is experiencing it because we all crossed a critical

threshold together some hundred years ago. That's when the number of people, products, ideas—the number of objects—in our system finally reached a critical mass of relationships, triggering a phase change. The old structures that brought us to this point gradually crumble under their own weight, and nothing will save them. After twenty-five hundred years, the fundamental model of the Western world has outlived its usefulness."

I didn't even pause to draw breath—I plowed ahead.

"According to those who live in the old mind, today's world is confused, chaotic, postmodern, derailed, doomed. Their old laws no longer apply, and the new complexity eludes them. What they fail to grasp is that the society is not collapsing into chaos, the solid state is simply turning liquid. They are witnessing the dawn of a new world."

Imagine me ramming it down his throat for half an hour. I know—I'm sorry, Nina. I still can't do it any other way.

I imagined his sixty-five-year-old mind, exhausted by vain attempts to hold off the avalanche breaking off inside him. Give me an Aristotelian mind, and I swear that it's not whether I break it but when. In time, I'd lead him to the question of what the Church should do in the new times. Then I'd know that I had sown a seed of doubt and that it would grow. And I'd advise him—Reverend, trade the Bible for Wikipedia.

Except he asked an entirely different question, and that was, truly, somewhat surprising.

"And are you planning to charge this woman of yours like you have me?"

Caught off guard, I merely shrugged.

"And you're telling me about relationships?"

"I probably just can't put it across."

He nodded, kind of compassionately. "Sit down." He pointed, and we finally sat. "You feel like you've come upon something exceptional, correct?"

I admitted that that could be the case.

"Do you think you're the first to think in this way?"

"Most definitely not. Among philosophers and mystics—"

"You spoke of the Cathars. Their thinking is close to yours?"

"Not literally, but there are parallels."

"And the Cathars believed in Jesus Christ."

"What's your point?"

The reverend sat back in his seat, eyeing me calmly. "Could Christ have known what you've been telling me?"

"How am I supposed to know? I'm not too into Christ."

"You don't say? And why is this the second time you've come here to lecture me about Christianity?"

I was getting ready to object, but he softly repeated his other question. "Could Christ have known?" I gave it a moment.

"He could," I admitted. "There's still Christian gnosis."

"Yes. And have you read what the Quran has to say about Christ, or what Sufi mystics knew about him?"

I hadn't.

"I would be happy to point you toward books in the university library that not many people read. Perhaps then, you won't judge Christ as quickly as you judge medieval Churches."

"Thank you," I replied carefully.

"And if you thought that Jesus was a character you respected, one you could learn from, one you could engage in dialogue with, well, then we could talk about it together. Then I'll also be happy to welcome you at Mass sometime. But don't come here to preach to me again. It's childish."

"I don't know, Reverend, whether I'll ever come to a Mass. I'd rather see a world without religion."

"Yes. Demolish everything and start from scratch." He shook his head. "You're contradicting yourself. The Church's authority bothers you, but you'd like to cram everyone with *your* idea of what they should think."

I didn't say anything.

"I'm happy people think about Christianity. Other students also stop by for a quick visit and we end up talking more than they wanted. Very clever, a little kooky—we're in Cambridge, after all—but a lot of them also share a grave sin."

Some Pavlovian reflex must have slipped past me because the priest calmed me.

"They sin against the one commandment that didn't make it into the Ten Commandments. And yet it's a great sin, perhaps the greatest."

"You're some reformer."

He shrugged. "The omitted eleventh commandment is 'Thou shalt not omit.'"

"Omit?"

He nodded.

"You're implying I'm omitting something—and I can talk my head off to keep from missing a thing!"

"Precisely. Good luck with your woman." He moved to stand.

I did not understand. "So you won't help me."

"Sorry. Moving a bathtub into my chapel really is impossible."

Well, that's all for today's conversation. It wouldn't have hurt this much if he'd speared me with a crucifix.

Oh, and he threw a remark over his shoulder with a laugh. "She'd think you'd gone completely bonkers, anyway. I don't know much about these things, but there must be better ways of charming a woman."

It's an inhuman effort just to write. How easy it seems now to say, "I love you, Nina, and I want to always be with you." But I fall asleep alone.

It's still not clear to me what he meant about omission. But if it was supposed to be spiritual comfort, it didn't work.

I am not simply trying to cause us to be together by creating a perfect *moment*. Rather, I conjure time, weaving situations past and future to bring me, you, and the universe into harmony. When and how this will happen, I don't know. But the universe is willing. I ran into the Pembroke string quartet at the Eagle pub and laid out my plan over lunch. They agreed immediately. A scrapped Victorian bathtub

appeared, discarded on the side of the street. The only remaining problem is the padre. I've spent the whole week visiting him. I speak of cosmology, the history of social networks, intellectual property laws, and why the Church and the army attract the same sort of freaks. He sticks to his own: mercy, forgiveness, omission.

⌃

He still doesn't want to lend me the church. Rules are rules. And I patiently insist: love is love. When we bid each other farewell, it almost looks like we both pity one another. How could we not … after all, he is, just like me, only a pawn in the defining conflict of the era, the battle of Hierarchy versus Network.

I see battlefields everywhere: is the Church a Hierarchy or a Network? Is the climate change movement solidifying the existing Hierarchy (by promoting a fear larger than all previous fears) or a grassroots shift to include nature in our Network? Is the infrastructure of the internet a Hierarchy or a decentralized Network? And the European Union—Hierarchy or Network?

They are all both at once—a duckrabbit. That's why conversations on these topics are difficult: one side sees the duck, the other sees the rabbit. Still, the answers can only come from the members of these entities. Nothing distinguishes a Hierarchy from a Network but the members' own perception. The Church can be a Network, the internet can be a Hierarchy. There is nothing keeping the Hierarchy alive but the slave's mind. And the Network is protected by nothing but the catalyst's own free thought.

I wrote that perceiving something as a relationship rather than an object makes it look completely different. Actually, it even *behaves* differently. It is only (and precisely) the members' own choice that determines if a group will behave as a Hierarchy or a Network. Their choice projects onto the values. Rules. Focus. Forms of power.

These questions are the two-hundred-year-long fight that Nietzsche foretold, the bloodied battlefields of Worldwide War. The third war rages concurrently on a thousand fractal levels, and a victory or a loss on one of them ripples through all the others.

Internet neutrality matters, as does climate change, as does my love for you. The trenches run to the core of Earth and through, to the center of the galaxy and right on through—right through every mind. We, the people living in these glorious times, have the rare opportunity for a discussion across two gigantic civilizational paradigms—without any understanding whatsoever. What a privilege! We are halfway through. The millennial philosophical shift will accelerate and intensify for a hundred years before society catches a breath of self-awareness to reflect on what it's become and to realize the depth of its potential. So much will be reconfigured. So many barriers will be removed. Everything will change—everything except love. It will be bloody but unstoppable, and in the end, the Hierarchy will succumb. And the Network won't win.

Today I came to evening Mass. I did it as a sacrifice. I sat in the first row so he couldn't fail to notice me, and I obediently knelt, clasped my hands, and prayed to the cuddly Universe.

After Mass, he walked to the sacristy and I remained where I was. He took his time, knowing I'd be waiting.

He sat next to me and prayed, presumably for my soul, and then he asked without turning his head, "Why do you do this to yourself, Adam?"

"I've told you everything. Now I just have to persist."

"You have to?"

If I had to, I'd insist on it for a year. "Your choice," I stressed, "will resonate throughout the world. It is part of—"

"It'll end badly, trust me."

"It hasn't ended yet."

He prayed again and then started talking. "Your endless exhortations that you have the right to use a sacred building for some private madness of yours—that won't work on me. Not one bit. Yet it's better that you're talking to me instead of drinking in a pub. You might not hear what I'm telling you at all—"

"I do."

He smiled.

"You see—" He searched for words for a moment. "If I stand my ground, I'll give you the perfect excuse to blame me for the rest of your life. That is not loving your neighbor as I understand it. So please, do what you need to do to see where your path leads. Find out. Whether I am doing good or evil—let someone else be the judge."

I tensed. "So you agree?"

"Next Sunday at 11p.m."

I yelled and hugged him.

"On Monday morning, there will not be a trace, do you hear?"

"Reverend Father, they must have reserved a rocking chair for you up in heaven."

The path keeps opening up. What used to be cloudy takes shape, slips from imagination into reality, and resounds with thunder. When it ripens, it'll hit you like an avalanche of love. I didn't wait for anything and called you. You know it from here onwards. We talked for a bit and then I asked whether you'd meet me at the Pembroke chapel, midnight on Sunday. You wanted to get out of it, but I insisted gently, like Marquis would do. And you agreed. Hallelujah! I've got a week for the preparations and I'll have to hustle hard to get it all done in time. But frankly, Nina, give me a week and I'll make the pope a heretic.

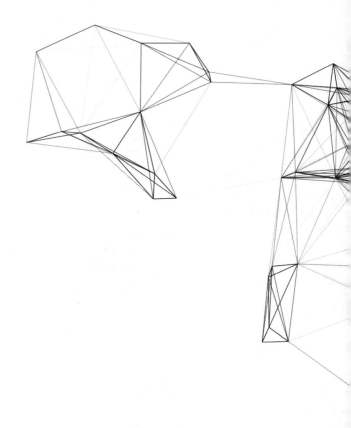

The Illusion
of Opp

usion

osites

The sun is but a morning star.
—Henry David Thoreau

The events of this diary, as I read back through them now, seem older than the year that has gone by. In the end, I didn't have the strength to finish the writing, nor a reason to. By some accident I didn't burn the diary but put it away instead. I only found it now while moving house. There's still no reason to finish it except for a certain feeling that closing a chapter is good. Good for what, I'd rather not guess. But I see I picked up a pen again. I see myself writing. And the memories come out as lively as if the night in the chapel were yesterday. So it seems like I'll write it and observe myself while I do, wondering why I won't just let it lie.

Fighting Marquis for the love of a woman is a battle lost in advance. Had I faced him head on, I would be beyond ridicule exactly three sentences later—and that would in fact be merciful. All I knew about charm was a collage of his own triumphs. And that is precisely what gave me the strength to face him: resisting the challenge of the impossible is utterly impossible. I breathed in the force of paradox. Without Marquis being both my teacher and my foe, I would never feel this powerful. And frankly, he wouldn't be his present self without you, and you wouldn't be who you are without me. The three of us are no longer separable. And so I breathed in—as you would say— to leap into the Sun.

My weapon was boldness. I had to delight and disturb you, fluster and seize you all at once, use a resonance between the past and the future so powerful it would displace your very meaning of the present moment. Recalling the three days prior to Sunday, I still feel the bliss. In an elation that touched on ecstasy at times, I glided through the Cambridge parks. Pedestrians and cyclists passed me, changed me and became me, the sunlit streets became me, the food and the coffee psychedelically became me.

For three nights, I would light a bonfire in the fields outside the town. I lured my consciousness to the third eye. Between my two hemispheres, I awaited you. In my dreams, images floated from the past. I channeled them into objects of desire. Hundreds of them. Photographs, a bottle of the champagne we drank in Prague, candles, a large bowl of fruit, the sharpest knife, flower petals, and ice cubes.

THE ILLUSION OF OPPOSITES

I hacked all the cubes into heart shapes. When I could no longer bear the silence, I sang and danced, rubbing them against my body. I chanted in mysterious tongues, calling the wave of Tōhoku and its might. My arms trembled with power and flew into the air of their own accord, searching for the paths of the planets above. I stroked the ancient souls of those cosmic giants and asked them for help, and they sighed and rolled slightly, gently shifting their paths toward a powerful synchronicity.

On the last day of my trance, the spirit of Tōhoku appeared. He introduced himself with thirty-three names, of which I remember Ereshkigal; Astaroth, the Grand Duke and Demon of Admeasurements and Proporci manifested to Faustus as Ishtar, prince of the haunted; Erlegkhaan; then Medusa the lethal Gorgon, Glasya Labolas of the Last Words of Solomon with griffin's wings, known to Eliphas Levi as the Captain of Manslaughter and the Loving Foe; Ta-Lai Milarepa of the Eagle Clan; and, one more I recall, Mighty Marquis Andrealphus the Great Geometer and Peacock. The spirit showed me how to arrange the objects of desire on the floor for the strongest effect— by using the golden ratio together with the Fibonacci sequence—and offered to remain present during my encounter with you. I thanked him sincerely.

At exactly 11 p.m. on Sunday I stood in front of the chapel gates with a bathtub, two buckets, a big canvas bag containing an array of tools, and precisely one hour to create an avalanche. Excitement ran down my spine, but I was calm as a samurai. I dragged the Victorian tub under the altar so it would be clearly visible from the entrance and took half an hour to fill it with warm water. Sixty or seventy

candles kept the temperature up, and another thirty longer ones burned spread around the chapel floor. Large photographs from our days together were thrown around under the guidance of the spirit and flower petals were strewn among them. I arranged the fruit bowls and the champagne by the tub and carefully set the portraits you drew of me against wooden holders from the chapel's inventory. The symbols of our most romantic moments together—from Prague to Tokyo—were perfectly composed into a live bonsai of our life. At quarter to midnight, the four musicians arrived, and, instructed not to talk, they silently took their places around the altarpiece and began to play their first careful tones. I stripped naked. Focusing my attention to the third eye, pulsating with the tension of opposites, I slowly submerged in the bathtub. You must have been steps away from Pembroke.

I felt nothing I could call control. I was a mere catalyst. At that thought, the spirit shouted in all its voices, "Hear, you who they called Adam, the Man! You are the strength of sound and the meaning of the word; you are the one who amplifies! The name you will bear from this day is Toito." I bowed to the gift and saw that I hadn't aligned the stars for one night only. My influence reached much further: through the life we would live to the people we would meet and inspire, our children and their friends … catalyzing decades to come. I was confident that with you, your laughter, and a worldview so different from mine, we would eventually manage to unite the two opposing paradigms.

I heard your steps before I saw you. You walked through the chapel to the bathtub, smiling and radiant. Then, you slowed down, looked around the floor and back at me. And you asked:

"Have you gone completely bonkers?"

The chamber music grew louder. From high above, the spirit shouted for me to remain in the third eye, and I saw.

✐

The vague feeling that's been following me for months finally collapsed into a tangible vision: the Universe as a portrait of man. It is

no coincidence that I have two hemispheres, separate and yet unified, one to process each side of reality. After all, it should be expected that a brain would gradually evolve to reflect the reality that shapes it. In this case, that reality is a duckrabbit. Not an illusion—it has a dual nature. Thus, we write:

$$network = hierarchy$$
$$information = matter$$
$$E = mc^2$$

The two sides of this Universe are its reverse and obverse. One side is material, local, objective. The other is Indra's net, in which all is connected. The two sides are the same and yet completely different. Each projects the other; they are mutual representations. The obverse mirrors the inverse, the inverse reflects what is mirrored ... in an infinite flow of shifts in representation. The tension between them keeps reality in existence: without matter, relationships would resolve immediately to their conclusion. Matter without relationships would turn to stone. Their dynamic balance gives the Universe a certain finite velocity.

Philosophy calls it dialectics. A thesis (object) produces an antithesis (object). The tension between them (relationship) eventually constructs a synthesis (an object). Repeat.

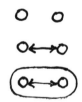

Elsewhere, the same is embodied in the Fibonacci sequence. Take the last two numbers (objects), add them together (relationship) to get the sum (object). Repeat. Observing the process for a while, it turns out that the well-known sign in the equations above (=) does not mean equality, as I was taught at school, but a change in representation.

Elsewhere, the same is embodied in the golden ratio, the simplest geometric expression of this alternation. In one dimension, it is drawn as a line split in such way that the whole is to the larger part as the larger part is to the smaller part:

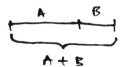

In two-dimensional geometry, it looks like this:

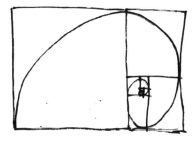

The repeated fractal self-similarity captures the mutual mirroring of two representations.

Elsewhere, the same is embodied as analysis and synthesis, $P1$ and $P2$, the two mental steps from objects to relationships and back again.

Elsewhere, the same is called consciousness, emerging from the mutual mirroring of two unequal hemispheres.

The form doesn't matter. Everywhere, two sides of reality mirror each other and mirror the image and so on. The unchanging relationship (proportion, constellation) of these two dimensions gives our reality its specific contours. It shapes galaxies, pinecones, and the double helix of DNA alike. It's the reason and proof of why our reality will never be fully grasped.

It is every conversation with you and the eternal
misunderstanding between man and woman.
It's the mystical image of a river: as it flows, it is at
once the same and different.
It's the grimace of a face that longs to glimpse itself.
It's the words of the Kabbalah, explaining God's
motive for creation:
"God did not see God."
It's a riddle of reality and story, which, on closer
observation, turns into the reality of the story and the
story of reality. Neither is any more real or fictional
than the other.
It's the Universe as a self-portrait, forever painting
the painter.

You asked whether I'd just had a heart attack or an orgasm, apparent-ly uncertain which would be worse. Nearly blinded by the insights, I closed my three eyes. I breathed deeply, returned to my samurai calm, and then attempted the impossible: to explain myself. And why I left you. I spoke of the whole time I was away, about my vision in Tōhoku, and especially, I tried very hard to explain that it's not some wacky abstraction. Relationships change our lives.

"Obviously." You shrugged. "Why are you in the bathtub? You got tats? On your fists? Jesus."

"I know, it's trivial in a way. But," I sweated and stuttered as I dived into the depth of the word relationship, struggling to yank my mind into some way to explain that I now know hundreds of its meanings.

"So is this why you wanted to meet?"

"Well ... I have been thinking about you the whole time."

"Yes, thinking," you said reproachfully. "Thinking all the time. You're still the same, Adam."

For heaven's sake! Speaking with a spirit with thirty-three names while having a bath in Pembroke chapel—is this really the mathema-tician you used to know? Well, damn right it is. Nina, meet Toito, the

rational mystic. He is rational, no doubt, for he shifts the very definition of rationality.

That's what I didn't say. Parting with my own shadow, I instead loudly said what I have been practicing since I packed up my backpack.

"I love you, Nina."

And I let go of myself and flew, an empty silhouette with a nameless love.

You smiled wide and touched my arm. "Where are you living, you silly? I've been with someone for a year and half now!"

Fair point.

"But I have to thank you. Marquis got rather nervous when you showed up," she giggled, "and guess what?" She couldn't stop laughing and clenched her knuckles. "He gave me the ring." The ouroboros of love that I have materialized.

"And you said yes."

She smiled. "Look, I wish you all the best, Adam. But I'm very happy now."

"Well, happy is a relative—"

"Listen to yourself! You are still the same. That's not who I want to be with, am I clear?"

Clear it was, the whole sadistic irony of my life. My fanatical research of relationships had ruined the one relationship that I really cared about. Emptiness beset me. We loved each other thoroughly and deeply but sadly, always one at a time. Stuck in opposites instead of harmony. While I continued to sink lower into the water, she walked around looking at the items scattered on the floor.

"This is freaky. You have to move on, Adam." She walked over to the portraits and stopped by the last one, surprised. "What is this?"

"Professor Gorgonuy painted me on the night when I decided we'd go to Japan."

"It's beautiful work. Why did you never show it to me?"

"Back then I thought I was going mad."

"What else is new?"

"Tell her," whispered the spirit, and I explained how Gorgonuy began to paint me in his basement flat and the miracle that happened when he finished the painting. I used the word miracle with

full awareness. I felt a tremendous weight was lifted off me, leaving me sad and elated at once.

"Amazing story, Adam. Now I understand why you went to Japan—not for me but for yourself."

"Just like you."

"That's … right." Something flashed through her face, an expression I knew but couldn't immediately place. "I would like to draw Professor Gorgonuy painting you. I see it so clearly. May I?"

I was grateful for the excuse to have her for a little longer. She sat down on the tub and started sketching.

We'd only repeat ourselves from here on, so we sat in silence. I wished for her to draw slower, hesitate, and trap a flash of uncertainty in the portrait. But her hand didn't even quiver.

"Nina …" I cleared my throat, and my gaze inadvertently slid down to the ring, and she knew what was on my mind.

"I'm in love, Adam." She caressed me one last time. "Get it already."

"That's great. Me too."

She tore the page from the journal and dropped it into the tub. I nearly drowned trying to catch it dry.

"Vltava," I gasped, and we both knew that time rhymes.

"Take care of yourself, and call me in a year." She kissed me on the cheek and left. I returned to myself, to that clueless place.

A half hour later, when the musicians chose to disappear and I still lay motionless in the bathtub, the reverend stepped out of the shadows. I couldn't even speak, let alone explain, but he just stood there, his head hung, present to my despair. What he'd been suggesting the whole time was clear.

That's all. My own journey has woven some unexpected turns since our farewell, never clear too long in advance. When I look back now and admire its proportional, geometric beauty, I see how it directly grows out of those strange days when the three of us fought for our full membership in the club of humans—so successfully that we even pulled those around us in, towards the epicenter of being, to the middle of the flock. And what more can one wish for in this world?

Flock Without Birds
© 2022 by Filip Dousek

INTERNATIONAL RIGHTS AND DISTRIBUTION
info@toitopublishing.com

———————

ISBN
PAPERBACK 978-80-907851-0-6
PDF 978-80-907851-1-3
MOBI 978-80-907851-2-0
EPUB 978-80-907851-3-7

WRITTEN BY
Filip Dousek

PUBLISHED BY
Toito Publishing

TRANSLATION
Filip Dousek

COVER DESIGN & TYPOGRAPHY
Jakub Gruber

COVER PHOTO
Lukas Cetera

EXPLORE TOITO'S LIBRARY
(unpublished texts)
www.flockwithoutbirds.com/library

JOIN MY MAIL LIST
(new book announcements, bonus materials etc.)
dousek.com/email

SIGN UP FOR NEWSLETTER
dousek.com/newsletter

———————

JOIN THE CONVERSATION AT

TWITTER
@fdousek

FACEBOOK
fb.com/flockwithoutbirds

INSTAGRAM
@filip.dousek

OR
www.flockwithoutbirds.com

Truth

is

a fallacy

Truth

is

a fallacy

EXPLORE TOITO'S LIBRARY
(unpublished texts)
www.flockwithoutbirds.com/library

JOIN MY MAIL LIST
(new book announcements, bonus materials etc.)
dousek.com/email

SIGN UP FOR NEWSLETTER
dousek.com/newsletter

———————

JOIN THE CONVERSATION AT

TWITTER
@fdousek

FACEBOOK
fb.com/flockwithoutbirds

INSTAGRAM
@filip.dousek

OR
www.flockwithoutbirds.com

WRITTEN BY
Filip Dousek

PUBLISHED BY
Toito Publishing

TRANSLATION
Ian Mikyska

COVER DESIGN & TYPOGRAPHY
Jakub Gruber

COVER PHOTO
Lukas Cetera

INTERNATIONAL RIGHTS AND DISTRIBUTION
info@toitopublishing.com

———————

ISBN
PAPERBACK 978-80-907851-0-6
PDF 978-80-907851-1-3
MOBI 978-80-907851-2-0
EPUB 978-80-907851-3-7

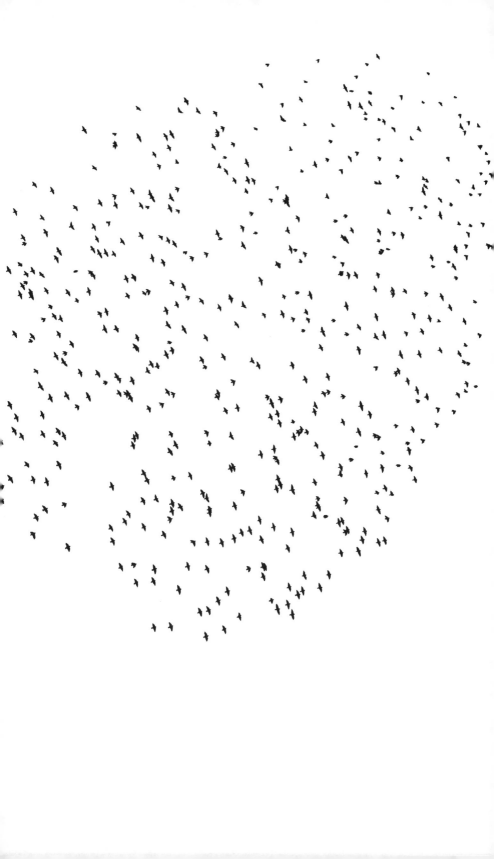